D0864255

REBEL

THE CHANGE, BOOK 3

Rachel Manija Brown
and Sherwood Smith

Book View
Café

REBEL
Copyright © 2017 by Rachel Manija Brown and Sherwood Smith
All Rights Reserved, including the right to reproduce this book or
portions thereof in any form.

First published in the United States of America by Viking, an
imprint of Penguin Group (USA) LLC, 2014

Second edition published 2018 by Book View Café Publishing
Cooperative
P.O. Box 1624
Cedar Crest, NM 87008-1624
www.bookviewcafe.com

Print edition 2018
ISBN: 978-1-61138-568-7

Cover by Augusta Scarlett
Interior design by Marissa Doyle

This book is a work of fiction. All characters, locations, and events
portrayed in this book are fictional or used in an imaginary
manner to entertain, and any resemblance to any real people,
situations, or incidents is purely coincidental.

Rebel

Other books by Rachel Manija Brown

*All the Fishes Come Home to Roost: An
American Misfit in India*
A Cup of Smoke: Stories and Poems

Other books by Sherwood Smith

Crown Duel
A Stranger to Command

CAST OF CHARACTERS

All occupations and ages are current as of the beginning of *Rebel*. Reading this list will not spoil anything that occurs in *Rebel*. Characters who do not appear in this book but are discussed in it are listed. Characters who are introduced in this book and whose appearance would be a spoiler are not listed.

Citizens of Las Anclas

Ross Juarez. A prospector; also assists Mia Lee with mechanical jobs. Has the power to communicate with crystal trees. Exact age unknown, but about 18 or 19.

Kerry Ji Sun Cho. Formerly Kerry Voske, crown princess of Gold Point. King Ian Voske and Min Soo Cho's daughter. Changed: can create invisible objects from force fields. A patroller; also works in the town stables. 18.

The Callahan Family

Bob Callahan. A trader. Left his family and Las Anclas years ago.

Martha Callahan. A clothing designer and tailor.

Henry Callahan. Their son, an apprentice carpenter, in Ranger candidate training. 18.

Becky Callahan. Their daughter, apprenticed to Dr. Lee. 17.

Grandma Ida. Mrs. Callahan's mother.

Grandma Alice. Mr. Callahan's mother. Killed in battle in *Stranger*.

Aunt Rosa Callahan. Mr. Callahan's sister. A weaver.

The Crow/Koslova Family

Tatyana Koslova. A rat breeder and trainer.

Noemi Crow. Her wife, a rat breeder and trainer.

Elizabeth Crow. Their daughter, the sheriff. On the town council. Changed: strength, speed, and a skull-like face.

The Diaz Family

Serafina "Sera" Diaz. Captain of the Rangers. Killed in battle in *Stranger*.

Francisco "Paco" Diaz. Her son, an apprentice glassmaker, in Ranger candidate training. Used to drum in the Oldtown band. 18.

The Lee Family

Dante Lee. A doctor. Changed: healer. On the town council.

Mia Lee. His daughter, the town mechanic. 17.

The Lowenstein/Nakamura Family

Ms. Lowenstein. The chief archer. Changed: cat's eyes.

Meredith Lowenstein. Her biological daughter, apprenticed to her mother, in Ranger candidate training. 17.

Yuki Nakamura. Her adopted son. 18. Left town to become a prospector in *Hostage*.

The Preciado Family

Mr. Preciado. A fieldworker.

Mrs. Preciado. A fieldworker.

Cisco Preciado. Their son, a fieldworker. 21.

Dominica Preciado. Their daughter, a fieldworker. 19.

Brisa Preciado. Has not yet settled on an apprenticeship. In Ranger candidate training. Changed: makes rocks explode. 17.

The Riley Family

Sam Riley. A patrol captain. Changed: far-seer.

Judith Riley. A horse trainer. Deaf. Her skill with horses may or may not be an actual Change.

Jennie Riley. Their biological daughter, formerly a Ranger, now the teacher at the one-room schoolhouse. Changed: telekinetic. 18.

Jose Aldana. Their foster son. Changed: earth-mover. An apprentice printer/librarian. In Ranger candidate training. 16.

Yolanda Riley. Their adopted daughter. Changed: controls the wind. An apprentice farmer. 15.

Dee Riley. Their biological daughter. One of the "Terrible Trio." 13.

Tonio Riley. Their foster son. Changed: bioluminescence. 10.

The Vardam Family

Ravi Vardam. Owner of a fruit orchard. Changed: chameleon skin. Killed in battle in *Stranger*.

Anjali Vardam. His wife, co-owner of the orchard.

Indra Vardam. Their son, a Ranger. 18.

Sujata Vardam. Their daughter, apprenticed to her parents, in Ranger candidate training. 17.

Priya Vardam. Ravi's mother, a judge. On the town council.

The Wolfe/Preston Family

Valeria Wolfe. The mayor of Las Anclas. On the town council.

Tom Preston. Her husband, the defense chief. On the town council.

Felicité Wolfe. Their daughter, the council scribe; also her mother's assistant. 17.

Will Preston. Their son. 11.

Julio Wolfe. Mayor Wolfe's nephew, a Ranger and a sentry chief.

Grandma Wolfe. Mayor Wolfe's mother, a retired teacher. Changed: firestarter. Currently living outside of town due to a difficulty controlling her power.

Other Townspeople Appearing in *Rebel*

Jamison Appel. The Guild chief. On the town council.

Anna-Lucia Benisti. The saloon manager and baker. Dr. Lee's girlfriend.

Peter Chang. A student. 13.

Clara. The Wolfe/Preston family's cook.

Nasreen Hassan. An apprentice beekeeper. 16.

Mrs. Hernandez. A miller, running for a place on the town council.

Laura Hernandez. An apprentice teacher. Changed: black cat-claws. 16. Killed in battle in *Stranger*.

Noah Horst. An ironmonger. Running for defense chief.

Tommy Horst. His son, apprenticed to his father. 18.

Luc Hsing. Owner of Luc's, a restaurant.

Zaida "Z" Kabbani. A student. One of the "Terrible Trio." 12.

Marina Lopez. A judge. On the town council.

Jack Lowell. The owner of the saloon. Sheriff Crow's ex-fiancé.

Tania Medina. A falconer. 23.

Alfonso Medina. A student and apprentice at the dairy. Tania's brother. Changed: gecko-like fingers and toes. 18.

Mr. McVey. A baker. Running for a place on the town council.

Sebastien Nguyen. A furniture maker.

Grace Nguyen. Sebastien's wife.

Josiah Rodriguez. The former town mechanic, now retired.

Hans Ruiz. A student. 14.

Constanzia Salazar. A weaver. Changed: a sparkling aura.

Rico Salazar. Constanzia's son. Changed: firestarter. 15.

Hattie Salazar. Constanzia's daughter. 8.

Grandma Thakrar. A brewer.

Nhi Tran. A student. One of the "Terrible Trio." 13.

Ms. Vasquez. A dairy worker.

Ed and Rick Willet. Brothers, troublemakers, town drunks.

Horses

Blackhawk. Jennie's favorite horse, a black mare.

Sidewinder. A buckskin gelding.

Tucker. A chestnut gelding.

Buttermilk. A palomino gelding.

Sally (Seattle Silver). Kerry's silver mare.

Nugget (Nebraska Gold). Kerry's gold stallion.

Penny (Pennsylvania Silver). Kerry's pregnant copper mare.

Tigereye (Tennessee Bronze). Yuki's bronze mare.

Rats

Peach, Ren, and other trained rats. Owned by Trainers Crow and Koslova.

Wu Zetian. Felicité Wolfe's golden rat, specially trained.

Kogatana. Yuki Nakamura's gray rat.

Other Pets

Princess Cloud. Dee's pet, a larval pit mouth. Blown up in *Stranger.*

Rusty. Ross's burro.

Visitors to Las Anclas

Furio Vilas. A bounty hunter. Left town in *Hostage*.

Citizens of Gold Point

The Royal Family
Ian Voske. The king. Changed: silver hair.
Min Soo Cho. Kerry's mother. Changed: can activate the Change in other people.
Deirdre Voske. The former crown princess. Changed: storm-bringer. Died in *Stranger* after over-using her power. 19.
Sean Voske. The former crown prince. Changed: can evade notice; his power is active unless he consciously turns it off. Disappeared several years ago. 19.
Bridget Voske. The crown princess. Changed: can make matter decay. 13.
Owen Voske. A prince. Changed: telekinetic. 11.
Fiona Busisiwe Voske. A princess. Changed: can teleport small objects. 9.
Connor Voske. A prince. Changed: can make flowers bloom. 7.

Other Citizens of Gold Point
Shanti Bankar. A soldier. Changed: can create electricity. Killed in battle in *Hostage*.
Santiago Flores. Kerry's boyfriend. King Voske's personal body-guard. Changed: can make rocks heat up in fifteen minutes.
Luis Zavaleta. King Voske's personal healer. Changed: has the uncontrolled power to burn people with a touch; can also use it to heal.

·1·
ROSS

ROSS JUAREZ SCANNED THE crowded town square of Las Anclas as warily as if they were an anti-Changed mob ready to run him out the gates.

He almost wished they were. He'd know how to handle that. But his first holiday in his new home was unexplored territory, and far more nerve-wracking.

The square had transformed overnight into a holiday marketplace lined with decorated booths selling gifts for Christmas and Hanukkah and New Year and winter celebrations he'd never even heard of before.

And that wasn't all. Every single person in that crowd knew how to give a present. Even if they were young enough to have never done it themselves, they'd grown up with gift exchanges. Ross was the only one with no idea what he was doing.

Then he spotted a slim figure poised as if waiting for the battle to begin. Kerry Ji Sun Cho, who had once been Kerry Voske, crown princess of Gold Point, also seemed to be inspecting the crowd for ambushes and enemies rather than gifts and friends.

While Ross knew he looked as uncomfortable as he felt, she appeared cool and haughty. But he bet she didn't feel so cool inside. She must have given presents before, so she couldn't be worried about doing that wrong. But he knew she was as certain as he was that some day King Voske would return to Las Anclas. And the two of them—Voske's renegade daughter and the prospector she'd helped to bring down his empire—would be first to get their heads put on pikes.

Kerry whipped around as if she'd felt Ross watching her. Like a pair of magnets, they drew closer until they stood together at the edge of the crowd.

"Expecting assassins?" Kerry's slanting eyebrows rose, adding to her tone of offhand joking.

"I wasn't." Ross scanned the crowd for weapons. "Are you?"

She dropped the light tone, leaving only raw honesty. "Always."

"I didn't mean—" Ross broke off, frustrated. She'd been teasing, like normal people did, and he'd replied way too seriously. Now she probably felt as weird as he did. "Yeah. You're right. Your father will send some eventually. But probably not today. Anyway, that wasn't it. I've never given a gift before. I don't know how. And—"

Ross stopped himself before adding, "I feel stupid." Kerry could probably see that for herself.

The sardonic twist to her sharp features smoothed into genuine sympathy. They'd only known each other for a few months, but they'd learned a lot about each other in that short time—first while Ross had been Voske's prisoner, and later when they'd fled through the desert after she'd broken him out and helped him blow up the Gold Point dam. She'd given up her life in Gold Point to save his, but she hadn't done it for him. She'd made that sacrifice for Mia, if she'd made it for anybody, but mostly she'd done it because it had been the right thing to do.

What did you even call that sort of relationship? Friendship seemed both too much and not enough. Ross and Kerry didn't make arrangements to spend time together, like Kerry did with Becky, Mia, and Meredith. But in those seven nights in the desert, they'd learned what haunted each other's dreams. He bet none of her other friends knew that.

Kerry tucked a strand of hair into her braid. The blue-black gloss reminded him of Mia's carelessly clipped bangs, just as the shape of Kerry's eyes made him think of Mia's eager gaze from behind wire-rimmed glass. But while he could often guess what was on Mia's mind by watching her face and body, Kerry's cool expression was less a window than a mirror of polished steel. She might be thinking about him or friendship or gifts or assassins, or something else entirely.

"Giving holiday presents isn't that complicated, Ross," Kerry said, simply but without condescension. "If you're going to a party with the person you have a present for, it'll have a time for gift-giving. If you're not, give it to them alone on the day of whatever holiday they celebrate."

"Right," Ross muttered. "Got it."

It was obvious once she'd explained it. But the whole idea of holidays, of crowds, of families — of all those things at once, of how important they were in Las Anclas, and of how he was the only person who was experiencing them for the first time — made his brain lock up like a rusty engine.

"And if you don't know what they'd like to get, ask someone who knows them well," Kerry advised. With that, she lifted her chin high and stepped into the crowd. People cleared a path for her without seeming to notice that they were doing it. If Ross had plunged in like that, he'd have collided with six people at once.

I'll ask about Jennie first, Ross thought. Lots of people knew her well, so she'd be easiest to start with.

He didn't pursue Kerry, as she and Jennie found each other's company awkward at best. But he spotted one of Jennie's adopted sisters at a booth selling potted plants, her head of prickly black hair bent over a writhing scarlet eater-rose in a glazed blue pot.

Ross made his way to her through the crowd, gritting his teeth against the ever-present murmur of *danger, danger, danger* thrumming through his body and mind.

Yolanda Riley looked up from the rose she'd been teasing with a fingertip. Its hungry petals snapped shut on empty air. "Hi, Ross. Need a guard flower? This one's nice and lively."

Ross shook his head. "No. I want a present for Jennie. Do you know what she'd like?"

"You picked the right person to ask!" Yolanda looked as delighted as if he was doing her a favor rather than asking for one. "She could always use a good weapon. Or maybe jewelry. She loves that, too. But she can't wear it in training, so that would be a special occasion thing."

Giving presents is *complicated,* Ross thought to the absent Kerry.

Something for special occasions made sense for a Christmas present. But he didn't want to saddle Jennie with a gift she had to be so careful with that she couldn't have fun wearing it, like the embroidered shirt of Paco's that Ross had borrowed for the dance, only to spend the night worrying that he'd spill something on it.

That wouldn't be a problem with a weapon. But he happened to know that Jennie was already getting one from someone else. And while he was sure she'd love it, she'd gone through a lot of bad times recently and they'd all involved fighting. He didn't want to risk a present that might come with unhappy memories attached.

That brought him back to jewelry. Was it really only for special occasions? Ross said, "I've seen her train wearing hair beads. Do those count as jewelry?"

"Oh, absolutely." Yolanda's voice rose with enthusiasm. "She loves beads."

Relief! "Then I'll get her some."

"Great! But if you want it to be a surprise..." Yolanda peered around the crowd.

"Jennie's at the schoolhouse, reviewing lesson plans. Oh, and I want something for Mia, too. She's working on an anti-raccoon electric fence at the Vardam orchard, and she'll be there for at least another three hours." Then, remembering how intent she'd been when he'd left her there, he added, "Or till I drag her home for dinner."

"I can't help you with Mia," Yolanda said with a shrug. "I mean, obviously something mechanical, but I don't know anything about that stuff. But I can make sure you don't buy Jennie beads she already has."

Yolanda jostled her way down Main Street. Ross followed more cautiously. He could stifle his impulse to flee, but he couldn't stop wanting to. The entire town seemed crammed into the square, talking and laughing, buying, selling or trading, but he and Kerry weren't the only ones who didn't seem relaxed. Some conversations had a tense undertone, and now and then he caught the quick arrow of a glare. But though he was used to being the target of a town's distrust, none of it was aimed at him. Instead, the glares focused on Mr. Horst, the ironmonger, who towered over a knot of people on the far side of the square.

Ross hoped he'd stay there, and that the jewelry was some-where else. He wanted nothing to do with that Changed-hater.

Yolanda led Ross past a booth selling decorated baskets, embroidered bags, and carved boxes. Ross slowed, wondering if Mia might want a box for nails or bolts. Then he spotted a line of booths crammed with fancy food.

Dr. Lee's girlfriend, Anna-Lucia, was selling jars with contents bright as jewels. Ross bent to read the labels: prickly pear jelly with rosemary, grapefruit marmalade, pomegranate jelly, spiced apple butter, habanero-honey barbecue sauce. It had been more than six months since he'd come to Las Anclas, but he was still impressed by its wealth and variety of food. And though he could now read with ease, his ability to look at writing and know its meaning still felt almost magical.

Yolanda impatiently waved up a gust of wind to ruffle his hair. "Jennie doesn't want jam. That's something you'd get for your grandma, not your girlfriend."

"My girlfriends could get it for me," Ross said. "*I'd* like it."

He let Yolanda lead him away. At least he knew better than to buy other people something he wanted himself. But he still wasn't sure what to get Mia, who was picky about food, and could invent anything she'd need or want. And he'd never seen her wear jewelry, even to a dance.

Ross spotted old Mr. Rodriguez, the retired town mechanic, manning a booth of tools.

"Wait, Yolanda," he called.

She turned impatiently, then saw the booth. "Oh. That's Mia stuff, all right."

Fireplace tongs, household and kitchen implements, gardening tools…and there, hanging from the ceiling, was a revolving tool rack. Mia stored her tools in boxes and on her table, and was constantly hunting for and tripping over them. That rack could hang over her table so she could reach up and grab whatever she needed.

Ross fingered the scrip in his pocket. He'd saved most of the payment he'd gotten from Mr. Preston in exchange for his ancient book. For the first time in his life, Ross could walk into a shop and buy anything in it. He was used to spending only what he absolutely needed to survive, because who knew when he'd be able to get more. But now he had enough scrip to buy a small house. Thinking that he couldn't afford anything but bare essentials was a habit, nothing more. He *wasn't* poor.

That realization should have made him happy, but instead, it unsettled him. It was like everything else that day: the friendly smiles, the abundance, the gifts, having people to buy gifts for. It was good, but so different from his previous life that it felt unreal. As if he might touch something solid, only to feel it dissolve under his hands. And then he'd open his eyes and find himself lying alone in the desert, with Jennie and Mia and his entire life in Las Anclas nothing but an incredibly vivid dream.

Ross wished he hadn't thought of that. Now he'd probably have a nightmare about it. He laid his palm on the booth wall, rubbing his fingers along the rough cloth over hard wood. Everything was solid and real. "I'd like the tool rack."

Mr. Rodriguez smiled as he lifted it down. "I think I know who this is for. In fact, I had her in mind when I made it. So, Ross, how are you enjoying the market?"

"I've never seen anything like it before," Ross replied.

Mr. Rodriguez snorted. "It was better in the old days. When the traders sailed in from Catalina, *then* it was a sight to see."

An old lady said, "Before Tom Preston kicked them out!"

"Yeah," a man chimed in. "And that's not all we lost. Remember their plays? I miss those more than the traders."

Mr. Rodriguez wrapped the tool rack in old newspaper. Ross caught a glimpse of a headline: TENTACLED TOMATO TRESPASSES ON PEACEFUL PUMPKIN PATCH! He bet Jennie had written it. She liked matching letters. And exclamation points.

"That's why I'm voting for Noah Horst for defense chief." Mr. Rodriguez gave Ross a weirdly intense stare, as if he was making a speech, not having a conversation. "Regardless of his personal opinions about Changed folk, he's promised to set those aside and go talk to the folk at Catalina. If he gets elected, the traders and musicians and actors are coming back."

Then Ross knew the source of the tension beneath the holiday cheer: the upcoming election.

In which he, as a new citizen, had a vote.

It would be his first election—yet another first—but it didn't seem as meaningful to him as it did to everyone else. Mr. Horst and the current defense chief, Mr. Preston, both hated the Changed. Mr. Horst had threatened Ross, and Mr. Preston had sent the bounty hunter to kill him. Sure, Mr. Horst had declared that he now saw the value of different people living together in harmony, but Ross didn't believe it. Dr. Lee had remarked over dinner that Mr. Horst would say black was white if he thought it would win him the election.

Ross had asked Mia if he *had* to vote, and she'd looked so horrified at the idea of having the right but not using it that he'd dropped the subject. But he still didn't see what difference it made. He didn't want either of those bigots running things.

An earnest man stuck his head out from a booth selling bright-moths in decorative terrariums. "Safety is more important than fun. As long as Tom Preston's defense chief, we'll never see Voske again."

Mr. Rodriguez pointed dramatically at Ross. "That's because of this young man here, *not* Tom Preston."

Ross reached for his package, hoping to take it and go, but Mr. Rodriguez held it tight.

The old mechanic declaimed, "Ross Juarez saved Las Anclas! And he did it with his Change power. If he'd been run out of town like the Catalina folk, this square would be filled with Voske's soldiers. And instead of holiday banners, it'd have our heads on pikes!"

Ross wished he hadn't heard that. The harder he tried not to think about it, the more he vividly he recalled staring at the ground in Gold Point, lest an upward glance confront him with a smooth white skull. Desperately, he shoved a handful of scrip at Mr. Rodriguez.

A woman looked up from the hammer she was examining. "You know the rules. No campaigning until a week before the election."

A chorus of dismissive noises rose up, with Mr. Rodriguez speaking loudest. "We can still *talk* about it! This isn't Gold Point!"

To Ross's relief, Mr. Rodriguez finally took his scrip and

released Mia's gift. Ross bolted back to Yolanda. Much as he didn't like touching people he didn't know well, he grabbed her elbow to hurry her away.

"It's okay, Ross. No one will get in trouble for early campaigning. It's a rule, but it's not a strict one." Wistfully, Yolanda added, "I wish I was old enough to have a vote."

I wish I could give you mine, Ross thought.

Mrs. Callahan's voice blared out, loud enough to make him jump. "Embroidered silks! Fine ribbons! Party dresses! Everything altered to order!"

Her booth was filled with fancy dresses and coats, shirts and pants, skirts and blouses, even scarves and hats. Especially scarves and hats.

It's like Felicité Wolfe turned into a place, Ross thought.

"Oh, do you mind if I take a quick look?" Yolanda begged.

"Go ahead." Ross squelched his urge to dodge Mrs. Callahan. Fair was fair. Yolanda had waited for him.

Yolanda rushed in to sort through the ribbons. Behind her back, Mrs. Callahan's upper lip curled in disgust. Ross wished Yolanda could go somewhere else. She had to know exactly what the dressmaker thought of Changed people, but no one else sold ribbons.

Mrs. Callahan turned her glare on her son, who had been yawning over the coat display. "Henry!"

"Silk embroidery," Henry announced with the enthusiasm of a seller of week-old fish. Then a much more sincere grin split his face. "Felicité!"

Ross snatched up the nearest skirt and hid behind it, hoping no one would ask him who he wanted it for. It was too small for Jennie, too big for Mia, and a shade of green halfway between mold and vomit.

Felicité minced in, her curls bouncing. The last time Ross had seen Felicité, her hair had been bright red. It was now a rich brown, a shade or two darker than her skin. She flipped up her curls in a dramatic gesture.

Henry caught the hint. "Oh, your hair! It's so pretty." He wound a curl around his finger as she leaned over the counter to kiss him.

"I had it dyed the exact shade of Grandmère's ancient mahogany chiffonier," said Felicité. "It came from France in the time of my ancestress, Queen Marie Antoinette."

Yolanda stifled a snicker. Felicité claimed descent from every royal person named in the Las Anclas history textbooks. Ross bet if he prospected a book that mentioned some new queens, she would suddenly remember that she was related to them, too.

"It's exquisite, dear," Mrs. Callahan cooed to Felicité. "But then, you always are. You have such impeccable taste. Are you shopping for your parents or your friends?"

"Don't tell, but I have some of your lovely dresses in mind for my friends. And maybe a greatcoat for Daddy. But not on this trip." Felicité's voice set Ross's teeth on edge. It was so sweet—too sweet. Like a handful of sugar crammed down your throat.

She stooped to pet her golden rat, Wu Zetian. Ross edged another step back. Felicité had used that rat to spy on Jennie and Mia and Yuki, and gotten them thrown in jail for weeks. Though Felicité had denied it, Ross was sure she'd trained Wu Zetian to spy on the entire town.

And he wasn't the only one who'd figured that out. When he'd first come to Las Anclas, everyone had stroked Wu Zetian and tried to coax her into their laps. Now people eyed her suspiciously and stepped out of her way.

Felicité stiffened as Kerry strolled up. The former princess turned a razor-edged smile toward Felicité, then offered a hand to Wu Zetian.

Of course Kerry doesn't care that the rat's a spy, Ross thought. *She's used to much worse spy-masters than Felicité.*

The golden rat tipped her head, giving Kerry the perfect angle to scratch between her round pink ears.

"Hello, Wu Zetian, you delicate darling." Kerry spoke in a weirdly sweet voice.

It wasn't until Ross caught a flash of rage tightening Felicité's face that he realized that Kerry was imitating Felicité. It was subtle, probably to prevent Felicité from accusing Kerry of mocking her, but clearly deliberate.

Felicité scooped up her rat, then turned her back on Kerry and gave Mrs. Callahan a charming smile. "May I borrow Henry?"

"Of course, dear." Mrs. Callahan replied pleasantly, but her expression hardened into contempt as her gaze fixed on Kerry. But when Kerry picked up a lace frill, the nastiness wiped off Mrs. Callahan's face like she'd used a dust rag.

"Come on in!" Mrs. Callahan said with a huge smile.

The dressmaker was only trying to drum up business, but that grin bore an unpleasant resemblance to the fake smiles the Gold Point townspeople plastered on because they feared King Voske's spying. Felicité's smile was fake, too, but hers was more convincing; Ross would never have known it wasn't sincere if he hadn't happened to be looking at her for the single second she'd let her fury show. His skin crawled.

Felicité set Wu Zetian down out of Kerry's reach. Then Henry and Felicité marched off, arm in arm, the spy rat following after.

A couple of people glanced from Wu Zetian to the sky, probably checking for Voske's spy hawks. Ross couldn't help glancing up as well, but his view was blocked by the booth's cloth ceiling.

When he lowered his gaze, he caught Mrs. Callahan staring at the fingerprint scars on his throat. He ducked his chin, letting his hair fall forward to hide them. Fake smiles, spies, the burn of Luis's fingers — everything reminded Ross of Gold Point. His heart was pounding and he felt slightly dizzy. Like he was trapped in the hell cell, with the thick granite walls closing in on him. A painful weight compressed his chest. He had to run, get out of the crowd, get somewhere safe under the open sky —

"Hey, Ross."

He jumped, but it was only Kerry. She pointed to some embroidered blouses. "I want to get one of those for Jennie. What colors does she like?"

Ross forced himself to breathe. To try to relax. He'd come to buy a present for Jennie, and he wasn't going to run away without one. He *wasn't* in Gold Point. He'd flooded the hell cells himself, with Kerry's help. He was in Las Anclas. He was safe. He was home.

"Bright ones," Ross said. "Orange, yellow, red."

"Thanks." Kerry lowered her voice. "I've got another question for you. Should I get a gift for Paco? Brisa said I shouldn't because he won't get one for me, and then it'll be awkward. Becky said it'll hurt his feelings if I don't, since he's my brother. Meredith said I could try but he'd probably throw it in my face. What do you think?"

"I don't know Paco that well." Ross thought of suggesting that she ask Jennie, who knew Paco as well as anyone now that his mother Sera was dead and his boyfriend Yuki had left. But Jennie was the last person Kerry would want to ask about anything.

Kerry's sharp eyes narrowed, but to his relief, she only said, "You go diving with him, and I wanted to ask another guy."

"Okay." When they dove in Yuki's sea cave, Paco seemed calm and friendly. He never mentioned Kerry, but if he saw her, he'd go silent and grim. And if she didn't leave, he would. "Don't give him anything. I think Meredith was joking, but I don't think he'd like it, either. And he definitely won't be hurt if you don't."

For a disquieting moment, the grimness that tightened Kerry's sharp features made her look just like Paco. Just like *Voske*. Tension gripped Ross's neck.

Then she gave a brisk nod and lifted a scarlet blouse with embroidered golden starbursts. "Thanks. Would Jennie like this?"

The tension eased. "She'd love it. She's beautiful in red *and* gold. And she likes embroidery." Ross added, "Mia likes pink. And ruffles. Lots of ruffles."

Kerry gave him a thin, secretive smile. He knew Kerry liked secrets. "I've got something else in mind for Mia."

◆ ◆ ◆

Ross opened the door to the Rileys' house. He'd known it would be crowded for Christmas, but the sheer number of people crammed inside drove him back a step. Then he made himself stop. Breathe. Give himself time to calm down.

As Dr. Lee had suggested to him, he made himself look at the people as individuals rather than as a crowd. If he thought of them as a mob, they'd feel dangerous. So he searched out people he knew, people who were harmless. Yolanda Riley. Jose Riley. Grandma Riley. A toddler with the Riley dark skin and curly hair making a grab for a shiny Christmas tree ornament, her oversized bat-like wings fluttering through the cut-outs in her dress.

To Ross's surprise, the little girl rose a few inches above the ground before a man and a woman lunged to snatch her away from the fragile glass bell. He'd never before seen a winged person who could actually fly. Usually their wings were too small to lift the weight of their body. And though still a child, the girl had the big Riley frame she'd obviously inherited from her mother.

For the first time, Ross realized just how many Rileys there were. Even the half- and step-cousins from Jackalope Row had gathered, in addition to all the scattered aunts and uncles and grand-nieces and nephews.

Jennie emerged from the group. She wore a crimson dress embroidered around the neckline with holly leaves. Her black hair, which was usually in bead-tipped braids, stood out in a puff around her face. It reminded him of the first time they'd danced together, alone in the backyard. The low cut of her dress, displaying her cleavage, reminded him of another dance, the one where she'd worn Meredith's too-tight dress. He'd spent half the night wondering if it would split right down the middle. It had sure looked like it might.

Ross took a deep breath, trying not to blush or stare, and caught a quirk of mischief in her smile. If she knew what he was picturing, she obviously didn't mind.

"Come on in, Ross." She took his hand, her grip warm and strong and reassuring. "Have a seat."

She seated him between herself and Mia, who instantly grabbed his hand under the table and squeezed it. Mia, too, had dressed up, in her own way. He recognized Dr. Lee's second-best button-down shirt, well-made but much too big for her, plus a pair of her father's pants, baggy and crammed into shiny boots. She'd confessed earlier that she was afraid that if she wore a dress, some disaster would ruin both it and the evening.

Ross didn't have to be introduced to anyone right away, because he already knew everyone within speaking distance. Jennie had probably set that up on purpose, to make him more comfortable. She was so thoughtful and kind, knowing what people wanted and making sure it happened. And it made him feel warm inside to know that she'd been thinking of him before he'd even arrived.

As the food passed from hand to hand, he relaxed incrementally. Everyone was warm and friendly. He was attending a party of friends and relatives, not a gathering of bandits or a subtle battle conducted in words and glances, like those horrific meals at Voske's palace. It was a family dinner, like normal people had every day. Just...bigger.

By the time the honey-basted ham, roast turkey, and side dishes had been replaced with a dried apple pie, a lemon meringue pie, blackberry turnovers, a cornmeal cake topped with candied orange slices, and a quivering caramel flan, Ross was actually enjoying himself.

"A slice of everything, Ross?" suggested Jennie.

"We'll have to roll him home," Meredith teased.

"We'll have to roll *you* home," Jennie said with a grin. "You've never met a dessert you didn't want seconds of."

The winged toddler fluttered over and made a grab for Ross's gauntlet. Her father again rushed forward, but Ross said, "It's okay." The girl's attention didn't bother him. She was only curious. Mia's gauntlet was an extraordinary piece of work, clever and beautiful and finely made. No wonder it had caught the little girl's eye.

Ross held out his hand so the child could touch the shiny metal. "She can't damage it. And it doesn't hurt."

"Little mechanic," Mia said approvingly. She leaned over to indicate the part the toddler was prodding. "This is called a rivet. Can you say that, April? *Rivet.*"

"Rivet," April repeated clearly. As she traced it, she leaned on Ross's leg, her solid toddler's body oddly light.

"Hollow bones?" Ross asked her father.

The man beamed and nodded. "But strong. No more danger of breaking than anyone's. Dr. Lee examined her. Her wings grow in pace with the rest of her body, so he thinks she'll still be able to fly as an adult. If she can, she'll be the first in the history of Las Anclas."

"The first flying Riley," said her mother, joining them. "You can't keep her out of anything. She hardly ever breaks things, though."

April smiled proudly. Ross could tell she was repeating a

parent's words as she said, "I'm *careful*."

Mr. and Mrs. Riley passed around dessert plates. Everyone in the family turned toward Mrs. Riley when they spoke, so she could read their lips. Even for the most trivial remarks and silly jokes, they made sure to include her. It reminded Ross of…

He grasped at a fleeting memory, a tall man with black hair down to his shoulders: his father. Had his father also been deaf? That felt…wrong, but not far wrong. Had he been disabled in some other way, like Ross was now?

He had been. Ross was suddenly and completely sure of it. But he had no idea how, or why he knew, or why he knew the fact but not the detail. He tried to reach further into the memory. Black hair… Brown skin… Stone dust, filling his throat, choking him…

"Ross?" Jennie peered at Ross, her dark gaze concerned. "Are you all right?"

The memory slipped away before Ross could grasp it, leaving him puzzled and frustrated. Instinctively, he lowered his face to hide his feelings, pretending to inspect his plate. "Sure. Just wondering where to put all this."

"That's never been a problem before," Mia piped up, then laid her warm hand on his thigh under the table. There were so many people crowded around that Mia and Ross and Jennie were pressed close together. Every time Jennie turned, her hair brushed against his cheek, soft as a cloud.

Paco sat opposite Ross, smiling at a joke Jose had made. But the smile didn't reach his eyes. It didn't look fake. But it didn't look truly happy, either. Ross had barely known him before his mother Sera had been killed, but he had a vague recollection of an easygoing boy who joked and laughed, and a sharper one of the passion and fluid ease with which Paco had played his drums.

Paco made no music now.

In the distance, the town bell clanged three times.

"Watch change!" a little girl yelled.

"Present time!" the rest of the kids chorused.

"When the table is cleared," Mrs. Riley said.

Ross watched, filled with emotions that he only partly recognized. Like his surprise at how even the youngest kids moved with the easy precision of a military drill, everyone knowing their job and how to work with each other. And the familiar awkwardness at being the only one without a place.

But he wasn't the only one. Mia, Meredith, and Paco didn't join in, either. It was only a chore for Rileys and a few selected visitors, like Dee's best friends, Z and Nhi, who held dishes over the sink while Dee sprayed them with a miniature waterspout.

But Mia and Meredith sat back and chatted, while Ross couldn't stop himself from watching for suspicious shadows or the glint of steel. He *knew* he was safe. But he couldn't make himself *feel* it. And all that family togetherness, which should have made him more relaxed, inexplicably made him more on edge.

What's wrong *with me?* Ross thought for the millionth time.

Half the time the Rileys make him feel more safe than he'd felt in his entire life, and half the time they made him want to run and hide. But he had no idea what triggered the difference. And his father—how could Ross be so sure that he'd had a disability, but have no idea what it had been?

Why didn't he remember things the way everyone else did, like a story? Why did his story-memory start a couple years ago, and everything before that was nothing but tiny pieces that popped into his head every now and then, half the time for no reason that he could figure out, and disappeared the moment he tried to remember more?

When the kitchen was clean, the smallest kids ran to the Christmas tree and began handing out gifts. The teenagers and adults gathered their chairs into small groups.

Meredith turned cheerfully to Ross, saying, "I gave my gifts at Hanukkah. But I should have gotten *you* something. I could bake you a pie later."

"Sure. Thanks." Now Ross felt awkward. It hadn't occurred to him to get her a present. He'd assumed gifts were only for people he was especially close to or people he'd done something special with, like diving with Paco or shopping with Yolanda.

But Meredith didn't seem upset. Maybe he should get her something and hold on to it until and unless she actually produced the pie. He could ask Jennie what the equivalent of a pie was. That was exactly the sort of thing she'd know.

Yolanda happily opened her presents, including the one Ross

had hastily bought while her back was turned. He'd guessed from her purchase of pink ribbons for a blouse she was sewing that she'd enjoy pink shell bracelets to go with it. She was wearing the blouse now. Yolanda delightedly slid on the bracelets, then made wind swirl around her wrists. The bracelets spun around and around, while the ribbons on her sleeves fluttered like streamers.

"I have a gift for the whole family," Paco called out.

Mr. and Mrs. Riley unwrapped a beautiful stained glass window worked into a rising sun.

"It's to replace the window that got broken when Mia blew up the pit mouth," Paco explained.

Snickers arose as everyone looked at Dee. She defensively clutched the fluffy white kitten in her lap. "If I hadn't smuggled it in, someone else would have, sooner or later. They're cute in their larval form."

"They *are*," Z said loyally.

Nhi nodded. "Anyone could have made that mistake. Anyone!"

Everyone over the age of thirteen looked extremely dubious at that statement, but no one argued.

Ross waited nervously as Jennie picked up his embroidered bag. Her face lit with a lovely smile as she poured the beads into her cupped palm. Blue and white agate shone in the firelight, swirled together like a cloudy sky on a summer day.

"Oh, if I was wearing my braids, I'd put these in right now. They're gorgeous, Ross." Jennie shook her hand, making them click together. "I like the sound, too." With a wicked smile that hit him in the heart—and headed down south—she added, "They'll feel smooth as silk against my neck. Stone stays cool for a long time, even on hot days. When you see me wearing them, remind me to have you touch them."

Ross could only manage a nod, then Mia thrust a sheet-wrapped cylinder into Jennie's lap. Ross saw that Jennie guessed what it was as soon as her hand closed over it. A spasm of pain tightened her features, and he knew she still missed the Rangers.

"Everyone knew it was Jennie's sword," Mia had told Ross indignantly, while she was making the new sword's hand guard. "It only *technically* belonged to the Rangers. None of them will use it. Frances said it would feel like stealing. Mr. Preston could've given it to Jennie for her service or just so it wouldn't be wasted. But he kept it *because* she loved it."

Jennie's smile at Mia was wistful but pleased. She brandished her new sword so firelight ran down the watered steel. It was perfectly balanced, Ross knew.

"I didn't make the blade, of course," Mia said, as apologetically as if that might ruin the gift. "It's from Dad and me. We split the cost of the steel and the swordsmith's fee. I made the grip myself. It has your initials inlayed in bronze. And that's sort of partly from Ross, too, because I used his hand to model it. Did you know that your hands are exactly the same size?"

"Yes, I've noticed." Jennie's smile at Mia was sister-sweet, but it turned wicked again when she glanced at Ross. "Thank you so much, Mia. It's exactly—"

Mia beamed. "I'm so glad you like it! It was so horrible when Mr. Preston kicked—um, I mean, I'm so glad you like it!"

Jennie's hand tightened on the hilt, her knuckles paling. Ross knew that tension all too well. And he knew how to break it, too.

"Hey, Mia. Time for your present." Ross pointed to her package, which was almost as big as she was.

Jennie cast him a grateful look, and he felt her body relax against his. They both had memories they'd never get out of their heads, of things done that could never be undone. But they didn't have to think about them every single second.

Mia's gasp of delighted surprise when she opened her gift was everything Ross had hoped for. "How clever! Mr. Rodriguez designed it, didn't he? It's got his style written all over it."

She threw her arms around Ross, her silky hair brushing his cheek and her warm body pressed tight against his. He felt her lips move against his throat as she said, "It's exactly what I always wanted, only I didn't know I always wanted it until now. So it's a perfect surprise. And now I'll never stub my foot on my wrench again. It's the best present ever."

Mia released Ross, then peered earnestly into his face. As if she wasn't sure he'd understood exactly how much she liked it, she added, "Ever! *EVER!*"

Ross grinned. "I believe you."

Jennie made a rueful face as she handed Mia her present. "I wish I'd given you this first. Now it's got a lot to live up to."

Mia yanked the cloth bag open, then shook out a peach-colored dress decorated with rows and rows of blue ruffles, with blue forget-me-nots embroidered around the neckline.

Her body would be hidden beneath the ruffles, much as her father's baggy shirt concealed it now. The dress wasn't Ross's taste—he liked how comfortable she looked in her old overalls, and he *really* liked her shirts with those tempting little rips she never remembered to repair, so bits of her skin showed unexpectedly when she moved—but it was exactly the sort of thing Mia adored.

Sure enough, she let out a delighted little squeak. "It's beautiful. And the ruffles! All those ruffles! And you did it all yourself, Jennie, didn't you?"

"Meredith helped embroider the forget-me-nots," Jennie said, as Meredith grinned proudly.

"I love them." Mia's happiness lit her from within, making her prettier than ever. "It's beautiful work, and I needed a new dress. I could never wear my mother's pink dress again, after it turned out to be see-through—I mean, after Ross saw through—only because it was wet, but still—"

Everyone else seemed confused, but Ross had known what she meant from the word "pink." The night Voske had attacked Las Anclas, he and Mia had stumbled into her cottage, drenched in rain. She'd turned on the lights, and he'd seen her with silk plastered to her body, translucent and paper-thin. He'd seen *everything*.

A rush of blood flooded his face as he remembered how he'd stared, then realized that he'd been staring, then bolted outside. And how he'd stood there in the icy rain, burning with an inner heat and longing to go back inside. To look for just one second longer. To stop looking, and touch...

Mia's face was fiery red as she hurriedly concluded, "Well, anyway, the silk was ruined. It's just a keepsake now. But this one, I'll wear."

Jennie handed Ross a bag decorated with embroidered poppies. He pulled out a shirt of blue cotton, tailored exactly to his size. Three tiny stars were embroidered over the pockets, in silver, red, and blue.

Jennie indicated the stars. "I was thinking about the dance when I made it. Red for my favorite color, blue for Mia's, and silver for your night sky."

My night sky.

Jennie and Mia had given him the sky before. When he'd thought he was dying in Voske's hell cell, he'd remembered holding hands with the girls beneath the skylight they'd installed in his room. Ross held the shirt tight to his chest, wishing he could hold Jennie instead. Mia, too. But though Mia had already grabbed him and the whole town knew he was dating them both, he couldn't bring himself to embrace either of them in front of onlookers.

"Thank you." The words came out in a choked whisper. They felt totally inadequate, and he couldn't get out any more. But when he looked up at Jennie, he could see that she understood.

Mia jumped up. "See how you like it." She handed him an oddly shaped bundle wrapped in drop cloths and tied with a bow.

Ross tugged at the knot, but it was too secure for one hand. He reached with his left, but he couldn't undo a knot with the gauntlet. And if he took it off, his fingers wouldn't close tightly enough. He began to turn aside to hide his difficulty, bracing himself against a familiar rush of self-consciousness and shame, but it didn't come. Everyone watching him already knew about his hand. And none of them cared.

Then it hit him: he didn't care, either. He handed the package to Mia. "Can you undo this knot?"

Blushing furiously, Mia opened the package. "Sorry. Sorry. I just wanted it to look nice. And not fall out."

She shoved it back at him. Ross took out a weapon resembling a long horse pistol. He turned it over, fascinated. The barrel was solid except for an indented cradle with an odd crosspiece. It was beautifully made, with the elegant simplicity and precision that was the hallmark of Mia's work, but what *was* it?

"Wait! Wait! Here's the rest of it!" Mia handed him a quiver of cut down crossbow bolts.

Then Ross saw what it was: a one-handed crossbow, specially

designed for his right hand.

He had the same problem with ordinary crossbows that he'd had with the knot: his gauntlet was strong but lacked dexterity, while his bare left hand was weak and had a limited range of motion. He couldn't pull hard enough with his left hand to crank a crossbow; his right was strong enough, but his left couldn't grasp the weapon.

But this crossbow had a piece on top that he could jerk back with his left palm to crank the bow. He picked up a bolt with his left hand and slid it into the cradle along the barrel. He didn't put his finger on the trigger, of course, but he could see that the crossbow could be shot exactly like a gun.

Like Jennie's gift, Mia's was more than it appeared on the surface, and much more than just a nice thing to own. Both girls' presents said, *I thought hard about what's important to you and what would make you happy.*

He hoped his gifts had said the same thing.

"It's amazing, Mia," he said. "I wish I could try it out right now."

"I'll go with you," she offered. "I might want to improve something!"

"My turn." Paco handed him a small package. Ross was glad Kerry had asked his advice, because otherwise it would have never occurred to him to get anything for Paco.

The paper was easy to unwrap, revealing a fine leather sheath. Ross took his belt knife out of its much-repaired sheath and slid it into the new one. It fit perfectly. He thanked Paco, then handed him his gift.

As Paco slowly held up the fine shirt embroidered with folklorico patterns, Ross said, "I wanted to make up for ruining your shirt in the battle."

Paco's expression seemed calm and friendly, but Ross's stomach clenched with the unspoken tension that silenced the entire room. Giving Paco a dancing shirt was obviously the worst thing he could have done.

And apparently everyone knew why. Except Ross.

"Thanks," Paco said. His Adam's apple bobbed as if it cost him an effort to speak.

Ross was relieved when Mr. Riley cleared his throat. He was an imposing figure, broad-shouldered and immensely tall, his immaculate white suit a startling contrast to the near-black skin that Jennie had inherited. His dreadlocks were pulled into a long ponytail.

"All right, everyone," Mr. Riley announced in his rumbling voice. "Time for church. Put your gifts away."

The party broke up as some said their good-byes, while others started tidying up.

"Are you a Christian, Ross?" Mrs. Riley's voice was over-enunciated, as she couldn't hear her own words, but he had no trouble understanding her—or her kindness. "You're welcome to attend Christmas Eve service with us."

"Yes, I am," Ross began, then wondered why he'd said that. He couldn't *remember*. "I mean, I'm not sure."

He fixed his gaze on the floor, but he knew everyone was staring at him. If there was anything worse than having his early memories in bits and pieces, it was the way everyone looked at him when he stumbled over questions they thought were obvious.

But he'd said yes when Mrs. Riley had asked. The night of the dance, when Sheriff Crow had given him a piece of fry bread, memories had flooded back with its smell and taste. Maybe if he went to church, he'd remember more.

Still looking down, he muttered, "I'd like to come."

At the midnight mass, he stood between Jennie and Mr. Riley with a candle clutched in his good right hand. Voices rose and fell in the cadences of prayers and psalms. None of it was familiar, and he wished he hadn't come. Though he knew everyone, he felt isolated, an intruder.

Then a phrase jumped out at him. As it echoed in his mind, he heard a man's voice saying, *"Loving mother of the Redeemer, gate of heaven, star of the sea,*
assist your people
who have fallen yet strive to rise again."

He saw a woman kneeling on the floor. Her head was bowed, hiding her face, but he could see her hugely rounded belly. The statue of a peaceful-faced woman in blue robes loomed above her, with one hand stretched out above the woman's head.

The Virgin Mary, Ross remembered. *Mom's getting her pregnancy blessed.*

Ross's excitement at the prospect of a baby brother or sister rose up vividly within him, along with a child's over-serious debate over which he wanted more. He could feel the rough wood beneath his knees and smell the sweet scent of smoke rising up from a swinging metal container. For the briefest of moments, he was not merely remembering the past, but re-living it.

Then a present thought intruded: *This is my chance to find out what Mom looked like.*

The images instantly began to fade. As he tried to raise his head to see his mother's face, the memory vanished.

Ross was back in the church in Las Anclas, a young man alone in a crowd. He stood lost and silent as a chorus rose up around him, speaking words at once alien and familiar.

"Forever and ever, amen."

·2·
JENNIE

THE RUDDY DISC OF the sun sank behind Jennie Riley as she and the rest of Pa's perimeter patrol headed for the back gate. Beside her, Kerry rode Nugget, the prehensile-tailed royal stallion. Slanting rays of sunlight struck his coat to beaten gold.

Jennie suppressed a grin when she saw the sentries on the wall watching Nugget rather than the horizon. It had been a month since Kerry Voske — Kerry *Cho*, Jennie reminded herself — had fled to Las Anclas with four shimmering royal horses. But nobody had tired of admiring them.

Sally's silver coat glistened with ethereal beauty as she playfully flicked her tail at her rider's head scarf. Of Kerry's original four horses, Penny was too advanced in pregnancy to be ridden, Nugget only allowed Kerry to ride him, and Kerry had given the bronze mare Tigereye to Yuki Nakamura when he'd gone off to prospect alone.

That left Sally to be awarded as a hotly contested mark of Kerry's favor. When Kerry's friends Brisa, Meredith, or Sujata went on patrol, Kerry loaned them Sally in strict rotation. But those girls were in Ranger training now, and Jennie wasn't there to train them.

Once again, she heard Mr. Preston's angry, contemptuous voice: *I want you to know one thing, Jennie Riley. No matter what else happens, you are banned from the Rangers for the rest of your life.*

Jennie slapped her saddle, stopping herself from replaying

those words over and over. She didn't deny her loss, but she could choose to focus on the present, not the past. Jennie was a teacher now, and the Rangers were no longer her business. But the plots and ploys that affected her students were.

What was Kerry's real reason for bringing Sally on patrol? The ex-princess had changed her name, but not her nature. Jennie was certain that Kerry used-to-be-Voske calculated even her most casual actions. Especially those. Mia wasn't on patrol and didn't care about horses anyway, and Kerry's other friend, Becky, was working at her apprenticeship at the surgery. That freed up Sally for some manipulative purpose. Jennie was sure that the reason a delighted Nasreen Hassan was riding Sally was because Nasreen was Felicité's friend, and Kerry meant to steal her away.

As the patrol rode through the gates, Alfonso Medina used the gecko-like pads on his bare fingers, toes, and heels to scurry straight down the wall. He stopped a few feet above Jennie's head, upside down with his black hair hanging in his face.

"Hi, Alfonso," she said.

Alfonso was a year younger than her, and he'd been shy and quiet his entire life. When she'd started teaching, Jennie had discovered that he was one of the smartest in the class, with a particular gift for science. She'd thought he might apprentice as a veterinarian or in some other science-based job, but when she'd last asked him, he'd said he'd work at his family's dairy. Jennie couldn't argue with that—the Medina dairy was quite prosperous—but she wondered how happy he'd be following in his family's footsteps. She'd never gotten the impression that wealth was important to him.

Maybe he wants to take over the cow breeding, Jennie thought. *It's genetics, and I know he's interested in that.*

Alfonso lifted one hand, his pads coming loose from the adobe with a soft popping sound, to pluck a grasping eater rose tendril from his wrist. "I have a message from the mayor. She'd like to speak to you at your earliest convenience. She's at Wolfe House."

"Thanks, Alfonso," she said.

"You're welcome." With that, he scuttled backwards up the wall. Jennie watched, enjoying his agility and lack of self-consciousness.

Pa leaned over, his saddle creaking. "I'll take Sidewinder to the stables. *At your earliest convenience* means earlier than convenient."

Jennie handed off the reins, trying not to be annoyed. If anyone had the right to give her orders, it was the mayor. But she couldn't help thinking that when Grandma Wolfe had been the teacher, Mayor Wolfe wouldn't have dared to summon her mother. It was more likely to have been the other way around.

As Jennie neared the forge, she saw that its windows had been soaped with big green letters saying **VOTE HORST! BETTER DEFENSE!** Brightly dyed strips of green cloth festooned the eaves. Campaign week was already in full swing.

In one week, the town would vote for defense chief, mayor, and a new council member. Voting age was eighteen, so it was Jennie's first election. She'd watched previous ones with excitement, longing for the day when she could vote. She'd imagined herself passionately campaigning, making stirring speeches for her favorite candidates, and turning the tide of the election all by herself.

Just my luck, Jennie thought glumly. *My first election...and I don't have a favorite candidate.*

Mayor Wolfe was running unopposed; no one had the nerve to take her on. Jennie didn't care for the mayor personally, but Las Anclas was a well-run town. Jennie would vote for her. She felt indifferent about the two candidates running for Judge Vardam's place, but she'd eventually pick one.

Much tougher to think about was the race for defense chief: Mr. Preston vs. Mr. Horst. Talk about a choice between two evils!

Jennie's shoulders tensed as she approached the crowd. Mr. Horst stood on a box by his forge, bellowing like the clang of a hammer on an anvil. "Are you enjoying Tom Preston's drills that drag you from your own valuable work and your precious free time? Voske was defeated! DEFEATED! And yet Tom Preston works us harder than ever, in drills specifically designed to fight off an enemy who's GONE! So I ask you now: DO YOU FEEL SAFER?"

"NO!" shouted the watching crowd.

Jennie started to roll her eyes, then considered Horst's question: *Did* she feel safer?

No.

But not because the drills were unnecessary. She'd seen Gold Point's vast army. Last summer Voske had underestimated how many soldiers he needed to conquer Las Anclas, but he wouldn't make that mistake again.

Jennie was certain that Voske would come back. It was a terrifying thought.

"Vote for me," Horst roared out. "I'll give you a strong defense. A smart defense! Not more training—better training! Not more weapons—better weapons! And I will respect the intelligence and the time of the people of Las Anclas!"

As the crowd cheered, Mr. Horst's son Tommy passed out green rosette pins for his supporters. Everywhere in sight, political allegiances were proclaimed in colors. The jail was the only building without decorations. The sheriff and her deputies were forbidden from campaigning, since it was their job to keep the peace. But beyond the jail, the brewery bristled with little red flags for Mr. Preston. And the crowd there was even bigger.

Tommy Horst stepped into Jennie's path. Not many people could loom over her, but he'd grown almost as tall as his father.

Tommy shoved a rosette into her hand, forcing her to either take it or give him and his father the direct insult of dropping it on the ground. Annoyed, Jennie clenched her fingers, squashing it.

Tommy didn't seem to notice. With a smug grin, he said, "Glad to have your vote, Jennie. I bet Mr. Preston's regretting kicking you out of the Rangers now!"

He turned to give out another rosette, and Jennie knew that he hadn't meant to manipulate her into taking one. That was the sort of trick Kerry or Felicité might play, but it was way too subtle for Tommy. He'd just assumed that her personal feelings about Mr. Preston were all that mattered to her.

Jennie stuffed the rosette into her pocket. She'd get rid of it later. As far as she was concerned, neither man had earned her vote. Her insides still roiled with fury and betrayal whenever she thought of Mr. Preston. But would Mr. Horst have made better decisions in Mr. Preston's position? And what did Mr. Horst mean by "better weapons" and "better training" anyway? The lack of specifics made Jennie suspect that he didn't know himself. He made weapons, but he didn't design new ones. Only Mia did that.

Jennie reached the brewery, which was almost hidden by a crowd wearing red rosettes. If it wasn't for those, she'd have taken the rally for a raucous, drunken party.

"Free beer!" A woman's piercing call was followed by an uproarious cheer.

That explains a lot, Jennie thought.

Grandma Thakrar, the brewer, presided over a giant keg, assisted by a pair of her grandchildren. One handed out glasses of beer, and the other pinned a red rosette on the person who took it.

"Empty glasses go there!" Grandma Thakrar pointed to a grandchild holding a tray. Jennie watched the boy dunk the tray into a rain barrel. A fourth grandchild used her Change power to evaporate the water on each glass. Then the clean, dry glasses were returned to the beer barrel. It was an impressively organized system, running as efficiently as a Ranger drill.

Jennie spotted both the Willet brothers unpinning their rosettes and sneaking to the back of the line. Two of her most unruly students, thirteen-year-old Peter Chang and fourteen-year-old Hans Ruiz, stood at the head of the line in unimpressive disguises consisting of their fathers' boots and caps pulled low over their faces.

A grandchild started to pour Peter a glass of beer. Grandma Thakrar yanked it out of his hand. With a sardonic chuckle, she knocked the boys' caps off. "Drinking age is eighteen. Come back in five years. Next!"

The crowd laughed as the boys slunk off, scowling.

Grandma Thakrar peered down the line at where the Willets were hiding their faces much as Peter and Hans had. She yelled, "And no double dipping! Don't think I don't remember who already got served!"

The Willets slumped away, muttering. Ed bumped into Jennie, beer fumes so strong that Jennie hoped they wouldn't permeate her clothes. She ducked around the two—just to collide with a man carrying a brimming glass of beer.

Her arms flew up in an instinctive block—useless against liquid. The entire pint leaped out of its mug and drenched her.

"Sorry," muttered the guilty party. Then he chuckled and said to one of his cronies, "It's not double-dipping if I didn't drink it.

Let's get back in line!"

Not only was Jennie soaked in strong-smelling beer, but her white shirt was now virtually transparent. She folded her arms over her breasts, wondering if it was worse to make the mayor wait while she walked home to change, or to arrive at Wolfe House soaked in beer.

No, it was definitely worse to keep Mayor Wolfe waiting. Better to get it over with, whatever it was. Jennie dropped her arms and shouldered her way through the crowd. She couldn't get any wetter, and no one was looking at her anyway when there was free beer to be had.

With a grin, she thought, *Too bad Ross isn't here.* He'd *appreciate the view. And no amount of free beer could distract him.*

She wondered if Ross even drank beer. He'd had dinner once at her house when wine had been served to the eighteen-and-overs, and once at the saloon when Jack had given the table free tequila shots. Both times, Ross had accepted one drink and made it last for the entire meal, as if he feared drinking enough to affect his ability to fight. Even during a peaceful dinner with friends, he hadn't felt truly safe.

Like going to church or Luc's or a family dinner, having a few drinks sometimes was a good and ordinary thing for Jennie, but something Ross either had to steel himself to do, or wouldn't—maybe couldn't—do at all. *There might be a whole lot of things Ross will never relax enough to do.*

The idea unsettled her. She strode faster, as if she could leave it behind. By the time she reached Jack's saloon, she felt like she was trying to outrun her own mind.

Jack's saloon was banner-free. Sheriff Crow stood on the porch, watching the crowd. The Changed skull side of her face was as expressionless as ever, but the other side was taut with stress. She rubbed her forehead as if she had a headache. Jack quietly set a tray table beside her. It held a glass of lemonade decorated with a sprig of mint, a dish of shortbread cookies, and another dish of sliced oranges.

Sheriff Crow's tense face relaxed into a tender smile, completely different from her usual quirk of dry amusement. She and Jack had once been engaged, and while that was over now,

Jennie had sure never seen her smile like that at anyone else. "Thanks, Jack. You really don't have to."

"Of course I do," Jack replied easily. "You won't take a chair. It makes me look like a bad host, having you stand there without even refreshments."

"Your chairs are too comfortable. If I sit down, I'll never get up."

"I'm sure I've got something uncomfortable somewhere. Maybe in the basement. If you don't drink my lemonade, I'll go fetch it."

"Guess I've got no choice, then." Sheriff Crow took a long drink of the lemonade, then set down the glass and returned her gaze to the crowd. Without looking at him, she reached out to brush her hand against Jack's. He curled his fingers around hers, but made no further movement toward her.

He's like me with Ross, Jennie thought. Careful. Letting the sheriff set the pace. Offering things, but in a way that made it easy for her to say no if she didn't want them.

Usually Jennie didn't want to know what the older generation were up to. But those two weren't that much older than she was. Jennie wondered if she *should* watch them. Maybe she'd learn something. Sheriff Crow wasn't Ross and Jennie wasn't Jack, but...

Several voices from the crowd rose in anger.

"It's about time the poor folk got a say on the council!"

"You're just too lazy to work!"

As the first speaker pulled back his fist for a roundhouse, a whoosh of air buffeted Jennie. With her Changed speed, Sheriff Crow caught the punch before it landed.

"Break it up." She levered down the man's arm, then spun to catch his opponent's attempted slap. Holding the men apart, Sheriff Crow said, "Both of you. Go home, or go to jail."

Jennie could see why the sheriff had a headache. There were hours to go before nightfall, and six days to go before the election. As Sheriff Crow gave the scowling fighters a hard shove in opposite directions, Jack stayed on the porch, waiting for her to return to him.

Is that the lesson? Jennie wondered. *Be patient, and let him come to you?*

But that reminded her that someone was waiting for her, and it wasn't Ross. Jennie hurried toward the Hill, dodging a group of children playing tag. The shadow of a hawk passed overhead. The kids stopped to shout up at it, their hands cupped around their mouths.

"Hey, Voske! You stink!"

"And your socks stink!"

"You're never gonna get us!" A girl shook a tiny fist at the hawk. "Come again and we'll kick your butt from here to Catalina!"

As the bird continued on its flight, the kids cheered.

"We scared him!" a boy yelled. "Look at him flying away!"

Jennie doubted that the hawk was one of Voske's, though it amused her to imagine him getting a report that the seven-year-olds of Las Anclas thought his socks stank.

After Kerry had revealed that Voske spied on people with the help of an old prospector, Pru, whose Change power let her hear and see through hawks, Las Anclas had taken measures to ensure that he could never use that against them again. Not only did the Rangers make regular searches for Pru, but Mr. Preston had warned every trader who had visited the town, knowing that they would pass it on wherever they went.

Jennie gave her reeking, beer-stained shirt one last hopeless brush as she approached Wolfe House. It was as imposing as ever, lording it over Las Anclas from atop the Hill. Three of its wings were visible from where she stood, the whitewashed walls ochre in the fading light.

As she passed the stumpy spikes of the trimmed rosebushes, the windows began glowing golden. But not in Felicité's room, Jennie was glad to see. Felicité would undoubtedly hear all about Jennie's beer-soaked visit. But at least she wouldn't see it. Or smell it.

A servant opened the door. As Jennie placed her shoes on the rack, she heard a very deliberate sniff. Even the servant was sneering at her. Jennie was debating whether explaining would make her look better or worse when the mayor walked in.

It was clearly not Jennie's day. Mayor Wolfe was always elegant, without a hair of her chignon out of place, but as if she'd set out to create the worst possible contrast between their appearances, she wore her single most intimidating outfit. Mia called it the Button Dress. It was a close-fitting, severely cut gown with about fifty polished obsidian buttons in two lines down the front, making her glitter as if she wore shining armor. Jennie supposed it *was* armor, of a sort.

"Please excuse my—" Jennie choked off a gulp of laughter as she thought, *smell.* "—appearance. The brewery is giving out free beer, and a guy with a mug bumped into me."

"I expect that a certain element in town is positively swimming in it. And I am quite aware that you are not among them. A least, not voluntarily." The mayor smiled in an apparent attempt to put Jennie at ease, but no one could relax in the presence of the Button Dress. "Please come into the parlor."

Jennie was relieved that at least the mayor understood about the beer. Then she took in the meaning of the parlor invitation. If her summons had been purely business, she would have been invited into the office. The parlor meant it was at least partly personal. Jennie couldn't imagine what personal matter could involve her and the mayor, but it couldn't be anything good.

Jennie gingerly sat on the parlor's least fancy chair, which was still embroidered satin, and reminded herself not to lean back. She remembered Mia's account of her disastrous visit to Wolfe House, when she'd demonstrated her collapsible cudgel and accidentally knocked a candy dish flying. The bowl was now atop a mantelpiece, well out of reach of the guest chairs.

They've Mia-proofed the parlor, Jennie thought, stifling a grin. If that was even possible. If Mia ever returned, it would probably be with a long-distance weapon.

The mayor smiled graciously. "As you know, Felicité's eighteenth birthday is coming up. She would like to celebrate it with her graduation. I brought you here to ask for your honest opinion. Do you think she's ready?"

At that, everything became clear. If the mayor needed to know this far in advance, she must be planning a party that involved the entire town.

Jennie glanced at the half-circle of scars on her hand. Months after she'd been bitten, they were still pink, extremely noticeable against her dark skin. She might bear the marks of Felicité's teeth till the day she died.

Jennie longed to say, "No, she needs at least another year. Poor thing, she's just not very bright."

She took a deep breath to keep her voice calm and business-like. "Yes, I think she's ready. I know Grandma Wolfe wanted her to read all the histories and town records in our library. She hasn't finished, but she could do that on her own." *Let Felicité's laziness be someone else's problem.*

"Are there any other areas of concern?" Mayor Wolfe asked.

If Felicité found a subject boring, she put in the minimum of effort, then stopped. But her mother undoubtedly knew that, so Jennie could phrase it delicately without worrying that she'd be misunderstood.

"She's shaky on science and math, but I've taken her as far as she can go with those. In terms of physical training, she's competent with a crossbow. But when it comes to hand-to-hand combat..." Jennie was at a loss for delicate phrasing there. Felicité refused to even put in the minimum of effort. She'd go through the motions, but at half-speed. Jennie had literally never seen her exert herself enough to sweat.

"She's not ready to fight," Jennie said bluntly. "And I don't think she ever will be. She should never be given a battle position where she could end up facing an enemy at close quarters. But academically, she's ready to graduate."

"Thank you for being so honest," Mayor Wolfe replied. "I was primarily concerned about her academics. There are many people who can't or don't fight, but they serve in other ways."

Jennie had certainly never seen Mayor Wolfe train. She couldn't even imagine it.

"Thank you, dear." Buttons flashed as the mayor rose. *Dismissed.*

Jennie jumped to her feet, a waft of drying beer rising with her. She couldn't get out the door fast enough. As it closed behind her, she grinned, imagining the mayor ordering the sniffing servant to clean her chair and light scented candles. The interview had been a success after all: Jennie would finally get Felicité out of the schoolhouse. As far as Jennie was concerned, they could then avoid each other for the rest of their lives.

She walked down the hedge-lined path, alone in the dimming light. Everyone in town who wasn't at Wolfe House must be out campaigning.

Or almost everyone. Someone stood on a ladder leaning against a lamp post, working on the electrical cable. A very familiar someone, a wiry figure with broad shoulders and narrow hips. Of course he wouldn't be campaigning.

"Ross?"

A curtain of black hair swung aside as Ross peered over his shoulder. "Jennie? Hang on. Almost done."

He connected two cables, working deftly with his right hand. The lamp flickered to life, bathing him in golden light.

She remembered the first time she'd seen him, in outgrown jeans and a baggy shirt, his collarbones and wrist bones and cheekbones far too prominent. Some boys his age were thin because they'd grown so fast that their weight hadn't caught up with their height, but it had been obvious that Ross wasn't getting enough to eat. Or enough human contact. He'd spoken so softly that she could barely hear him and looked her in the eye maybe twice in half an hour, for about a second per glance.

He must have had such a hard life, she'd thought. And then, at his first glance up, *He's got beautiful eyes...*

He'd lost weight during his time as a prisoner at Gold Point, but had put some muscle back on since he'd returned. And he'd finally acquired some clothes that fit. He wore a simple work shirt, but his shoulders and arms filled it out nicely, and the white cotton was a perfect contrast to his smooth brown skin and glossy black hair.

And his body wasn't all that had changed. He'd always been a brilliant fighter, but when he'd first arrived, he'd relaxed while they were sparring, then tensed up the instant they stopped. But now when he practiced at the workout sessions at the Vardams' clearing, he helped his junior partners, advising Jose on his stance or straightening Becky's wrist, and sat down and talked during the breaks.

And, of course, when he'd first arrived, he'd flinched from any touch but sparring practice. Now he not only let her touch him, he reached out to touch her. To pull her close, caress her body, draw her in for a kiss. There was nothing hesitant about his kisses now. Once he'd gotten past the first awkwardness, he kissed like he sparred, with ease and passion and skill, his body moving in perfect sync with hers. The chemistry between them had never faded. If anything, it had gotten more intense. She could feel it between them now, a heat that traveled from his body to hers through ten feet of empty air.

When would he be ready to do more than kiss and touch? They'd never gone farther than him taking his shirt off, and touching her beneath hers. She was sure he was dying to see her with her blouse off, but whenever she started to lift it or move his hands to do the same, he'd freeze and she'd feel his heart speed up in a way that had nothing to do with desire. And then she'd back off until he relaxed again.

It wasn't sex specifically that scared him, that was obvious. He reacted the same way in all sorts of non-sexual situations. She'd been pleasantly surprised when he'd agreed to go to church with her, but once the service started, he'd looked tense. More than tense—haunted. There'd been a moment when she'd thought he'd run out, and she still had no idea what had set that off.

But Jennie didn't think it was some long-forgotten moment that made him freeze up when their touching went past a certain point. She had a sense that what unnerved him was a feeling or atmosphere—not something sexual in itself, but something that came along with sex. Closeness, maybe. Safety. Relaxation. Trust. Intimacy.

After all this time, part of him was still that wary boy who couldn't meet her eyes.

A surge of impatience rose in her, but she squashed it down. People were ready when they were ready. Some early, some late. Some never.

What if it is never? Jennie thought, unable to stop herself. *Will I be satisfied with just kissing and a little bit of touching, forever?*

It been so easy with Indra…

Sex had been easy with Indra, Jennie corrected herself. Other things hadn't been. They'd broken up because he'd wanted to move in together, and he hadn't let it go when she'd told him she wasn't ready. She couldn't do the same thing to Ross that Indra had done to her.

"Finished," Ross said, indicating the cable. "Not even a raccoon could undo that."

As he climbed down and stowed his tools in his carryall, she admired the long lashes that brushed his cheeks. He had no idea how handsome he was, but that only added to his attraction. It was like he was something special and precious that only she knew about.

Well. Only her and Mia.

Remembering Jack and Sheriff Crow, Jennie held out her hand to him, then waited. Ross glanced around warily, then came to her. His strong arms closed around her. The steel gauntlet stayed at her waist, but he slid his bare hand up her back. Whether he was doing it on purpose or not, the slowness of his touch sent delicious shivers through her nerves. He toyed with the agate beads he'd given her, making them click together, then moved her braids aside and laid his palm on the bare skin of her neck.

Jennie swallowed, her breath catching. Ross pulled her head down and tilted his head back. His hair fell away from his face, and their lips met. And then Jennie stopped thinking of anything at all, and melted into his kiss.

When they finally broke apart, Ross gave a puzzled sniff. "Did someone spill beer on you?"

Jennie laughed. "Okay, I'm going home to take a bath now."

"I'll walk you," Ross said. If Indra had said that, he'd have meant, "to bathe with you." But Ross clearly just meant, "to your house."

Don't push, Jennie reminded herself.

"Thanks." She took his hand. That, he had no problem with. She gave him a run-down of her afternoon as they walked down the Hill.

Ross looked more and more alarmed as she described the mob scene. "Is that still going on? I came here to get away from it. Mia's locked herself in her cottage."

"Campaigning will probably go past midnight. Or until Grandma Thakrar's beer runs out. And then it'll all start up again tomorrow morning."

Ross's dark eyes widened. "There isn't any way to Mia's that dodges everyone, is there?"

"Not unless you want to walk the sentry wall all the way around Las Anclas."

"I might," Ross muttered. "Is it going to be like this until the election?"

He looked so horrified that she stifled a laugh. "Afraid so."

As they passed the Callahan house, Ross gave it a wide berth. Jennie felt the same instinct. It looked like any other house, but ever since she was small, she'd avoided walking too close. Maybe it was it the way the windows were always shut tight and the shades drawn, even at the height of summer. It felt...wrong.

Maybe it was just that Mrs. Callahan lived there. She was never at a loss for an unkind word. Whenever Jennie had to deal with her, she had to work hard not to snap back. It was as if anger was contagious.

"*I'll* walk *you*," Jennie said as they turned at Pottery Circle. "If anyone tries to electioneer at you, I'll wave beer fumes in their face." She sniffed at herself. "Horse, too."

Ross gave her the sweet, elusive smile that always kindled warmth inside her. "Deal."

His shoulders and jaw tensed as they approached the town square, as if he expected someone to attack him at any second. Jennie dropped back a step, guarding his flank, and saw him relax a little.

As they reached the surgery, the door opened and a pale face peered out.

"Hi—" Jennie began.

Becky's gaze traveled past her and spotted the crowd beyond. The blonde girl's wariness flashed into terror. She ducked back inside and slammed the door.

"Jennie?" The voice was unmistakable: sugar with a faintly sour edge. Like burnt caramel.

Ross whipped around; Jennie turned more sedately.

Felicité Wolfe was a walking campaign declaration, gold and red from head to toe. Her dress and long scarf were crimson, while her parasol and huge sunhat were gold.

Who goes around with a parasol and a hat? Jennie thought, not for the first time. In the evening, too.

Felicité's golden spy rat trotted at her heels. Jennie choked down a snicker at the thought of Wu Zetian voting for Mayor Wolfe with her tiny pink paws.

"Jennie!" Felicité exclaimed, as if she couldn't recognize Jennie from the back. "Just the person I wanted to talk to."

Ross froze at Jennie's side. She knew exactly how he felt. She'd done her best to avoid Felicité outside of the schoolhouse, but Las Anclas was far too small for that to last forever.

Felicité's gaze dropped to Jennie's hand. Jennie had made it through years of Ranger training, a battle, multiple encounters with dangerous animals and plants, and a fight with the formidable Kerry Voske without acquiring any major scars, only to be bitten by Felicité. It still made her angry. Her only consolation was that Felicité was undoubtedly reliving a memory that must fill her with equal rage, of Jennie tying her up, gagging her, and locking her in a fruit shed all day.

Jennie waited in silence until Felicité said, "Did you talk to my mother about my graduation?"

"Yes," said Jennie.

She'd make Felicité ask her for it. But Felicité seemed to have resolved to make Jennie volunteer the information. Neither girl spoke. The tension between them was palpable.

Ross spun around and bolted into Mia's cottage, slamming the door behind him. Jennie wished she could follow him. But Ross could get away with things like that. Everyone was used to it. The expectations placed on Jennie were entirely different; people whose opinion she cared about would be shocked and disappointed if she simply fled from unpleasant situations. She held her ground.

Felicité broke the silence.

"Mother trusts your judgment, so I'm sure you gave me a good report. Thank you very much." Felicité gave Jennie an extra-sweet smile.

Now Jennie had to tell her, or she'd look childish. Resigned, Jennie said, "I said you were ready to graduate. You can start planning your party now."

But Felicité didn't move. She must have some other agenda as well.

Here it comes, Jennie thought.

Sure enough, Felicité flicked invisible dust off her crimson sleeve, smoothed her scarf, and said, "I know you and Daddy have had some serious differences."

Jennie had to marvel at Felicité's way with words: "serious differences," meaning that he'd thrown her in jail, called her a traitor, and forever banned her from the Rangers. For doing the right thing. And in return, she'd revealed to the entire town that he'd tried to have Ross murdered.

Those were more than differences. Those were actions that neither would forget or forgive for the rest of their lives.

"But I know you're much too mature to let personal matters sway you from what's best for the town." Felicité paused as if waiting for a response.

Jennie smiled. There was no longer any reason to hold back from doing something she'd longed to do for years. She held out her hand, tugged with her mind, and jerked a smooth lump of metal from Mia's yard. It smacked into her palm. Jennie looked into Felicité's eyes as she used her Changed power to tug the metal from one hand to the other as if she was juggling.

I dare you to call me a mutant, Jennie thought. *The way you called Ross a mutant in front of every teenager in Las Anclas.*

Felicité's jaw clenched. Then she spoke in her accustomed sugary tone. "Yes. You are, as everyone knows, one of the best fighters in town. And who trained you? Daddy—"

"Sera Diaz," Jennie said, her heart constricting.

Felicité's lips tightened, then she dipped her head in acknowledgment. To Jennie's surprise, it seemed sincere.

"Sera *and* Daddy," Felicité corrected herself. "But defense is my father's charge. He can protect Las Anclas. You know how well he trains people, and you know that people are the strength of the town. Not machines, like Mr. Horst thinks."

Jennie couldn't help agreeing, but that only annoyed her more. She kept silent.

"I'm confident that you'll vote for the safety of Las Anclas," Felicité went on. Then the sugar dropped out of her voice, leaving a startling echo of Mr. Preston's steel. "Because you and I and

Daddy know, Voske is coming back."

Jennie counted to five inwardly, then said, "Are you done?"

That would have wilted most people, but Felicité said brightly, "I am indeed. Are you going to talk to Mia, too?" Her crimson skirts swishing, she marched up to Mia's cottage, leaving Jennie to follow.

It was a masterly maneuver, Jennie had to admit, worthy of the mayor herself. With Jennie behind Felicité, Mia would have to open the door.

Felicité knocked. Sure enough, Mia opened it. Her black hair stood up in tufts and her face was flushed. Her glasses flashed as she glanced wildly from Felicité to Jennie, then back to Felicité.

"Come, Wu Zetian," Felicité said, calmly inviting herself in.

Then she stopped dead in the doorway. Jennie smothered a laugh as Felicité's gaze flicked from the two engines sagging Mia's narrow bed, to the work table piled with the guts of another engine, to the overloaded wheel that spun lazily over the table, to the crammed shelves threatening to fall inward. Then Felicité pulled her skirts tightly against her thighs, her nose wrinkling as if an army of invisible stink bugs paraded across the floor, and strode inside.

Ross lurked in the background, looking as flustered as Mia, one side of his shirt pulled out of his jeans. He and Mia had obviously been doing…something.

Jennie's heart jolted with a complicated rush of emotions that had recently become quite familiar. A little bit of jealousy, a little bit of feeling left out, a little bit of pride in Ross and Mia for doing something Jennie knew wasn't easy for them, a little bit of happiness that they were happy, a little bit of pleasurable anticipation at getting her turn, a little bit of embarrassment. And probably some other little bits of feelings that Jennie hadn't even identified yet.

That was the thing with Ross. Everything was always so complicated, because *he* was complicated. But the thought of giving him up gave Jennie an absolutely straightforward stab of pain in the heart. And so did the thought of taking him away from Mia. Not to mention that it wasn't Jennie's decision to make. All three of them would have to agree, just as the three of them had agreed on this relationship. Awkward as it was, Mia and Jennie both dating Ross had made them all happier than they'd been on their own. Even if it did sometimes feel…weird.

Felicité looked from Mia to Ross to Jennie. *She* clearly thought it was weird, which made Jennie feel less weird. Anything Felicité disapproved of had to be a great idea.

Felicité cleared her throat. "I wanted to remind you all that a vote for my father is a vote for the security of Las Anclas. This is a matter of safety, not personal feelings. We all know it was his skills that saved the town during the battle, until you were able to do…what you did."

Felicité didn't even look at Ross, but she still nearly choked on her last words. He'd saved the town, Felicité included, but she spoke as if he'd done something shameful and repulsive. Jennie wanted to slap her.

Felicité went on, "While I respect Mr. Horst as an excellent ironmonger…"

Mia interrupted her. "You're right. I *should* set aside my personal feelings. He *is* an excellent ironmonger." She picked up a wrench and gazed at it fondly. "I've had this wrench since I was ten, no, since I was eight. It's my very favorite wrench, and he made it."

Jennie smothered a laugh as Felicité first looked baffled, then aggravated. Then her features smoothed out. "Yes. Well, regardless of his skills in other areas, the vote is not for town ironmonger. It's for defense chief. And in that area, my father is the clear choice."

Ross spoke up from the corner. His voice was low, but it carried. "He tried to have me killed."

Even Felicité didn't have an answer for that. A heavy silence fell as Felicité looked around as if seeking inspiration. Then she straightened her shoulders with a little twitch, and the treacly voice was back. "You've got six days to think it over. Don't forget—"

She stopped as a shadow blocked the light from the door, which Mia had left open.

A tall figure stepped through—Tommy Horst inviting himself in. He too looked around, but his big features lengthened with awe. "Wow, Mia. Nobody told me you had such a cool room!"

Jennie nearly strangled herself trying not to laugh. Mia turned bright pink. "Oh, um, well, would you like to get a better look at my engine? I could explain exactly —"

Tommy looked confused, torn between the engine and his original purpose. Then he cleared his throat and boomed out, "Vote for Dad, and he'll give this town a strong defense. A smart defense! Not more training — better training! Not more weapons — better weapons!"

"Better weapons?" Mia cut in, her eyes bright with interest. "What sort of better weapons?"

Louder, Tommy repeated, "*Better* weapons! In fact, over Christmas dinner, Dad said he wanted to talk to you about them."

Mia beamed at him. "I'd love to!"

"Mia, Daddy has always involved you in discussions about new weaponry," Felicité pointed out.

Mia recoiled, looking hunted. Behind her, Ross was trying to back into the wall.

Jennie said firmly, "We just finished a long day of work. Our dinners are getting cold. We've got the rest of the week to talk about this."

Using her teacher posture, Jennie stepped deliberately toward the two invaders until they were forced to bump chests or back out. They backed out, and Jennie shut the door on them.

Ross and Mia instantly sank down on the bed in relief, squeezed into the tiny spaces between engines.

Ross rubbed his head in a gesture that reminded Jennie of the sheriff's. He probably had a headache, too. Jennie sure did.

"Is it always like this?" Ross asked. "I mean the election."

"More or less," Jennie said.

Ross looked from her to Mia, then at the door. Jennie could see that he was going through some inner struggle. She waited, knowing not to rush him. Mia idly twisted a screw on the nearest engine.

Finally, Ross turned to Mia. "I've been thinking about trying the ruined city again. Want to go with me?"

"Yes!" Mia dropped her wrench in excitement. It bounced, skittering across the floor until Jennie put out her foot to stop it.

"Jennie?" Ross asked.

"Yes." Jennie tried not to read too much into why he'd asked Mia first. Mia had desperately longed to get into those ruins ever since she and Jennie had been kids, while for Jennie, it was just one of many adventures she'd enjoy. The ruined city itself was more important to Mia than it was to Jennie, and Ross knew that. It didn't mean he liked Mia better.

Jennie smiled at them both. "I think we'd all love to get out of town."

·3·
FELICITÉ

THE CROWD AT JACK'S saloon pressed in on Felicité, but she held her ground. Mother was barely an inch taller than Felicité, but people made way for her.

Think yourself tall, Mother had told her once. *Move as if no one is there, and people will step out of your way.*

Ed Willet lumbered in her direction, his arms swaying. Felicité briefly thought herself tall, then realized that Ed was drunk enough to walk into a wall. She snatched up Wu Zetian and hopped aside. Her sore toes pinched painfully in her beautiful shoes.

The porch railing shook as Ed collided with it. Jack Lowell, who stood on the porch beside Sheriff Crow, bent to check the wood for cracks, looking as pained as if Ed had crashed into him.

The sheriff gave him a rueful smile, grotesque on her half-face, and patted his shoulder. "If it can survive Ed Willet, it can survive campaign week."

Ed blinked in puzzlement, as if the saloon had materialized just to halt him, then roared at Ricardo Horst, "You're an idiot! King Voske is coming back."

"In a hundred years," scoffed Ricardo. Like his cousin Tommy—like all the Horsts—he was an annoying loudmouth.

"He'll be back within the year." Sebastien Nguyen spoke quietly, but the conviction in his voice carried more force than Ed and Ricardo's yells. "And Noah Horst won't know the first thing about defending this town."

"An excellent point, Mr. Nguyen," Felicité said, delighted to find someone speaking reasonably. For once.

Ricardo sneered, "Gold Point's gunpowder's swamped. They're in mud up to the armpits!"

Once again, Mr. Nguyen's soft voice broke through the shouts of agreement and dissent. "My point exactly. Las Anclas turned back Voske's army, captured his daughter and turned her against him, and then dealt him a devastating, humiliating blow. Voske's pride—maybe even his survival—is at stake. From all I've heard, he'll feel that he *has* to defeat us. And soon, before his own people smell weakness and turn on him."

"That's what I said," Ed Willet bellowed. Like a bull about to charge, he lowered his head as he turned back to Ricardo. "Idiot!"

"You're the idiot, Willet," Ricardo retorted. Then, with a drunken laugh, he added, "Idi-*et!* Get it? Will-*et*—Idi—"

Ed swung a slow, heavy punch. Sheriff Crow neatly caught his fist in her open hand, bringing Ed to a halt. As Ed looked confused, Ricardo stepped around her arm and aimed a slightly faster punch at Ed. The sheriff captured it in her other hand.

"Boys—" she began.

As if Ed and Ricardo's punches had been matches tossed into dry grass, a completely new fight broke out all around Felicité. She looked wildly for a weapon—an escape route—someone to protect her—

A rush of air resolved into Sheriff Crow pitching Ed and Ricardo to the side. Her long black hair flew out as she spun to break up the brawl. Felicité was briefly transfixed by the sheriff's yellow snake eye, embedded in skin stretched tight over bare bone. Then, to Felicité's immense relief, it turned away from her to fix on Ed. He froze, cowed by that nightmare skull.

"Quiet." The sheriff didn't yell, but her voice cut through the hubbub as effectively as her unnatural strength. "Name-calling isn't campaigning. People will want to vote against your candidate just to spite you."

Ricardo straightened his shirt cuffs, making a show of not caring. "So who are you voting for, Sheriff?"

Coolly, she replied, "My vote is my business."

"Why don't *you* run for defense chief?" Grandma Torres shouted. "We all saw you whup Tom Preston! You could kick

Voske all the way back to Gold Point."

Felicité forced down her anger before it could show on her face. It was true that Sheriff Crow had defeated Daddy in a duel to win his position as sheriff, though as far as Felicité was concerned, using mutant powers was a kind of legal cheating. True, the monster sheriff was stronger than Daddy. She was stronger than anyone alive. But Voske fought wars, not duels. Felicité opened her mouth to say so.

"I like my job just fine," Sheriff Crow replied. Felicité closed her mouth. "Now, break it up, all of you. Ed, this is the third fight you've gotten into in two days. If I have to lay hands on you one more time, I'll keep you in jail a week instead of overnight. And then you won't be voting at all."

Ed Willet slouched away, muttering. Much of the crowd went with him.

The sheriff stood ramrod straight until Jack slid an arm around her waist. Then she turned into him and rested her head on his shoulder. Her unbound hair fell forward, hiding her monster face and sheriff badge.

For a surreal moment, Felicité felt as if time had run backward, to one year ago. So much had happened in that time, she felt dizzy with it. Elizabeth Crow had been a beautiful Norm archer, engaged and happily expecting a baby. Everyone had known long before she'd begun to show from how Jack waited on her, constantly offering her drinks and snacks and cushions, though no one would comment on a pregnancy before it was announced. It was bad luck. Too many pregnancies were lost early. And worse things than that could happen.

Felicité had thought the worst thing was both mother and infant dying, like Mia's mother and baby brother. Then she watched Elizabeth Crow walk out of the surgery after losing her baby. And for the first time in Felicité's life, she saw a monster face to equal her own.

Jack leaned his blond head on Sheriff Crow's shoulder. She put her arm around his shoulders, rubbing the side of his jaw with a finger in a careless lover's gesture. Jack gave an audible sigh and tilted his head, offering her more of his throat to caress. Every line of his body spelled out contentment.

A wave of bitter fury blazed through Felicité, propelling her out of her exhausted haze and sending her stumbling away. Jack loved his monster — had never stopped loving her — would keep on loving her if she turned into something even more hideous, or never touched him again. Elizabeth Crow had done nothing to earn that pure, unshakable love, and there was nothing Felicité could ever do to make anyone love her like that.

Life was so unfair.

As she made her painful way home, she regretted her elegant high heeled shoes. After an entire day walking all over town raising support for Daddy, she couldn't tell which hurt worse, her feet, her back, her throat, or her head. Even darling Wu Zetian's whiskers drooped. Felicité was halfway up the hill before she remembered that she no longer needed to carry her rat, and thankfully set her down.

She wished she'd trained Wu Zetian to bite people. Maybe she should teach her to "accidentally" claw anyone who used the phrase "better weapons."

Felicité stepped into her home and peeled off her shoes. She actually had blisters! And six more days to go. She limped into the parlor, where Mother was being served lemonade by the kitchen maid.

"Did you just get back, Mother?" Felicité asked. "I hope your feet did better than mine."

Mother lifted her skirts, displaying her walking shoes.

Long skirts were so...old. Felicité liked the contrast between her full skirts swinging at her knees and her slim legs and elegant feet. She had never worn ugly shoes, ever.

"I'll wear my boots tomorrow. Anything for Daddy," Felicité said, suppressing a sigh. No one would see bandaged blisters in boots.

Mother didn't answer. Her back was straight and her forehead smooth, though Felicité could see by her closed eyes that she too was exhausted. "I'm so glad no one dared run against *you*."

Mother opened her eyes. "It doesn't do to become complacent. There is always the possibility of a vote of no confidence."

"I'm sure you'll get elected for your fifth term." Felicité couldn't imagine anything else. Mother had won her first election when Felicité had been barely a year old. "I haven't heard a word against you. But that Tommy Horst—"

Felicité broke off, hearing her angry shrillness. She was too tired and upset to control her voice, and Mother admired discipline above all else.

Daddy walked in. The sun lines in his face had deepened to grooves. She hadn't seen him so exhausted since the battle. But he smiled as he bent to kiss Felicité on the cheek and Mother on the lips. "Now there's a heartening sight, my two favorite women in the world."

"How was your day, dear?" Mother asked.

"Long. But I've got a good group of Ranger candidates. Ah. Thank you." He took a glass of lemonade from the maid. "How were your days?"

"You have very...enthusiastic supporters." Mother leaned back, more evidence of her weariness. "But I wish one of them would point out that the person who will profit from investing in weapons rather than people is Noah Horst himself."

Felicité burst in, "Ricardo Horst started a fight when Mr. Nguyen said Mr. Horst won't be able to defend us when Voske returns."

Daddy didn't seem surprised. "He won't. Horst has done a good job running drills under my direction, but he's never held command in actual combat."

"I don't think Mr. Horst believes that Voske is coming back," Felicité said. The lines around Daddy's mouth deepened, so she changed the subject. "Tommy Horst bores everyone with that same stupid speech about 'better weapons.' I tailored all *my* speeches to the individual."

"Smart thinking, darling." Daddy drained his glass and set it down with a thump. "Did you convert anyone?"

Felicité smiled with pride. "A few, I expect. Including one who I think will surprise you. She may never admit it, but I'm sure I won you Jennie Riley's vote."

Daddy stopped cleaning his spectacles with his linen handkerchief, looking thoughtful. "If that's true—and if you say it is, I'm sure it's so—you'll make as good a mayor as your mother. Between her Change and our personal history, I assumed her vote would go to Horst."

"I'm sure the Changed adults have not forgotten that Horst was the first to volunteer to drive away those unfortunates from Catalina ten years ago," said Mother. "He only altered his tune when he decided to run for defense chief. Nobody switches their beliefs overnight. It's embarrassing to see what a hypocrite he's become."

Felicité flung back her hair. "I heard people saying his promise to bring back the Catalina traders and players is just to get votes, not because he thinks it's the right thing to do."

Daddy put his glasses back on, his blue eyes narrowed. "It's *not* the right thing to do! Look at Gold Point. That's what you get when you encourage those mutants. Voske deliberately chooses monster women to have children with, so he can get more monsters to make war on Norms. We don't want that kind in Las Anclas. Remember that delegation from Catalina, Valeria?"

"Such an unfortunate day," Mother said.

"Unfortunate! Darling, you're brilliant and beautiful, but you need to be careful with that kind heart of yours. Keep it for the people who deserve it." Daddy softened his criticism with a kiss. To Felicité, he said, "We kept you indoors to protect you. But their leader was a hideous woman — if you can even call her a woman — with slimy purple skin, like some mutant underwater creature you'd net and throw back in. And the man she was with was even worse. Like something from a nightmare. Those are the kind of...*things* Horst wants to invite into Las Anclas."

Felicité tensed, conscious of how dirty she was. Not just untidy and dusty, but filthy, inside and out. She stood up. "I'm going to take a bath. I have a date with Henry later. I hope he remembers. Is he still practicing?"

Daddy smiled. "He must have been eager for your date. He left before I did."

Felicité rushed upstairs. She locked her bedroom door, then her bathroom door, leaving Wu Zetian outside. As always, she rattled the doorknob and pushed against the door to make sure it was securely locked. Only then did she run her bath.

She undressed before the full-length mirror hanging on the bathroom door. Dust and grime smudged her face, but her body looked clean.

Felicité imagined how some observer might see her. Her slim waist highlighted the curves of her breasts and hips. Her legs were long and elegant, and her shoulders were exactly wide enough. She admired the creamy brown of her skin and the new mahogany of her hair. While Daddy's blue eyes would have made a striking contrast to her hair and skin, the tilted brown eyes she'd inherited from Mother suited her just as well. But she was glad she'd gotten Daddy's nose. It was so distinguished. Everyone said she had such a pretty face.

She was perfect.

Gritting her teeth, she turned the mirror to the wall.

Why had she even looked? She used to bathe without thinking about her body. All she'd had to do was turn off the light and think about pleasant things until she was dry and a Norm again.

Kerry's voice spoke in her memory, lilting with arrogance as she'd bragged about her Change power. *"I remember my father saying, 'You're going to be the pride of Gold Point.' And then he picked up one of the roses and put it in a golden vase for everyone to admire."*

Felicité smashed her foot into the water, splashing it all over the floor. Great. That was stupid. She'd have to clean it up herself, or risk stepping in the damned puddle and making those damned scales grow.

She toweled her foot dry and used her dirty clothes to mop the floor, then flung them into a corner for the maid to launder.

The bath was full. She shut the water off, then froze with her hand on the faucet.

Felicité's belly tightened with horrified anticipation. She faced nothing but a porcelain bath filled with clean water, but she felt as she had when she'd stood with Daddy during the battle of Las Anclas and watched the first Gold Point soldier collapse, writhing and screaming. She'd known what would happen, known she shouldn't look, and known that if she didn't close her eyes, she'd see something that would haunt her for the rest of her life. But Felicité had kept her eyes open, and watched obsidian branches burst from the back of the dying soldier, clawing their way upward toward the brightening sky.

Felicité closed her eyes, then stepped into the water.

One foot, then the other. Now the hard part was done. She lay back into the tub. As always, there was a moment of quiet bliss. Some part of her couldn't help enjoying the simple pleasure of heat and weightlessness, of soft warmth on sore muscles.

Then the Change began.

The first sign was the tiniest prickle, not even painful. Then she tingled all over as silvery scales emerged to disfigure her skin. Her toes and fingers itched as hideous webs stretched between them. Then came the painless but horrifying sensation of her neck splitting open on either side. That was the gills forming.

Felicité tried to force her thoughts away from her monstrous transformation, but it was impossible. A membrane slid over her eyes. The flesh of her nostrils started to pinch together. Felicité needed to move fast if she wanted to get clean. How horrible, if she had to get out, dry off, and then bathe *again*. She ducked her head underwater and roughly shampooed her hair, trying to think of anything but the terrible secret that she had to keep forever.

She'd think of Henry. He was lovely to think about. He had such nice muscles in his shoulders. She loved to run her hands over them, and down his lean, flat stomach. She imagined them lying in bed together, touching each other. She could smell his scent of clean cloth and fresh sweat. Their hearts beat together, his fast, her slow…

Felicité jerked upright, her eyes widening. Her heart *was* beating slower. She could count one, two, three between beats. Then she felt an even more alarming sensation: behind her ribs, her organs were shifting.

She leaped out of the tub, snatching wildly for the towels. Felicité rubbed them over her body as fast as she could, desperate to drive away the Change.

She'd been such a fool. Ever since she was thirteen and she'd first become a monster, she'd known better than to let herself linger too long in water. If she stayed wet for longer than it took to wash her hair, some horrifying inner Change always started. She knew intuitively that if let it continue, she would never Change back. She'd be a monster forever, and Daddy wouldn't just give that look of disgust and loathing to other people. He'd give it to her. She'd never again be Felicité Wolfe, his beloved daughter.

She'd be a nameless, hated *thing*.

Felicité turned the mirror out so the maid wouldn't wonder. Her skin was still tingling, but her heart beat normally and her organs had returned to their proper places. She forced herself to look in the mirror, afraid of what she might see. But to her relief, though her neck and chest had a few scratches from scrubbing too hard, the monstrous scales were gone.

She was a Norm.

Willing herself to believe, she murmured to the mirror, "You have always been a Norm. The Changed are other people. You will never Change."

Her chin came up, smooth and elegant. Her brown shoulders straightened.

Relaxing, she reached for her clean clothes, and a pair of pretty low-heeled sandals.

Felicité tugged at her emerald scarf, making sure it was knotted tight. She would never risk exposing her throat again. Five months after the battle, not a day had gone by that she didn't remember with horror how she'd begun to Change in the torrential rain. Only quick thinking and luck had prevented Daddy from discovering that she was a monster.

Henry had probably already arrived, so she took the time to walk gracefully toward the stairs. Nothing was wrong. She, like her mother, had poise and style.

Sure enough, Henry stood at the foot of the stairs, looking up at her. She tossed back her glorious hair and straightened her spine.

Henry's eyes widened with appreciation. She gave her mahogany-hued curls another toss. Good. He was staring at her hair, not her throat. It had been worth every tedious minute she'd spent applying the expensive dye. She was a Norm whose only reason for dyeing her hair that autumnal shade was because it was pretty.

Her parents and her little brother Will had gone out. She had the house to herself. Smiling, she went down to meet her boyfriend.

"Felicité!" Henry greeted her with a passionate kiss. "Wow, you look gorgeous. You're the prettiest girl in the entire town."

Another kiss. "You know, I wake up every morning and think of how lucky I am that you like me, too. I was so sure I'd pine for you forever, and you'd never even look at me. Let's go to Luc's. I want to show you off."

Felicité loved Luc's, but even the thought of walking all that way made feet throb anew. "Would you mind if we stayed here?"

"I wanted to dance all night," Henry protested.

Felicité became aware of the faint sound of music. She opened the parlor windows, and saw a string quartet on the neighbors' lamplit terrace halfway down the Hill, playing for a party. "We have our own music. It's more romantic."

Henry gave in at the word 'romantic.' "I could dance with *you* all night. Here, there, or anywhere."

His arms closed around her, and she slid her feet out of the sandals. It was so surprising and wonderful how Henry, the class clown, had turned out to be the only true romantic her age. She wondered if she'd never noticed before, or if he'd grown up, or if she'd brought it out in him.

They waltzed around the parlor. Other boys she'd dated had been clumsy or inattentive, but Henry was quick to follow her cues. It was so intimate to dance barefoot, alone with her boyfriend in an empty house. Her blisters only stung a little. She loved the feeling of Henry's steady hand on her waist, caressing the curve of her back…

Her dress stuck to her back after his hand moved on. Was she sweating already? A few drops of her own sweat weren't enough moisture to start her Change, but Felicité had never dared to find out how many it would take.

She stopped dancing and patted her face with her lace-edged handkerchief. "Would you like to say hello to Wu Zetian?"

"Sure." Henry made an exaggerated but graceful bow.

Felicité curtseyed, smiling. She knew from his eagerness what he really wanted to see — her bedroom.

They walked upstairs hand in hand. She sat on her bed, her skirts spread out around her. Henry promptly sat beside her, careful not to crush her skirt. Good. Eager, but not *too* eager.

"Wu Zetian," Felicité called.

The golden rat ran out of her petal-pink rat house and rose

sweetly on her haunches, her bright gaze fixed on Felicité. She was as clever and beautiful as Felicité's ancestor, the ancient empress she was named for.

Wu Zetian was as much of a delight to Felicité now as she'd been on the first day they'd met, when Felicité had been taken to the rat trainers as a surprise present for her thirteenth birthday. Felicité had known of the golden rat in the litter, but had never guessed that the beautiful creature was destined for *her*.

"Wu Zetian is brilliant. As well as a darling." Felicité daintily kissed the tip of her rat's nose, then flicked her left pinkie finger. At that signal, Wu Zetian scampered back into her house.

"I wish I was a rat," Henry said wryly.

Felicité playfully kissed him on the nose. "There. Satisfied?"

"No. But if I was a rat, I couldn't do this." He brought her chin up with a finger. "Or this." He brushed his lips over hers, and Felicité rewarded him with a real kiss.

Henry was as good at kissing as he was at listening. Ignoring her skirts, Felicité adjusted herself so they sat hip to hip. He edged her back until they leaned against her pile of silken pillows. She ran her fingers up his arms. One thing to be said for that interminable drilling—his arms had taken on some enticing definition.

Henry had a light touch in exploring her own curves. She kissed him again, confident that he would not be disappointed in what he found. But the touch of air on skin warned her that he was doing more than just exploring. Three, four of her blouse buttons had come undone, and he was busy on the fifth. Felicité jerked aside.

Henry sat up, then frowned. "Oh, no. Did I do that?"

Felicité's entire body flashed cold with fear. Dreading what she would see, she looked down. But it was only a few pink scratches across her smooth Norm skin.

Henry leaned forward. "Let me kiss it better."

She longed to let him, but an echo of the terror she'd felt held her back. She forced herself to chuckle as she buttoned her blouse up to her throat. "Wu Zetian got into my bathroom while I was bathing, and the silly thing scratched me when I took her out."

Henry grinned, returning his fingers to the buttons. "Lucky Wu Zetian!"

She caught herself tugging at her scarf again, and captured his hand. "I'm not ready for undressing. When I am, I'll tell you."

"Or undress me. Which you can do any time." He gave her a hopeful grin.

Felicité tried to smile back, but it felt hollow. Henry had been so dexterous that she hadn't caught him until he'd nearly undone her entire blouse. What if those sensitive fingers discovered her scales, or reached up beneath her scarf and found gills? She shivered.

"Are you cold?" Henry asked. "Come here. I'll warm you up."

Felicité pulled away. She had no gills. She had no scales. As long as her skin stayed dry, she was a Norm. As long as she never permitted anyone's naked, sweaty body to press up against her bare skin, she was safe.

"Or just I could undress," Henry suggested.

"Any undressing has to wait for The One." She instantly wished she could take back those words. Maybe it was time to offer him dessert downstairs. Better to break up the romantic mood than risk a discussion of The One.

"Who's The One?" Henry asked.

Felicité read the jealousy in his narrowed eyes and compressed mouth, and enjoyed a little thrill of power. "No one. Yet."

Henry relaxed and ran his fingers through her silken curls. "He might be me."

She made herself smile. "You never know."

"Don't worry," he said earnestly. "I won't push you."

"I know."

He went on in that same serious tone, so different from his loud clowning voice. "We're used to knowing each other as kids at school. But we're about to graduate, so maybe we should try out what it's like to be together as adults."

Felicité stroked his hands, glad to abandon the subject of The One. "I meant to talk to you about that. I'll be graduating on my birthday. It'll be a couple weeks after the Ranger selection, so what do you think of my party being for my birthday and graduation, and you becoming a Ranger?"

"Great idea. My family..." Henry hesitated. "We don't really do parties."

Felicité tried not to let her pity show. Poor Becky certainly would never have had any birthday parties if Felicité hadn't thrown them for her. Not for the first time, Felicité wished she hadn't lost Becky's friendship. If only Becky hadn't fallen in love with a Changed mutant! But Felicité didn't see any way to make an overture to Becky that didn't start with an apology for everything she'd said about Changed people and a sincere vow that she wasn't prejudiced, and she couldn't do that. She just couldn't.

Brisa will throw her a party, Felicité assured herself. *Becky will be fine. She has other friends now. She doesn't need me anymore.*

That line of thought didn't feel much better than the first. She was relieved when Henry spoke.

"What I'm really looking forward to is my first patrol as a Ranger," Henry said. "Wouldn't it be cool if we fought some bandits?"

"If you're lucky, you can celebrate that at the party."

She hadn't meant to start making out again, but it was so sweet to kiss Henry. He was so good at it. Then he stroked her jawline, his fingers pushing beneath her scarf. A jolt of alarm thrummed through her nerves, and she pulled away.

Henry let her go at once. Then he leaned toward her, his grin wicked. "Let's play a game." He ran his fingers through her hair, making her shiver with pleasure. "It's called Secrets. I tell you one, you tell me one. Whoever knows a secret that the other one doesn't gets to kiss them. Anywhere they want."

"Through clothes." Felicité recognized the emphasis on that 'anywhere.'

"Sure," Henry said easily.

She loved hearing secrets, but she was sworn not to discuss council meetings or anything involving town business. However, she'd never made any vows regarding people's personal lives.

"I've got one about Indra," Felicité offered. Handsome Norm Indra Vardam, perfect in every way—except for his taste in girls. He was dating Nasreen now, but Felicité watched him closely, and she was certain that he still secretly pined for the monster Jennie Riley. "Sujata told me he sucked his thumb until he was seven."

Henry's laugh blew back a lock of her hair. "That's great!"

"My kiss." Felicité kissed behind his ear. He blushed delightfully.

"My turn. You know how Alfonso Medina got those disgusting gecko fingers?" Henry splayed his fingers in mockery. "His father isn't his real father. His mother had an affair with a Changed neighbor."

"And got a monster." Felicité eyed his crooked fingers, but she didn't need that cue to put disgust into her voice. A person with reptile features was unnatural and horrifying. "That's what you get for lying and cheating. Anyway, I knew that. Mother mentioned it one time."

Henry grimaced. "You know all the town secrets. That's hardly fair."

"Tell me one about yourself, then."

"I have a big one." He paused, frowning. "I don't know if I should tell you this. I don't know what you'll think."

Felicité wrinkled her nose, hoping he wasn't going to tell her that his father, who had left five years ago to "go trading with the Saigon Alliance," had no intention of ever coming back. Everyone knew that already, and a depressing secret like that would ruin the mood.

But Henry's voice was light and teasing. "In school... About a month before the battle, I..." He hung his head. "I hate to admit it."

She let him squirm, then laughed. "You put that flying roach in my desk, didn't you?"

He blushed again. "I didn't mean to scare you. I mean, I knew it would, but I did it so I could rescue you. I thought it would impress you. It was a stupid idea."

"You're forgiven. But no kisses for that!"

He looked adorably rueful, which Felicité found charming. "Okay, your turn."

Felicité combed through her treasure chest of secrets. Should she share something about herself?

She considered him in the soft darkness, tall and broadening so nicely through the shoulders, his fair hair outlined by the flickering candlelight. Who would have thought he could be so interesting? She wouldn't have expected his courage in battle, either. When it had been down to the ten of them, running to intercept Voske's strike team of thirty, Henry had been fearless. Even when the crystal trees —

She wasn't going to think about the battle.

Henry kissed so well. She steered her thoughts toward that, and smiled into the darkness. "When I was little, I used to pretend something about myself that I thought made me more special. Can you guess what it was?"

"I can't imagine anything that would make you more special than you already are," he said fervently.

His wrong answer was even better than the correct one. "I used to imagine that I was a princess."

"You *are* a princess," said Henry. "From now on, that's what I'll call you. But only I get to."

She could tell that his thrill was real. He wasn't putting on a show of being romantic just to please her — he was absolutely sincere. She kissed him again, then waited eagerly for his secret. But it turned out to be a boring one about her cousin Julio flirting with someone else's fiancée. Felicité didn't care about Julio's unending string of girlfriends. It was time for better secrets.

Personal, but not *too* personal.

"I never had a crush on anyone until I was nearly fifteen," she said. "Want to know who it was on?"

"Indra Vardam or Carlos Garcia," Henry said resignedly. "All the girls love tall, dark, and handsome. Though if it was Julio, I guess that would be good for a laugh."

"No, no, and ugh," Felicité said. "Though you're right about dark, and you're close about handsome. It was Elizabeth Crow."

When Henry's jaw dropped, she said quickly, "Before her Change, of course."

"I get it. I never had a thing for older women, but if I had, I might have fallen for her too. She used to be beautiful." In a low soft voice, he added, "It's so cool that you trusted me enough to tell me you had a crush on someone who turned into a monster. Poor Felicité! Was it awful for you when she Changed?"

She shook her head. "No, I was crushing on someone else by then. But you see why it's a secret."

Henry nodded emphatically. "That ugly mutant face of hers

gives me the shudders." He closed his eyes. "Your kiss. Surprise me."

Felicité took her time selecting a place for her kiss. But the joy had gone out of it. She could never let him see her own ugly mutant face. He could never be The One.

·4·
KERRY

NOBODY SYMPATHIZED WITH AN ex-princess.

Kerry scorned pity. But still, there were these...holes in her life, these little frustrations that crowded her day, that nobody else even noticed, much less understood.

Take brushing her hair. She'd rarely ever had to do it. She knew how, of course. Totally different from knowing how to pull a brush through your hair was doing it every day, especially after wind and sweat tangled it unmercifully, and your body was so tired every muscle ached, and you just wanted the maid to draw a hot bath then massage your scalp while you lay in the clean hot water with your eyes closed, soothed by the gentle tug on your scalp.

Well, the days of maids were gone. And while Becky Callahan was perfectly willing to brush Kerry's hair for her, Becky had a very full life. She couldn't be summoned by a snap of the fingers whenever Kerry wanted her.

And that wasn't even considering the little braids done up so cleverly into a coronet, Kerry's favorite style in Gold Point. It was elegant, and comfortable whether she was dancing or sparring. But when she'd tried to duplicate it, the braids inevitably came down around her ears. And none of the back braids were even, she'd discovered one day when Felicité Wolfe had said in that poisonous voice of hers, "Very interesting style in parting, Kerry. A Gold Point fashion?"

Kerry had cadged a hand mirror from Becky, and craned her

neck looking into her little mirror—to see her scalp looking like a ragged patchwork quilt under the lopsided braids.

Ever since then, Kerry kept her hair in a single braid, pinning it up to fight or to ride. She pinned it up that morning and ran to the stables in the soft pre-dawn air.

The sky blushed pink over the eastern hills, heralding the sunrise when Kerry met Mia and Ross, who'd stopped to visit Rusty, Ross's burro.

They were just leaving, so Kerry went with them toward the gate. The silence of Main Street and the pearly light made her feel enclosed in a bubble of her own creation, safe from all harm. She'd always imagined that if her power was visible, her swords and sticks and shields would glow with that same translucent light. But it was a childish idea, and immaturity was a sign of weakness. She'd never told it to anyone.

As she led Nugget toward the back gate, with Mia and Ross walking beside her, Kerry thought, *I could tell Mia.*

Mia wouldn't think getting odd ideas was weak or wrong. She'd be interested and speculate about why the objects Kerry created were invisible, and whether there might be any way of making them visible, to see if Kerry was right. And if Kerry asked her not to mention it to anyone else, Mia wouldn't.

The sun had begun to rim the eastern hills when Mia began talking about the election. Ross, unsurprisingly, was silent. Kerry suspected that he, like her, had no interest in the topic, but was letting Mia go on about it rather than risk hurting her feelings. Mia had confided once that people sometimes outright told her she was boring them and how crushed that made her feel. Kerry had no intention of hurting her, but she could change the subject so tactfully that Mia would never notice. With her idea about her power, for instance.

But while Kerry was still debating over whether she minded letting Ross know too, Mia spoke to her. "So who *are* you voting for, Kerry? Or haven't you made up your mind yet?"

"I can vote?" Kerry had assumed that as the town's former enemy, she wouldn't be allowed.

"Sure. You're an adult citizen." Mia squirmed and reached behind her back, trying to shift her backpack. Before Kerry could do anything, Ross helped her distribute its weight more evenly across her shoulders. "Oh, thanks, Ross."

As if my vote matters, Kerry thought. *As if anyone's does.*

Oh, maybe *some* elections were legitimate. Even in Gold Point, the craftspeople really did elect their guild leaders. The race between the Mrs. Hernandez and Mr. McVey might be real. Both candidates held similar positions in the town hierarchy—a miller and a baker—so giving one the job rather than the other didn't have any clear benefit. But there was no way Mr. Preston would lose *his* race, regardless of the actual voting. People in power didn't give it up peacefully—it had to be taken from them by force.

Mia was one of the most brilliant people Kerry had ever met, but even she was as naïve about politics as the rest of Las Anclas's citizens, campaigning so enthusiastically for their sham election.

Kerry recalled Father saying, *People will believe anything that preserves their illusion of comfort. Learn to manage their gullibility, and you'll have as strong a tool for holding power as an elite cadre of soldiers on duty around the clock.*

Though Kerry hated her father with the same passion with which she'd once admired him, she couldn't deny the wisdom of his words. He was hard and cruel, not stupid. He understood people like Mia understood machines and Ross understood the desert. Kerry wouldn't follow in Father's footsteps, but neither would she rebel to the point where she automatically disbelieved everything he'd ever taught her. That would make her as gullible as she'd been when she'd believed everything he'd said.

A tall figure awaited them at the gate, instantly recognizable among the field workers ready to go out to tend the crops: Jennie, with her magnificent new sword slung across her back.

Jennie greeted Ross and Mia, then turned to Kerry. "Coming with us?"

Kerry detected an edge beneath the friendly teasing. Like many in Las Anclas, Jennie was still wary of her. Kerry could hardly blame them. If she'd been them, she wouldn't have trusted the turncoat daughter of the town's worst enemy either.

No, Jennie, I have no intention of horning in on your adventure, your best friend, or your boyfriend, Kerry imagined replying, before she decided that those weren't Jennie-type worries. She corrected it to one that probably was: *No, I won't run off to Gold Point and get back in Father's good graces by telling him everything I've learned about Las Anclas.*

As if that would even work. She'd burned her bridges with her father for good. But nobody could understand that who didn't know Father, and in all of Las Anclas, only Ross and Mr. Preston did.

"I wish," Kerry replied lightly, making sure there was no edge to *her* voice.

"Oh, I wish you could, too," Mia said with sincere regret. "But Ross can only hold hands with two people at a time."

Jennie chuckled, and even Ross smiled. Mia didn't seem to notice that she'd said anything funny.

"Well, if you ever decide to live up to that 'I'm madly in love with Ross' letter you left for your father…" Jennie said to Kerry.

There was no sharpness in that joke. But it hurt Kerry in a way that Jennie couldn't have intended.

When Kerry had returned to Las Anclas with Ross, one of the first things she'd done was to catch Mia alone and make her promise to tell no one about Santiago. Kerry had seen how gossip traveled in this tiny town, and didn't want condolences that would bring more pain than comfort. Mia had understood that and promised to say nothing, not even to Jennie.

As the dawn watch bell clanged, the sentries opened the gates. Mia quivered with excitement, but Ross tensed. Jennie moved into a guard's position beside him, alert and ready, and he visibly relaxed.

It was like how Ross had helped Mia with her backpack. He'd known what she needed and did it without her having to say anything, because he knew her so well and paid her such close attention. Santiago and Kerry had been like that too, passing each other salt shakers, checking for eavesdroppers, and giving each other back rubs, all without having to ask. She could almost feel the solid muscle of his shoulders softening under her hands . . .

Kerry swung into Nugget's saddle, suddenly desperate to get away from the tender awareness between Ross and Mia and Jennie. But there was no escaping her own loss. Santiago would never ride beside her again, and every reminder of him was like opening a wound.

"Find some great artifacts!" Kerry saluted them, then rode away before anyone could say anything awkward.

Then she groaned, recognizing that she'd done something awkward. They didn't salute in Las Anclas.

Nugget tossed his head, sending the glittering strands of his mane flying. The sun had crested the mountains, lighting his shimmering coat. Kerry gave him what they both wanted: the signal to gallop.

"Hoo, look at him go!" Jose Riley yelled from the sentry post.

Kerry grinned fiercely. Nugget permitted no one but her to ride him, but she'd seen him run in the corral and knew his magnificent gallop, with his tail flying out behind him like a streak of gold.

She only slowed when they reached the shore. The fishers had launched on the ebbing tide, visible as tiny dots on the blue expanse. She was alone on the beach.

It still surprised her how casual the townspeople were about the ocean. Kerry vividly recalled her first glimpse of that extraordinary expanse of water, blue as a sapphire that day, and in constant motion, stretching out to meet the sky. She'd visited the beach nearly every day since, finding it different shades, sometimes full of whitecaps, other days smooth. Once, angry with surging waves. Why didn't the entire town come out every day to look at the ever-changing sea?

The empty beach was deserted, as if it belonged just to her. Kerry rode onto a wide spit of land that extended into the ocean, inhaling the sea brine and listening to the soft splash of the waves. Morning birds chattered as they rose in a flock of gray wings. She was solitary, but the ocean's peace made her feel less lonely.

Nugget's ears twitched, and he tried to wheel away from the ripples foaming up the sand.

"Easy, Nugget. It's not going to attack you." She stroked his neck, but he didn't calm. Instead, he tried again to get off the peninsula, forcing her to rein him in.

That was strange. She'd taken the stallion to the beach more than any of her other horses, and even ridden him once through the lapping waves. He hadn't liked that, so she hadn't done it again. But the waves themselves shouldn't bother him.

Kerry scanned the area to see what was upsetting him, but there was nothing but water, sky, and sand. She shrugged. Horses did sometimes suddenly decide that things were scary when they'd never been frightened of them before. Sally had once been badly startled by her own watering trough! Kerry often wondered what was going on in horses' minds, or what they were seeing that humans could not.

"Ghosts," her sister Bridget had once suggested, her eyes bright with ghoulish glee. "Horses can see ghosts. So can cats. When it seems like they're startled by nothing, that's why."

Kerry had always secretly enjoyed how unabashedly strange Bridget was. Her little sister was completely herself, unworried that Father would think she was creepy or weird or immature. Even at thirteen, Bridget had still enjoyed suddenly thrusting her cupped hands at people's faces, then opening them to reveal something alarming: a live scorpion in a glass jar, perhaps, or a dissected fetal pig.

Sean was the sibling Kerry loved. But at that moment, Kerry missed all of them, not only Bridget: Owen's earnestness, Fiona's delight in high places and "flying" with the help of her mother's gravity-negating power, and little Connor's sweetness as he crouched in a field, watching wildflowers bloom under his outstretched hand. And Mom: what would their relationship have been like if Kerry hadn't left? The brief taste of what it could have been—love and compromise and conversation instead of a constant battle of wills—made Kerry wish for more.

I am *haunted,* Kerry thought. *I'm haunted by everyone I left behind.*

But gone was gone. She patted Nugget again, trying to fix her mind on what she had, not what she'd lost. "You're spooked by your own shadow. It's nothing."

A hiss and splash made him sidle. Then the blue water heaved up as if something big was under it.

A red claw the size of a horse's head lashed out of the waves.

Kerry jumped, and Nugget tried to rear. As she struggled to control the stallion, a scarlet creature lunged out of the water. It resembled a crab grown to the size of a wild boar, with clacking claws and tentacles that writhed like a nest of snakes.

Kerry wheeled Nugget to race back to safety. But another crab-creature scuttled up onto the spit, blocking their path back to the beach. Its claws extended, clacking together threateningly.

She eyed it warily. Nugget could probably jump over it, but she didn't know how fast it could move. Those claws looked strong enough to snip through a horse's ankle. It would be safer to kill the thing. Kerry materialized a sword and studied the creature for a weak point. But except for its swiveling eyestalks and waving tentacles, it was covered in armor plates.

Something splashed behind her. Kerry looked over her shoulder. Two more crab things crawled out of the ocean and lumbered toward her.

At least they're slow, she thought. *Though maybe they can move fast, and they just haven't yet.*

She was alarmed, but not terrified. She'd been attacked by creatures before, and felt confident that she could handle one medium-sized beast. Kerry urged Nugget toward the thing blocking their way back to the beach, her sword upraised. She'd slice through the eyestalks and have Nugget leap over it while it was blinded.

A wave of panic swept over Kerry.

That thing is going to kill me!

Her heart pounded and terror drenched her in sweat. The sword vanished from her hand. She couldn't breathe. Couldn't move.

A desperate glance behind her showed that the other two crab things were closing in. She and Nugget would be sliced to bits by those razor claws if they stayed where they were.

They couldn't go forward. They couldn't go back. Her only chance was to ride into the ocean. Her heart pounding, she urged her stallion toward the waves.

Nugget balked. She yanked on the reins and dug in with her heels. He had to obey her, or he'd get them both killed!

"Move!" Kerry screamed. "Move! Into the water, you stupid thing! It's our only chance!"

Nugget's ears flattened. He tossed his head, eyes rolling, and planted his hooves in the sand. No matter how hard she tried, he wouldn't budge. And the crab things were almost on them.

Kerry had to abandon the horse. She leaped free of the saddle and bolted for the safety of the water. Her foot splashed in surging water when five iron bands closed around her arm and yanked. The world spun around her.

Father loomed over her, gripping her tight. She recoiled in terror, a shriek bursting from her lips.

"Kerry!"

That wasn't Father's voice.

"Kerry?"

It wasn't Father.

"Paco," she breathed. Then she gasped, "Look out!"

Kerry tackled Paco, knocking them both to the damp sand. A giant red claw snapped shut where their ribcages had been.

Then her terror vanished, as abruptly as it had seized her. As Paco rolled to the side, she materialized a sword and slashed through the crab monster's eyestalks. It thrashed around wildly, its tentacles lashing and its claws snapping on empty air.

Kerry and Paco scrambled to their feet. Her heart still banged against her ribs, but with excitement and ordinary fear, not the unreasoning panic she'd felt before. What had she been thinking, abandoning Nugget to run into the water that the monsters had come from?

Where *was* Nugget? She couldn't see him anywhere. Her heart lurched at the thought that the crab-creatures could have gotten him.

"On your right!" somebody yelled.

Kerry whipped up her hand and created a shield. A tentacle splattered across it. For an instant, she stared in fascination at the suckers clinging to the shield's invisible surface. Then Paco swung his sword, slicing the tentacles. They fell away.

"Get back on the beach!" a hoarse voice bellowed.

An entire patrol was battling a horde of crab-creatures on the beach. To Kerry's immense relief, Nugget plunged about higher on the strand, well away from the fighting. But more crab things scuttled from the waves, keeping her and Paco trapped on the spit. As Kerry fought them, she caught glimpses of the battle on the beach.

Her friend Sujata dodged one crab monster, then leaped over another. A tentacle coiled around Indra's ankle as he used his machete to hack through the legs of the biggest creature yet. Sujata snatched up her fallen bow, cranked it, and shot, severing the tentacle around her brother's ankle.

I hope the patrol leader saw that, Kerry thought. Sujata was trying out for the Rangers, and that had been a Ranger-worthy shot if Kerry had ever seen one.

But everyone was fighting hard. Anna-Lucia, the pastry chef, gripped a staff in both hands and slammed it down on a crab-creature. It bounced off the shell, but the blow staggered the thing. Indra's machete smashed down on its sectioned neck. The tiny severed head rolled down the sloping beach into the ocean.

Indra's gaze caught Kerry's. "Get back to shore!"

Paco swung his heavy sword, sending it crunching through the carapace of the last crab monster blocking their way. The thing twitched, then lay still.

It looked like the battle was over. All the crab-creatures seemed to have been killed.

Then three more lumbered out of the ocean.

Paco grabbed her wrist. "Come on. I don't think they'll follow us off the beach."

The ocean surged up in a giant wave, too huge to dodge. Kerry only had time to hold her breath before it smashed into her and Paco, knocking her off her feet. She tried to clutch at him, but her hands closed on water. Freezing brine filled her mouth and nose. The wave rolled on, leaving her sprawled on the sand. She staggered to her feet, wiping salt water out of her stinging eyes. Paco was scrambling up beside her.

A crab-creature the size of a house rose from the waves.

"Run!" Paco shouted.

As a claw the size of Nugget lunged toward them, they clutched each other's hands and bolted off the peninsula. Arrows flew in a rain toward the great crab-creature, bouncing off its shell with a rattle like hail. When she and Paco reached the patrol, Sujata grabbed him and Indra grabbed Kerry, then everyone ran for dry land. Kerry glanced over her shoulder, nearly falling, and saw one last immense tentacle slap down a few inches behind her foot.

They stopped, panting, at the palisade where Nugget stood. The beach was littered with dead crab-creatures. A few live ones scuttled back into the sea. The huge crab-creature was still in the water. Its eye stalks extended several feet, then swiveled to glare at the patrol. Then, with a loud hiss, it slowly sank beneath the waves.

The entire patrol let out a breath of relief. The blue water stayed calm and peaceful—deceptively peaceful, Kerry thought as she stroked Nugget in apology, wondering again why she'd abandoned him. It was so unlike her.

Paco approached her, his fox-like features taut with annoyance. "What was wrong with you? Why did you jump off your horse and try to run into the ocean? We were all yelling at you to get back on the beach."

"You were? I didn't hear it." Kerry confessed, and turned away from his angry face, so unsettlingly like their father's. She addressed the rest of the patrol. "I don't know what got into me. I never panic like that. And I didn't see any of you until Paco grabbed me."

Anna-Lucia wiped sweat and tentacle slime off her forehead with a shaking hand. "I know what that thing was. It was a queen lobster."

"I thought those were just stories to scare little kids out of swimming without supervision," Sujata said.

Anna-Lucia shook her head. "You know how rabbits cast illusions?"

"Small illusions," Sujata remarked, slinging her bow over her shoulder. It was true. Rabbit illusions were fuzzy and vague, sometimes so much so that it was hard to tell what they were trying to make you see.

"Well, queen lobsters cast strong ones," Anna-Lucia said. "We're lucky that one went after Kerry instead of the fishers. They can make people leap out of their boats in a panic. And then they're easy pickings. I don't think we've had one in Las Anclas for fifteen years," she finished. "They usually like deeper water. But I remember one thing from fifteen years ago: they're good eating."

Another patrol member, Dominica Preciado, took a step

toward the beach. "Do you think the big one's gone? Let's take them to Jack's for a feast!"

Indra and Sujata made identical faces of disgust. They were vegetarians, Kerry remembered.

A little doubtfully, Kerry said, "Well...I like Dr. Lee's crab dumplings."

"You almost turned into a queen lobster's human dumpling," Paco said. His slanted eyebrows quirked as he grinned, transforming his face.

Kerry didn't think she'd ever seen his smile before. She'd have remembered. It didn't look at all like Father's.

Then he turned his back to clean his sword, and the moment was gone.

·5·
ROSS

ROSS, MIA, AND JENNIE walked down the hill overlooking the ruined city and the crystal forest that surrounded it.

Since they'd shared a quick breakfast at dawn, they'd walked in a comfortable silence. Ross enjoyed their steady rhythm, his steps matching Jennie's, with Mia taking one and a half quick steps to every one of theirs, plus an occasional hop that set her tools jingling.

As their feet hit the sand, his heart was full of...

Even inside his own mind, Ross couldn't bring himself to give more than a cautious poke at the word "love." The more he heard it spoken, the less he felt like he knew what it really meant.

The Oldtown Band was always singing about love—wanting it, getting it, losing it, dying for it. And people in Las Anclas used the word so easily: "I love Luc's tacos!" "I love that song!" When Mia had unwrapped Kerry's Christmas gift, a pretty dress that Kerry had called a hanbok, she'd said, "Oh, Kerry, I love it!"

Mia had obviously been sincere, but could you really love clothes? Ross's leather jacket was comfortable and had seen him through thunderstorms, swarms of stinging insects, and battles. Jennie had told him how good he looked in it, prompting him to wear it every time he knew he'd see her. He'd never give it away, but he wouldn't say he *loved* it.

People *liked* clothes. They *liked* songs. And they used the word "love" to mean "like," just as they sometimes said, "Do you like her?" when they obviously meant "Do you love her?" But understanding that brought him no closer to understanding what love — real love, between people — truly meant.

Ross glanced down at his hands. Mia's clever little fingers curled around his left, adjusting to his limited range of motion. Jennie's strong hand, exactly the same size as his own, enfolded his right. A warm feeling swelled in his chest as he looked at those two hands holding his. No one but Jennie and Mia had ever made him feel that way. That had to be love.

Right?

But if it was love, shouldn't he feel the same way about them both? The way he felt about Jennie wasn't the same way he felt about Mia, except where it sort of was. Maybe he thought about them differently, but loved them in the same way. Or wanted to love them in the same way.

And that brought his thoughts straight to sex. At completely the wrong time, when he was about to risk his life. But when was the right time? Whenever he kissed either of them, it felt like the right time. But Mia would get nervous and jittery, and that would unnerve him, and they'd both back off in confusion. And Jennie would keep going, as if she was walking down a road she knew by heart, but for some reason her confidence made *him* panic.

He'd told them once that he loved them, but he'd never been able to say it since. Every time he thought of admitting it, even to himself, he tensed up, sure that someone would come and take them away. Like his family had vanished, going to bed one night and gone forever by the next morning.

Ross raised his head, preferring to face the possibility of his own death than keep thinking about his past. The forest of singing trees glittered coldly in the rain-washed morning light. A wind blew strong and cool, but the leaves stirred of their own accord or not at all, occasionally chiming in the distance. The rainbow patterns of light they cast across the yellow-brown sands reminded him of the hills above Gold Point, when Voske had forced him to prospect in the ruined city.

A sweet tinkle was followed by a soft pop, then a squeal. All three of them jumped.

The squeal became a scream as surprise turned to pain, and then trailed off. Ross caught himself clutching at his left arm, and made his hand drop.

"Rabbit," said Jennie. She breathed out, slow and controlled, revealing that she was nearly as tense as Ross. "Or maybe a wild rat."

He had assumed that since he'd gotten through the singing trees near Gold Point, he could get through the ones near Las Anclas. But now that they'd reached the forest, he found the idea much more intimidating. This forest was more than twice the size of Gold Point's, and many of the trees were far, far bigger. While the Gold Point trees had been born from the deaths of desert animals, and bore the dull colors of their fur, most of the trees here had obviously been created from the deaths of humans. They glowed with the brilliant colors of clothing dye.

The brightest trees grew out of the ancient road, splitting it with emerald or sapphire or topaz roots. Those were the remains of the prospectors and other travelers who had tried to walk this way before him.

It had been easy enough to push aside the death memories of rats and coyotes and mountain lions. Animal emotions were so different from those of humans that their memories didn't sink hooks into his mind. Though animals felt pain, they didn't burn with the desire for revenge or grieve for the children they'd left behind. Now that he saw hundreds of human-born trees lined up like an army, he wondered if he was about to get them all killed.

Mia huddled inside her shirt as if the cool wind had turned to ice. "You think we could still talk to each other if we become trees?"

"That's not funny." Jennie hefted her pack higher. "Let's review, guys."

"I go ahead. You watch me. I'll give you a signal if it's safe." Ross raised his hand high. "You'll know if it's not."

Mia gave him a shove. "That's *really* not funny."

"When you get to me, take my hands," Ross went on. "I might not be able to see or hear you, but I should still be able to feel you. Whatever happens, don't let go. I have to convince the trees that you're with me."

"And then we explore!" Mia said happily. "There could be rooms and rooms of perfectly preserved artifacts! On neatly labeled shelves."

He knew she was joking, but maybe only barely. "You know, even though humans won't have picked it over, animals nearly always get in and knock things around."

"But animals haven't been able to get in, either." Mia pointed to an amethyst branch swaying in a way that had nothing to do with the wind, sending up a barely audible melody. "No one has. That's why I'm so excited!" Then she sobered and turned to Ross earnestly. "If you're okay with it. Don't do this just because I want to get in. I hope *you* want to get in. You shouldn't risk your life for me. Not that it's risky for you! But—"

Jennie shook her gently. "Mia. It's okay. First sign that it's not working, we turn around and go home. Right, Ross?"

He flexed his fingers. "I'm going now."

Mia flung herself on Ross, nearly bowling him over. Her fingernails dug into his shoulders, but he didn't care about that because that...*feeling,* whatever it was...flared up inside him. He bent down and kissed her hard. She was so warm and so brave, and she believed in him in a way he didn't believe in himself.

Both she and Jennie. When Mia let him go at last, he instinctively reached for Jennie. She stepped into his arms and lowered her head to kiss him just as hard, but before he could panic—just as his muscles began to stiffen—she let go and stepped back.

He had to walk away right now, before he lost his nerve. He hefted his pack.

"Watch for the signal." His voice came out a croak, but neither girl laughed.

"Okay." Mia's voice trembled.

He squeezed her warm little hand, then walked down the rise.

Fifty feet from the nearest tree, he stopped, closed his eyes, and stood before his mental wall. His blood-red tree and the obsidian grove were faint with distance, but he could hear the forest singing. The trees were always singing. The sounds made by the leaves were merely a part of their voices, a single instrument in the melody.

Ross could hear their music, but he couldn't understand it. Cautiously, he listened harder– listened deeper. He brushed against the earliest memories of the trees, of the deaths of the people and animals they had grown from, but his mental walls kept those at a safe distance.

He opened the door a crack. The trees seemed curious. They were used to only speaking to each other. He saw himself as the trees saw him, a figure of red heat standing on an expanse of white-hot earth. Casting his mental net wider, he saw that image multiply by the perceptions of hundreds of trees.

Ross tried to make the trees see as he did: not as many beings sharing thoughts, but as one. The figures merged back into a single image. He sent out a picture of himself as the trees saw him, but walking forward, hand in hand with a tall girl made of heat on one side, and a small one on the other.

The trees waited.

Ross tried to approach, but he couldn't get his feet to move. For a frightening moment, he didn't even know where his feet where, or how to find his own body again. Then he found a double awareness, of himself in the mental landscape and himself in his own body.

His legs seemed to be a mile away, but he made them move. One step. Two.

The trees waited.

He could feel when he was within range of their deadly shards, because the trees knew as well. But none attacked. As he neared, images drifted past, not of their own origins but of their neighbors'; not of deaths, but of the moments before.

A man with a yellow beard, leading a mule. They had become the dusty gray tree and the pale one beside it. A woman in bright steel armor. That was the silvery tree up ahead. Two tall figures and three small ones, stumbling through a moonless night. That was the cluster of five trees off to the side, their branches intertwined.

Ross pushed his own vision at the forest: Mia and Jennie walking up to him and taking his hands, and then the three of them walking safely past the trees.

The trees seemed to consider this. Ross waited for them to send a picture back at him, of crystal branches sprouting from three bodies. As soon as he thought of it, that image echoed through the forest, raising a shimmering chorus of chimes. Ross held his breath. The image faded, replaced by his own picture, repeated a hundred times from tree to tree: three heat-figures, walking safely, hand-in-hand.

Hoping he was interpreting that correctly, he sent a slow message down the many miles to his hand. It felt heavy as an ox, but he dragged it upward.

Then they waited, Ross and the trees.

·6·
MIA

MIA HAD WATCHED ROSS approach singing trees before. She and Jennie stood by while he spoke with the black grove that had taken over the cornfield. Like many true Change powers, his unique symbiosis was obviously getting stronger and easier to control with time and practice...

...and telling herself all that didn't make Mia any less scared. She turned to Jennie, hoping that Jennie's confidence would rub off on her.

But Jennie looked worried. "He's got to be in range now."

Mia answered automatically, "Range is twenty feet. He's at ten."

Jennie's fists clenched. Mia made what she hoped was a reassuring noise.

Ross took another shuffling step, then swayed. Mia wanted to rush out there and grab him, except that would probably get them both killed. She patted her crossbow, not that a bow would be of any use. Mia wished she had her flamethrower, even though the range was so short. What she needed was a long-range weapon that could stop the shards. A hose that sprayed glue? If it was thinned enough to flow easily, would it be sticky enough to trap the shards?

Her heartbeat galloped as Ross walked right up to a tall moonstone tree and touched its trunk. A slim branch dipped down to brush against his hair, crystals chiming with shivering sweetness. Jennie's body tensed beside Mia.

Then Ross turned toward them. His hand rose slowly, fingers spread.

Mia's mouth dried. "Let's go."

The rasp of steel shivered on the bone-dry air as Jennie drew her beautiful new sword. Mia admired how heroic she looked brandishing it. And the grip fit her hand perfectly.

I *made that,* Mia thought with pride. *Well, me and Mr. Garcia.*

Jennie stepped in Ross's footprints, clear in the dust. Mia followed, counting mentally. Thirty feet. Twenty-five. Mia hesitated, but Jennie didn't, so Mia scrambled to catch up. Twenty. If any of the fragile-looking globes hanging from the faceted boughs exploded now, they'd all be dead.

They passed a huge gray tree, its mighty branches glimmering in the sunlight. Leaves chimed sharply. Mia wanted to close her eyes, like a kid hiding from monsters under the bed. No one had ever come this close to these trees before and lived.

No one had ever come this close to any singing trees and gotten a good look at them, either. Mia had gone near some before, but every single time she'd been too scared or too worried about Ross to examine them, or it had been the middle of a battle. This time, she wouldn't miss her chance.

An amber seedpod the size of a cantaloupe hung above her shoulder, so close that Mia could see the individual shards crammed inside. They were thin as needles, sharp at both ends. The shell looked fragile as a soap bubble. She edged away. Other pods were smaller, probably immature. The shards inside those seemed stuck together, blunt, not fully formed.

Jennie touched her arm. Mia flinched.

Jennie beckoned: Mia had drifted off the path. She sidled hastily behind Jennie. When they reached Ross, Mia took Ross's left hand as Jennie closed her fingers around his right, leaving her sword-arm free. His eyes were closed but his long lashes fluttered as if he was dreaming.

Mia didn't dare speak. Loud noises could shatter glass. Maybe even soft noises could break those glassy pods. She gave Ross's hand a gentle squeeze. His weight shifted, one foot sliding forward. Mia and Jennie stepped with him, and together they walked through the forest.

No birds sang. The sunlight filtered through the jewel-colored leaves and the air felt oddly cool. Mia was tempted to brush her fingers against a trunk to see if the trees were cold, but decided not to risk it. She'd tell Dad. He'd be interested, even if no one else would. Kerry might, too. She liked knowing how things worked.

Step by step they traveled, until an enormous sapphire tree loomed up ahead. She wondered how old it was.

Ross jolted to a stop. Jennie shifted her grip, slipping her arm around Ross's. Mia switched hands and slid her other arm around his back. He was trembling, and she could feel every knob along his spine. She resisted the impulse to hug him to her—to stop everything—to keep him safe, to *be* safe, but it was too late for that. She gritted her teeth and kept her arm in place for support, mentally counting heartbeats and wondering how far she would get before her last. And if she would ever know the final number.

A glittering blue branch bent toward him.

Terror thrilled through Mia. She felt Jennie trying to tug Ross backward. Mia shifted, ready to move, but Ross dug his heels in. Mia couldn't stop a whimper from escaping her lips as a single gemlike twig bent down, closer and closer until it caressed his face. Mia ducked. Ross shuddered, but held his ground. The razor edges of the twig drew two lines of blood from forehead to jaw.

Tears slipped down Mia's face as she thought of all the kisses she would miss. They both would miss. All three of them would miss. Or maybe he and Jennie had done more than kissing and why not because Jennie was beautiful and smart and experienced and she was only weird little Mia who'd gotten older but never grown up, just like Mr. Preston had said...

Ross took a step. And another. Fifty-six, fifty-seven heartbeats...they were still alive. Four steps, sixty-five heartbeats, and they'd passed the great sapphire tree. Maybe they would live?

Twice more Ross stopped, his chin lifted, his eyes wide but focused on nothing, like blind Alma Preciado. He wore the same intent listening expression as Alma, though Mia heard nothing but a whispering breeze, and now and then a faint sweet tinkle that made her skin crawl.

Was he listening to the trees? Talking to them? Negotiating with them?

If they lived, she would stop dithering. That was a promise. She was not going to die without ever having sex! With Ross. She didn't want to have sex with anyone else. But how could she actually make that happen?

One inner voice counted steps as another babbled, half excited and half in panic. Did Ross want to have sex with her? Sometimes she thought yes, sometimes no. What if he'd thought about it, but then looked around her cottage, and…should she move the engine off her bed? Would that be too obvious a hint? And if she did, where would she put that lovely, lovely engine, that might become the heart of an actual tractor, if she lived to build it?

Step, step, past trees more colorful and varied: bloodstone, garnet, aquamarine, jade; silver, gold, bronze, steel. Even the black trees were metallic like iron, not shiny like obsidian.

A sharp chime overhead made Mia jump.

If we live, I'll tell Ross we should have sex!

Ross didn't waver.

Jennie moved with him, her sword upraised. Mia scrambled to follow. It was such a relief to have Jennie with them. She did everything better than Mia. She was *experienced.* Mia hadn't asked about her and Ross because she didn't want to know. But if one of them already knew what to do, wouldn't that be better than two people who had no idea? Other than to get the engine off the bed.

Yes, think of good things. Like exploring a treasure trove of ancient machines with her best friend and boyfriend. That would have been the fulfillment of her wildest dreams, except that before Ross had come to Las Anclas, it wouldn't have occurred to her to put a boyfriend into her daydreams. It just went to show that even Mia could dream too small. She had to be the luckiest girl in the world. Maybe she'd find a flying carriage!

Light flashed from beyond the trees. Ross didn't pause, but continued straight into a grove of twisted bronze and golden trees. When it looked as if he'd smack his head into a branch, Jennie cupped her palm over his head and pushed it down. Ross bent, but walked on. The view ahead broke into threads of emerald light. As they got closer, the strands resolved into brilliant vines that draped over the trees, creating a solid-seeming wall of green.

Mia reached to shove aside the nearest fall of vines, then snatched her hand back with a yelp. Several cuts beaded up with blood. The leaves had been hard and sharp as knives.

"I have leather gloves in my pack," Jennie whispered, her breath warm at Mia's ear.

Mia stretched out her arm behind Ross to extract the gloves, one for her and one for Jennie. Then Jennie used her sword to part the vines. They slithered down the edge with a scraping noise, striking purple and gold sparks. Mia pulled more vines away, creating a doorway.

Light dazzled them.

"It's like a rainbow," Jennie whispered.

Color shimmered and flashed, glittering and coruscating with such intensity that Mia was half-blinded. She couldn't make sense of anything she saw. The ground was silver, the horizon emerald, and the air a kaleidoscope of brilliant motion.

Then she began to make sense of her surroundings. The moving shapes were butterflies! They filled the air, some smaller than her thumbnails, some large as her cats, swirling and fluttering, their wings intricately patterned.

They stepped through, letting the curtain of vines fall behind them. Fragile objects shattered and popped under her feet. Jewel-like pebbles and broken glass lay scattered across a carpet of silver moss.

Mia's first find was right there at her feet, an intricately carved little copper box. With an excited squeal, she stooped to pick it up. It stuck to the ground, then came free with a sucking sound. Hundreds of tiny waving legs clung to the underside. She flung it away with a yelp.

Ross started. "What was that?"

He pulled his hand free of hers, shaded his eyes, then clutched at her shoulder for support. "I have to sit down."

"Not here!" Mia caught him around the ribs. "Everything's either sharp or has legs!"

Jennie prodded a bare patch of glittering moss with her sword. Nothing wriggled, jumped, or broke. "Try this."

Ross sank on to it and put his head down between his knees.

Jennie crouched beside him. "Are you all right?"

Mia didn't catch what Ross muttered in response, but she guessed that it was "Yeah." He added, more clearly, "I'll be fine."

She sat down, close enough that he could lean on her if he wanted to. He was breathing hard and fast, as if he'd run all the way through the forest.

The ancient road continued into the ruins, but it was rippled with large mounds covered in silver moss and delicate flowers with a glassy sheen. Much bigger structures, also coated with moss, lined either side of the road. Some were almost as high as the Las Anclas bell tower, but the jumbled shapes made them hard to identify. Beyond those, a slim white tower rose higher than the tallest tree, gleaming in the sun.

Mia wiped her face on her sleeve. The lack of wind made the air even colder, but she was sweating with exertion and nerves. She could taste static on her tongue. Clicks and whirrs, rustles and chimes sounded all around her, shrill and sharp; some came from the trees and some from the flying insects, but others were unnervingly hard to pinpoint. The air smelled metallic and acrid.

Ross lifted his head, the blood from the sapphire tree cuts already drying on his face. His skin was pale beneath its natural brown, and he pressed his fingers into his temples. He reminded her of the victims of heat exhaustion who flooded the infirmary every summer. Mia fished a bottle of her father's headache elixir from her backpack and pushed it into Ross's hand. He drank it without seeming to notice the bitterness. Jennie, who seemed to be thinking along the same lines as Mia, took the emptied bottle and gave him her canteen.

Ross looked better by the time he returned the canteen to Jennie. He tugged at the silver moss, stretching a few strands out. When he let go, they sprang back into place.

"How can it be so different in here?" he asked. "I've never seen anything like any of this."

"It's isolated," Jennie replied. "Nothing comes in, nothing goes out. Grandma Wolfe said that some islands have plants and animals that only exist in that one place, because they kept evolving and mutating right where they were. I guess that's been going on here for hundreds of years."

A dragonfly darted between two blue butterflies drifting near Mia. With a flick of indigo wings, one butterfly dropped so that its hair-thin legs brushed the dragonfly. There was an electric spark and a sizzle, and the dragonfly's wings stilled. Before it could fall, the butterfly's legs wrapped around it and bore it away.

Ross got to his feet. "Let's take a look around."

The vines that had been green within the forest were silver on the city side, creating what looked like an impenetrable wall. Ross took out a stake with a red cloth streamer and pushed it into the earth to mark where they'd come from. The color, which would have leaped out against the desert sands, blended into the rainbow pebbles like camouflage.

Ross shrugged. "I guess we'll see it when we get near it."

Mia pointed to the tower. "Let's go to that! It's in perfect condition, and look how clean it is. It must be full of cool stuff."

With a concerned glance at Ross, Jennie suggested, "Let's start with something a bit closer."

Ross shaded his eyes. "I think these structures by us are fallen buildings."

"Let's go! Let's go!" Mia took an eager step, and her foot hit a small oval object. It skidded into a plant with golden leaves and opalescent flowers. A flower fell and shattered like glass, and the object flipped open on a hinge. She grabbed it with her gloved hand, inspected it for legs, then held it out. "Look what I found!"

"I've seen those," Ross said. "Some towns trade for them. You don't know what they were for, do you?"

"No, but you can use the little wires inside them. First find!" Mia added, "First non-legged find!"

"Remember Princess Pit Mouth," Jennie warned her. "Make sure anything you put in your pack isn't alive."

"I'd be amazed if this reproduced." Mia popped her find into her pack. One step and she'd already gotten a good artifact. This place was a prospector's dream—and an engineer's.

Ross pointed at a mound. "Let's try that one."

There were regular rows of square outlines along its side, like windows, but they were overgrown with metallic moss and gemlike nests. With a chitter and a whir of wings, iridescent dragonflies rose up, zipped overhead in a tight spiral, then aimed straight for the sky.

Ross inspected the fallen building. "We'll have to cut through here."

They sawed through a mat of moss and shoved aside a tangle of vines, revealing a black crevasse. Ross lit his lantern and held it inside. Glowing white shapes flapped away. The light gleamed off transparent bubbles stuck to the walls and floor. Some were cloudy and dark, filled with mounds of dust. Others held objects, perfectly preserved: another hinged oval like the one Mia had found, a steel fork, and–

"Books!" Jennie exclaimed. "Three of them!"

"Wait." Ross threw out his arm, stopping her from scrambling inside. "See that crack in the floor?"

It took close examination for Mia to spot a faint, jagged line. "Yeah, I see it."

"Don't step over it, or go within a few feet of it. The rest of the place looks okay. But don't touch the walls, and stand back when you break the bubbles." Ross tested the floor with his crowbar before he cautiously stepped inside and beckoned the others in.

Jennie went straight for the bubble containing three bound books, grinning like it was Christmas all over again, and tapped it with her sword. It popped into nothingness, like a soap bubble, and the books flew into her outstretched hand. All three had pictures on the cover, of children in odd, bright clothing, and were titled *The Homework Club*. The volume numbers were five, nine, and twelve.

"Children's books." Jennie sheathed her sword and cradled them like babies. "I think. I wonder if the rest of them are here, too."

Mia's attention was caught by a wooden rectangle jammed up against the wall...not a rectangle. A door. It was a door lying on its side.

Her entire perception of the room shifted. They had come in through a window, and that door should lead to another room. She darted toward it. The door was ajar, and when she peered into the darkness, she saw a glint of metal.

She was about to point it out when Jennie exclaimed, "More books!"

The corner of another book stuck out from a pile of broken furniture.

Ross tilted his head. "Don't try to pull it out. We'll have to brace it first."

As Ross and Jennie extracted tools from their backpacks, Mia held up her lantern to the dark room. The glint of metal resolved itself into a large square of black glass attached to a metal box, with a row of buttons at the bottom. Mia bent down further, until her glasses scraped the door frame. The largest button was marked POWER.

Excitement shivered along every nerve in her body. She put down the lantern and leaned in to peer through the crack. Her left hand rested against the door to steady it. With just that tiny bit of pressure, it pivoted and toppled into her hands. Mia staggered under its weight before she managed to lay it down.

"What are you doing?" Ross called out. He sounded alarmed.

"I was bracing it," Mia explained hastily, eager to get to the machine. "Ross, there's a machine that says power!"

She snatched up her lantern, bent low, and stepped through the doorway. White specks were drifting down. She looked up. More flakes of plaster pattered down to her face and sprinkled her glasses.

"RUN!" Ross shouted.

Mia lunged for the machine—the find of a lifetime—but two sets of hands clamped onto her arms, dragged her away, and flung her through the window.

She landed outside in a sprawl, her backpack thumping down on top of her. A body slammed into her, squishing out her breath.

"Ow!"

As Jennie rolled off her, Mia heard things crashing and collapsing. Plaster and dust billowed out from the window.

The three of them sat there, frozen, until the noise stopped. The dust began to settle as Ross got to his feet.

"It's probably safe to go back in now," Mia said hopefully.

Both Jennie and Ross swung around. "No!" they said together.

The find of a lifetime, and it had probably been crunched to dust. And Ross and Jennie were looking at Mia like she was out of her mind. "It said *power*."

·7·
ROSS

ROSS FOLDED HIS ARMS tight across his chest, trying to stop himself from shaking, as he watched the dust billowing out the window. They'd come so close to being caught in the collapse. If they hadn't been crushed to death, they'd have been trapped under tons of concrete, to slowly suffocate or die of thirst.

But we did *escape,* he reminded himself.

He watched Mia and Jennie, making himself see and believe that they were alive and unhurt, until his pounding heartbeat slowed. Jennie brushed dust from her hair, then smiled down at the books she'd made it out with. Mia glared at the dust clouds, obviously wishing she could go back in.

Nothing bad had happened. They'd had a close call, but that was it. Everything was fine.

Then Ross remembered that he'd left his crowbar and pry bar inside. They'd once belonged to his grandmother, and he'd carried them ever since she'd died. Voske had stolen his pack when Ross had been dragged to Gold Point, but Kerry had retrieved it for him when they'd escaped. And after all that, his precious tools were trapped beneath a pile of furniture in an unstable structure that he didn't dare go into again.

Now that the dust had settled, his crowbar was temptingly visible. Jennie followed his longing stare.

"Maybe I can free it." She extended her hand. The crowbar jerked a half-inch, then stuck. A piece of wood fell from the top of the heap, and the building gave a grinding groan. More dust sprinkled gently down. The whole thing was ready to collapse at any second.

"Sorry about your tools, Ross." Mia hung her head like a scolded puppy.

"What happened in there?" Ross asked. "Did you say you were bracing it? Bracing what?"

"Well, the door looked a little wobbly, and I remembered what you said about bracing things. So I put my hand on it—gently!— and the whole thing fell on my head." She peered up at him from beneath her bangs, half-hopeful and half-skittish, as if she wasn't sure if he'd forgive her or yell at her. "I'll make you a new crowbar. A *better* crowbar!"

Despite the loss of his tools, Ross had to laugh. Mia was so sweet and her eyes were so bright and eager, it was impossible to stay mad at her. "I did the same sort of stuff when I started learning to prospect. Next time, just let me check first before you brace anything."

Mia instantly perked up and pointed to the closest fallen building. "How about that one?"

It took no more than a glance to see how unstable that one was. Ross shook his head. Though it had been true that he, like Mia, had been over-eager when he'd started out, he meant to keep a close eye on her for this prospecting trip and any others in the future. Brilliant as she was, there was something about her that made him think she wasn't really the prospector type.

Too fearless, he decided at last.

The part of her that loved machines spoke louder than the part that cared about safety. Oh, she was cautious enough in her own cottage, but nowhere near as cautious as Ross. She'd admitted that she'd repeatedly burned off her eyebrows. If she saw another ancient machine that said *power*, he'd better be there to grab her.

"Why don't we try the white tower? That one that looks intact," Ross suggested.

"At least I got the books." Jennie carefully tucked them into her pack.

Now, Jennie would make a good prospector, Ross thought.

It wasn't surprising. She was good at everything he'd ever seen her do—fighting, teaching, dancing, even sewing. And now prospecting. She'd probably picked up some of the skills training with the Rangers, learning to scrutinize the environment for danger. He wondered how happy she really was at the schoolhouse. When he'd studied there, it had felt huge and crowded. Overwhelming. But for Jennie, it seemed too small. Or maybe it was that she was too big for it. Not physically, but . . .

"What are those metal poles?" Mia asked, pointing down the road. "Ever seen those before?"

Ross shook his head and started walking. It bothered him to be so close to his grandmother's tools and be unable to reach them.

"It would take ten of us to lift one," said Jennie. "But imagine having all that metal!"

"We wouldn't have to lift them," Mia replied. "I could build rollers and a pulley system."

Ross kept going. The tools were gone. There was no point thinking about things that had already been lost. He'd find new things.

He stopped at a building with an open doorway. It was overgrown with metallic vines but structurally intact, not even an inch off its foundations. This time Mia stayed well back, though she was quivering with eagerness, like a pup on a leash. Ross had been like that with his grandmother. The memory made him smile as he shaded his eyes from the light glinting off the vines.

"Jennie, can you test the floor?" he asked.

Jennie used her sword to prod at the debris that mounded the floor. What had looked like a heap of moldering cloth vanished like a rabbit illusion, revealing a furry creature the size of a small dog. The creature's fur writhed, and hundreds of pinprick eyes opened. It had a mass of tiny babies clinging to its back. With a shriek, the creature leaped for the opening, skittered over Mia's foot, and vanished into another building.

The girls backed away, Mia shaking her foot madly. Ross tried not to laugh as he peered inside. A speck of crimson gleamed amidst the gray-green mold. He checked for eyes, then plucked out a folding knife. It was rusted shut, but he knew the type by the bright red handle. A good soak in oil, and it would be a valuable multi-purpose tool.

Mia reached out to pet it—she owned one herself—then

pointed. "What are those mounds over there? The ones in a row. I don't think that's a natural formation."

Once she'd called them to Ross's attention, he recognized them. "Those are vehicles. I saw a row like that in the ruined city of Gold Point, but I had to pretend I didn't know what they were so Voske couldn't get them."

Mia bolted across the silvery road. Ross pursued her, delighted that he could finally get to explore one and intent on preventing her from getting herself into trouble.

But to his relief, she didn't attempt to fling herself inside. Instead, she stayed at a safe distance and looked to Ross. "What do we do? I don't want to do anything wrong."

He inspected the mound. It looked stable, and he didn't see anything living on or in it other than a few harmless-looking bugs. "Let's start by scraping off the moss."

The silvery moss peeled off more easily than he'd expected, coming away in curling sheets like paper. The underside was sticky and smelled acidic, and he warned the girls not to touch it. Soon they exposed a rusted metal body with glass windows, and rotted seats and a round rudder wheel inside.

Reverently, Mia whispered, "It's a *car*. Maybe it still moves!"

Jennie circled it. "I see a wheel, but where's the rudder to steer it along the road?"

Mia pointed to the front. "In there. The engine has to be in there, too. Let's get it open!" She hopped from foot to foot. "Oh, this is even better than I hoped! A real car, with a *complete* engine!"

Ross, too, was thrilled. He'd seen pictures in rare books of cars. Legend had it they'd sped along the roads faster than the fastest deer could run. Legend also insisted that planes—another item he'd seen in Jennie's books—actually flew in the sky, though he could not imagine how those thin metal wings would flap hard enough to lift a tube that seemed capable of holding a hundred people. But he'd never seen examples of either. They had stopped working when the world changed, and then had either been trapped inside the ruined cities or long since salvaged for their parts.

Even if it was impossible to make the car move again, just seeing one made all the pain he'd gone through with the singing trees seem worthwhile. It was like finding that ancient book that only Yuki could read. It had been far more than a valuable relic. That book had changed his entire life. Without it, he'd never have made an enemy of Voske—never been struck by a shard from a crystal tree—never come to Las Anclas—never met Mia or Jennie.

Ross wondered if the car, too, would somehow prove to be more than a precious discovery. But while he was standing and thinking, the girls were busy running around and examining the vehicle.

Jennie exclaimed, "I see a crack. I think this is a lid! Give me your crowbar—sorry. I'll use mine. It's smaller, but it should be okay."

They levered up the lid and exposed a mass of engine parts, rusted almost solid. Swarms of brilliant blue creatures fled from the light and scuttled off along the road, squeaking shrilly.

"Ugh!" Mia exclaimed. "Why do they always run over *my* foot?"

"They like you," Jennie said with a grin. "Maybe you smell good to them."

"It's probably metal or oil," Mia said. "They were living in an engine, after all."

That warm feeling filled Ross's chest again, at Jennie's joke and Mia taking it seriously and his realization that Mia might well be right. The girls were being so themselves. That little exchange had so much of what made him...

He again hesitated over the word *love*.

It's what makes me want to be with them, he concluded.

Then he shut down the thoughts and pulled some tools from his pack. Ross lost all sense of time as they poured oil over the engine and worked part after part free. It was as thrilling as his very first prospecting trip. So many parts were completely new to him. He only realized how much time had passed when they were down to components that were too heavy to lift or had corroded into nothingness.

Mia rubbed a forefinger over the engine block that not even the three of them could lift. "Maybe next trip we could get this. Okay! Let's go to the next car."

Ross looked up at the sky. The sun had changed position;

they'd spent about three hours over that engine. "I don't want to be caught here at dusk. Who knows what might come out. Let's scout out that tower, then go back through the forest and camp in the desert. If there's nothing in the tower, we can open another car tomorrow."

"Good idea." Mia spotted a steel nut on the ground, and snatched it up to stuff into her bulging pack.

Ross opened his mouth to warn her about what looked like a golden millipede heading for her foot, but he was too late. In a flash of glinting light, the thing leaped onto her boot and began scurrying up her leg.

With a shriek, Mia kicked out violently, sending the thing flying. "I *definitely* don't want to spend the night here."

She smacked her glasses up her nose, then brushed herself off all over. "Ugh, I can still feel things creeping on me."

Jennie patted her shoulder. "Let's walk fast. Don't give anything a chance to crawl on you."

The tower was much larger up close than it had seemed from the other end of the street. Ross had never seen anything like it before. It was smooth and clean, made of hexagonal panels six feet square, all glistening like white glass. There was one entrance, a hexagonal hole at ground level. A soft, deep thrumming hum emanated from the hole, unceasing and steady, regular as the tower walls. The air wafting out smelled of hot metal, like a forge.

He reached into the hole, holding up the lantern. Light flashed and flashed again against the glass interior, reflecting from wall to wall and nearly blinding him. A squeaking noise arose and was drowned out by the rise of the hum. As his eyes adjusted to the brilliant light, he saw that the floor was covered in arm-sized white larvae, writhing and keening and blinking their enormous faceted eyes.

The hum intensified until his skull and teeth buzzed. From the top of the tower, bees the size of large dogs flew down in descending circles, their bodies pulsing and their glittering stingers sparking. They were headed straight for Ross.

"Bees!" Ross shouted, yanking his head out. "*Giant* bees!"

He reached for a knife, then remembered that he had a better weapon. He'd spent every spare minute before the trip practicing with Mia's gift. As Jennie and Mia fell into position beside him, slapping bolts into their own crossbows, Ross dropped a bolt into his, shoved the lever back, aimed, and shot the first bee to fly out of the tower. It fell out of the air and landed with a splat.

Two bees emerged, but were hit by crossbow bolts. It looked like Mia and Jennie had gotten one each. But as he and the girls reloaded, more bees emerged. All three crossbows jerked up and twanged. Three more bees fell to the mossy road.

Silence. They backed warily from the opening. Ross let out a breath of relief. Then a tremendous buzz bludgeoned their ears. The entire swarm of gigantic bees boiled out of the opening.

"Run!" Ross yelled.

He and the girls stampeded. Jennie sprinted ahead. Mia lagged, her overstuffed pack weighing her down, and her short legs taking three steps for every one of Jennie's strides. Ross grabbed her arm and dragged her along with him.

Mia pitched forward, knocked off-balance by her pack. Ross fell with her, trying to cushion her body with his own. They slammed into one of the flowered mounds, which crumbled beneath them like dry sand. Something writhed under his chest. His yell was echoed by Mia's shriek. They dragged each other up and staggered away.

Giant termites crawled out of the broken mound, fanning out their translucent wings, then took to the sky.

Ross again grabbed Mia and ran with her, wishing he could ditch her pack. But it was strapped on tight, with far too many buckles to quickly undo. He clenched his jaw in the anticipation of pain, certain that stingers would stab him from behind at any moment. Their only chance was to get to the crystal trees and hope the bees wouldn't follow.

The angry humming rose to a high-pitched screech. Still running, he glanced back. The termite swarm hit the bee swarm in mid-air. The insects immediately attacked each other. Stingers jabbed, pincers snapped. Bees and termites spiraled overhead, locked in furious, glittering combat.

Ross slammed into something hard. He fell, taking Mia with him. He'd run straight into one of the vine-covered poles. Vines slithered down, tangling their arms and legs. Glassy leaves and flowers shattered all around them. They fought their way free. Ross hadn't felt any pain, but Mia's face and hands were slashed all over with hair-thin cuts.

Jennie pulled Mia to her feet. Ross scrambled after them. Blood and sweat dripped into his eyes, blurring his vision.

They didn't stop until they reached a wall of shining vines. By now the singing trees seemed like a refuge. Skidding to a stop, Ross closed his eyes and opened the door in his mind.

Chimes rang out a warning. These trees didn't know him. This wasn't the same part of the forest they'd entered from. Desperately, he pushed the door open wider, throwing his mind open to everything but the death memories.

The girls became heat shapes. The small one crouched, scrabbling, while the taller one stood with her hand raised high. Ross couldn't see the flying insects, only the disturbances they made in the air. The air rippled near the larger shape—Jennie—and then smoothed out as she slashed her arm down.

A distant voice called out, "Are you done?"

Chimes rang out a warning. Ross shouted, "Don't distract me!"

The trees here were ancient, their memories confusing and many-layered. The humans they recalled were dressed in strange clothing and doing strange things. As curious as Ross was about those images, the trees were much more curious about him. They could see out of his eyes the same way that he could perceive with their senses. That was why the trees were letting him live.

"Now!" Ross yelled.

He couldn't feel the girls taking his hands, but he could see them approach the heat-figure that was himself. Then he was lost in the images: rivers of light, metal carriages, moving paintings. Everything was so bright, so loud, so overwhelming.

The song of the trees and the rush of images faded away, leaving him bewildered. Where was he? *Who* was he?

"We're out of range," a voice was saying. "Ross, we're safe now, you can stop."

The words made no sense...oh.

The heat shapes... That's me and the girls.

"Ross, can you hear me?"

He couldn't seem to fit himself back into his body. For what felt like an eternity, he struggled with a crucial task he couldn't quite remember how to do.

Then he recalled the wall of concrete and the steel door standing ajar. Ross stepped through the door.

His body was as heavy as if he was bearing up a ceiling. He couldn't hold himself up. Hands caught him and lowered him to the ground. Even with his eyes closed, everything seemed to be spinning. A white-hot spike of pain stabbed from behind his eyes to his jaw.

"Ross!" He recognized Jennie's voice, though it was higher than usual. "Ross!"

Someone was shaking him. It was Jennie—he knew the grip of her hands. It made his head hurt even more.

"Don't," he managed to say.

Jennie didn't seem to hear him, or else he hadn't spoken aloud. She kept shaking him.

He caught her hands, his fingers clumsy. "Stop it. I'm just tired."

"He's exhausted," Mia said. A different set of familiar hands brushed his hair off his forehead as he lay on the sand where he'd fallen. "He had to go through the forest twice, without enough time to rest in between. Right, Ross?"

"Yeah." He felt a little better now that no one was shaking him, and Mia's cool hands stroked his aching head. "I'll be fine."

"There's blood all over your face," Jennie muttered. She didn't sound reassured.

"It's only glass cuts," said Mia. "From when we fell into the flowers. See, I have them, too."

Ross forced his eyes open. Mia's face and hands were bleeding, but Jennie was the one who looked as if she was in pain.

A movement past Jennie's shoulder caught his eye. Over the distant sand dune, a figure flew through the air. It was a person, with long black hair streaming behind them. He blinked, wondering if he was still seeing a memory from one of the crystal trees. The figure—a young girl—landed lightly on the sand, then leaped again, impossibly high, holding a dagger upraised to kill.

"Jennie!" Ross dragged his arm up to point beyond her.

Jennie and Mia both spun around, Mia staggering from the

weight of her pack. Jennie whipped out her sword. In a backswing too quick to follow, she sent the girl's knife spinning.

"Surrender!" Jennie shouted. "I won't hurt you!"

The girl leaped at Jennie, dodging her sword with impossible agility, and knocked Jennie flat on her back. The sword flew from Jennie's hand, and the two girls began wrestling in the sand.

Ross struggled to get up, but the world spun dizzily around him. He managed to make it to his knees, but pitched forward when he tried to stand and ended up sprawled on the ground again.

Mia stood guard over him, her crossbow poised.

"Leave him alone!" the girl shouted. She tried to head-butt Jennie, then gasped, "Two against one? Really brave of you!"

"Stop fighting!" Mia yelled. "He's with us! We're not trying to hurt him."

"They're my friends," Ross said, but his words were lost in the shouts and gasps.

Jennie pinned the girl down. Her voice was jagged and breathless as she gasped out, "All three of us escaped the forest."

"Liars. No one goes there." The girl twisted her head to the side, grunted with effort, and lashed out with one leg as if she had no bones in her body. Her foot flew out at an impossible angle and kicked Jennie hard in the ribs.

Jennie winced. "Ross, tell her we're your friends."

The girl abruptly stopped fighting, her eyes widening with shock. "Ross? Ross *Juarez*?"

Before Ross could speak, the girl hissed out her breath. In a blur of movement, she writhed out from Jennie's grip. In an instant she was beside him, her mouth open wide with horror. Ross blinked. His vision was blurred with blood and sweat, but she looked strangely familiar.

"Santa Maria," the girl gasped. "The crystal trees."

Ross realized what she must be thinking. He pulled his shirt up and wiped the blood off his face. The girl still looked so horrified that he forced himself to sit up, though the effort left him even more sick and dizzy.

"I'm not hit," he said. "I'm fine."

The girl sat back on her heels. He watched her expressive

face—her strangely familiar face—as her horror turned to confusion. "Then it's true what they say. You command the trees?"

"Well…" Ross was way too tired to explain what it was really like. He could never quite put it in words anyway. "Yeah. Sort of."

"But you're hurt." The girl's voice rose to a frightened pitch. "You're covered in blood."

He tried to make himself sound reassuring. He could see now how young she was, fifteen at most. "I got cut by some flowers."

"Flowers?" The girl's voice rose incredulously.

"Glass flowers," Mia explained. "We were chased by bees."

"*Bees?*"

"Giant bees." Mia held out her arms in giant bee size. "A whole swarm of them."

"Bees," repeated the girl, now sounding contemptuous. "You were attacked by bees and flowers."

"Who are you?" Jennie asked. "Where did you come from?"

The girl jerked her thumb over her shoulder. "The west road."

But she didn't look to Jennie as she spoke. Her gaze was fixed on Ross, intent and hungry. She seemed to want something from him, though he couldn't imagine what.

The last light of the sun illuminated her face. He *knew* he'd seen her before. But he couldn't think where. The long black hair. The thick fringe of long eyelashes. The prominent cheekbones. Maybe she looked a little like Sheriff Crow?

"I'm Summer," the girl said. "Summer *Juarez*. I've been looking for you, Ross."

My sister? I have a sister?

Even looking at her half-familiar face, Ross couldn't believe it. It felt like a dream.

A blood-red haze dimmed his vision. Inside his head, crystal bells rang. The door in his mind had swung open, allowing the trees to try to communicate with him. It made his head ache. He struggled to close the door.

Behind him, in the still, hot air of sunset, a few trees chimed. The sound spread until the entire forest was ringing out a warning like a rain of metal on glass. Everyone started nervously, even Ross.

Ross stumbled to his feet. "We have to get farther away."

Jennie and Mia grabbed his arms. Summer stared at him as he staggered away and she followed. His head throbbed. He wanted to say something to her but he couldn't put any words together.

They fled across the dunes until the ringing in Ross's mind faded, allowing him to concentrate. He found the steel door inside his head and slammed it shut. The chimes stopped.

They were behind one of the dunes. Rays of sunset slanted across Summer's face, giving it a red-gold tone. Two tiny crescents of light shone in her black eyes.

Jennie was the first to speak. "Let's make camp here."

Ross sat down and slid off his pack without taking his eyes from Summer. If she hadn't been there, he would have stretched out on the sand and let exhaustion overtake him. But she was his *sister*. He had to…

But he didn't know what to do or say. He should be overjoyed, but he only felt stunned. Slowly thoughts returned, little wormy things trailing old emotions. Old pain. A memory slithered into his mind.

His mother stumbling through the darkened streets, her belly huge with pregnancy. His father supported her, trying to hurry her along.

A pair of bony arms swept Ross off his feet.

"I'll carry Ross," Grandma whispered, her voice hoarse and urgent. "We'll wait for you at the tunnel."

Then the memory vanished, the way they always did. What tunnel? He had no idea. All he knew was that he'd never seen his mother again.

"I thought Mom was dead," Ross said.

"You left her for dead," Summer snapped.

Another memory hit Ross, so harsh and vivid that he mentally staggered with the force of it.

His father lay broken and unbreathing, half-buried in stones and dust. Ross touched his cheek, then jerked back his hand from that stiff, cold flesh. His grandmother dug frantically to find his mother in the rubble of the fallen tunnel, until she finally gave up. The dust choked him, and the sound of his grandmother's harsh sobs echoed in his ears. Her hands held him too tight, in a grip close to pain, as she pulled him away.

"She's gone," Grandma said. "This will have to be their grave."

The memory ended as if it had been cut off with a knife.

"We thought she was buried," Ross said slowly. "There was a tunnel. It must have fallen in."

"They blew it up," Summer exclaimed. "How can you not know that? You were *there*. Mom said they tried to kill us all. And they got everyone but Mom because she was out looking for you. She came back and found everyone dead. She waited and waited, but you never came back to find her."

"I was four," Ross protested, though guilt wrung through him. Why *hadn't* he returned? No, he had. He snatched at one of his few memories. "I did go back. But it was years later. All I found were skeletons. Where is she?"

Summer folded her arms across her chest. Her black eyes didn't blink. Ross became aware of the sounds of Mia and Jennie setting up the camp. Of course they were listening. He felt like someone had broken his head open and was prying at the inside of his skull.

Summer still hadn't answered.

"She's dead. Isn't she." He didn't make it a question.

"Yes. *Years* later." She said the phrase exactly as he had. It took him a second to realize she was accusing him.

Jennie stepped up and dropped a load of firewood and three canteens between them. "Ross, why don't you make up the fire? Summer, if you're going to camp with us, would you mind fetching the water? The stream is that way."

Summer hesitated, then grabbed first the canteens and then her pack, which she slung it over her shoulder as she marched away. Ross remembered when he'd carried his pack everywhere because he didn't trust anyone not to rob him, even for the few minutes it would take to collect water.

He couldn't help feeling relieved to see her go. Then guilt punched him in the gut. After all the time he'd spent imagining that someone in his family had survived and maybe someday they'd meet up again, he couldn't believe it had gone that badly.

"I was sure my mother was dead," Ross said, not even knowing who he was talking to. "I was *sure*. It never even occurred to me that she might not be."

"I know." Jennie laid a gentle hand on his shoulder. "I don't think Summer really blames you. Meeting you must be as much of a shock for her as it is for you. She probably thought *you* were dead."

"And she just turned up here?" Mia asked. "That's an awfully big coincidence. Wait! Unless you both came from somewhere much nearer here than I thought. Did you?"

Ross shook his head. "It took me years to get this far west."

Jennie cast a suspicious look in Summer's direction. "I wonder how she knew to come. That is, if she did come looking for you."

"Talking about me?" Summer appeared from behind a boulder, sloshing canteens in her arms.

"How did you find me?" Ross asked.

Summer gave him an angry glare. "You're famous. You single-handedly destroyed the Gold Point empire. You captured the crown princess of Gold Point and turned her against the king. You control the crystal trees, but people say you have other powers, too. You blew up a dam with the power of your mind, you teleported out of a canyon, and..." Her mouth pursed skeptically. "And you can make people like you? Huh. Not sure I believe that one."

A sound like a kitten's mew distracted Ross. It was Mia trying to stifle a laugh.

He blushed hotly. "I didn't do *any* of that. Where did you hear that stuff?"

"It's everywhere!" Summer flung her arms wide. "Every trader! Every traveler! Every person in every town is talking about *you*."

Ross was tempted to run straight back into the crystal forest.

"It's a little exaggerated," Jennie said. Ross recognized the voice she used in the classroom to calm down angry or over-excited kids. "He can control the singing trees, but that's it. King Voske kidnapped him to try to make Ross work for him, but Ross escaped and blew up the Gold Point dam. With gunpowder. But he didn't do it singlehandedly. Princess Kerry helped him. And he didn't kidnap her, either."

Mia spoke up helpfully, her glasses winking in the ruddy light. "Jennie did that."

Summer glared at Mia. "You think you're so funny." She

turned her glare on Ross. "The only thing that's true is that the stories about you are total lies. I came all this way, I lost everything I had, and for what? I thought you were some big hero! I thought all I had to do was find you, and you'd fix everything. We'd ride off together and be gunslingers, and every town would want to hire us, and we'd be rich! And what do I find? A guy my own size who has to have two people to defend him because he can't even get up off the ground!"

Jennie cut in. "That's enough—"

A streak of crimson split the sky. The eerie keen of a cloud viper rose to a near-painful pitch. Mia flung herself down with her hands covering her head, Jennie yanked her sword from its sheath, and Summer leaped backward twenty feet. Ross grabbed his belt knife and threw it.

The winged snake thudded to the ground at his feet. It writhed for a second, then lay still. Its attack crimson faded in death to its usual mottled camouflage of sky blue and cloud white. Ross drew his knife from its heart.

"Thanks, Ross!" Mia scrambled to her hands and knees, peering at the dead snake. "What *is* that thing? It looks like a king snake with wings."

"It's a cloud viper," Ross said. "I thought they only swarmed in mountains. This one must be a scout."

Summer's voice was less belligerent as she cautiously rejoined them. "Yeah, I never saw one in the desert before."

"I wish I could leap like that," Mia said wistfully. "That was twenty-two feet. That must be fun. Except when you're scared."

"I wasn't scared, just startled." Defensively, Summer added, "They're not dangerous unless you're slow and alone. The venom only paralyzes you. But if no one else is around, the scout flies back and brings the rest of the flock. And then they all strip you to your bones before you can move."

"Well, that one won't be going back." Ross peered up at the sky, though the cloud vipers' camouflage made it difficult to see a flock. At least the sun was setting. Wherever this one's nest mates were, they'd be settling for the night.

Mia fished through her pack. "Ah!" She pulled out a small, sharp knife and a glass vial.

"And gloves?" Jennie reminded her.

"Of course." Mia brandished a pair.

"What are you doing?" Summer's lips curled in disgust. "You can't eat those things. Well, they won't make you sick or anything, but they're gross. I hate snake."

Mia gingerly pried its jaws open. "Extracting the venom."

"Ugh," Summer sneered. "You're weird."

Ross looked from one girl to the other. He wanted to defend Mia, but Summer was his sister. In all the times he'd imagined that someone in his family had survived and he'd meet up with them again, it had never gone like this. Once again, he was completely at a loss for words, or even thoughts.

His face itched. The blood from the glass cuts had dried and pulled at his skin. Grateful to have something to do, Ross poured some water from his canteen into the palm of his hand and started washing off his face and throat.

Summer stepped close. "Not a bad throw with the knife."

"Thanks," Ross muttered, scrubbing harder.

"Hey, what happened to your throat?" Leaning in much too close, Summer said, "Is that a scar? It looks like a hand print!"

Ross ducked, turning to make his hair fall to hide the scar. He couldn't have explained even if he wanted to; his jaw was locked shut. He could almost smell the hell cell: granite and blood.

Jennie walked in between them. He'd never been more relieved to hear her teacher voice as she said, "Who wants first watch?"

·8·
BECKY

BECKY CALLAHAN STOOD OUTSIDE her home with one hand on the doorknob, unable to force herself to turn it. Her stomach churned with anxiety and nausea, and she gulped air to fight it.

A window had been left open a crack, allowing her to hear the clink of metal against china. Mom had started dinner without her. That meant Grandma Ida was eating with them. And it was Henry's day to cook. Her stomach roiled even more.

Becky wished she could run back to the surgery. But Dr. Lee had said he was going to eat at Jack's. He'd invited Becky, but he was just being kind. He couldn't really want her company for dinner after having her around all day at work. And he'd insist on paying for her meal, because he always did on the few occasions when she accepted his invitations, and then she'd feel guilty about taking his hard-earned scrip.

Worst of all, if they were alone together without work to distract them, Dr. Lee would begin asking questions. They'd be gentle but probing, as if he was feeling for painful spots on a patient's body. But he was feeling for painful spots in her life—in her family. She couldn't tell him, and she hated to lie. He was so kind. It made her feel even guiltier than letting him buy her dinner.

She couldn't go back, so she had to go in. Every moment she stayed outside would only make her later and get her in even more trouble.

Becky forced herself to walk into the dining room. The transition from the warm glow of sunset to the stuffy gloom half-blinded her. She wished Mom would leave the curtains open, like most people in Las Anclas did. But then any passerby would be able to see inside the house, and gossip. Mom hated the idea that people might talk about them.

Becky slunk to her chair and sat down, wishing she was invisible. But of course, her entrance didn't go unnoticed.

Grandma Ida paused in lighting the lamp, her wrinkled features tightening with scorn. "So her majesty deigns to join us? In my day, we waited for our elders and stood behind our chairs until they were seated. You young people have the manners of wild goats."

Becky wondered if Grandma Ida actually wanted her to get up and stand behind her chair. But if she did, her grandmother would scold her for being mocking, or maybe ask why she was standing around doing nothing when the moth holes in the curtains were still undarned. There was no right thing to do when Grandma Ida was in a bad mood.

Mom's voice rose, angry and defensive, as she said, "If I've told them once, I've told them a thousand times to be here at six sharp. It's little enough to ask, when I have to work all day."

Nothing ever changes, Becky thought dully.

When her father's mother, Grandma Alice, had been killed in the battle of Las Anclas, Becky had been horrified at her own hope that their family would be happier without her. Grandma Alice and Grandma Ida had hated each other and constantly dragged the rest of the family into their fights. Becky still felt guilty over that secret hope, feeling it was somehow her fault that nothing had changed. Grandma Ida's venom filled the space Grandma Alice had left.

Becky's churning stomach growled, and she looked at the table, to find Henry's usual excuse for dinner: leftovers and a few vegetables thrown into a pot of water and left to boil while he did something else. Judging by the unappetizing lumps at the bottom, it was leftover ground turkey boiled with roughly chopped, unpeeled turnips, baking potatoes, and parsnips. The dirty scum floating on top meant the vegetables hadn't even been washed.

Becky knew that Henry cooked badly in the hope that she or Mom would do it for him rather than eat one of his revolting stews. His ploy often worked.

She picked up the ladle and fished around for the least unappetizing bits. If she didn't eat, she'd get the lecture on wasting food, so she took a couple potatoes as Grandma Ida started in on Henry about his table manners.

As Grandma Ida went into the familiar drone about how in her day, children showed adults a proper respect, Henry shot Becky a quick, covert grin. He helped himself to a turkey lump, minced off a tiny portion, and lifted it delicately to his mouth with his pinky finger curled. If they'd been alone, Becky would have laughed, but her grandmother's presence made her nervous. If Grandma Ida noticed that he was mocking her, she'd get even more angry.

Grandma Ida interrupted herself halfway through her lecture on Proper Gratitude, and thumped her fork down. "I can't even cut these potatoes!"

Becky had just discovered that herself.

"Sorry, Grandma Ida." Henry didn't sound at all sorry. "I was helping Mr. Preston campaign, and I got home late. Becky wasn't around to give me a hand, so I did the best I could."

Grandma Ida shot Becky a disapproving glare.

"I was working, too," Becky said to her plate, and stuffed an unappetizing bite of nearly raw potato into her mouth.

Mother stabbed at an undercooked parsnip. "I wonder what Noah Horst is thinking, blabbering on about inviting those mutants at Catalina. I know for a fact that he doesn't like monsters any more than we do."

"He's a hypocrite." Grandma Ida nodded so sharply that the silver pin holding up her bun bobbed like a rooster's comb. "But all the Horsts are like that. His grandmother was the biggest liar in town."

"Well, Noah won't get elected. Not if my Henry has anything to do with it." The bitter lines of Mom's face smoothed out as she looked at Henry with pride.

"That's right." Henry grinned, shoving aside the rest of his tasteless turkey. Becky wondered if he had already eaten. Maybe he'd left training early, claiming that he was needed at home, and went to Luc's instead. "In between all my Ranger training, I got at least twenty people switched from voting for Mr. Horst to voting for Mr. Preston."

"Where's your crystal ball, Henry?" Grandma Ida snapped. "I'll believe that when I see the vote. And as for your training, it's a waste of time. You haven't lasted six months in any of your apprenticeships. You'll never make the Rangers."

"Henry *will* be chosen as a Ranger," Mom said, glaring at her mother. "He's practically living at Wolfe House these days. I wouldn't be surprised if he ousts Julio Wolfe one of these days. That fool is too busy carousing to lead a chicken, much less a patrol. He'll never last as Ranger captain. But my Henry is another story. Never mind the Rangers—we're eating dinner with the future defense chief."

Grandma Ida snorted. "That will be Will Preston, Martha. Use your wits."

Becky stabbed at her lump of uncooked potato. Her fork skidded off its impenetrable surface. "May I be excused?"

As soon as she said it, she realized that she'd made a horrible mistake. She was so stupid. She *knew* not to draw attention to herself.

Mom turned on her, two angry red spots flaring on her cheeks. "Don't think you're fooling me. I know you're sneaking off to visit that mutant girlfriend of yours. How many times have I told you that you're forbidden to see that monster?"

Becky's throat tightened with unshed tears. Mom thought Brisa wasn't good enough for Becky, but it was the other way around. Brisa deserved a girlfriend with the courage to stand up and defend her, but Becky was too much of a coward to do anything but sit in miserable silence.

"What did you do to drive away the one decent friend you had, that pretty Felicité Wolfe?" Grandma Ida demanded, then turned her scowl on Mom. "This is your fault, Martha. If you actually minded your children, Becky would have a nice Norm girlfriend that she'd be proud to bring home for dinner. A girl from the Hill!"

Mom shot back, "When you tell me how to be in two places at once, *Mother*, I will be glad to mind my children *and* run my shop in order to keep food on this table."

Becky stared at her plate. Dirty grease was congealing around the raw potato. Her stomach made a nauseating flip-flop. If she didn't get out of there fast, she'd throw up right there on the table. She flung down her napkin and ran.

Behind her, Mom screeched, "Rebecca Callahan! You get back in here! You better not be going to that dirt-grubbing monster!"

Tears blinded Becky's eyes as she fled down the path. Dusk had fallen. The street lights blinked on overhead, twinkling like stars. A sob forced its way up from inside her chest as she ran, and she hoped no one saw her. But most shops were closed for the night. Becky slipped past them as if she was invisible.

As she passed the stable, Becky dared a quick glance at Tucker. She was glad to see that he was finally walking without a limp. But Mrs. Riley, who was grooming Blackhawk, must have felt the vibrations of Becky's feet. The motion of her currycomb stopped, and she started to turn her head. Becky couldn't even face anyone as sweet as Mrs. Riley. She couldn't bear to see anyone but Brisa. She backed away and fled.

Chatter and music carried from Luc's, so she avoided it and instead ran along the path between the wall and the gardens, grateful for the lack of street lights on the poorer side of town and hating herself for her own relief. Becky was the biggest coward in town. Nobody else was terrified by ordinary, friendly people.

She ran until a stitch pierced her side and her breath burned in her throat. Then she stopped, bent over and gasping, at Brisa's house. It was one a row of old adobe bungalows, no different from the others, but it was the one Brisa lived in. The sight of it sparked warmth in Becky's heart. Light glowed in its windows—*their* curtains were never drawn—and though the air was cold, the front door stood open, as it always did at dinnertime, welcoming any visitors. Laughter and happy voices spilled out, along with the smell of fresh tortillas and spicy salsa.

Becky wiped her eyes as she slunk closer, uncertain if she even meant to go in. Maybe she should turn and go, leaving no trace of her presence, like the ghost she sometimes wished she was.

"Becky!" Brisa charged out, her arms already open wide, her glossy black pigtails and red ribbons streaming behind her.

Becky felt stupid for even considering leaving as she sank into the delicious warmth of Brisa's strong arms. The painful knots in her stomach and heart loosened as Brisa swayed back and forth, hugging Becky against her lovely, soft curves.

Becky buried her face in Brisa's hair, inhaling her scent. Brisa always smelled fresh and flowery, like a summer morning. When Becky had told her once, Brisa had laughed and attributed it to the flower petals she used to stain her fingernails to match her ribbons. But it was Brisa's own scent. Becky could smell it even when Brisa's petal stains had worn off, or she was dusty and sweaty from training, or she'd just stepped out of a bath.

"Did you hear?" Brisa asked, her breath warm against Becky's cheek. "Or is this just a wonderful coincidence?"

"Hear what?"

Brisa laughed, and Becky felt the vibration through her own body. "Wonderful coincidence wins. Come on in and help us celebrate Cisco's good news."

Becky peeked over her girlfriend's shoulder and spotted Brisa's oldest brother Cisco. Like Brisa, he was round—more than round, he was enormous—and his smile shone bright as the sun as he embraced tall, elegant Tania, Alfonso Medina's older sister.

"Becky! You're just in time for the toast to Tania and Cisco!" Mrs. Preciado said.

Brisa pulled Becky inside, and her sister Dominica pressed a cup of dandelion wine into her hand.

"Cisco and Tania?" Becky repeated, trying to catch up.

"We're getting married!" Cisco said.

The entire family cheered and raised their cups. Becky copied them, doing her best to smile. Everybody clinked their glasses. The wine was sweet on Becky's tongue, with a bite of citrus and a hint of summery grass. It went down her throat like golden sunshine.

"Now, let's eat," Mr. Preciado called out.

"Come on, Beck," Brisa said. "You look hungry."

"I don't want to intrude." Becky's voice came out in a rabbity tremble. "I just…"

"There's more than enough for a little thing like you." Mr. Preciado's voice boomed out. "Squeeze up, boys."

He pointed to the two youngest, who poked each other, laughing. But Brisa tugged Becky to the other end of the bench. "No, sit with me."

Becky despised herself for how she cringed inside just walking across the crowded room. The Preciados were friendly, and they really didn't mind her being there. And she wasn't the only guest: Alfonso Medina sat with Cisco and Tania and a couple of his cousins. Everyone was talking and laughing as if they genuinely liked being crowded in like this: three generations of family and friends, happy just to be together.

That was something Becky never got at home. Ever.

Brisa slapped a hot corn tortilla on Becky's plate, piled it with eggs scrambled with cactus and onions, and topped it with fresh salsa. "Eat up! I made the salsa. It's your favorite."

Anything Brisa made would be Becky's favorite. But it did smell good. And though she hadn't thought she could face food when she'd come in, once it was in front of her, the gnawing emptiness in her belly faded into simple hunger. Though she only had one haunch on the bench and was pressed so tight against Brisa that her right arm could barely move, she felt better than she had all day. The eggs were spicy and delicious, and the lightly sautéed strips of cactus gave it a fresh, green crunch.

Becky gobbled up two tacos, then stopped, embarrassed at her greed. But no one even noticed, except for Mr. Preciado, who simply passed her another. One of the boys made a joke, and Becky felt Brisa's curves shake with laughter. It made Becky want to cuddle up even closer, if that was possible.

For the millionth time, Becky marveled that someone as gorgeous and sweet and playful and outgoing and all-round amazing as Brisa had picked Becky for her girlfriend. She still had no idea what Brisa saw in the town mouse, as Henry called her. In her darkest moments, Becky worried that one day Brisa would realize her mistake and find some other girl to love. And then Becky would have no one at all.

After dinner, everyone pitched in to do the dishes. Becky's happiness faded at the thought that at her house, all the dirty dishes from tonight would be waiting for her in the morning. Henry had cooked, so Becky had to do the dishes. Tomorrow was her day to cook. Brisa would offer to help if Becky mentioned it, but that was why Becky would say nothing. Neither Becky nor Henry ever brought anyone home.

Brisa cupped Becky's face in her hands. "What's wrong, sweetie? Headache? Cramps?"

"It's nothing." Becky had been as slow to get her period as she was at everything else, but it had finally happened a couple months ago, years after the other girls their age. "Just me being silly."

"You're never silly." Brisa shook her head, making the trailing ribbons tying up her pigtails ripple all the way down to the small of her back. "I don't think you're silly enough. We need to work on that."

Though Becky didn't know why, Brisa's words made her eyes sting with unshed tears. She stood up, wishing she hadn't drunk that wine. She had to get out of there before her emotions flooded out and ruined everything for everyone.

"Becky?" Brisa asked uncertainly.

Then Becky thought of something that would distract Brisa — and herself. "Let's go visit Aunt Rosa."

Brisa gave her a wicked smile. "And her guest bedroom?"

Becky prickled all over with heat, and not just from embarrassment. She nodded.

"Mom! Dad!" Brisa called out. "Becky and I are going to her aunt's place."

As Brisa's parents told them to go ahead, the younger kids launched into the kissing song. "Brisa and Becky, sitting in a tree…"

"You're next, you two," Cisco bellowed.

They hurried out, Becky blushing and Brisa laughing. Becky held Brisa's soft hand tight, trying to think of nothing but that she was about to spend the night with her wonderful girlfriend.

But she couldn't forget that in the morning, Brisa would go off to weekend Ranger training, while Becky would have to return to the dirty dishes and her mother and her grandmother and Henry, in a silent, bitter house where no one was ever glad to see anyone else.

Becky could escape from her life for a few precious hours. But in the end, she always had to go back.

·9·
MIA

THE WALK THROUGH THE desert and back to Las Anclas seemed endless, especially compared to how short and fun it had been the other way around. As they neared the town, Mia weighed the positives and negatives of the trip on an imaginary scale.

Bad: Ross had barely said a word all day.

Good: She had cloud viper venom and a plan for a new weapon.

Bad: To keep the peace with Summer, Jennie had spent the entire walk back as teacher-Jennie, as opposed to Mia's-friend-Jennie, so even when Ross took off to "scout ahead" (or escape Summer, Mia suspected), Mia still couldn't talk to Jennie about...with Summer around, Mia was too embarrassed to even think the word *sex*...about Ross.

Good: She had cloud viper venom and a plan for a new weapon.

Bad: Summer hadn't stomped back into the desert or disappeared in a puff of smoke. Mia felt guilty putting that under 'bad,' since she *was* Ross's sister. She looked too much like him not to be. But she seemed to hate them all, Ross especially, and that was obviously making him miserable. He looked as haunted as he did when he woke up from a nightmare—as if he was *in* a nightmare. And Mia couldn't comfort him, because he flinched if anyone came near him. She was sure she could if she could get him alone, but Summer was there.

Mia couldn't help glaring at Summer's back. She was so small to be so awful. And that made Mia feel guilty all over again. It seemed unfair and immature to dislike a fourteen-year-old. But if Ross felt like he was back in a nightmare from his past, Mia felt like she was back on the schoolyard. Summer gave Mia the same walking-on-eggshells anxiety as the girls who'd bullied her at school when they were all ten.

Good: She had cloud viper venom and a plan for a new weapon.

Since "cloud viper venom and a plan for a new weapon" only counted twice no matter how often she thought it, Mia's mental scale was weighted so far toward bad, it was about to tip over.

But much more had happened than finding Ross's sister, she reminded herself. Her appearance had cast such a dark cloud that Mia had nearly forgotten their thrilling trip into the ruined city, where they'd had adventures and made incredible new discoveries. And Mia had roughly twenty-two percent of a car engine. A *car engine!* That should count as three or four good things. Or twenty-two.

Mia stacked twenty-two weights atop the two for 'cloud viper venom' and 'plan for new weapon' on her mental scale, and watched with satisfaction as it plummeted toward 'good.'

The rumble of horse hooves startled her. The perimeter patrol halted atop the ridge, silhouetted against the crimson sunset. Mia was too nearsighted to see who was riding, but two horses shone silver and gold. Kerry was on patrol, then; only she rode her golden stallion.

As they scrambled up the dusty footpath, Mr. Riley's booming voice called out, "Jennie? Who's with you?"

Jennie shouted back, "Ross's sister."

The patrol burst into an incomprehensible chorus of exclamations and questions. Ross held up his hand, shading his gaze from the sun. Or hiding his face. Mia bet he'd make his whole body disappear if he could. He sure looked like he wanted to.

Mr. Riley raised his voice. "Anyone who wants to return to town now can go. I'll escort the explorers to the gates."

By then Mia was close enough to see the patrollers. Only Mrs. Tehrani and Mr. Garcia took off. Mia glumly watched them go. They were both notorious gossips who'd rather be first to announce the news than stay longer and get more to say. By the time Summer arrived, the entire town would know that Ross had a sister. Mia hoped they'd stare at Summer instead of at Ross.

"We've got news, too." Meredith nudged Sally forward, making her silver flanks shimmer. "Kerry almost got eaten by a queen lobster!"

"Kerry, are you—" Mia started to say, but was interrupted by Summer asking, "What's a queen lobster?"

"It's telepathic and the size of a house," Kerry replied with relish. "Jennie, did you get into the city? What did you find?"

"Are you all right, Kerry?" Mia belatedly got out, then felt stupid. Obviously she was. Summer made sure to catch Mia's gaze before she rolled her eyes. Hot blood rose to Mia's face. It was exactly like the schoolyard, where she could never say anything right that wasn't an answer to the teacher's question.

Kerry ignored Summer and replied to Mia as if she appreciated being asked. "Yeah, I'm fine. She got into my head, though. I'll tell you about it later."

Kerry didn't like revealing 'weakness.' But she'd tell Mia. That made Mia felt a little less schoolyardish. Jennie had protected her back then, and Jennie and Ross and Kerry would stand by her now.

"Dad once told me about queen lobsters," Mia said. "They're powerful enough to get into anybody's head. Guess we won't be doing any swimming for a while."

Meredith urged Sally closer. "I didn't know you had a sister, Ross."

After a pause that Mia knew would become an endless silence if they waited for Ross to reply, Jennie said in her teacher-voice, "Ross didn't, either. They were separated as children. Summer heard about him and came to Las Anclas to meet him."

Summer pulled a face that made Mia imagine a newspaper headline hovering over her head, reading AND I WISH I HADN'T.

"Ross, is your sister going to stay in Las Anclas?" Mr. Riley asked.

Ross finally opened his mouth. "Will I need to speak for her at a council meeting?"

"*She* can speak for herself," said Summer rudely.

Mr. Riley replied as if she'd greeted him like a normal person. "Welcome to Las Anclas, Summer."

He tucked his dreadlocks behind his ears, then leaned down from Sidewinder to offer her his hand. She hesitated, then gingerly held out hers as if she expected him to grab it and then knife her. Her tiny hand vanished into his huge one as he shook it.

"How old are you?" Mr. Riley asked.

"Practically fifteen." Summer announced it as if she expected someone to call her a liar.

Mr. Riley again ignored her tone. To Ross, he said, "You won't need to speak. She's a child."

"I've been traveling and fighting and surviving in the desert for *years!* By myself," Summer added hastily, tossing her long black hair. "I'm not a child!"

You're a brat, Mia thought. *You probably survived because everything ran when they saw you coming.*

Mr. Riley spoke again to Summer. "In Las Anclas, fourteen is a child. But Ross is nineteen and out of school, and that makes him an adult. If he takes responsibility for you, there's no need for a council meeting. Do you take responsibility for Summer, Ross?"

Probably nineteen, Mia thought. Ross still didn't know exactly how old he was, or when his birthday was. She wondered if Summer did, but couldn't imagine him asking her.

When he'd first come to Las Anclas, Mia had taken responsibility for him. And she'd had a terrible moment when she'd thought her trust could have been misplaced. If it had, Mia would be legally responsible for any crimes he committed. Of course, Ross had turned out to be absolutely honorable and trustworthy. But Mia wasn't so sure about his sister.

"Yes, I do. She's my sister. And my guest." Ross spoke with a gritty tightness, as if he'd already resigned himself to taking the blame for Summer's misdeeds.

To Mia's annoyance, Summer didn't seem to understand or care about the risk Ross was taking on her behalf. She didn't even thank him. Instead, she indicated the royal horses. The red light of sunset made Nugget's coat glisten like molten gold. "Do guests get to ride those?"

"That depends," Kerry said. The westering sun lit her profile, highlighting her sharp features. "How's your riding?"

Summer lifted her head proudly. "I can ride anything with four legs. I was practically born on horseback."

Mia tried really hard not to look at Ross.

"I'll judge that for myself." Kerry saluted Mr. Riley, then clicked to Nugget. His tail whipped up as if he was saluting too, then they galloped off in a golden streak.

"Why's that girl acting like she owns those horses?" Summer demanded of no one in particular.

"Because she does." Jennie smiled. "That's Kerry Cho, the former crown princess of Gold Point. Those are royal horses."

"Oh!" For the first time, Summer looked genuinely impressed.

Mr. Riley cleared his throat. "Summer, you might want your brother to keep your weapons for you."

"What?" She clutched protectively at her knives. "No!"

"It's a rule for guests and visitors," Jennie said. "And Pa's right. If you don't let Ross hold them for you, the sheriff will confiscate them."

Summer gave her fiercest scowl yet, then practically flung her holstered knives at Ross. "Don't mess with them."

"I'll keep them safe," he said, but instead of being reassured, his sister rolled her eyes and sneered.

Mia shifted her knapsack to her other aching shoulder.

Ross tapped her arm. "Hey, Mia. Want me to take something else out of your pack?"

She regretfully shook her head. "You've already got most of it. Only about..." She peered at the gates. "525 yards to go."

"Give me a turn," Jennie offered. "I have free hands now." She had sheathed her sword and unslung her bow at the first sight of the patrol.

Mia gratefully relinquished her pack, which Jennie easily carried into town. As she'd dreaded, virtually the entire town had assembled at the gate. Ross ducked his head and hunched in on himself. The crowd made her nervous, too. Especially since they stared at both Summer and Ross, and since he was beside her, that meant that they also stared at Mia. She wished she hadn't given Jennie her pack. Now she had nothing to hide behind.

Summer strode along, glaring at the crowd with a challenging lift to her chin, as if she hoped they would all pick a fight with her so she could beat them up.

"Where will your sister stay?" Jennie asked Ross.

Jack's saloon, Mia hoped. *With the Rileys. Anywhere but Dad's house.*

Ross turned to her, his dark eyes full of appeal. Her words felt pulled out of her by tweezers, but she couldn't deny him anything he wanted that much. "We can ask Dad. About the second guest room."

Ross had time to say, "Thanks, Mia," before questions started peppering them from all sides.

Mia tugged her knapsack from Jennie. She didn't need to go the surgery; Dad would never refuse to take in Ross's long-lost sister.

"Good night," she muttered, hoping Ross would come by later. Without Summer.

That reminded her of the promise she'd made to herself in the crystal forest. They *had* all gotten out alive, so she had to ask Ross if he wanted to have sex. It was her turn for a date with him, too. But she'd rather sew her lips shut than mention dates, much less anything else, in front of Summer.

Jennie turned her teacher smile on Summer. "I'll see you at school in the morning."

"School?" Summer yelped as if she'd been stung by a giant bee. "What? Why should I have to—"

Mia fled to her cottage, feeling like a coward at every footfall. She slammed the door, then feverishly unloaded her new engine parts and lined them up. Then she re-organized them. Once. Twice. Three times. Her fingers moved like a machine, her gaze fixed on the bed. Should she move the engine, as a hint? Should she not move the engine, in case Ross got the hint and fled before she could even ask?

Ross never showed up.

·10·
ROSS

ROSS MIGHT NOT KNOW much about love, but the one thing he was sure of was that families loved each other. It didn't seem to matter whether they were birth relatives, adopted, or related by marriage. Once they were family, as far as he could tell, the love just happened. Different families expressed it in different ways, but it was always there.

He'd seen the joking camaraderie between Mia and Dr. Lee, as much friends as father and daughter, and the fierce loyalty between Yuki Nakamura and his adoptive sister and mother, Meredith and Ms. Lowenstein. The Rileys were close and affectionate with each other, while the Preciados were cheerful and easy-going. Mr. Horst and Tommy were a lot alike, and the Vardams were close to one another. Even Mr. Preston seemed human when his son was around, and he obviously thought his wife and daughter were the most perfect beings to ever walk the Earth.

How had things gone so wrong between Ross and his sister?

His return to Las Anclas with Summer had been one of the most depressing days of his life, and that was saying a lot. He had no idea what he should have done instead, but it was obvious that everything he had done was wrong. Though Summer had cared enough about the *idea* of him to track him down, she didn't seem to like him, let alone love him.

He'd hoped she was only shocked, as Jennie had suggested, and suspicious, as he'd been when he'd first come to Las Anclas. Maybe, like him, she'd loosen up once she saw that no one would harm her. But so far, she'd alternated bragging about unlikely feats with complaining about everything and insulting everyone.

She'd even been rude to Dr. Lee, who was not only the nicest and most patient man Ross had ever met, but he'd cooked a great meal and offered her a free room in his own house.

It had been one of the best meals of Ross's life—lobster dumplings, lobster in garlic-chili sauce, butter-poached lobster, bean shoots sautéed in sesame oil, and six different types of kimchi: cabbage, cucumber, squash, radish, chestnut, and apple. But it was hard to enjoy the food while Summer complained. Dr. Lee's girlfriend Anna-Lucia dropped by to deliver a cake of layered custard and crisp sheets of pastry, but when she caught one of Summer's furious glares, she politely declined Dr. Lee's invitation to join them.

How could Summer clean her plate, and shovel in seconds, without ever saying anything nice? Ross tried to prompt her by complimenting each dish and repeatedly thanking Dr. Lee, but she never followed his lead. He wasn't surprised that Mia never showed up though she could undoubtedly smell the food from her cottage. She could probably hear Summer from her cottage, too.

By the time she went to bed in the room next to Ross's, slamming the door behind her, his head was splitting. Dr. Lee silently offered him a hefty dose of willow bark elixir.

"Ross," Dr. Lee began.

The last thing Ross wanted was advice or sympathy. He couldn't stand the thought of talking to anyone about his sister, even Dr. Lee.

"Thanks." Ross gulped down the elixir and fled to his room.

He lay in bed and looked up at the stars through his skylight, but they didn't calm him.

She's my sister, he kept thinking. *I should love her no matter how she acts. Dee brought home a pit mouth, but it didn't make Jennie love her any less.*

But it was another thought that kept him awake all night, no matter how hard he tried to push it away.

She's the only family I'll ever have. And she hates me.

The next morning, Ross waited for Summer's stomping footsteps coming down the stairs before he emerged from his room. Dr. Lee had either given up or decided that she might prefer simpler food, because he served only plain scrambled eggs. Summer ate just as much and just as rudely, then announced that she wasn't going to school and no one could make her.

Dr. Lee spoke in a polite but firm tone that Ross had never heard before, one which made disobedience unthinkable. "Ross, take your sister to school."

Ross moved immediately. To his surprise, Summer did as well. They were halfway to the schoolhouse before she started criticizing the buildings, the gardens, and the entire concept of school. But before she could carry out her threat of jumping over the wall, they spotted Becky, Brisa, Sujata, Meredith, and Kerry walking together. Summer fell silent and followed them.

Ross remembered how awkward he'd felt on his first day, and sympathized. But Jennie would put his sister at ease, like she'd done for him—if Summer gave her the chance.

Once they reached the schoolyard, Summer crossed her skinny arms across her chest. "You don't have to walk me inside. I'm not a toddler." She strode forward, head held high, and never looked back.

Ross gave up. She obviously didn't want him around. At least Jennie would keep her from getting into too much trouble.

He retreated to Mia's cottage, hoping to spend some time with someone who'd actually be happy to see him. But she didn't answer his knock, and when he peeked in the window, he saw her fast asleep on the floor with a wrench lying across her open hand.

Despite his disappointment, Ross had to smile. That sight was so Mia. He longed to go cuddle up beside her, but he had work to do. And he figured he'd better be around in case Summer did decide to flee the schoolhouse.

He occupied himself with his day's jobs, half-expecting to see his sister stomping by on her way out of town. But the morning passed quietly.

At noon, he returned to the surgery. Dr. Lee had lunch waiting for him. This time he'd cooked with Ross's tastes in mind. All the kimchi was back on the table, along with barley tea, noodles in black bean sauce with chunks of lobster, a salad of dandelion greens in oil and vinegar, and almond cake for dessert.

Ross cheered up as he attacked the food, not forgetting to tell Dr. Lee how delicious it was. Dr. Lee explained that there had been so much lobster that Jack had preserved everything he couldn't serve fresh, drying some and storing some submerged in jars of oil.

"The dumpling filling last night was from the oil-preserved lobster," Dr. Lee said. "This lobster was dried, then reconstituted by soaking it in water. Do you have a preference?"

"They're both delicious. I like this sauce better than the dumpling sauce, though."

"Good. Once you're done, you can take a lunch box to Summer."

"So...she's still here?" Ross asked cautiously. He didn't want to admit that he half-hoped that if she stormed out of the school, she'd keep right on going.

"Give her time," Dr. Lee advised, as if he'd known what Ross was thinking. "I suspect that she's had as rough a life as you had. People don't get that angry without a good reason. Try not to take it personally. Remember, when Summer first saw you, she thought she was coming to your rescue."

"That's true," Ross said. "But she didn't know who I was. She just thought Mia and Jennie were attacking me."

"So she protects people she thinks need help, even if they're strangers." With a smile, Dr. Lee asked, "Does that sound like anyone you know?"

"Sure," Ross said, wondering what Dr. Lee was getting at. "You. Jennie. Mia. Sheriff Crow. Mr.—"

Dr. Lee stopped him with a laugh. "I meant you, Ross. Anyway, she obviously has a good heart beneath the bravado. Remember how long it took you to adjust to Las Anclas, and how you felt when you first came here. She may have some similar feelings, but shows them—or covers them up—differently."

"Thanks."

Ross relaxed and enjoyed his almond cake. Dr. Lee's suggestion made a lot of sense. Maybe Summer was scared, just as he'd been, but expressed it by yelling and complaining instead of running and hiding. He could sympathize with the fear, and that made him less annoyed by the rest.

As he headed for the schoolhouse, he wondered how Summer's first day had gone, and if she knew how to read. If she didn't, maybe he could coach her. Mia's coaching had helped him a lot.

Before he even reached the schoolyard, he heard a hubbub of angry voices, with Summer's rising above them all. His heart sank.

"You don't talk like that to my friends!" Dee shouted.

"I'll say whatever I like to whoever I like!" Summer yelled. "Especially when it's true. None of you know anything about *real* dancing. You're just hopping around to a beat."

"Then show us some real dancing," Dee demanded.

"No way!" Summer snapped. "You wouldn't know it if you saw it."

"Chicken," Meredith taunted. "I bet you don't even know how to dance."

As Ross reached the schoolyard, he spotted a half-circle of girls under the big oak tree, facing Summer.

To Ross's alarm, Summer's fist flashed out at Meredith with her full Changed speed. Meredith yelped and fell, then her foot snapped out from where she lay, hitting Summer's knee with a perfect side thrust kick. Summer toppled and landed on top of her.

As Ross dropped the lunch box and bolted for them, the girls began rolling around, grappling and punching. Sujata grabbed Meredith's arm just as Ross reached down for Summer.

An elbow smacked him in the nose, sending a lightning bolt of pain through his head. He gritted his teeth, then caught Summer's wrists and twisted them behind her back. Then he yanked the struggling girl to her feet and held her tight, keeping her away from Meredith. Sujata had Meredith in a similar hold, as the younger girls shrilled angrily at Summer.

Jennie arrived at a run, followed by half the school. "What's going on here?"

"She made fun of me." Summer writhed in Ross's arms. Her Changed agility made her slippery as a snake, and he nearly lost his grip on her. He barely managed to keep hold of her as she kicked out at Meredith.

"She's been making fun of everyone the whole day," Meredith shot back, struggling against Sujata's grip.

"Meredith," Jennie said. "She's only fourteen."

"I can fight anyone, any age!" Summer shouted. "And I can beat them, too."

Meredith rolled her eyes, then subsided, looking embarrassed. "You're right, Jennie. From now on, I'll just ignore her."

Sujata let go and Meredith walked away, brushing dust off her clothes and bright red curls.

Then Jennie turned to Summer. "Fourteen is much too old to behave like this. Up until last summer, thirteen-year-olds went on patrol in Las Anclas."

"I killed my first man at thirteen," Summer retorted. She tossed her hair back.

Ross caught a lock right in the mouth and spat it out. He let go of one of Summer's hands and spun her around. "I was twelve. And it's nothing to brag about."

Jennie put a hand on each of their shoulders. Ross relaxed at her touch, but Summer jerked away.

"We know you're tough, Summer," Jennie said. "But so is everybody else here. If you want to prove it, save it for training. That's not what you're here to learn." She glanced behind Ross. "Your brother brought you lunch."

He felt Summer stiffen at the word *"brother."* Like Dr. Lee had suggested, Ross tried not to take her reaction personally. But it still felt like a slap in the face. He released her and retrieved her lunch box, using the time his back was turned to try to keep his feelings off his face.

To his relief, Summer only had eyes for the lunch box, not him. She snatched and opened it, not even bothering to sit down first. Ross had seen Dr. Lee's packed lunches before, and he could tell that it had once been beautifully arranged. But not any longer. The little container of sauce for the noodles had come open and mixed with the salad dressing. Noodles, chunks of lobster, kimchi, and seaweed had all mixed together, topped with crumbs that had once been a piece of almond cake.

Summer reached in and grabbed a handful. With her mouth full, she said, "Not bad." Then she noisily sucked in a hanging noodle.

Ross had no idea if she was trying to annoy and disgust him,

Jennie, or anyone who happened to be watching, which was half the schoolyard, but he'd had it. He yanked the box from her hands. "Eat it at the table. After you clean up."

He turned his back on her and headed for the nearest table, hot and tense with anger, embarrassment, and the knowledge that everyone was watching him to see if his sister would obey him. His chest was so tight he could hardly breathe. He hated to be caught in some attention-attracting scene, and Summer couldn't seem to do anything but make them. He half-hoped that she'd take off. For all he knew, if she followed him it would only be to throw the lunch in his face.

Summer caught up with him. "Gimme my lunch. I'm starved."

"Only if you promise to eat right." Ross searched her face for something that would make him *feel* like she was family rather than just knowing it. But all he saw was an angry girl radiating dislike. "You know how to use utensils—I saw you last night. Were you trying to embarrass me? Why?"

"Of course I know how," she fired back. "The fork was covered in sauce."

Ross didn't believe for a second that she cared. But rather than argue, he led her to a bench. "Go wash your hands. I'll try to put it back together. Dr. Lee's food deserves to be eaten right."

Summer opened her mouth, then hesitated. Ross had the feeling she'd had second thoughts about whatever she'd been about to say. "Yeah. It *is* pretty good."

She gave him a half-smile—the first he'd seen from her—then leaped into the air. Ross watched her float halfway across the schoolyard to a chorus of gasps and exclamations, land, and then leap to the hand pump. But even more than the incredible grace of her Change power, it was her smile that caught his attention. Was it his mother's smile? His father's?

Ross wiped off the fork, then used it to try to reconstruct the lunch. There was a soft thud as Summer landed behind him. He looked up. The entire population of the schoolhouse was following her. Ross couldn't help trying to press himself into the bench.

She leaped again, and landed sitting beside him with her legs folded beneath her. It was the most amazing move he'd seen from her yet.

"You're really good with your power," he said.

Summer gave him that half-smile again, then took the fork and announced, "Yum. I haven't eaten like this for *years*."

Ross did his best to ignore the fascinated onlookers and focus only on his sister's face. It was odd how familiar she looked when he'd never seen her until the day before. She must look like his parents, but he couldn't remember their faces. She didn't look like him, except maybe for her eyes. He'd seen those same dark eyes looking back at him in the mirror.

Becky's soft voice interrupted his thoughts. "Where did you come from, Summer?"

Summer leaned back, folded her hands behind her head, and raised her voice so the entire schoolyard could hear. "I've been traveling all over the desert. Making my own way. Hunting. Fighting."

She stuffed her mouth with noodles as the crowd whispered.

"Fighting what?" Will Preston asked. "Bandits?"

Summer's hands twitched as if she wanted to clench them into fists. But her voice was relaxed as she said, "If it has a weapon, I've fought it. Or teeth. Or claws. Or poison. Once I got attacked by a sand tiger, but I jumped on its back and strangled it with my bare hands."

Ross dared to glance up at the crowd. All the little kids and some teenagers looked impressed, though others seemed skeptical. But though they'd seen Summer leap, her struggle with Meredith had lasted only seconds. Ross had seen her fight *Jennie*. He could easily believe she'd strangled a sand tiger.

"We don't have sand tigers here," Rico said.

"But we've learned about them in school," Hattie Salazar piped up.

"They were all over the place Ross and I come from," Summer said. "Mom said that in our town, they had to shut up all the livestock, even the bulls, before sundown. Right, Ross?"

Ross couldn't meet her eyes. His chest and throat tightened, making it hard to speak. "I don't remember."

"Of course you don't," Summer said impatiently. "You were too little. But Grandma would have told you. You remember that, right?"

The only thing that stopped Ross from getting up and leaving was that it would draw even more attention to him. Staring at the table, he muttered, "No."

Summer's voice rose with anger and frustration. "You don't remember Grandma telling you about sand tigers. You don't remember the Norms trying to kill us. What *do* you remember?"

"What?" Rico exclaimed.

"The Norms tried to kill you?" Yolanda said indignantly.

"That's horrible," Becky murmured.

Summer smacked Ross on the arm. "I asked you a question, Ross. What do you remember?"

The harder he tried to recall his grandmother telling him about his town, the harder it was to remember anything at all. Especially with his sister and the entire school watching him fail at what a ten-year-old could do with ease: remember their own lives. Humiliation burned through his body, making his eyes sting and his vision blur.

What was wrong with him?

"Nothing!" Ross burst out. "I don't remember anything, all right? Stop asking me!"

Ross had no idea how Summer or anyone was reacting. He wouldn't look up now if he had a pistol held to his head.

Summer spoke again after a moment, sounding more confused than angry. "Well, anyway, the Norms tried to kill all the Changed in my town."

"A Changed person tried to take over our town." Will Preston's accusing tone was just like his father's. "Maybe something like that happened there."

"Are you blaming people for *being murdered?*" Yolanda demanded. "People like—"

"I want to hear the story," Rico interrupted. "Summer, did you have to fight your way out?"

Ross cautiously looked up, his heart pounding from anticipation and dread. He desperately wanted to know what had happened, but he had a feeling that once he'd heard the story, he'd wish he hadn't.

Summer finished a last leaf of watercress kimchi and licked her fingers. "I wasn't actually born yet, but Mom told, uh…"

She broke off, then licked her fingers again with a flourish, as if challenging everyone to mind her manners. But no one spoke. They obviously all wanted to hear her story.

"Yum," Summer announced loudly. "Well, Mom told me what happened. There were never many Changed people in our town. Maybe one family in ten. And the town was much smaller than Las Anclas. Mom said most Norms never liked us. They just put up with us because they needed every hand to keep the town going."

She glanced at Ross, who hastily ducked his head. His muscles were so tight that his jaw ached and his hands were shaking. He pushed them against his thighs, hoping no one would notice.

Mom said. Ross couldn't remember a single thing Mom had said, or even the sound of her voice.

Summer went on, "Mom said she only found out exactly what happened afterward. We'd had a drought for three years in a row. One greedy Norm guy started secretly meeting with other Norms and blaming it on the Changed, plus everything else bad that had ever happened. He said we were using our powers to drive out the Norms. He convinced them that if they kicked out all the Changed, the drought would end. And also, then the Norms could take over everything that the Changed people owned, houses included."

"I've heard of that happening," Brisa said. She sounded unusually subdued. Becky reached out to clasp her hand.

Ross wished Mia were there to hold *his* hand. Then he glanced around for Jennie. But she was out of reach, watching and listening intently—not just to Summer, but she watched the entire school. Jennie had to be a teacher now, not a girlfriend.

Ross was so tense that he flinched when Summer spoke again. "A mob of Norms got together in the middle of the night and started rousting the Changed families out of bed. Mom said she realized later that they probably hadn't intended to kill anyone, just to kick them out. But of course, some of the Changed started fighting back. At the time, all Mom knew was that she got woken up by yelling and fighting. Dad's Change was that he could only see heat. If everything was cold, he was blind. He looked out the window and said there were hot spots all over town, people running around and houses burning."

Once Summer mentioned Dad's power, Ross remembered it. But it meant more now than if he'd learned it before he'd come to Las Anclas. Ross, too, could see heat when he was linked with the crystal trees. His father was dead, but not entirely gone: Ross could see as he saw. That realization was so overwhelming that he missed Summer's next few sentences.

He forced himself to pay attention as she went on, "A Changed friend of hers banged on the door and shouted that the Norms were killing all the Changed."

Summer spun around to stab a finger at Ross, making him jump. "Mom and Dad and Grandma grabbed *you*. And ran."

Images flickered in his memory, quick as lightning. Gray ash drifting down on his father's black hair. Bodies lying still in the street. Little black pools reflecting the firelight.

That must have been blood.

Once he had that thought, the memories faded.

"And then my family split up," Summer said.

Another memory thrust itself to the surface: his grandmother's strong hands yanking him off the ground. His face buried in her shoulder. Her jolting strides as she ran. His father moving away as he helped Ross's mother into a grove of trees, as arrows zipped through the air all around them. Ross reached out his hand...

Summer's voice broke through the memory. "The Changed who made it out of town hid in a tunnel in an old mine, but Grandma wasn't there. Once things seemed to die down, Mom went to look for her and *you*."

Ross gritted his teeth as she again pointed at him. It was hard enough having to hear this story without her calling everyone's attention to him every few minutes.

"Mom's Change had to do with her eyes, too," Summer said. "When Dad first came to town, they spent hours talking about how the world looked to them. It was how they fell in love. Her eyes were golden as an eagle's, and she could see an ant dance on a hillside a mile away."

Little Tonio Riley piped up, "Pa can do that! But his eyes are brown."

"She saw that half the town had burned down," Summer said.

"The crops had burned, too. And she saw a gang of Norms closing in on the tunnel at the other entrance. Before she could do anything, they threw in a bunch of barrels of gunpowder and lit the fuse. The whole tunnel collapsed. Mom had to run for her life. She never found Grandma. Or you."

Summer stared straight at Ross, her tone and black eyes accusing. "She didn't hear about it till years later, but the town never recovered. Everyone died or left. It's a ghost town now."

"Ghost town? Cool!" Will Preston exclaimed.

Jose spoke in a calm tone that was more crushing than if he'd yelled. "Changed people getting murdered is cool?"

Before another argument could break out, Jennie stepped between Jose and Will. Like Dr. Lee had, she spoke in a tone that could not be disobeyed. "Recess is over."

Everyone but Jennie and Summer took off. As he left, Will remarked to the boy beside him, "If the Changed people had just left, nothing bad would have happened."

Summer started to rise, radiating fury. Jennie grabbed her shoulder, forcing her back into her seat.

"Will's only eleven," Jennie said. "Argue if you want, but no fighting. It's not fair. He wouldn't stand a chance."

Summer settled down, but Ross was sure it wasn't because of Jennie. He could feel her gaze on him like a pair of burning coals. It made him feel guilty. He wanted to leave. He wanted her to go. He had to say something, but he had no idea what.

He'd finally learned the story of his past, but it was only a story. He knew now that Mom's eyes had been golden, but he still couldn't picture her face.

"You can go inside now," Jennie said to Summer.

She let out a long-suffering sigh, but hitched her pack over her shoulder and leaped toward the schoolhouse.

Jennie sat beside Ross. "Are you all right?"

"Yeah."

"I wasn't sure if I should let that go on or not." Jennie looked as uncertain as Ross felt. It wasn't an expression he'd often seen on her face.

"You chose right. I did want to know what had happened." Ross pressed his hands to his eyes, trying to push back the memory of his father lying dead. Out of everything he couldn't remember, why couldn't he have lost that memory, too?

"I remember..." He hesitated, distrustful of anything in his mind, then went on. "Yeah. I'm sure this happened. I touched my father's body. The blood was still wet. Mom couldn't have been far away. If we'd gone in the right direction, we would have caught up with her. I should have known—"

Jennie put her hand on his shoulder, squeezing his tight muscles. "How old were you, Ross? Four? You couldn't possibly have known. Anyway, you weren't making any decisions. Your grandmother was. Remember what happened to me after the battle? Once you start blaming yourself for stuff you had no control over, there's no end to it. You didn't set those fires. You didn't blow up that tunnel. And you couldn't possibly have known that your mother was still alive. Ross, none of that was your fault."

"No?" Ross got up. He had to get away, to breathe. To be alone. "Tell that to Summer."

·11·
JENNIE

THE BLEAK ANGUISH IN Ross's face made Jennie hurt as much for his sake as when she'd first heard that he'd been captured by Voske. She longed to run after him. But she was losing classroom time, and she'd lose more getting the younger students to settle down and focus on something other than Summer.

Jennie went into the schoolhouse and raised her voice over the buzz of talk. "We still have lessons. Anyone who keeps wasting time now stays after to make it up, while everyone else watches the Ranger selection ceremony."

Instant quiet fell. She gave out assignments, then observed the busy classroom. Felicité was absent, probably out campaigning on the theory that she was as good as graduated. Jennie was fine with that. Everyone else, even Henry, got to work, from little kids puzzling over their letters to teenagers doing math. Summer's glossy head bent over a slate as she chalked a simple equation.

Jennie couldn't help wishing someone would act up so she'd have an excuse to stay and supervise rather than attend the ceremony. She couldn't bear the thought of watching from the sidelines as the other Rangers welcomed their new brothers and sisters. No matter how much loss and grief and guilt was tangled up with her time with the Rangers—Sera's death, Jennie's breakdown, the endless terrible choices she'd had to make, and finally getting banned for life—she loved them, too. She'd loved being a Ranger.

Jennie bit her lip, forcing her emotions down. So she wasn't one. She was lucky to have a meaningful job that she enjoyed. And, she reminded herself, one where she'd never have to make snap decisions with other people's lives depending on her choice.

Her gaze stopped again on Summer. When Ross had first come to the classroom, he'd known the advanced math and science that a prospector needed. But he knew no history and couldn't read. Summer, four years younger, was nowhere near as far along in math and science, but could read and write easily. She also knew some history. Jennie wondered where she had learned what she knew, but Summer wasn't saying.

Several hours later, the big pocket watch on her desk ticked out the time to go. *Time to face it.*

"School's out," Jennie called. "Good work, everyone. And good luck to the candidates!"

Chalks and slates clattered as everyone clustered around the Ranger candidates: Jose, Sujata, Brisa, Meredith, Tommy, and Henry.

Henry gave a war whoop, pumped his fist, and charged out the door. The other candidates followed, visibly excited but, unlike Henry, also nervous. Jennie couldn't imagine Henry being chosen. Whatever else she could say against Mr. Preston—and there was plenty—he'd never put the town's safety in the hands of a boy who couldn't bother to show up for practice on time and didn't take it seriously when he did.

Jennie grimaced as she wiped down the chalkboard. After days of inner struggle, she had decided to vote for Mr. Preston. Much as she despised Felicité, she had to agree with her campaign speech. Mr. Horst simply wasn't qualified. And though Jennie would never forgive Mr. Preston, she trusted him to protect Las Anclas.

All the same, she'd never tell anyone how she had voted.

She reached out with her mind and pulled at the chalks, smiling as they flew into her hand like a storm of frost-bitten sticks. The slates followed. Once they were stacked, Jennie left the schoolhouse, sure that she'd dawdled enough that no one would be around to ask where she was going.

Paco and Jose were waiting for her.

They didn't seem to be together so much as standing near one another. She turned to Jose first. "Is there a problem at home?"

"No." Jose shifted from foot to foot, his skinny body tense. "Jennie, you're coming to the Ranger ceremony, right? Whether I get in or not, I'd like you to be there."

The hope on her foster brother's earnest face made Jennie's perspective shift, as if she'd looked into a magnifying glass. The Ranger ceremony wasn't about her. It was about the hopes and dreams of Jose, her brother, who would be hurt if his big sister didn't show up. Meredith and Brisa and Paco might not take it so personally, but they were her friends, too. They'd be disappointed if she skipped something so important to them.

"Of course I'm coming, Jose," Jennie said. "I wouldn't miss it."

"Wish me luck!" With a look of relief, Jose ran off before he could hear her response.

"I came to ask you, too," Paco said. "Were you really planning to go all along?"

"No," she admitted, after making sure Jose was out of earshot. "But I've got a brother and friends who want me there. And to be honest, I don't want Mr. Preston thinking I'm a coward."

"No one would ever think that."

Jennie studied his unsmiling face, trying to see an echo of his mother. But Sera's easy smiles, once so much a part of Paco, were gone, leaving only Voske's sharp bones and upswept eyebrows.

Paco's dark eyes were his own. His emotions were impossible to read, but she sensed some intense feeling. Loneliness? It was strange not to know. He used to be so expressive, speaking with his face and body—and most of all, his music—more eloquently than with his words.

She spoke impulsively. "I wish Yuki was here."

Paco didn't react. At least, not visibly.

"But I'll be there," Jennie concluded, feeling awkward.

"Thanks." Paco walked away quickly, alone.

By the time Jennie reached the Ranger yard, the sun was sinking toward the ocean. Last summer, it would have still been high overhead, and she would have come to start Ranger practice.

She turned her thoughts firmly to the present. The families of the candidates were gathered around, along with most of the town's teenagers and kids old enough to be excited, and a host of curious townspeople. Ross, Jennie noticed, was not there. Mia and

Summer were, though separated by the crowd.

Ross must have been desperate to be alone after hearing Summer's story. Jennie couldn't imagine what it must have been like for him to think himself solitary, discover a sister and have her reject him, and then have his lost history dropped on him like a boulder. Jennie was so lucky to have a family who loved her.

Chill washed through her nerves as she thought again about Summer's story—the murder of the Changed, the destruction of the town. It couldn't ever happen to Las Anclas. The Changed were too large of a minority—one-third, not one-tenth. But it was horrifying to think that nothing but their sheer numbers protected them. If the Rileys were the only Changed family, would they live in fear of being rousted out of town some night? Ten years ago, Jennie had watched Mr. Preston drive away the boatful of desperate Changed people from Catalina.

Everyone old enough to vote remembers that, Jennie realized. Summer's story would be all over town by the end of the day.

Mia beckoned frantically. Jennie hastened to her side, placing one more body between Mia and Summer. Though Mia probably didn't need to worry about Summer. The girl was totally focused on the Ranger candidates. She'd gotten an earful about the Rangers from the other students, and though it would probably kill her to say anything good about Las Anclas, she obviously thought fighters were cool.

A shout rose as the Rangers ran onto the field and lined up. They were in full uniform, weapons included. If Jennie had been with them, she'd have worn her sword in a harness across her back. And she'd have stood beside Indra, tall and proud with his machete glinting at his belt, looking toward Sera at the head of the line.

But Jennie and Indra had broken up, and Julio Wolfe stood where Sera should have been. There was no place in that line for Jennie any more.

"Quiet!" Mr. Preston called through his bullhorn. When the crowd of spectators had ceased whispering, he handed the bullhorn to Julio. "Candidates, step forward."

Except for the distant cry of seagulls, there was no sound as the seven candidates formed a line. They wore practice clothes and bore no weapons. They hadn't earned them yet.

"Meredith Lowenstein," Mr. Preston said. Even without the bullhorn, his voice carried easily across the crowd.

She stepped out once more, a small, determined figure. Her copper hair glittered in the setting sun as she stood alone, awaiting her fate.

"You've done very well in training," Mr. Preston said. "I have no issues with your discipline or your physical skills. You'd make a good Ranger. However, you'll make a *great* archer. I have to consider not only the Rangers, but the defenses of the entire town. I'm turning you down for the Rangers only because I think your skills are more needed elsewhere."

Jennie shot a glance at Ms. Lowenstein, captain of the archers. Though there was no love lost between her and Mr. Preston, Meredith's mother nodded slowly in agreement. Meredith looked disappointed as she stepped back, but not heartbroken.

Mr. Preston turned his head. "Jose Riley, step forward."

Jose wiped his trembling fingers down his pants, then stepped forward.

Mr. Preston smiled as he said, "Jose, you've also done very well in training. Your discipline is impressive, especially considering your age. I'd like you to continue in Ranger training and try again next year. You're only sixteen. If you keep at it, some day I expect you to join the Rangers. If not next year, then the year after that."

Jennie wished she could give Jose a consoling pat on the back, though she was sure she wasn't the only one who'd warned him that no one had ever become a Ranger at sixteen, though it was technically within the rules. But the tension went out of his shoulders, and he even managed a grin. He seemed encouraged rather than let down.

Jennie recognized Mr. Preston's fond expression as he watched Jose step back. She had to force herself to stop gritting her teeth. Mr. Preston used to bestow that smile on her. It said silently, "You may be Changed but I like you in spite of it." She wondered how long it would be before Jose realized what it meant.

"Brisa Preciado," Mr. Preston called next.

As Brisa bounced forward, ribbons streaming in the sea breeze, cold fingers gripped Jennie's hand. Becky had edged up to her, pale with anxiety. Over Brisa? Or over the crowd, which Becky didn't like any better than Ross did? Jennie squeezed her hand reassuringly, but Becky stayed tense.

Jennie knew Mr. Preston well enough to catch the slight crease of annoyance between his brows as he said, "Brisa, I didn't expect you to stick it out this long. So I commend you for that. I'm also…impressed…with your enthusiasm. But." He bit the word off. "Your physical skills are not up to our standards, and you lack the necessary discipline. Thank you for trying."

Brisa broke out of the line and bounced back to Becky. Jennie stifled a laugh at Mr. Preston's no-longer-subtle irritation at that breach of procedure.

Becky released Jennie to hug her girlfriend. Brisa said cheerfully over Becky's shoulder, "It was way more fun when you were running our teams, Jennie. I really only stayed because I like hanging out with Meredith."

Jennie couldn't help but grin as Mr. Preston actually rolled his eyes.

"Thomas Horst," Mr. Preston said.

Tall Tommy stepped forward with a martial strut.

"Tommy, you're a good, strong candidate," said Mr. Preston. "Your discipline has improved enormously, and so have your skills. I'm glad to see you learning focus and applying yourself. You didn't quite make the cut this year, but you came so close that I'm confident that you will next year, if you keep up the good work."

Tommy's shoulders slumped, then he straightened and joined the rejected candidates. Mutters arose from his family. Jennie caught, "The election," and "Pure prejudice." But Tommy, like Jose, looked more encouraged than disappointed.

"Henry Callahan," called Mr. Preston.

Henry also stepped forward with a martial snap, though his was exaggerated almost to a parody. Muffled laughter emerged from some teenage boys in the audience.

Neither the mockery nor the laugh escaped Mr. Preston. His look of disapproval deepened. "Henry, you're strong and you like fighting, but you lack discipline. Let me give you some advice.

There is an inverse proportion between how much you talk about killing enemies, and how capable you actually are of doing so. Talk less, train more."

Jennie waited to hear if Mr. Preston would invite Henry to try again next year. Henry also seemed to be waiting. But Mr. Preston waved him back to the line of rejected candidates without another word. Henry's ever-present grin faded, then tightened for a heartbeat into an anger Jennie had never seen before. And Felicité looked almost as shocked as she had when Jennie had stuffed her into the fruit shed. Had Felicité actually expected Henry to be chosen?

Mrs. Callahan's voice rose shrilly, "I never thought I'd hear prejudice from *that* quarter. In that case..."

Henry shrugged and tossed his floppy hair back, grinning like always. As if he didn't care. And maybe he didn't. But it sure looked as if Felicité did.

"Sujata Vardam." Mr. Preston's voice easily drowned out Mrs. Callahan's remark that Noah Horst had *her* vote.

Sujata glanced at Indra as she stepped out of the line. A tiny, private smile passed between brother and sister. Jennie knew how much Indra had been working with Sujata outside of training. A pulse of regret squeezed her heart. She longed to spar with him again. Just as friends, of course.

Mr. Preston also smiled. "Sujata, I confess that I was very surprised to see you enter training at all. And I also confess that I wasn't expecting much. But you completely surpassed my expectations. I don't know which is better, your skill or your discipline, but both are more than sufficient to guarantee you a place on my team. Sujata Vardam, welcome to the Rangers."

The crowd broke into cheers.

Sujata's solemnity melted into a brilliant smile. It was met by looks of pride from Mr. Preston, her brother, and her family in the audience. Julio came forward and handed her signature weapon, a pair of highly polished dark wood double sticks. Sujata thrust them through her belt.

Then she was passed down the line of Rangers, shaking hands and getting slapped on the back. When she came to Indra, he caught her up in a hug and swung her around in a circle. Then he set her down beside him, a part of the line.

Sujata stood straight and proud, claiming her place amongst the Rangers.

A long, fluttering sigh escaped Jennie's lips. Right there, beside Indra at the end of the line: that had been *her* place.

Mr. Preston called out, "Paco Diaz."

Paco, the last of the candidates, stepped forward.

Mr. Preston spoke with surprising gentleness as he said, "Paco, I only wish your mother were here for this moment."

Unshed tears stung Jennie's eyes. She bent her head, letting her braids fall to hide her face, only realizing as she did it that she'd learned that trick from Ross. Jennie listened, breathing as Sera had taught her, until she felt safe to hold up her head again.

"Sera was proud of you, whatever you did," Mr. Preston went on. "But she loved to see you put your best effort into a task, and practice until you were brilliant. You've done that here. Your discipline is superlative and your skills are undeniable. You've worked hard for this moment, and you've earned it. Paco Diaz, welcome to the Rangers."

Julio came forward to give Paco his sword.

Jennie must have worn out her envy on Sujata; she felt none as she watched Paco move down the line, shaking hands. But neither was she as happy for him as she'd have liked to have been. Was it really what he wanted? His face was expressionless, and, unlike all the other candidates, his tension hadn't relaxed after he heard Mr. Preston's choice.

But becoming a Ranger was a huge achievement. Jennie added her applause to that of the crowd as Paco took his place beside Sujata.

Mr. Preston held up his hand, stopping the cheers before they could die out. "Our new Rangers have a lot in common. Both of them always were strong and quick and physically capable of being great fighters. But both of them intended to do something else with their lives. As you probably remember, Sujata meant to inherit her parents' orchard, and Paco was dividing his time between glass-making and music."

Another, smaller cheer went up.

Mr. Preston raised his voice. "And then Voske attacked. I

happened to see both Paco and Sujata fight in that battle. Paco stood beside Yuki in the last defense of the gates, and Sujata was one of the archers who kept the enemy from rallying at the broken wall by the south forge."

Rustles and whispering rose up. Jennie caught quite a few suspicious or hostile looks directed at Kerry, though none, to Jennie's relief, at Paco. But Kerry, who had joined Brisa and Becky, seemed unconcerned. Well, Kerry could handle some dirty looks. She was one person Jennie didn't need to protect.

"Both of our new Rangers lost a parent in that battle," Mr. Preston went on. "That changes a person, for better or for worse. Sujata and Paco took their loss and turned it into purpose. I'm proud to welcome them both."

Another cheer rose, even louder than before. Sujata rubbed her wrist across her eyes, while Indra laid a hand on her back. Paco stood unmoving, his gaze fixed on the ground.

Indra cupped his hands around his mouth and shouted, "Hey, come celebrate at Luc's! It's our treat!"

His broad, handsome smile swept over the teenagers, and went right past Jennie without an instant's pause. The crowd broke up, all going in different directions. Summer took off in floating skips, ignoring the murmurs that arose at each long, slow leap. Paco went with the Rangers, but unspeaking and unsmiling, alone in the crowd.

Indra had shut her out. Paco had shut the world out. Those entirely different hurts melded within Jennie, becoming a single, deeper pain. It made no sense. Paco had lost his mother and Jennie her mentor in the battle; Sera's death had nearly destroyed Jennie with guilt and seemed to have drained the joy from Paco's life. But Jennie and Indra had broken up earlier, and Jennie had only been banned from the Rangers months later.

Logical or not, everything felt as if it had come together at that one moment, instantaneous and irrevocable.

Sera, falling…

Jennie tensed, waiting to be caught in an endless repeat of that memory. She shut her eyes and reached for a different image, sitting in Dr. Lee's kitchen while he once again listened to her recount Sera's death. Usually, he'd then walked her through every decision she'd made, gently but relentlessly making her see how impossible it had been to foresee or prevent. But that time, his question was unexpected: "Who's living who you love?"

Startled, Jennie had begun naming people. Her family. Her friends. Her students. People who'd taught her or simply been kind to her. When she'd come to the end of a list so long that it had surprised even her, Dr. Lee had said, "Of all those people, who do you miss the most?"

Jennie had replied without thinking: "Mia."

And then she'd walked outside, come face-to-face with Mia, and talked to her instead of avoiding her.

At the time, their meeting had felt memorable because Mia had confessed that she was plotting to release Kerry Voske—an act which had led to so many things, both good and bad, from losing the Rangers to saving Ross's life. But in retrospect, Jennie remembered it as the moment in which she'd turned away from the past and the dead, and moved toward the present and the living. Toward love.

I can't stray from that path, Jennie thought. *I have to keep going forward.*

Most of the crowd was gone now. But Mia had hung back, eyeing Jennie. Either Mia wanted more guards if she had to be around Summer, or she was hoping Jennie wouldn't want to go to Luc's either and Mia would have an excuse to stay away.

Jennie's heart lightened. She'd do whatever Mia wanted her to do, and no matter what else was going on, she'd enjoy her friend's company.

"Waiting for me?" Jennie said with a smile. "Where do you want to go?"

"Ah." Mia glanced around. "Actually, I was thinking of staying right here."

Jennie looked at the abandoned practice ground, puzzled. "To train?"

Mia made a face. "No, no! To talk. In private."

"About...?" Jennie inquired. But she could guess from Mia's nervous fidgeting and uneasy glances at townspeople way out of earshot. Mia only got that way when the subject was Ross. And relationships.

"Sex." Mia's eyes flickered furtively.

Or sex, Jennie thought, blinking.

"Because you know all about it!" Mia burst out. "And I don't know anything. At all! Nothing!"

"Okay," Jennie said, wondering how Dr. Lee's daughter could have possibly avoided learning about a biological basic like sex. Well, maybe Mia could manage it. Before Ross had arrived, she'd seemed disinterested or disgusted at schoolyard talk that even remotely touched on the subject.

"I know this is your night with Ross. Ugh, I feel weird even saying that. But maybe it's only that *I'm* weird. Or that I'm weird about sex," Mia added with a sigh that seemed to come all the way up from inside her scruffy work boots.

Jennie relaxed at that. At least she wouldn't have to explain anatomy. Probably. "Remember how we agreed that we'd figure out how to make this work, instead of getting in a stupid fight over it? Well, talking like this is how we figure it out. So what are you feeling weird about? You know the basics." Mia's look of horror deepened, prompting Jennie to add, "Right?"

"I know what goes where and how to not get pregnant," Mia muttered, turning bright red. "Dad made sure of it before I had my first and only date. I mean before Ross. I was so embarrassed. But I was scared, too. And I still am. Even with Ross. Not *of* Ross! Of sex. And I don't even know why."

"If you're not ready, you're not ready," Jennie said. "Some people aren't until they're a lot older than us. And some people just aren't interested. Ever. Do you *want* to have sex with him? I mean, even though you're scared, too."

Mia's head dropped so her glossy hair hid her face. Jennie wondered if she too had learned that movement from Ross. Before he'd come to town, she'd only fiddled with her glasses.

"Yes." Mia's voice got softer and softer until Jennie had to crane her neck to hear her. "When we kiss. And sometimes just thinking about him."

I'm advising my best friend on how to have sex with my – her – our boyfriend, Jennie thought. *This is the weirdest conversation I've ever had.*

It was so strange, she didn't even know how she felt about it, other than incredibly awkward.

Pretend it's not Ross, Jennie told herself. *What would you tell Mia if she was asking about anyone else?*

Once she had that idea, she felt on surer ground. "Take it one bit a time. Sex isn't one thing you do all at once. Do you enjoy it when he does something? Or when you do something to him? If you don't, you either try something else, or say no."

"I know *that*." Mia squirmed, looking even more embarrassed. "It's the part before the bits that's getting me. How do you start? Do you just say, 'Well, Ross, how about some sex?'"

Jennie inwardly shook with laughter, but managed not to let it out. "Sure, why not? Most guys his age would say YES as fast as they could get the word out. Asking is the easy part."

"But this isn't most guys! This is Ross!" Mia's words tumbled out until she was almost tripping over her own tongue. "What if he says no? What if he runs away? What if he says yes, but wishes he hadn't a second later but is embarrassed to say? What if I'm bad at sex? What if it's a horrible disaster that embarrasses both of us? It would always be *there*, between us. Haunting us, like a—a sex ghost. So we'd both think of it every time we look at each other. And don't say memories can't be like that because they *can*. I know you've seen Ross when he's remembering something awful. And—"

Mia broke off, but she didn't need to say, *And you know too.* She took a deep breath. "Also, I think Ross is scared, too. But I don't know why."

"Then talk to him. Take things one step at a time." Pretending Mia was talking about someone else had made the conversation easier for Jennie, but Mia was right: Ross wasn't most guys, and Jennie *didn't* know how he'd react. But she knew one thing that was true for everyone. "Nobody knows how to have sex the first time they do it. I sure didn't."

"So there's no...mathematical formula that everybody knows but me."

"Mia," Jennie said, "one thing I promise you. Everybody had to begin somewhere. And every couple figures out their own math."

·12·
ROSS

ROSS WOULD HAVE LIKED to walk straight out into the desert after hearing Summer's story, but he couldn't leave town. He couldn't even hide somewhere alone inside town. If anything happened with Summer, people would need to find him.

He compromised by offering to do extra sentry duty, though he'd already done his week's stint before going to the ruined city.

"I know lots of people would rather watch the Ranger ceremony," Ross explained to Ms. Lowenstein. She'd given him a sharp look but accepted, releasing a delighted Fernando Herrera to the training grounds before leaving herself.

Ross paced back and forth, watching the sun set over the shining ocean water. Directly under the fiery ball of the sun, something like a soap bubble shimmered in the air. Before he could tell if it was a trick of the light or something else, it vanished into the mist that shrouded Catalina.

The peace of walking under the open sky, as alone as you ever were in Las Anclas, allowed him to shut out his thoughts. But he was still on edge, and jumped every time a shout or cheer arose from the Rangers' training grounds.

A final cheer, followed by silence and then music drifting from Luc's, told Ross it was over. Ms. Lowenstein returned to the command platform. He wondered if Meredith had made it into the Rangers—her mother's yellow cat eyes gave nothing away—but wasn't curious enough to start a conversation. He'd find out soon enough.

He continued to pace as the grays and brilliant pinks of the sunset deepened to purple and deep red, then to a velvety black. Stars winked into being as the creatures of the night emerged. Coyotes yodeled to each other in the desert. Beacon cacti glowed softly in green and gold, their brightness and radiant heat luring unwary creatures close enough touch their tranquilizing spines. Then the snakes that lived among their roots would emerge to finish off the sleeping victim. They bit off chunks rather than swallowing creatures whole, leaving enough scraps to feed and fertilize the cacti.

A flash of memory: a man's slow, deep voice explaining how the beacon cactus captured and stored sunlight by day, but only enough to keep them alight a few hours past sunset.

Could that voice have been his father, who could have seen for himself that the cacti held heat as well as light?

Ross had no idea. But if a day was so cloudy or rainy that the sun never came out, the cacti wouldn't glow that night, so the explanation was probably right. Jennie would know for sure, he supposed.

He carried the crossbow Mia had made for him—before, he'd had to check out a pistol to do sentry duty—but never had reason to draw it. Ross might feel unsettled, but the night was peaceful.

The bells rang the change of watch. Ross considered volunteering for another shift, but he knew Ms. Lowenstein would turn him down. She didn't want exhausted sentries who might miss something.

Ross reluctantly headed back to the command post. He'd managed to avoid thinking about Summer for a few hours, and hoped the break might give him some new ideas. But it hadn't. He couldn't change himself into the wandering gunslinger she'd imagined, he couldn't change Las Anclas to suit her better, and he didn't know how to change her mind.

A shadow moved behind him. A familiar scent of dried herbs and roses drifted to him on the breeze, telling him who was coming as much as her soft footfalls and curvy, broad-shouldered silhouette. His heart lifted.

"Hi, Jennie," Ross said. "Who are the new Rangers?"

"Sujata and Paco," Jennie replied.

He heard the sadness and regret behind her pride. Then Ross felt guilty for leaving her alone to watch others get something she deserved but could never have.

"I should have gone with you," Ross said.

To his surprise, she chuckled. "No... No... Just as well you didn't."

Ross stiffened, instantly wary. "Did Summer do something?"

Jennie smothered another laugh—what was so funny?—but spoke seriously. "Not at all. She watched, but she was perfectly well-behaved. Last I saw, she was at the stables, peeking at the royal horses. Penny's near her time. I think Summer's hoping if she checks in enough, she'll be around for the birth."

Ross relaxed as Jennie accompanied him back along the wall, recounting the ceremony. Ordinarily Ms. Lowenstein came down hard on sentries chatting while on duty, but she trusted Jennie to keep watch while talking and he was about to turn over his watch anyway.

Meredith met him at the command post. "Hi, Ross." To Jennie, she said, "Guess the 'great archer' is back on her *real* duty."

Ross smiled at her dead-on imitation of Mr. Preston.

"Are you disappointed, Meredith?" Jennie asked.

"Nah. Well, sort of. I liked the idea of riding out to find bad guys. But I liked fending them off from here too." Meredith thumped her bow on the sentry wall, her frizzy hair gleaming red-gold in the torchlight.

"And it probably doesn't hurt that everyone else got 'train harder' or 'thanks but no thanks' or 'shut up and go away,' but you got 'you're too good to lose to the Rangers,'" Jennie teased.

Meredith grinned. "Did you see Henry's face? I thought for a second he might punch Mr. Preston."

"If he'd brought that fire to training, maybe he'd have had a chance," Jennie said thoughtfully.

Meredith snorted. "Not likely. Henry has one moment of being serious once a year, and that was it."

Her laughter floated behind them as Ross walked down the steps with Jennie.

"Ross, what do you want to do?" Jennie asked. "Indra invited everybody to Luc's. Do you want to go?"

She left the choice to him, as she always did. He appreciated how she never made him feel trapped, but ever since Summer's arrival he'd begun to wonder how much of teacher-Jennie, as Mia called her, was mixed with girlfriend-Jennie. She had the exact same calming note in her voice that she used on the schoolyard.

I'm not her student, Ross thought.

He wasn't made of glass, either. So he didn't like crowds. But Jennie liked dancing, and Ross liked — maybe even loved — watching her dance.

"Yeah. I do." If he looked around to see if anyone was watching them, he'd lose his nerve. So he didn't look. Instead, he fixed his gaze on Jennie's beautiful face, her full lips, her skin like the night sky, and he put his arm around her waist.

He felt her startled inhale — he could feel every breath that she took — and then she moved to do the same to him, laying her palm flat against his side. He could feel her warmth through her clothes, too, just as she must be able to feel his.

Teacher Jennie vanished. Now she was *his* Jennie, who moved with him as if they were one person in two bodies, whether they were dancing or fighting or merely walking side by side. Her breathing matched his, deep and controlled with an occasional tiny stutter, as if she was having trouble keeping her hand in place. As if she wanted to touch him more.

That *was* why. He knew it the same way he knew how to move with her, and she with him. They could read each other's bodies like some Changed people could read minds.

"Meet at my place?" Jennie asked. "I want to put on something I can dance in."

She brushed at her teacher clothes, sending up a gritty puff of chalk dust.

"Sure. I want to wash up and change, too." It had been six months since Ross had gotten regular access to hot baths and clean clothes, but the pleasure of it hadn't worn off. He'd sometimes spent years in one outfit, and in winter it and he had often stayed grimy for months.

He was too self-conscious to kiss Jennie right there below the wall full of alert sentries, so they squeezed hands and parted.

Later, Ross thought. *In private.*

He'd rather have kept thinking of Jennie, and the curve of her waist under his arm. But as he reached the surgery, he couldn't help looking for Summer.

The building was dark and empty. Ross didn't know whether to be relieved or worried, but he forced himself not to go check the stables. She was safe within the town walls, and he was not going to let her take over his life or even ruin this one night. Tonight was for him and Jennie.

Ross bathed and changed into the blue shirt Jennie had made for him, the new pair of jeans he'd finally got around to buying from Mr. Kim, and his old leather jacket.

He hesitated over his gauntlet, then left it on the table. If he'd been going out with Mia, he'd have left it on, just to see her never-fading delight at her handiwork. But Jennie wouldn't care, and he wanted to touch her with both hands.

Downstairs, he checked himself in the mirror while cats wound around his ankles. Would Jennie like what he chose? His gaze fell on the handprint scars across his throat, and he turned away from the mirror. Of course she would.

Jennie waited for him outside her house. The bright-moths living under the eaves cast a flickering light over the low-cut red dress that clung so temptingly to her curves, the one she'd worn to teach him to dance. The same way he could sense her next move before she made it when they sparred together, he knew that she'd selected the dress because it was his favorite.

She often unbraided her hair to go dancing, but tonight her braids still swung around her face as she stepped toward him. His smile broadened when he saw she was wearing the agate beads.

"It's like Christmas all over again," she said with a laugh.

Ross smiled, but didn't reply. There had to be watching eyes from the windows overhead. Jennie's little siblings never missed a chance to spy and tease.

Ross and Jennie walked close together, but not touching. Instinct said, *later.*

At Luc's, music spilled out the open door in a wide shaft of golden light and tempting smells. Ross heard crowd noise, and fought the urge to run. The voices and laughter made it clear that everyone was having a good time. It was just a party, like normal people enjoyed. He didn't hear Henry, and that laugh would have been impossible to miss. Even better, he didn't hear Felicité's voice, which too often reminded him of the chiming of the crystal trees. He didn't see her, either, and even in this crowd, her enormous hat would have caught his eye.

The person he did see was Summer, perched high on a barrel across from the musicians, the lamplight glittering in her eyes. Her head whipped toward Ross, sending her curtain of black hair swinging. He instantly dropped his gaze. She was not going to ruin his night with her anger or contempt.

Jennie murmured in his ear, "She's not watching you."

Relieved, Ross raised his head. Summer had turned her attention to the dance floor, where Kerry was dancing with Alfonso Medina. He moved lightly for a guy his size, but Summer only had eyes for Kerry, and Ross could guess why. Kerry danced like a fighter, her movements strong and precise, graceful but not romantic. Alfonso was her partner, nothing more; Kerry appeared to be teaching him the dance.

A brown hand waved from the crowd. Inside the hot room, a cool breeze rippled Ross's hair. He laughed.

"There you are," Yolanda exclaimed. "I held places for you!"

She pointed to the bench where she, Jose, Brisa, and Becky sat, along with Brisa's sister Dominica, and Fernando Herrera. They squeezed over, making space for Ross and Jennie.

"Congratulations on the invite to try again," Jennie said to Jose, and when he grinned, shaking his head, "Mr. Preston doesn't say that unless he means it."

"He sure didn't invite me," Brisa said, laughing. "He sounded like he wished I'd quit before he had a chance to tell me to go away!"

"Did you want him to invite you?" Becky asked in her barely-there voice. Ross had to lean in to hear her.

"Getting up before dawn every day to exercise till every muscle in my body hurt? Are you kidding?" Brisa retorted.

"Then why'd you stay?" Jose asked.

"Didn't want to be a quitter." Then, with a laugh, Brisa added, "And to annoy Mr. Preston. The glare he gave me every morning made it all worthwhile. I've been wanting to get back at him ever since he kicked you out, Jennie. And tried to kill *you!*"

Brisa looked straight at Ross. He started to duck, then made himself meet her gaze. It was only Brisa, being unexpectedly protective of him. He'd had no idea that she cared. Ross managed a smile. "Thanks."

Jennie, who had frozen when Brisa had mentioned her, relaxed her body in the deliberate way that Ross knew so well. "Sweet revenge, *and* you're in the best shape of your life. Good work, Brisa."

"Yeah!" Brisa flexed her arm. She was as plump as ever, but her biceps bulged visibly beneath the soft layer of fat. She offered her tensed arm to Becky, who stroked it and murmured something Ross couldn't catch. "Come on, let's dance and celebrate my escape!"

Laughing, Brisa slid her arm around Becky's waist. The girls rose as one and joined the dance floor. The band was playing a lively tune, but they moved at their own, slower pace, arms tightly wrapped around each other, heads leaning together, black hair mingling with blonde.

A waiter plunked down a tray of tacos and a jug of tamarindo. Savory and tart smells wafted up. Ross helped himself to everything, but Jennie only filled her glass.

She took a long drink, her head tilted back and her neck arched gracefully, then asked, "Want to dance?"

He already had a taco in hand, so he held it up, relieved to have an excuse. He did want to dance, but not in this crowd; he wanted to dance alone with her in her own backyard, just the two of them under the stars. "Go ahead."

Indra came up, his arm around Nasreen. He was in dancing clothes, not his Ranger uniform: white pants and a long white tunic split up to his hips, embroidered in black. Nasreen wore a deep purple dress and a lavender scarf wrapped around her hair and throat, the end trailing gracefully down her back to the same length as Indra's braid.

Ross wondered if Indra had stood in front of a mirror and examined his clothes, hoping to please the person he was with. Maybe Nasreen had, too, and Brisa and Becky. Maybe all the couples here had. The world seemed to shift around Ross as he tested the idea that he wasn't so different from anyone else in the room. He might not like being in a crowd, but he was still part of it. He wasn't an outsider any more, he was just another guy on a date.

Indra nodded pleasantly at Jennie, who nodded back with a smile like his...*exactly* like his. Measured, not spontaneous. Then his smile vanished. "Have any of you seen Paco?"

All heads shook.

"This is his party, too," Indra said. "I sent Sujata to see if he went back to his room."

Sujata appeared out of the crowd. She, too, wore a split tunic and pants, hers in blue embroidered with white. Like Nasreen, she wore a scarf, but hers was blue gauze and wrapped only around her throat, leaving her black hair uncovered.

"Paco's at the back wall," Sujata said. "He took over Henry's turn at sentry duty."

Indra frowned. "Why would he do that?"

"Maybe he felt sorry for Henry," Sujata said, but she didn't sound as if she believed it. "I told Paco he should come, but he said he couldn't abandon his post."

"If Henry really cared, he'd have taken training seriously," Jose said. "Where is he anyway?"

"Probably off with Felicité," Sujata said, rolling her eyes. "Bet he'd have skipped out on sentry duty anyway. It's not right. Paco should be here. He's a Ranger!"

Indra looked at Jennie, not Sujata, as he said, "Maybe Paco wants some private time to let it sink in."

Jennie nodded, but avoided Indra's gaze. "Just enjoy the evening, Sujata. We're here, so let's celebrate. Who wants to dance?"

Ross noticed that Jennie's invitation seemed directed at everyone but Indra, though he was still watching her. Indra started to reach out to her but Jennie turned her head away. He smoothly moved to take Nasreen's hand, and they headed for the dance floor.

Ross wondered what that had been about. Indra and Jennie used to date, but that was over now. Something to do with the Rangers? With Paco?

Ross's senses had sharpened, noise and light and smells clear and distinct. It wasn't quite danger sense, but close, as if he were missing something important. Was he ever going to really understand other people?

Tommy Horst shouldered his way through the crowd, his height and bulk easily moving others aside. "Jennie? How about a dance?"

He sent a challenging glance at Ross as he spoke. That, Ross understood. But he wasn't threatened. If Jennie agreed, it was only because she wanted a dance partner. Ross raised his taco and smiled. Tommy looked confused.

"Sure." Jennie nodded at Tommy, but without taking his offered hand.

Once they were in the middle of the dance floor, Tommy cleared space with his big body and long reach. Others looked at Jennie, then stepped back, giving her room. By now Ross knew that he wasn't the only person who thought Jennie was one of the best dancers in Las Anclas.

She twirled, sending her skirt flaring out in a scarlet circle. Tommy followed along, giving her support when she needed it, and once lifting her over his head. But Ross's attention was on Jennie alone as she stamped and leaped, now impressing him with the speed and complexity of her hand gestures, now making his whole body burn as she dropped down and slithered along the floor in an unexpectedly sensual movement.

His breath caught, then caught again as Jennie launched herself into the air, going from a lying position to a flip.

The crowd cheered. It was an amazing, impossible-looking move. But a different kind of warmth, slower and deeper, filled Ross as he realized how long she must have spent practicing it in secret. And that she'd revealed it now, for the first time, for him. He knew it even before her bright gaze caught his, and she flashed a private grin his way.

As he watched her strong, graceful body whirling about the room, he wanted to watch her dance forever, but he wanted to take her away from Luc's, and be alone with her.

Ross *could* be alone with her. He could do anything he wanted. All he needed to do was say yes.

A familiar panic rose within him, but he neither fought it nor gave in to it. He stayed where he was, watching Jennie dance.

When the music ended, Tommy stepped away and Sujata took

his place. The girls mirrored each other's movements in a complicated dance Ross had never seen before, though they had obviously danced it many times before. Sujata moved well, but Ross
barely noticed her. He only saw Jennie, her beaded braids swinging and her hips swaying in provocative counterpoint her scarlet
blouse barely containing her breasts, her skirt flaring out, her eyes
reflecting the lights, he soft lips parted in the joy of movement.

She was so beautiful.

Every now and then she looked straight at him, catching his
gaze and holding it long enough for him to get her message: *For
you.*

She finished her last dance—a solo—and made her way to his
side. "Want to go?"

Outside, Ross breathed in the fresh air, then caught a whiff of
burning pine. No one used pine as firewood. It burst into showers
of sparks that could float in all directions and set the bone-dry
weeds aflame. The smell was gone in another breath, but he and
Jennie stood watching the hills until they were sure no fire
threatened the town.

"Thought I smelled smoke," Jennie said.

"Me, too." As he spoke, he realized how unnecessary the
words were. They'd both known what the other was thinking and
doing.

They reached out, lacing their fingers together. Her palm was
damp but warm, as was his. He let her lead him, and was
unsurprised to find her heading for her home rather than his.
Unusually, all but one of the windows were dark.

"Grandma," Jennie said, indicating the square of light. "The
little kids are asleep, Ma's at the stable with the pregnant mares,
and everyone else is dancing at Luc's or talking politics at Jack's.
Want to dance in the backyard?"

Once again, she'd read his mind—his body—maybe it was all
the same thing. This time he was the one who led her to the yard.
The sweet scent of night-blooming jasmine filled the air, the stars
shone brilliant overhead, and the bushes hid them from view.

Her arm slid softly around him, one hand clasping his, one flat
on the small of his back. He followed her movements, remembering their very first dance.

"One-two-three," he counted, smiling.

Jennie laughed. "You don't need that anymore."

Then they were waltzing, their bodies keeping rhythm without him having to think about it. He laid his cheek against hers, feeling her soft skin and the smoothness of the agate beads as her braids slid forward and back, forward and back. Like she'd said, they were cooler than her skin and his, making his breath quicken at every slide. She smelled of fresh soap and sweat, of dried rose petals and herbs, a scent he could never mistake for anyone else's.

Their dance slowed and slowed, until they were simply swaying in each other's arms. When she lifted her face to his, offering him her beautiful lips, he kissed her. Fire kindled deep inside him, along with a sense of foreboding. They'd kiss for a while, and then something would go wrong—

No.

Jennie had taught him to dance, and they'd taught each other to fight better. She could teach him this, too. He was not going to let himself be ruled by fear.

The kiss deepened. Jennie knew what she was doing, and Ross followed her lead. Then, boldened by the soft noises of enjoyment she was making, he tried out nibbling, and all the things you could do with your tongue. It *was* like sparring, or dancing: if he only paid attention to her body, he could feel what she liked. And so long as he kept going rather than stopping, she too could learn what felt good to him.

When she lifted her head, he knew what she was going to say. "Do you want to spend the night?"

He gulped back a surge of panic. He had nothing to be afraid of. This was Jennie, whom he trusted with his life. And he did want to. He wanted her as desperately as he feared...something.

Ross nodded. But there was something he had to ask. "Mia...?"

He couldn't put the words together, but Jennie seemed to know what he meant.

"She won't be mad at you or me," Jennie said. "It might be awkward, I don't know. But we've talked about it. No one's cheating. We'll work it out. And you and Mia can do whatever you like, too. But I think it might go better if you're not both experimenting for the first time."

Realizing how much he was relying on Jennie's experience, Ross nodded again. He knew how nervous Mia got when she had no idea how to do something she thought she should know how to do, and he was exactly the same way. But that thought brought back all his anxiety. He *didn't* know what he was doing.

Jennie caught his hands in hers. "Ross? *Do* you want to?"

Ross closed his eyes and breathed in Jennie's scent. For once he'd let his body be the leader, and not his memory or mind. "Yeah. I do."

He barely felt his feet hitting the ground as Jennie led him to her bedroom. He felt half-dazed, half intensely aware of Jennie's presence, her breathing, the brush of her dress against his legs. His pulse pounded in his ears.

And then they were standing alone in her bedroom, with the door closed.

"What do I do?" His voice came out so hoarse, he half-expected her to change her mind on the spot.

Instead, she gave him a slow smile that told him how much *she* wanted *him*. She wasn't doing this as a favor or a lesson. She might be experienced, but that didn't make her own desire burn less than his. "Anything you want. If I don't like it, I'll tell you. But I have a feeling that whatever you do, I'll like."

She took his hand and tugged him to the bed. And then she proved as good as her word.

When he felt clumsy and awkward, she chuckled and said, "Practice makes perfect. Want to practice till we get perfect?"

He hadn't expected to laugh, but he did. "Let's try."

And then he couldn't think at all.

At last they lay side by side. Exhausted, amazed, exhilarated, he realized that it was the first time he'd ever shared a bed with someone. Sleeping fully clothed out in Mia's yard wasn't quite the same. Then he fell into a deep sleep, holding Jennie close.

And when he woke from a dream of Voske's hell cells, cold with terror, Jennie was there to lay a comforting hand on his shoulder, and to be understanding when he had to dress and go outside in the open air, alone, and breathe.

·13·
FELICITÉ

THE DISASTROUS RANGER CEREMONY wasn't the first shock of Felicité's day.

A few older teenagers on the verge of graduation, who'd been released from school after lunch to do sentry duty or work their apprenticeships, had repeated Summer's stupid story to everyone they'd seen. Within an hour, everyone in town was repeating it as if nothing else had ever happened anywhere.

At first Felicité hadn't been worried. Schoolyard chatter had ever been important to adults. But all afternoon, she heard references to Summer's story, followed by variations on a theme: "That town is *gone,* all because someone powerful decided to throw out the Changed. I don't like them myself, but I don't want Las Anclas to go up in flames. When Tom Preston kicked out those Changed folk from Catalina, the same thing could have happened to us. That does it. I'm not voting for him."

After all her hard work campaigning and everything Daddy had done for the town, an obviously exaggerated yarn told by a fourteen-year-old vagrant seemed to have destroyed everything.

But a Wolfe never gave up. Felicité hurried about town, reminding everyone how Daddy had turned away King Voske's attack, saying that Daddy had no intention of throwing out Las Anclas's Changed folk, and pointing out that Summer was a child and a braggart who had probably made up the entire tale to get attention.

It was all in vain. Most people ignored her, but several sharply informed her that even if Summer had made it up, they'd heard of similar things happening before. "Maybe that particular story's not true," Mrs. Hernandez said. "But it's happened elsewhere. It could happen here. Liar or not, we should thank that girl for reminding us."

Felicité could make no dent in that illogic. After the Ranger ceremony, she turned her back on Luc's. She had nothing to celebrate. Felicité wanted to comfort Henry after his crushing disappointment, but he'd vanished.

Well, he knew where to find her. And she'd help him more by interceding with Daddy than by giving him useless consolation. She spotted her father walking with Julio, who loped off toward Singles Row, leaving Daddy alone.

"Hello, darling. Long day on the campaign trail?" Daddy said.

Felicité quickly rehearsed her words and manner. She couldn't sound like Mrs. Callahan or even like herself a year ago. She was almost an adult now. If she acted like one, she'd be treated like one.

"I'll be glad when it's over," she said, glancing up at his face. That line between his brows told her that she didn't have to repeat Summer's story or its implications for the election. He knew.

Daddy liked people to get to the point. So she said, "How do you choose the Rangers?"

His glasses flashed as he turned to her. His stride didn't falter, but he slowly removed the spectacles and slid them into his shirt pocket. Her question had surprised him; he was giving himself time to think before he spoke. "You know what qualities I look for. You've heard me talk about it with your mother. And with Sera. Or did you have someone specific in mind?"

In her most mature voice, she said, "I know I'm not a fighter. But I know Henry, and he hasn't been the class clown for a long time. You saw how well he fought in the battle. And real fighting's more important than training, isn't it?"

Daddy rubbed his chin. "In my experience, they go together. And I'm not as impressed with his real fighting, darling. Yes, he has the skills, and he's brave. But I saw him disobey an order to see if the front gate line needed reinforcements. Instead, he chased after wounded soldiers who were already retreating. Based on what he's said in training, I imagine he was trying to rack up his kill count. That's not what I want in a Ranger."

Felicité found that hard to imagine. She'd seen plenty of people running around wildly during the battle, confused by the noise and chaos or uncertain of whether changing circumstances meant previous orders were still in effect. Most flagrantly of all, Ross had made completely unauthorized use of his secret Change power. "Maybe Henry didn't hear the order."

"It's possible." But Daddy clearly didn't believe it. "Regardless, he lacks discipline. How can his teammates count on him in the heat of battle if he can't even show up for drill consistently? He's like Will and his friends, enthusiastic in spurts. Henry's eighteen going on eleven."

As they headed for home, Felicité tried not to let her disappointment show. She couldn't argue that Henry was consistently enthusiastic about *her*. Why was Daddy so sure Henry wouldn't apply himself if he was given a second chance?

"I see," Felicité said. "But Daddy, you must've thought this for a while. Why didn't you tell me so I'd be prepared?"

His thick eyebrows rose in surprise. "I didn't know it mattered to you. I realize he's one of your flirts, and that's fine. But that has nothing to do with the Rangers, surely?"

"No, of course not," Felicité said. "I just like to stay informed."

She liked how smooth she sounded—exactly like Mother when a council member sprang something unpleasant on her. Mother never let her true emotions show during council battles.

Felicité let Daddy change the subject, joining him in guessing what they might find for dinner, but she fumed inside. *One of your flirts.* Daddy hadn't the slightest idea how important Henry was to her. He didn't even realize that Henry was her boyfriend, not a "flirt."

She couldn't inform Daddy now, when he'd just finished telling her exactly how much he disapproved of Henry. But she saw a side of Henry that others didn't. She had to figure out how to show it to the world.

She was unsurprised when Henry didn't show up for dinner—he undoubtedly didn't want to face Daddy—and guiltily relieved.

All that campaigning had given her a headache. She confessed as much, retreated to her room with a bottle of headache elixir, scrubbed herself with a barely damp towel, and went to bed.

She woke the next morning with a sense of doom, as if she'd had a nightmare. But the day before had been all too real.

Felicité put on one of her prettiest silk gowns, the eggshell blue that set off her mahogany hair, wrapped a darker blue scarf around her neck, topped it with a white straw hat, and tied a blue ribbon around Wu Zetian's neck. Then she wrapped her blistered toes and set out early to campaign before school.

No one even responded to her arguments. The best she got was a fake compliment or two on her dress. She thought of her own praise as the sweet clinking of golden coins, but the words she received clunked like the iron junk in Mia's yard. And then everyone pointedly waited for her to go out of earshot before they returned to their conversations.

The sun was barely out, and she already had a headache. At the schoolyard, she caught Henry's eye as he practiced archery. *His* smile was sincere. But everyone else was clustered around a small figure on the porch, their voices rising shrill and excited.

Summer, Felicité thought grimly.

Then she saw who everyone was squealing over. Felicité gasped with surprise, then with joy. "Grandmère!"

The last time she'd seen her grandmother had been after the battle, the tiny old woman exhausted with the effort of defending the gates with her fire powers.

Guilt clutched at Felicité's heart. She easily could have visited her grandmother in the fireproof adobe home outside the gates that she'd exiled herself to until she could control the power she'd gained with menopause. Her mother had gone every week. But Felicité had always found an excuse. She couldn't bear the thought of being present if Grandmère had a hot flash and was forced to rush outside to throw a fireball into the desert sand. Felicité wanted to remember Grandmère as an elegant, controlled Norm.

Now she had Grandmère back, and she appeared as she'd been when she'd presided over the Wolfe house and taught in the schoolhouse, exquisitely dressed and poised. Her white hair was upswept and pinned with iridescent abalone combs, and she wore black silk pants and a blue silk coat with embroidered crimson phoenixes swooping around its frog closures.

"Yes, I'm back," Grandmère said, opening her arms with a smile.

Henry joined the crowd, saying in a mock-solemn voice, "Grandma Wolfe, will you be setting any fires? I just want to be prepared." He jerked his thumb at the water pump. "Shall I get a bucket?"

Some little kids snickered. Felicité glared at him. That was exactly the sort of joke that had kept him out of the Rangers.

Henry, catching sight of her, looked contrite. "Sorry. Just kidding!"

"It is a fair question," Grandmère said seriously. "However, you will be glad to hear that I have complete control of my powers now. And if Jennie says I may, I might even pop some corn for you later in the week."

Felicité pulled her scarf tight, choking back her disgust. Surely now that Grandmère had learned to control her power, she'd do the right thing and never use it.

Jennie threw open the schoolroom door. "Grandma Wolfe!"

"Hello, Jennie," Grandmère said, smiling.

"Would you like to come in and see how we're doing?" Jennie asked.

"Perhaps another time, dear," Grandmère said. "I just stopped by to say hello. And to pick up my granddaughter, if she may be excused for the morning."

"Of course," Jennie said in that annoyingly superior teacher voice of hers, as if she were twenty years older than Felicité instead of barely one. "She's about to graduate anyway." She said it as if she couldn't wait.

Then Jennie's smugness slipped. As uncertainly as a child, she added, "You have complete control of your powers? Are you moving back to town?"

Felicité could barely control her glee as she realized what that meant. Jennie was about to get booted out of her job—for the second time! She'd have to go hunting for an apprenticeship at a humiliatingly old age.

"Yes, and yes. But I have no intention of taking your job

away," Grandmère assured Jennie. "I have other plans."

To Felicité's surprise, a flash of disappointment tightened Jennie's face. Was she satisfied with nothing? Again with uncharacteristic awkwardness, Jennie said, "Oh."

Grandmère smiled at Henry. "I have not forgotten you, Henry. Would you care to join us at dinner this evening? My house at six?"

"Yes, ma'am!" Henry grinned at Grandmère, then Felicité. Maybe he wasn't taking his rejection from the Rangers as hard as Felicité had thought.

Grandmère petted Wu Zetian, who reacted excitedly—her poor pet, she must feel so snubbed by the town that used to love her—then placed her hand on Felicité's arm. They left the schoolyard, Felicité gladly thinking, *Soon it will be for the last time.*

"It's so good to see you again, dear. And I am so glad to see you developing your own style. Though perhaps fewer accouterments, charming as they are, would suit you even better." Grandmère indicated Felicité's scarf. "Sometimes less is more."

Felicité clutched at her neck. Rainclouds were passing in the north. The scarf would cover her gills if she got wet. It was the only thing that ensured that Daddy would never see..."No!"

Her grandmother gave her a puzzled look.

Felicité hastily recovered her smooth mayor's voice. "People know I like scarves, so I often get them as gifts. I don't want to hurt anyone's feelings by not wearing them. But you're right. My dress has too much embroidery to go with this one."

Grandmère patted her hand. "It is a touch formal for school. Oh, darling, I've missed you." She hugged Felicité tight. "I know who prevented you from coming to see me, as I'm sure you wanted."

Felicité winced inwardly. Grandmère and Daddy had never gotten along, even before her Change, but Daddy hadn't said a word against Felicité visiting. But since she had no better excuse, she let it slide.

"But perhaps it's as well to let matters rest," Grandmère went on. "I'm back, and looking forward to taking up my life again—a *new* life. Walk with me to the council office, where I am officially registering my candidacy."

"Candidacy?" Felicité repeated blankly.

"Yes. Now that Judge Vardam is retiring from the council, I am going to throw my hat into the ring and run for the council seat."

"But you…" Felicité shut her mouth on the word *'can't.'*

Grandmère laughed. "Why not? I am very well qualified. I served on the council for years, and I loved it. I only retired when your father became sheriff. It seemed inappropriate to have three family members with four votes."

Felicité knew that. But things were different now. There were already two Changed people on the council—the most there had ever been in her life. And neither Sheriff Crow nor Dr. Lee's seats were up for election. If Grandmère was elected, that would make three. Even if she always voted with the family, Felicité was sure Daddy would think it set a bad precedent.

"Congratulations! I'm sure you'll win," Felicité said, though secretly relieved that she couldn't possibly. No one could with only two days to campaign, not even Grandmère. "I'm glad you invited Henry to dinner. Did you know we're dating?"

"Yes, darling," Grandmère replied. "Henry seems to have grown up a great deal. He looked quite fierce in the battle. But I only caught a glimpse of him while I was running for the front gates. Even then, I wasn't sure I would be able to produce enough fire to make a difference. But all my practice paid off."

Felicité was horrified. Would Grandmère never stop talking about her Change power? How could she live with Daddy if she was talked like this?

But to Felicité's relief, a distraction appeared. Dr. Lee came out of the surgery and waved. "Mrs. Wolfe! I'm delighted to see you back."

"And I am delighted to be back, Dante," Grandmère said. "Come talk to me when you have a moment. I'm running for the empty council seat!"

"Congratulations," Dr. Lee said. "Well, that certainly simplifies my decision."

His reaction was echoed again and again as they crossed the town square. Felicité was torn between admiration at Grandmère's skillfully understated campaigning and alarm at its apparent effectiveness. Everybody seemed relieved that she was running.

Once she registered at the town hall, she seated herself on its verandah like a queen. The town came to her as she held court. Jack even brought her lunch.

By the end of the day, Felicité knew that Grandmère had won the council seat. She tried to be happy for her, and tried harder to watch and learn a master of politics in action. But all she could think of was the impending battle within her family.

Please, Grandmère, Felicité inwardly begged her. *Keep the peace. Act like you're not Changed, and Daddy will pretend you aren't.*

When the bells rang for the evening shift change, they took leave of the happy crowd and walked up the hill.

Grandmère looked around with obvious pleasure at her garden and house. "I see that everything has been kept up beautifully in my absence. Not that I would expect anything less."

Mother appeared in her office door, looking distracted. "Oh, there you are, Mother. Where have you been all afternoon?"

"Campaigning, of course."

Mother's smile was completely unsurprised. "I'm sure it went brilliantly."

So Mother had known in advance. Why hadn't she told Felicité? Daddy hadn't warned her about Henry, and Mother hadn't warned her about Grandmère. Didn't her parents understand her at all? Did they still think she was a child, even though she was about to graduate?

Grandmère went on, "I invited someone for dinner, Valeria. Henry Callahan."

Mother's smile widened. "I would have loved to have you all to ourselves, but I'm sure Felicité will enjoy that."

"We all will. She's found herself a charming young man. "

"Let me change," Felicité said, happy to hear Grandmère and Mother talking approvingly about Henry. Normal talk. Maybe she was having childish fears over nothing.

◆ ◆ ◆

Henry arrived promptly at six, in a new black linen suit that set off his light complexion and hair.

"You look quite handsome," Grandmère said. "Is that your

mother's excellent tailoring?"

"Yes," Henry said, turning to display the details. "It's the same design I wore to the dance, but that one got ruined in the battle."

"Cool," Will said enviously. He'd never gotten over spending the entire battle shut up inside, first in the schoolhouse and then the town hall.

"That was a fine suit. It's a shame it got ruined." Daddy smiled. "But perhaps the subject of battles is better left for after dinner."

Clara brought in their best silver tray with a steaming haunch of roast beef atop a hash of root vegetables. Daddy carved with his usual skill as the side dishes of sautéed green beans, corn bread, and baked pumpkin were laid out. Felicité breathed in the delicious scents. No fish, Henry at her side, everyone on their best behavior: it would be a wonderful night after all.

"Oh, Valeria," Grandmère said. "You didn't light the candles."

"It's so warm," Mother said.

Grandmère raised her hand dramatically toward the candelabra, commanding attention. Everyone froze, Daddy with his knife in mid-air and Will with his hand on a piece of corn bread.

"*No,*" Felicité tried to say, but it was too late.

With a soft *poof,* the candles burst into flame.

Daddy's brows lowered in anger. Sick with fear, Felicité groped under the table for Henry's hand. But Henry's jaw tightened, his lips pressing into a white line of horror. Felicité snatched her hand back.

"Grandmère," Will exclaimed. "You can't do that here—"

"William." Daddy's voice was sharp.

Will turned to Daddy. "But she can't do Change powers at the table!"

"Leave that discussion to the adults," Daddy said.

"But *you* said—"

"Will." Daddy's voice was commanding. "Leave the table."

Will instantly stood up.

"William, sit down and eat." Grandmère's tone also demanded obedience. Will stood uncertainly, looking from his father to his grandmother. "My use of my Change is not up to you, but—"

Daddy laid down the carving knife. It clinked hard against the platter. "Please let me discipline my own son."

"By all means," Grandmère replied. "When he has earned it. What exactly was it that you said that gave him the impression that I may not light my own candles at my own table?"

"It's a matter of decent manners."

Grandmère lifted her chin. Her combs flashed in the firelight like a crown. "My actions are *indecent*, Thomas? That is a first."

"I'm not going to argue with you about manners." Daddy's voice rose angrily. "But I won't have anyone endangering my family with those unnatural powers in my house."

"It's *my* house," Grandmère pointed out.

Daddy shoved back his chair, threw down his napkin, and walked out.

"Ma mère, was that necessary?" Mother asked softly.

"Valeria, I'm too old to pretend that I'm something I'm not. I have this power and I'm not going to hide it," Grandmère said. "Thomas will simply have to adjust."

"Mom...?" Will said plaintively, still standing.

"Sit down and eat," Mother said.

Will plonked down and went back to gobbling his roast beef, as if dinner was all that mattered. Grandmère launched into a practiced speech about being true to oneself, then gracefully led Mother and Henry into a discussion of the election.

Felicité could neither eat nor speak. She knew that Daddy would never adjust. Even if Grandmère apologized, Daddy would never forget how she'd flaunted her power in front of him.

Even Daddy's one-time Changed pet, Jennie, had never used her power when Daddy could see. Felicité had despised her as a hypocrite. But it had worked. Daddy had accepted her into the Rangers. And Henry had mentioned that once Daddy took over Ranger training from Jennie, Jose had stopped using his earthmoving power during training, though Brisa kept on exploding rocks whenever she felt like it.

Daddy loves his Norm children.

Felicité pulled her scarf tight around her throat.

She wasn't sure whether to be relieved that Henry acted as if everything was completely normal, or frustrated that he didn't seem to register how tense the meal was. He helped himself to a second slice of peach pie and scarfed it down before he finally noticed that everyone else was sitting there with empty plates. Even then, he stood up and waited as if he expected Felicité to invite him to her room.

He didn't get the hint until she said "Good night, Henry," and gave him a brief kiss on the cheek. Then, to her immense relief, he left.

Felicité fled upstairs. Wu Zetian ran up to comfort her. She always knew when Felicité was upset. Felicité cuddled her rat and waited with her door open a crack, listening for Daddy's footsteps.

When she heard them, she crept on to the dark landing, so she could see as well as hear. No light shone from under Grandmère's door. Daddy had probably waited for that before coming back. He and Mother stood by the front door with their backs to Felicité.

"I'm sorry I ruined your dinner, Valeria," Daddy said.

A kiss usually followed her parents' rare fights and apologies, but when Daddy leaned in, Mother stepped away.

"Thomas, what about tomorrow's dinner?" Mother asked. "And any dinner in which my mother lights the candles...like that?"

There was a long silence before Daddy spoke again. "If she does, she can do it before I come into the room. Compromise goes two ways."

Another silence, then Mother spoke so softly Felicité had to creep halfway down the stairs to hear. "This is proof that the Change is in the Wolfe bloodline. I have not yet reached menopause. What if I Change?"

"Impossible." Daddy spoke so forcefully that Felicité scooted back up to the landing. This was not a conversation she wanted to be caught eavesdropping on. "You don't want to, so you won't."

"Thomas, this is not a matter of wanting or not wanting." Mother's voice rose slightly with frustration. "Could I stop my hair from going gray? Does an infant choose to be born Changed?"

"No, babies don't choose. Their mothers chose for them. But anyone who Changes after childhood either wanted it to happen or didn't have the willpower to prevent it. You can see for yourself that your mother wanted it." Daddy sounded so reasonable.

Felicité's nails dug into her palms. Wildly, she thought that maybe she could convince Daddy, if he ever learned her secret, that she had been born Changed. Then he wouldn't blame her, just as he hadn't blamed Jennie and didn't blame Jose.

But it was impossible. Her parents had bathed her when she was a baby. She'd swum with all her schoolmates, and nothing had happened. She knew that; she'd thought all this through a thousand times before. She had never wanted a Change, but it had happened anyway, the month after she got her first period.

Felicité didn't want Daddy to blame Mother. She didn't want him to blame anybody. She just didn't want him to know. Ever.

"But you're not weak-willed," Daddy went on. "You're the strongest-willed woman in town. Nothing could ever happen to you that you didn't choose, and you'd never choose to become a monster. You have nothing to worry about."

"That was not what I meant," Mother replied. But Daddy drew her into their bedroom and shut the door behind them.

Felicité could hear nothing more. She returned to her room, numb with despair. Daddy was right. When other Norm kids nearing puberty had done their nighttime rituals to prevent the Change, Felicité had never bothered. She'd been so certain she was safe that she'd secretly laughed at the other eleven and twelve-year-olds who fell asleep every night reciting to themselves, "I will not Change. I will fall asleep a Norm, and I will wake up a Norm. I will not Change."

She was a monster, and it was her own fault.

◆ ◆ ◆

Felicité's last day of campaigning was the worst yet. Since she had to campaign for Grandmère as well as for Mother and Daddy, more people than Mrs. Callahan made remarks in her hearing about the "royal family of Las Anclas."

Felicité forced herself to treat the younger voters at Luc's, though she never wanted to see the place again. It helped that Henry accompanied her, dancing with anyone she asked him to as she offered the gold coins of her compliments before her carefully worded reminders about voting. She pretended not to notice that Tommy Horst wasn't there, though he was a regular at Luc's, especially when someone else was paying.

But there were other voters absent, like Indra and Sujata—and Paco, Jennie, Mia, and Ross, all new voting citizens. The only new voter who did show up was Kerry.

Felicité didn't trust her for a heartbeat. And it wasn't just Kerry. Despite the thousand false compliments Felicité forced herself to utter, and her generosity in paying for food and drink and the band, it felt as if everyone who did come ate and drank at her expense while smirking at her, then whispering as soon as her back was turned.

She wished they'd *all* whisper. She overheard the potter's assistant and two friends talking loudly about how "certain people" took it upon themselves to waste the town's money on that useless book of Ross Juarez's.

What could Felicité say? She had to pretend that she didn't hear them. When she walked home at last, failure dragged at every limb.

Her headache was back. So was another day's worth of sweat and dust. Again, she gave her skin a quick swipe with a barely damp washcloth, then scrubbed with a dry towel. The only good thing in the miserable day was skipping her hideous Change.

She fell into bed—and a nightmare of her gills opening up at the dinner table.

It was only a dream, she told herself. But the look of horror and revulsion on Daddy's face felt more real than the sheets under her hands.

Will was silent at breakfast, his expression as sullen as Felicité felt. On their way to school, he said, "I still don't see why Dad got mad at me the other night. I didn't do anything."

"It's the election," she explained. "Everybody is in a bad mood. It's not your fault."

"At least the election is today. I'll be so glad when Dad wins. Then he won't be crabby anymore." He ran off.

Though it was early morning, a line of citizens already waited to vote at the town hall. As she passed, Jennie Riley was waved inside. A spurt of irritation burned through Felicité. All that work, and when it really counted, she was still a mere child, unable to cancel out Jennie's vote with her own. For all Felicité's confident words, she knew that Jennie would vote for a donkey before she'd vote for Daddy.

At the schoolhouse, the kids were running wild, with a harried Sujata trying to marshal them.

"Felicité, help me get these brats in order," Sujata called. "Get Will."

Felicité pretended not to hear. Let Sujata play the boss and see how she enjoyed it.

Will's voice rose above the hubbub. "If you Change it's because you wanted to. You chose to be evil."

Felicité was appalled to hear Will talk like that in public. Summer leaped into the air. Her black hair streaming out behind her, she flew all the way across the schoolyard and slammed into Will, knocking him flat.

Felicité froze. The black-haired girl crouched on top of her brother, pinning him to the ground—it was just like the duel between Elizabeth Crow and Daddy, when the Changed woman had stolen Daddy's rightful position as sheriff.

Will screamed in pain. "My arm!"

Summer pulled back her fist to punch him, but Jose caught her wrist and Sujata grabbed her other arm.

"Stop that right now!" Sujata yelled, yanking Summer off Will. "Can't you see he's hurt?"

Felicité ran to her brother's side. Jennie came charging up, too. They crouched beside Will as he rolled back and forth, sobbing for breath. His hand was curled protectively around his wrist, which was already puffing up into hideous distortion.

Jennie snapped over her shoulder, "Get in the schoolhouse, all of you! Jose, fetch the first aid kit. Felicité, run and tell Dr. Lee." To Summer, Jennie said curtly, "And you can sit on that bench and wait."

Felicité ran. She found Dr. Lee in the infirmary, examining Grace and Sebastien Nguyen's infant son. Felicité's stomach clenched as the curling antennae on the baby's bald head swiveled in her direction.

"My brother broke his arm," she gasped. "Jennie's bringing him now."

Dr. Lee hastily handed the baby back to his parents. "A fine healthy boy."

◆ ◆ ◆

"Daddy carried Will home," Felicité told Henry.

They were sitting at a corner table for two at Jack's. Felicité loved the quiet adult voices murmuring below the sound of the duo playing guitar and singing old ballads. As far as she was concerned, she would never set foot in Luc's again.

Henry's pale skin and bleached hair looked its best by candlelight. He listened, his blue eyes reflecting the flames, as she finished, "And now all Will's friends are there, scribbling on his cast and talking like he fought Voske, a gang of bandits, and fifteen coyote packs."

"Don't forget the sand tiger," Henry said, grinning. He already looked less upset than he had after the catastrophic Ranger ceremony. "You missed Summer getting both ends of Jennie's tongue. She said Summer has to bring Will his work every day until he comes back to school. And she gets to write his work on his slate for him until the cast comes off. And if she injures anyone else, she gets kicked out of town."

"I'm surprised she stayed and took it."

"She didn't," Henry said. "Summer got up and announced, 'Fine. I'll go and Ross will go with me.'"

Good riddance, Felicité thought. "What did Jennie say to that?"

"She said, 'Ross isn't going anywhere. This is his home now.' Summer glared like she was going to try to break Jennie's arm. I was all ready to stop the fight, then Jose said, 'We don't want bullies in Las Anclas.' And Summer turned and walked—"

The saloon doors slammed open. Summer stood in a dramatic pose, skinny arms outstretched between the doors, feet planted wide, her scrawny body in baggy jeans and rumpled top silhouetted against the ruddy light of sunset. Her long black hair half-obscured her ragged travel pack hooked over one shoulder.

Jack looked at her over the tray of glasses he held. "Can I help you?"

Summer marched past him to the bar, the doors slamming shut behind her. She dumped her ragtag pack onto a chair, grabbed a mug of beer from a man just lifting it to his lips, and brought it to her own mouth.

Before she could drink a drop, Jack's hand reached down from behind her bony shoulder and nipped the mug away. As she gaped in surprise, he said, "Come back in four years. Can I get you some lemonade?"

He returned the mug to its owner and handed Summer a glass of lemonade without waiting for a response. She half-pushed the glass away, then seemed to change her mind and tasted it. Her scowl turned to surprise, and she took a bigger gulp. Then, as if to hide that she liked it, she turned around and leaned against the bar, glaring at the musicians. By the time the song was finished, so was the lemonade.

"No one can dance to that," Summer said scornfully. To Jack, she said, "Get me a room. I'm staying here now."

The entire saloon was watching in dead silence.

"Aren't you Ross's guest?" Jack asked.

"Not anymore."

Jack looked startled, then his expression smoothed out. "No, I'm sure you still are. Anyway, I can't give you a room. They're for adults. Go back to Dr. Lee. He'll have kept your room for you. I promise."

Summer stared at him, then darted a glance toward the customer beside her. He protectively clutched at his mug. With a final glare, Summer slung her pack behind her and stalked out.

"Good riddance," Henry said, laughing. "Though I have to say, school hasn't been nearly as boring since she showed up. I just hope she doesn't get herself kicked out before I get to graduate." His smile lessened, as if he was remembering the graduation party that was supposed to celebrate not only their graduation, but his appointment to the Rangers.

Felicité took Henry's hand. It was so unfair! Henry simply hadn't had enough time to develop the discipline that Paco had been practicing his whole life under his mother's direction.

Felicité had had such a beautiful dream: graduation, her birthday, Henry a Ranger, and they'd both be adults. And while Felicité gained the trust of the town, Henry would impress Daddy with his fighting prowess. Henry would look so good in Ranger night blacks. In a few years, he could take Julio's place as the head of the Rangers and Felicité could run for council. And years after that, when Daddy and Mother were ready to retire, they could be mayor and defense chief.

Nothing could ruin such a perfect plan. She had to convince Daddy that he was wrong about Henry.

"Finished?" Felicité leaned forward to whisper, "Let's go back to my room."

Henry dropped his fork on his half-eaten apple crumble.

◆ ◆ ◆

The moment they walked in, Felicité knew something was wrong. Grandmère was nowhere to be seen, and her parents sat silently on the satin couch.

Felicité turned to Henry. "I hate to do this, but my headache is coming back. Can we see each other tomorrow?"

Henry glanced past her at her family, and grinned as he backed away. "Feel better. We can celebrate the election results tomorrow."

Felicité shut the door behind him. Surely it was too early for any results? "Mother? Daddy?"

"The last vote was cast two hours ago," Mother said. "The results will be publicly announced once they inform the candidates. But you should know that I am still mayor, Grandmère is on the council—"

"And I am a private citizen again," said Daddy.

Though Felicité had spent the day dreading that news, it still came as a shock. "That's impossible! Somebody cheated. Who counted the ballots?"

"Judge Vardam headed the committee," Mother said. "There was no cheating."

"It was a landslide." Daddy slapped his hands to his knees, then got up. "So it's time to let it go. It's not like I don't have plenty to do. I've already spoken to Julio. Being captain of the Rangers didn't suit him as much as he expected. Too much responsibility, too little action. He was happy to step aside. I'll take this opportunity to overhaul our training."

Felicité had thought that if he lost he'd be furious. But as he leaned down to kiss Mother, he seemed in a better mood than when he'd been waiting for the results.

"Aren't you mad that a fourteen-year-old vagrant turned the town against you?" Felicité asked.

"Oh, if people hadn't already had questions, they wouldn't have listened," Daddy said. "That girl may have been responsible for the landslide, but I don't think she was responsible for the loss itself. Let Horst boil in my boots for a while, and see how he likes it. When I think that he'll soon be listening to Harry Tranh's interminable stories about how much better his grandfather was as Defense Chief in his day, and Julia Ford's uninformed opinions about weaponry, I want to send him a commiseration letter."

"And it's only one term," Mother added. "We shall see how peaceful things are. If not, the town will learn who can defend it."

Felicité looked from Mother to Daddy, realizing that they were certain it would not be peaceful at all.

·14·
BECKY

EVER SINCE THE MISERABLE day Henry wasn't picked for the Rangers, Becky had stayed away from home as much as she dared.

She divided her time between Brisa's home, her apprenticeship, and school. At the surgery, she went early and stayed late, finding tasks to do that would kill time. As she dusted and reorganized the cabinets, she couldn't help being glad that she was cleaning shelves rather than cleaning wounds.

She was a failure as well as a coward.

Dr. Lee kept watching her with concern and thoughtfulness, as if he was trying to make a diagnosis. Becky always felt sick with anticipation when she saw that look aimed at her instead of a patient.

"Is everything all right, Becky?" Dr. Lee asked.

She hated that question. He was so nice, but that only made it worse. She didn't deserve his kindness. Her stupidity and cowardice was her own fault.

"Of course," she replied, as brightly as she could. "See, I've steeped the kelp water, and ground fresh willow bark…"

Gently, he asked, "Is anything wrong at home?"

"It's fine. I'm done with my work, Dr. Lee. Good night!" She hung up her apron, stuffed her feet into her shoes, and ran.

She was lucky Mom was out. Becky slunk into her room without going near the kitchen. She left the lamp unlit, in case her mother came back and saw it. Becky hoped Mom was doing a fitting. Getting clothing orders might put her in a better mood.

She crawled into bed and curled up tight. It eased the ache when your stomach was empty. Rain began to patter against the window, then gradually increased to a downpour. The drumming soothed her to sleep.

Becky woke early. She stayed in her room until all noise ceased in the hallway. Henry had already slammed out an hour ago. Becky slipped from her room, hoping her mother had gone to the dress shop.

She walked into the kitchen. Silence. She reached for the bread box.

"There you are. I thought you'd come sneaking out."

Becky recoiled. Her mother stood in the hall, her face and body tight with anger.

"And look at that. Here you are, always thinking of yourself first. You get your filthy mitts off that bread box, and think about how much trouble you've caused this entire family."

Becky backed away.

Her mother advanced, her face mottled red. "You knew you had to help Henry with his chores so he could get to Ranger training on time. Instead, you ran off with your monster girlfriend and left everything to Henry and me. Because of *you*, Henry is not on the Rangers. And he's not earning scrip to keep this household afloat. And now you come sneaking in here to gobble down bread that you didn't bake or pay for. Get out of here."

Her mother raised her hand to strike. Becky hunched her head into her shoulders and dodged around the table. A hard slap stung her shoulder blade as her mother screamed, "You stop right now! Come back here!"

Becky staggered under the blow, jumped over a fallen chair and ran outside. She didn't stop running until she reached the stable, where she stopped, a hand pressed to the stitch in her side. Her stomach heaved, and she gulped air. She mustn't throw up. She hadn't eaten anything since she'd shared Brisa's lunch the day before. Throwing up on an empty stomach was so much worse.

The bell clanged out the time. She pushed away from the wall and headed toward the schoolhouse. Everywhere people busily weeded their gardens, their feet sinking into the new mud. Ordinarily Becky stopped to say hello to every cat and dog she met, for she knew everyone's pets, but now everything made her eyes prickle. Happy voices, the smells of food drifting out doorways as people left for work or school, even birdsong. It all made her feel worse.

She was the last one into the schoolhouse, but at least she wasn't late. Nobody gave her a glance as she slipped into her place beside Brisa.

"What happened?" Brisa whispered as Jennie passed out slates. "Was it horrible?"

"Worse than horrible," Becky breathed. "Mom is still mad at me about the Rangers."

"But it's not *your* fault Henry messed up his own chances," Brisa whispered indignantly.

"Yes, it is," Becky started to say, but her throat closed up.

Brisa rummaged in her pockets, and removed a plump brown bun wrapped in a cloth. She thrust it at Becky. "Fresh baked. I have two more in my lunch box. Eat up, Beck."

Becky pretended to nibble, but she felt much too sick to eat. Brisa was so good to her, so kind. Becky couldn't even thank her, or her voice would crack and everyone would stare at her. She slid the bun into her desk and tried to sink into the history lesson, but all she could hear was her mother screaming, *"It's all your fault."*

When Jennie dismissed the school for recess, Becky was still gulping air, trying to keep her throat from closing up. She knew that she'd start sobbing if she looked at Brisa's face, and saw her loving concern.

Becky jumped up. The world twisted weirdly. Off-balance, she grabbed onto the nearest chair for support.

Her hand came down on the battered leather jacket draped over Summer's chair.

The classroom vanished, and Becky found herself crawling over a cold stone floor in the back of an old, dusty building, the air hot and close. Fear and misery wrung through her at what she must do, but she had no choice. In the distance, voices rose and fell in a Latin chant. She crept toward the donations box, biting her lip from guilt. It was wrong to steal, and especially wrong to steal from a church.

At least Mom can't see me sinning.

Her small brown hand reached into the donation box, moving slowly to keep the coins from clinking against each other. She pulled out her hand…

Becky opened her eyes. She lay flat on her back. In the classroom. Cold air was blowing in from the door. Faces stared down at her: Jennie. Brisa. Sujata.

"Becky?" Jennie lifted a heavy leather jacket off her, and laid it over a chair. "You fainted. Are you sick?"

"I think she didn't eat breakfast." Brisa's voice rang high and sharp. It echoed in Becky's ears. "I don't think she even got any dinner!"

Jennie's look of concern mixed with suspicion reminded Becky of Dr. Lee. "Becky, as soon as you can stand, I want you to go straight to the surgery."

Becky started to shake her head, but Brisa said, "I'll take her."

"Thanks, Brisa." Jennie swung to her feet and backed away. "All right, everyone, let's give her some air."

Brisa took hold of Becky's hands—her own pale, freckled hands—and helped her sit up. "Come on. Lean against me."

As they walked to the surgery, Becky leaning against Brisa's warm side, she kept thinking, *What's happening to me? What was that?*

She'd treated people who had fainted from hunger or heat or exhaustion. But they always said that right before it happened their vision got blurry or the dark started closing in or they felt really sick, and the next thing they knew they were on the floor. She'd never heard anyone say, "I had an incredibly vivid dream and then I passed out."

At the surgery, Dr. Lee made her lie down on the examination table while he took her pulse.

"She didn't get any dinner last night!" Brisa burst out. "I could tell you—"

"Brisa," Becky said warningly. "I *skipped* dinner last night. And I overslept this morning and forgot to eat breakfast."

Brisa scowled. Becky knew she wanted to blurt out everything to Dr. Lee, but Becky had made her promise not to. Becky could see her struggling to keep that promise, and Becky was glad that Brisa didn't know one-tenth of what life was like at home.

"I'm fine," Becky said.

Dr. Lee frowned. "Becky. You know how important it is to eat regularly. You're still growing. I'll get you some breakfast."

As soon as he went out, Becky sat up and grabbed Brisa's hand. "There's nothing wrong with me. I guess I didn't get enough sleep last night, so I fell asleep on my feet. I even dreamed! The next thing I knew, I was on the floor."

Brisa looked puzzled. "What did you dream about?"

"It was really vivid — the most real-feeling dream I've ever had. I crawled into a church I've never seen before, and stole from the collection box. And the weirdest thing was, I was thinking about my mom, only it wasn't my mom at all! I was a little girl, but not me as a little girl. My skin was brown."

"Like Summer's?" Brisa asked. She stuck a ribbon in her mouth and chewed on it, an old habit she only did when she was thinking hard. "You know...you pulled her jacket on top of you when you fell."

"I was hanging onto it before I started dreaming."

Brisa's eyes narrowed. "Are you sure it was a dream?"

"What else could it be? I've always had these ugly freckles, and I've never seen that church. And I've never stolen anything in my life!"

Brisa patted Becky's hands. "No, no, that wasn't what I meant. I think..."

Before she could finish, Dr. Lee came back in with a plate of steaming biscuits spread with butter and honey. "Go sit out on the porch in the fresh air, and eat every bite. Then, and only if you feel up to it, you can go back to school."

"Thank you." Becky gritted her teeth at the sound of her tiny mouse-voice. Her hands shook as she reached for the plate. Brisa snatched it, chewing the ribbon impatiently.

Brisa managed to stay quiet until they sat on the porch bench. Then she spat out the ribbon, held up the plate, and said in a portentous voice, "Beck. I want you to touch this plate."

"Well, of course." Becky reached for a biscuit.

"No!" Brisa exclaimed, yanking the plate away. "You might faint again! Let me get ready to catch you." She slid her arm around Becky's shoulders.

Becky leaned up against her. She wondered vaguely what weird idea Brisa had gotten, but she couldn't bring herself to care. It felt so safe, so warm, so deliciously good to rest in her arms.

Brisa dumped the biscuits into her lap. "Now touch the plate."

Confused, Becky touched it with a fingertip.

"Hmm," Brisa said after a moment. "Try laying your whole palm on it."

Becky had no idea what had gotten into her girlfriend, but she obediently pressed her hand into the plate —

— and she was in the Lees' kitchen, putting a biscuit down on the plate. She had a man's hand! Mewing cats wove in and out around her ankles. She picked up the plate and took a step toward the door…

The world reeled sharply. Becky was back on the surgery porch, her head resting on Brisa's shoulder. She sucked in a breath.

Brisa clutched at her. "Becky! Becky!"

"I'm…" Becky trailed off. "I feel so strange."

"Did you dream again?" Brisa demanded eagerly.

"Yes! I had a man's hand this time. I put the biscuit…that was Dr. Lee's hand! Brisa, for a moment, I was Dr. Lee!"

Brisa had her lips pressed firmly together. She took hold of Becky's hands. "Shut your eyes. What do you see?"

Becky obeyed. All she saw was the reddish light filtering through her eyelids. "Nothing."

"And I was thinking of something so lovely." Brisa gave a wistful sigh. "I was remembering our first kiss. I thought you'd like to see yourself the way you look to me."

"Am I seeing other people's memories?" It was the only thing that made sense, but it was hard to believe.

Brisa grinned. "Congratulations, Beck. You've Changed."

"I can't have," Becky protested. "I'm much too old. Girls Change when they're twelve or thirteen."

"Girls Change when they start getting their periods," Brisa corrected her.

Becky wanted to argue, but Brisa was right. Becky's hormones had been just as slow as the rest of her: she'd only gotten her period that year.

Brisa went on, "And *this* is your Change. You're seeing

memories from stuff other people have touched." She tapped the plate. "Happy Change day!" She leaned in to kiss Becky.

For the first time, Becky pulled away instead of kissing Brisa back. What would her mother say? It was hard to imagine life at her house getting any worse, but this would do it. Dread knotted up her insides. Her mother would rather have Becky steal money from a church than be Changed.

Brisa's smile faded. "Becky? Maybe you better eat these biscuits. You just went really pale."

Becky shook her head. "I can't go home. Not like this."

"Sure you can. Just don't tell your mom." Brisa waved a biscuit at her. "Come on. Just one bite."

Becky's stomach was churning too much for her to even look at food. She laid her hands flat on the bench, gulping for air—and once again images flooded in: she was in the carpenter's shop, sawing wood as someone nearby sang a folk song. She inhaled the smell of fresh wood chips. Thunder rumbled outside.

Becky jerked her hands up. "I can't go around like this! I...I need gloves, or something."

"We can get gloves," Brisa said softly, rubbing Becky's shoulders. "Beck, you can handle this. I'll help you."

"I know that." Becky's voice wobbled. "But..."

"I know your family is prejudiced, but being Changed is cool. I love being Changed. Not to brag, but remember, I used my Change to help Jennie blow up Voske's ammo dump. We saved the town! And *my* family loves you. Mom and Dad will want to throw you a Change party."

"I can't have a party!" Becky exclaimed. "I can't tell anybody! Mom will hate me worse than ever!"

"So come live with me," Brisa said, rocking her. "Then it won't matter what she thinks."

"I *can't*." Becky pulled away just far enough to look into Brisa's face. "This is my family. I can't just walk away from them. And you don't have any room. I can't do that to *your* family."

Brisa huffed, blowing her pigtail ribbons so they fluttered and danced. "Nobody will care. They always say one more person won't make a difference. Come on, Beck, stop saying 'I can't.'"

Becky pulled away more. "I can't. I just can't!"

"Okay, fine." Brisa let go of Becky and stood up. The biscuits tumbled out of her lap, and she dove after them. But instead of scooping them up, she carefully picked them up, one by one.

Becky could see how hard Brisa was trying not to be hurt. It made her feel guilty, as well as sick and terrified. How could Becky yell at someone who was doing so much to help her?

"Let's go back to school," Brisa said to the dusty floorboards.

Becky started up, then sat back down. Three field workers were approaching the surgery. Two held the drooping third between them.

The man on the right said, "He's got bad heat cramps. Is the doctor busy?"

Becky stared at the sick man in the middle, his face twisted in pain, and his arms clutched over his stomach. Just like the man who'd been carried into the field hospital during the battle, with blood oozing out from between his fingers. Becky should stick around in case Dr. Lee needed her, but she couldn't face it.

"He's inside. I have to get to school." She turned and fled. Brisa ran silently beside her.

At the schoolyard, Becky was shocked to see that recess was still going on. It felt as if days has passed since Becky had laid her hand on Summer's jacket. If Becky could sense memories by touching objects, then Ross's sister had been that little girl who had stolen money from a church.

Summer sat alone on the fence, munching an apple. She was only fourteen, and the hand Becky had seen had been tiny. How long had Summer been a thief?

Becky didn't like that train of thought. It might have just been that one time. And the little girl had felt frightened and guilty. Maybe someone had bullied her into doing it. People were suspicious of Summer anyway, the same way they'd once been suspicious of Ross. And Ross had saved them all.

Becky decided not to mention the stealing. She knew too well what it felt like to be blamed no matter what she did.

When she and Brisa went inside, Jennie set down a stack of slates and came up to her. "Are you all right? You're still so pale."

"You can tell her, Beck. She can keep a secret." Brisa nudged Becky.

Becky bit her lip. Brisa meant well, but she'd just given away that there was a secret to keep. But when she looked up at Jennie's calm dark eyes, she knew that Brisa was right.

"I can tell you what happened," Becky said. "But it's important to me that you keep it to yourself."

Jennie held up her hand as if she was swearing a vow. "I promise."

Becky drew a breath. It was easier to explain now that she understood it herself. "When I touched Summer's jacket, I saw a memory that I'm pretty sure is hers. She was a little girl in a church." She gave Brisa a warning glance, then went on, "Then when I touched a plate at the surgery, I was Dr. Lee for a second. That is, I saw his hand as if it was mine. I can see memories when I touch things. And I can't make it stop."

Jennie reached into her desk. "Here. Try these."

"Your Ranger gloves!" Brisa exclaimed.

Jennie's hands clenched briefly, then relaxed. "I don't need them anymore."

Becky slid on the gloves. They were much too big—

—they fit her like a second skin. She was on the ground, wrestling someone bigger than her. Heat radiated from his body. He twisted her arm painfully behind her back, but she didn't mind. She was having fun. She laughed as she whipped her elbow toward Indra's face...

Becky swayed. Shut her eyes hard. Opened them. Breathed. She was still standing, with Brisa's arm around her waist. "It happened again. But I didn't faint." She flexed her gloved hands. "And it stopped. Maybe it only happens the first time I touch something with my palms, and it doesn't last."

"Good. Keep the gloves. You can alter them to fit your hands." Jennie peered at Becky's face. "Did Dr. Lee give you anything to eat?"

"Yeah, but I dropped it. We can share my lunch." Brisa shot Becky an anxious look.

Becky's belly twisted with guilt again. She quickly answered the real question. "Thanks, Brisa. I don't know what I'd..."

Brisa kissed her. "Don't apologize. Just be Becky, the girl I love."

When school got out, Brisa instantly invited Becky to her house. But Becky knew she had to go home.

She could hear her mother's voice from the street corner outside the house. "Henry, this was your chance to do something for this family. How long do you think Felicité Wolfe is going to keep dating someone her father threw out of the Rangers? So don't give me that backchat about not doing chores. You're cooking tonight. Get busy."

Becky stopped short. The shivering began at the back of her neck, and shuddered down into her belly. *Stop it,* she scolded herself. She couldn't stand there all night.

She forced her knees to unlock. One step, then another. She pulled the door open. It creaked.

Her mother's angry scowl shifted from Henry to Becky. "Where have *you* been? Why are you wearing those ridiculous gloves? Take them off and get busy. The laundry isn't going to do itself."

Becky pulled the gloves off. She'd alter them later, in the privacy of her room.

She picked up the laundry basket with her fingertips. She'd do the laundry, but she'd be very careful not to touch any of her mother's clothing with her palms. Becky didn't want any more of Mom in her head.

·15·
MIA

TONIGHT WAS MIA'S NIGHT with Ross.

She had promised herself that she was going to stop being squeamish, squirmy, and stupid. She really liked Ross. She really liked kissing Ross. And she really, *really* liked it when he pressed close to her and his wonderful strong hands would caress her so gently. Not just her face and her hair and her arms and her back and her waist, but when he slipped his hand under her shirt...

Her entire body burned so hot, she was certain that she'd turned bright red. Anyone who saw her would know exactly what she was imagining.

"Stop that," she said aloud. Then she cast a frantic gaze at her open window in case anyone had heard and instantly knew what she was talking about.

But they *wouldn't* know. She had to stop imagining the worst just because sex was something new, something that had nothing to do with math or science. She always knew where she was with machines. But with people?

"There is no mathematical formula!" Mia announced, then realized that she'd spoken aloud. Again.

She ran to her window and peered out. No crowd stood out there pointing and laughing. All she saw were a couple of birds twittering as they pecked for seeds.

It was time to be a grownup. She knew what she wanted, and she was going to have it.

"But first I need a—"

Bed. She couldn't bring herself to say *that* out loud.

Fighting another hot tide, she scowled at the two engines on her old, sagging camp bed. These were precious engines. One belonged to a tractor, and the other to a car. The parts she had so carefully brought out of the ruined city didn't fit either of them. That had been disappointing, but reasonable. Of course there were different kinds of car engines, just as tractor and car engines differed.

She simply needed more car parts.

"You're dithering," she muttered.

Bed. Engines. Should she move them off the bed? But it was so narrow. Could two people fit onto it, even if it were engine-free?

Her quick calculation of the width of the bed compared to the combined width of Mia and Ross told her it would be a tight fit. The person on the inside would be squished against the wall and the person on the outside might fall off.

The reasonable solution would be to make a bed on the floor. She was used to sleeping on the floor anyway. Why not make it nice? Ross would be coming over to the surgery for dinner as usual, and she could maybe figure out what to say between then and when they went to her cottage. If he didn't want to do anything, they could go somewhere else, anywhere else, so he wouldn't have to see the bed they wouldn't be using.

So *she* wouldn't have to see the bed.

Mia hauled out fresh sheets and blankets, putting the latter down first, for softness. She laid a sheet over that, then the nice coverlet her aunt had made her, which had been folded in a box ever since so she wouldn't spill oil on it. She spread it smoothly over the bed, picked up her pillow, then scowled again. Two people needed two pillows.

She ran to the surgery, peeked in to make certain Summer was nowhere around, and was immensely relieved to see no one at all. Mia darted in, snatched the last pillow from the storage closet, hid it under the sweater she'd brought, and scurried back to the cottage. Then she stood with it, wondering which end to put the pillows at. It was so arbitrary once you thought about it.

Mia forced herself not to get sucked into worrying about that. She had two pillows, and they'd go under the window. Which would be shut, with the curtain drawn.

With the bed taken care of, she bathed at the surgery, then put on her cleanest shirt and overalls.

The night started out well, First, Summer wasn't there. Mia watched Ross warily enter the kitchen, then relax when he saw the empty chair.

Nobody commented on Summer's absence. Dad dished up the steamed fish Mia had asked for, Ross's favorite noodles, tender snap beans, and for dessert, some of Jack's apple crumble that Mia had fetched herself.

When they left for the cottage, Mia reached for Ross's hand, her heart pounding in her ears like the throb of a generator. It seemed impossible that he couldn't hear it. But he simply closed his fingers into hers. Their hands swung between them, catching her attention. Now her hand felt too heavy. Her grip first felt too hard, then too soft. And how *was* she supposed to swing her hand, anyway?

"Want to get a head start on the Nguyen generator overhaul?" Ross asked.

Mia gulped.

Be an adult. Make your own formula!

"I thought we could...be together?" It came out in a squeak.

Even in the dim light from the surgery windows she could see his bewildered expression. "Aren't we?"

"*Together* together," she said. "You and me."

"Well, here we are." He squeezed her hand as started into the junkyard.

"What I mean is..." She remembered they were still technically in public, and whispered, "We could...you know."

"Oh. Oh!" His smile flared bright, then he slid his hands up her arms to cup her face. "Is that what you want?"

With his warm hands on her cheeks and his dark eyes looking into hers, what she wanted was to stay like that forever.

But she'd promised.

Mia couldn't speak, but she nodded hard. It felt like her glasses bounced on her nose. Had her glasses bounced? Did she look as weird as she felt?

"Great!" Ross sounded enthusiastic...or did he? Was he only

trying to sound enthusiastic? Did he really want to? Did he want to…with *her?*

But when he opened the door and saw the bed on the floor, his expression reminded her of how he'd looked when she'd given him his gauntlet, his cudgel, and his crossbow: like he was seeing not only what she'd given him, but all the work she'd put into it and how she'd felt when she was making it. Like he was seeing *her.*

"This is great, Mia," he said at last. "But I'm not very good about sleeping indoors. With someone."

So he's already been with Jennie.

Of course he had. Jennie was his girlfriend, too. And Jennie was experienced. Mia had half-expected it all along. And now she knew. It felt weird. But everything about sex felt weird.

Well, she was going to change that.

Remembering what Ross had actually said, she hurriedly pointed out, "Well, we won't be *sleeping.*" Then, before he could say anything else, she kicked off her shoes, prompting him to kick off his, and tugged him down to the floor-bed.

They started kissing. That was something she could do right, and she loved the way Ross kissed her back. She caressed his shoulders, and arms, as his hands closed around her. Oh, yes. This felt good.

Kisses and hands first, she thought hazily. *This subset of my mathematical equation has been proved.*

A fizzy warm feeling started up from her toes and filled her body, making her heart and lungs work faster. She added that to the building formula as Ross's breathing became as unsteady as hers.

Step two, she thought. *Remove clothing.*

She reached for the top button of Ross's shirt. He responded by unhooking one of her overall straps.

It's working, she exulted, *it's working! What was I worried about? This is easy!*

Knock knock!

Mia shot upright, her heart pounding in a completely different way.

Ross murmured, "Were you expecting anyone?"

"No," she whispered.

KNOCK KNOCK! The rap on her door became more insistent.

"Mia? Are you in there? I can see a light on!" It was Tommy Horst.

"Don't come in!" Mia yelled wildly, adding, "Explosives!"

She shot to her feet. Tommy would laugh at her if he saw what she was doing: stupid little misfit Mia, thinking she could have sex like a regular person!

Ross scrambled up, looking confused. Mia waved him toward the bed, then away from it. The bed! She had to hide it.

"I need to talk to you," Tommy called. "Can I come in?"

Frantic, Mia scooped up her carefully made bed and flung it behind her soldering setup. Too late, she remembered the half-empty canister of water she kept back there for dunking hot tools. Rusty, nasty-smelling water. Then she remembered to check herself. One overall strap was undone and flapping, and her shirt was pulled out. As her shaky fingers fumbled with hooks and buttons, she glanced at Ross. He sank down on to the work bench, shaking with silent laughter.

How could he laugh? This was the least funny experience of Mia's life.

Giving her overalls a last yank, she opened the door.

Tommy pushed his way in. "What explosives? Where are they?"

Ross's shirt was pulled out and partly unbuttoned, and he'd picked up a wrench even though there was nothing on the work table that you could use a wrench on. If Tommy looked at Ross, he'd have to know what they'd been doing.

Mia edged in front of Ross, trying to block Tommy's view. "What do you want?"

"Dad sent me. Now that he's defense chief, he needs to talk to you," Tommy went on in an important voice. "About new weapon designs. Like the six-shooter crossbows Mr. Preston's been mounting on the sentry walk. But *better!*"

"That's not actually my design. It was from Ross's book—" Mia came to an awkward halt. She didn't want to make Tommy think of Ross.

"Well, you're the one who made it. Anyway, he sent me to

invite you over to the forge to talk to him. Hey, are the explosives new?" Tommy added hopefully. "C'mon, you can show *me*."

"Okay, I'm coming," Mia said glumly. She'd obviously ruined her chance with Ross, so she might as well go.

Ross gave her a look that she couldn't interpret. Was he disappointed? Relieved? Something else entirely? Then he shrugged and gestured with his useless wrench. "Sure, Mia. I'll finish up here."

As she followed Tommy out into the darkness, she thought, *Maybe I* should *stick to machines. They're much easier than people.*

♦ ♦ ♦

Mia was still brooding over her sex failure as she trudged to Luc's the next morning.

Jennie would have known exactly what to do if someone banged on her door when she was trying to have sex. Jennie would never panic and hurl her best bedding into rusty soldering water. Why couldn't Mia be more like her?

Jennie had said some people never wanted to have sex at all. Dad had told her the same thing, and added that there was nothing wrong with that. Mia *wished* she didn't want to. That would make everything so much simpler. Before she'd met Ross, she'd thought maybe she was that kind of person, but that hadn't felt right either.

When it came to sex — and love and relationships and people — it always seemed like she was doing it wrong. It was like sparring. Everyone said to relax and stop thinking, but how could she relax when she couldn't stop thinking?

Ross was the only person she'd ever met who found people and feelings as hard and confusing as she did. But last night had proved how much he'd learned and changed, while Mia had stayed exactly the same.

For the millionth time, Mr. Preston's words echoed in her mind: *You don't understand anything unless it's made out of metal. You may officially be an adult, but you've never grown up and as far as I can tell, you never will.*

She was so depressed by the time she reached Luc's, she didn't even expect to enjoy fixing his broken compressor. But once she started, she got lost in her work. She'd sneezed three times before she registered that the tickle in her nose and singed smell wasn't coming from Luc's kitchen.

She raised her head, idly wondering whose breakfast was ruined, but the smell carried on the breeze was of burning wood, not burning food.

Instantly alert, Mia dropped her tools and looked around. Ribbons of white smoke rose lazily from the old harvest barn where they'd thrown the secret party for Kerry. As Mia opened her mouth to shout, a boy yelled, "Fire! Fire!"

A shovel leaned against the wall. She grabbed it and ran.

Peter Chang stumbled out of the barn, coughing. He smelled like smoke, soot, and stale beer. Mia slapped out a smoldering patch on his jacket, then checked for injuries and signs of smoke inhalation. He seemed unhurt.

In the minute it had taken her to do that, the thin streamers of smoke had become billows, and she could hear the greedy crackle of the spreading fire. Through the open door of the barn, she could see nothing but a solid curtain of white smoke.

Peter started to run back inside. Mia grabbed him by the back of the jacket. "Don't go back in there!"

Peter tried to free himself. "Hans is in the loft!"

A thin voice was barely audible over the fire's roar. "Help! Help!"

"The fire started right by the ladder," Peter gasped. "I jumped over the flames but I guess Hans didn't. I have to go back and get him."

Mia held him tighter as he struggled. "With smoke that thick, you'll pass out before you get five steps inside. Then someone will have to rescue *you*. You can't hold your breath long enough to run the length of the barn, climb the ladder, climb down—"

Footsteps announced the arrival of a crowd. Henry was at the forefront, with a bucket dangling from his elbow and one of Luc's water pitchers in his hand. "Form a bucket brigade!"

"Good idea," said Luc, who had run up with more buckets.

"I have five buckets in my shop," Mr. Nguyen shouted. "I'll get them."

"Hans is trapped in the loft!" Mia exclaimed.

Henry dropped the pitcher. It shattered at his feet. "What was he doing in there?"

"Doesn't matter right now." Luc raised his voice. "Sebastien! Bring ladders!"

"I don't have any," Mr. Nguyen called. "The closest one is at the south forge. I'll go get it!"

Henry turned to Peter. "Were you in there? What were you doing?"

"Nothing!" Peter said. Mia let him go, since he'd stopped struggling. He grabbed at Luc's arm. "We have to get Hans out!"

At the rate the fire was spreading, they'd never get to the south forge and back before Hans suffocated. Mia darted around to the side of the barn. Maybe Hans could escape through the trap door they used to pitch hay from the loft. But once she saw it, she realized why he hadn't already. It was twenty-five feet up and latched from the outside.

Mia ran to the front again. The wind whipped into the barn, briefly blowing aside the curtain of smoke. She caught a horrifying glimpse of the entire front of the loft aflame. The ladder lay in smoking ruins on the floor.

"Where is he?" Alfonso Medina came tearing up, barefoot and out of breath.

Peter pointed toward the loft. "Up there!"

Alfonso flexed his fingers and toes, then leaped onto the side of the barn. His gecko pads stuck tight as he scurried straight up the wall to the trapdoor. He worked the rusty bolt to the side, then flung the trapdoor open. Mia held her breath as he vanished into the smoky darkness.

He reappeared with Hans clinging to his back. Alfonso eased out the trapdoor, spreading his fingers and toes wide. Mia gasped as he slid an inch or two, weighted down by Hans. He froze for a horrible moment, hanging twenty feet above the ground. Then, inching one hand and foot at a time, he began to descend again. Though a crowd had gathered with hands upraised to catch them both, everyone was so silent that Mia could hear the popping sound of Alfonso's pads pulling off the wall each time he moved.

Henry was the first to catch them and help lower them down.

Hans collapsed to the ground, coughing, as townspeople moved to check him and thank Alfonso.

Sheriff Crow had arrived at some point while Mia had been watching the rescue. She bent briefly over Hans, then turned to Alfonso. "That was very brave."

"Town hero!" Henry said loudly as he clapped Alfonso on the back. "How's it feel?"

Alfonso blushed, ducking his head until nothing was visible but smooth black hair. "Anyone would have done it."

Sheriff Crow raised her voice. "Form a line! Pass the buckets along! If you're not working, get away from the barn!"

Alfonso turned away, obviously glad to lose himself in the crowd. Mia moved to join the bucket brigade. In the distance, the bell tolled the patterns for Fire and Southwest.

A girl flew through the air and landed beside her. A strand of black hair whipped into Mia's face as Summer made a grab for Grandpa Chen's bucket. "Give me that. I'll jump up and pour it right on the flames."

He yanked it back. "Get in line!"

"I can use my power," Summer insisted. "You need somebody up high. Just give me the bucket."

Grandpa Chen pushed her toward the back of the line. "You do as you're told."

Summer backed away. "You can't tell me what to do. If you don't want me to help, fine. I won't."

Peter's voice rose above the hubbub. "We didn't do anything! A bale of hay just burst into flames!"

As Mia passed along a heavy bucket, she saw Sheriff Crow talking to Peter and Hans.

"It was like someone dropped a match through the hole in the roof," Hans said. "We both looked up, but no one was there."

Grandpa Chen pointed a bony, accusing finger at the departing Summer. "*She* just said she could jump onto the roof."

"Are there any witnesses?" Sheriff Crow called. "Who was the first on the scene?"

Mia automatically raised her hand, then hurriedly grabbed the bucket Faviola was trying to pass her. "I was, I think. I mean, I was."

"I think the bucket brigade can function without you." The sheriff beckoned her closer. "Tell me what you saw."

Mia told her story, concluding with, "I didn't see anyone on the roof. But there was at least a one minute delay between when I first smelled smoke and when I got here. And the smoke had to have time to travel to me. So that would be..." She calculated. "...probably three and a half minutes."

Sheriff Crow turned to the boys. "What were you two doing for three and a half minutes?"

"Trying to put out the fire," Hans said defensively. "I tried to smother it, and Peter, uh, he tried to smother it, too."

"Yeah," Peter said.

Mia eyed the two nervous boys. If even she could tell that Peter hadn't tried to smother it, Sheriff Crow surely could, too. The sheriff turned her head deliberately, giving the boys a good look at her skull face and lashless yellow eye.

Ominously, she said, "What were you doing in the loft in the first place?" Before they could reply, she added, "And your explanation had better include why you both stink of stale beer. And why Peter also stinks of whiskey."

"Uh...uh...We stole—" Hans muttered.

Peter cut in. "Borrowed! We borrowed some of Grandma Thakrar's beer."

"It was left over from the campaign. No one was using it."

Sheriff Crow's snake eye didn't blink. "So you were hiding in the loft, getting drunk on stolen beer, when a bale of hay burst into flames. Are you sure you didn't do anything to set it on fire?"

"No!" both boys exclaimed.

"And how exactly did Peter try to put out the fire?"

Peter hung his head. "I threw the whiskey on it. It's liquid!"

Mia barely stopped herself from suggesting that he get extra coaching in chemistry.

Sheriff Crow glanced over the boys' heads at the barn. The bucket brigade had reduced the fire enough to prevent it from spreading, but the barn would be a ruin.

Mrs. Garcia spoke up from the end of the bucket line. "Someone used their Change power to set the fire. Rico Salazar can do that."

"So can Grandma Wolfe," Luc called from the front. "Are you going to blame her?"

Mia did not want an argument breaking out between Norms and Changed. She said, "Anyone can set a fire from a distance. Someone could have planted a fuse. Someone could have left two different chemicals that slowly heat up when they're mixed together. Someone could have—" Everybody was staring at her. "Well, there's lots of ways it could be done. It doesn't have to be a Change power. I could have done it. I didn't! But I could have."

Sheriff Crow turned to Mia. "You know a lot about fires. Once this is out, could you take a look at it and see if you can figure out how it started?"

"Sure. I mean, I can try." Mia meant to reply to the sheriff, but her voice came out in a nervous squeak that definitely carried to the entire line of onlookers.

"Good. We'll meet back here in the morning, when all the embers have gone safely cold." Sheriff Crow raised her voice. "My deputies will be guarding the barn, to keep it exactly as it was."

♦ ♦ ♦

Rain drummed on the remains of the barn roof as Mia picked her way through the ashy muck, followed by Sheriff Crow. The floor of the loft had collapsed, sending fragments of charred wood everywhere. She wasn't certain what she was looking for, but she figured that if she found anything unusual, she could deduce from there.

A stream of rain spattered her shoes. Mia looked up at the hole in the roof, checked her mental map of the barn from before the fire, and made her first deduction. "Sheriff Crow, I remember where the hay bale was." She walked to the place, then pointed back at the hole. "It's not in line with the hole. Not even close. If someone dropped or even threw a match, it would have landed on the floorboards."

Sheriff Crow nodded. "So we're back to a Change power or a fuse or some such. Or the boys were lying. But I don't think they were. See if you can find any remnants of a fuse."

Mia got down on her hands and knees. She had a lot of charred wood and ash to comb through. But it was much more interesting, though also more cold and smelly, than returning to Luc's generator. She wasn't sure how much time had passed before she finally found something different.

Wedged up against the southwest corner of the barn, half-buried in ash, was a chunk of a board with a hole burned in it. A weird-looking hole. Mia used the bucket of water she'd brought in with her to wash it off. It was even stranger when she got a good look at it.

A charred-edged hole shaped like a starfish or a flower had burned right into the center. The edges of the board were also charred. But everything between the hole and the edges wasn't burned at all. It was as if a perfectly symmetrical fireball had landed in the middle of the board, then leaped up and sprayed fire in all directions.

"I found something," Mia exclaimed.

Sheriff Crow crouched down to examine the board. "I'd guess that was caused by a Change power."

Mia said cautiously, "I've experimented with a lot of types of fire. And I've seen lightning strikes, in trees and on roofs. But I've never seen anything like this."

The sheriff straightened up. "Mia, don't mention this to anyone. But I'd like you to be there when I test our two firestarters."

A few hours later, Mia joined Sheriff Crow in an empty jail cell. As she stepped inside, a jittery feeling made her glance back to make sure the door wasn't closed, then shove up her glasses, then check the door again, then adjust her tool belt, then check the door again.

"Mia," Sheriff Crow said. "We're doing this in a cell because it's private and the walls can't catch fire. And I brought you here because I trust your opinion."

Startled, Mia shoved her hands into her overall pockets. Then she relaxed. She was here to observe an exciting experiment, not as a prisoner.

Rico Salazar came, looking as nervous as Mia had felt.

"Rico, don't tell anyone what I'm going to have you do," Sheriff Crow warned him. "Just say I asked you some questions."

"I didn't set the fire," Rico protested. "I don't play with my power. And I can't set fires by accident. I have to concentrate hard."

"No one's accusing you. I just want to see you set a fire here." The sheriff pointed at the board lying between two sawhorses. "Can you burn a hole in that?"

Rico closed his eyes and clenched his fists. A small flame appeared in the middle of the board, burning steadily. He opened his eyes. Apologetically, he said, "If you waited long enough it would burn a hole in it."

Mia and the sheriff examined the board. A small charred depression had been burned into the middle. There were no petal-like marks, and the fire hadn't jumped. Mia had never thought Rico would set fires anyway.

"Thank you, Rico," said the sheriff. "That'll be all."

He ran out of the jail. Sheriff Crow beckoned to Grandma Wolfe, who sat in the sheriff's chair, watching with interest. "Your turn."

"I have to admit, this is exciting. A hole, you say?" Grandma Wolfe got up and pointed at the board. A tiny fireball leaped from her finger. There was a white flash. A small, perfectly round, black-edged hole appeared in the center of the board.

Mia wondered, since Grandma Wolfe seemed to have excellent control of her power now, if she could have made petals if she'd wanted to. But she couldn't imagine her old teacher setting a barn on fire.

"I trust you'll tell me what you find?" Grandma Wolfe asked as she snapped out her umbrella.

"If we find anything, everyone will hear," the sheriff said. "Thank you for your time."

Once Grandma Wolfe left, Sheriff Crow took the board into her office. "Thanks for your help, Mia. I'll let you know if I need you again."

Mia was disappointed that her part in the investigation seemed to be over. It had been so interesting. And the mystery was still unsolved. "Do you know what happened now?"

"No more than you do. But since finding out how the fire was started seems to have hit a dead end, I'll start thinking about *why* it might have been started."

·16·
KERRY

KERRY WAS RIDING ALONG the broad streets of Gold Point. Everyone saluted as she passed. But Nugget seemed disturbed, tossing his golden mane and neighing urgently, as if he was trying to alert her to something wrong.

Father's coming.

Kerry jerked awake.

Father stood over her.

She flung herself backward with a strangled gasp, materializing a sword in her hand.

"Kerry!"

The winged brows and sharp cheekbones belonged to Paco. Bewildered, Kerry took in the scene. She was lying on the floor of a stable stall. Paco stood by her mare Penny.

"I took over for Mrs. Riley," Paco explained, his black eyes gazing down impatiently. "A horse on the dawn patrol got bitten by a coyote."

Kerry came fully awake as he spoke, remembering that she'd decided to sleep in Penny's stall because the mare was so close to giving birth. Feeling stupid, she let the sword disintegrate.

Penny kicked the wooden stall with a loud bang.

Kerry scrambled up to stroke the mare. "I think she's going into labor. The royal horses give birth very quickly. Especially their first."

"Everything's ready," Paco said.

Kerry and Mrs. Riley had already set up for the birth with

fresh straw, soap, and a bucket of hot water in case she had to reach into the mare to help the baby out, a horse stethoscope, and a bigger bucket for the placenta. But Paco must have re-heated the water for her. It was still steaming.

"Thanks," Kerry said.

They worked together as Penny labored, intent on the mare and saying little. In the small part of Kerry's mind that wasn't devoted to Penny and her unborn foal, she noted that Paco's touch with horses went beyond his excellent riding. Royal horses were temperamental, and that went double for a birthing mare. But Paco's hands were gentle and skilled, and Penny never so much as slapped him with her tail.

A bluish balloon emerged, then broke apart to reveal a tiny foal struggling to its feet, glittering like polished steel in the pale dawn light.

The foal chuckled softly. Penny's head came around, her nostrils fluttering. She gave a tender whicker as she nuzzled her baby.

"A colt," Paco said, wiping his forehead. "You're lucky. You'll have another stallion."

"A stallion," Kerry breathed, fizzing with happiness. Both baby and mother looked healthy. As the foal shook himself under his mother's tongue-bath, his hair glistened blue-white. "A steel coat. I love those."

Paco held out his fingers. The colt sniffed, then lipped them curiously before turning back to his mother. "How many colors are there?"

Before Kerry could answer, Penny began to strain again. Kerry made sure clean straw was waiting for the placenta. "Wait . . ."

"Here it comes," Paco said.

Penny gave a fretful snort and shook her coppery mane. Kerry and Paco waited until the mass of tissue landed with a splat, then checked it for missing pieces. If any remained inside Penny, she could get an infection.

"It's whole," Paco said.

"Good."

It was the longest conversation she'd had with her brother since the queen lobster attack, and the first with him alone. She waited for him to speak next as they cleaned the stall, moving slowly so Penny wouldn't get defensive. The mare watched them, ears flicking, but stayed calm. Paco said nothing. It seemed clear that if Kerry wanted to talk some more, she'd have to take the lead.

When the stall was fresh again, they left Penny and her foal alone to get to know each other. Kerry said, "You asked about the colors. There's gold, silver, bronze, copper, steel, platinum, iron...oh! Titanium. They're incredibly rare. I've never seen one."

"What color is titanium?" he asked.

"Rainbow. It's an ancient metal. But there haven't been any titanium horses in Gold Point for generations. I hope the genes haven't died out."

At the words 'Gold Point,' Paco's expression closed like a slammed door. "Looks like everything's fine. I'll haul this stuff to the mulch pit." He hefted the sacks of dirty straw and started out.

"Wait!"

Paco waited, his shoulders tight, but didn't turn around. This was their first real conversation, and she'd ruined it. She had to find something to distract him. Or something he could share.

"Want to help me name the foal?"

He shrugged.

"We name them after ancient places, and give them nicknames that start with the same letter," Kerry said. "Penny is Pennsylvania Copper; Tigereye is Tennessee Bronze. Can you think of an ancient place that would sound good with steel?"

"*We* don't name horses like that in Las Anclas," he said flatly. Two steps, and he was gone.

Kerry was disgusted with herself. First she'd mentioned Gold Point, then she'd let that "we" slip.

Maybe she should give the foal some boring Las Anclas name. But would that stop Paco from hating her? She doubted it.

She returned to the stall and watched the foal nuzzle under Penny's belly. It would be a long watch alone, waiting to make sure the baby nursed and passed his first dung. Kerry wished she had more company than Penny, whom she also had to watch for post-birth complications. A rat, maybe. A rat would be perfect. She'd told the Las Anclas rat trainers she'd like to buy a pup from their next litter, but she hadn't been told of any pregnancies yet.

Kerry wondered how Kogatana, Yuki's rat, was doing. She'd cuddled up to Kerry every night of that miserable trip back from Gold Point, when Kerry had been certain that everyone she liked in Las Anclas would be killed—right after Father executed her. Without Kogatana—and, she had to admit, without Ross—she would have lost her mind.

She knew now how hard Ross had worked to keep her going, talking much more than she was sure he was comfortable with.

"Yuki said that Kogatana means 'Little Sword' in Japanese," Ross had said as she sat shivering by the fire, unable to sleep. "*Ko* means little, and *katana* means sword. He said the 'k' changed to a 'g' because it was in the middle of the word. And he said that the best swords in the world were made in Japan."

Kerry stroked her new foal. His coat gleamed like a polished sword. She could nickname him Katana. But his real name would be Kansas Steel.

◆ ◆ ◆

When Kerry arrived at the Vardams' orchard for martial arts training, Brisa, Becky, Meredith, and Mia rushed up to her.

"How's Penny?" Becky asked.

"Oooh, I want to see the baaaby," Brisa cooed. "I love baby animals!"

"A stallion, huh?" Meredith said. "Bet he'll be a handful!"

"Is his coat really the exact shade of steel?" Mia asked. "Pure steel? Or steel alloy?"

As Kerry told them about Katana, she noticed a new addition to the group: Summer, perched high in a pear tree. Despite her precarious position, she managed to slouch, looking sullen and bored. But the angle of her head told Kerry that Ross's sister was listening.

Jennie had to be thinking of Summer, though she didn't look up; instead of joining the conversation, she'd withdrawn behind her teacher mask. Ross's gaze flickered between them, his hands twitching at his sides.

This should be interesting, Kerry thought, her tiredness forgotten.

Jennie announced, "Let's get started. Who wants to lead the warm-ups?"

"I will," Meredith volunteered.

Everybody lined up. Paco and Sujata no longer attended the group, now that they were Rangers, so the only people left who could truly challenge Kerry were Ross, Jennie, and Meredith. Jose and Yolanda were competent and had good spirit, but were younger and less experienced. Kerry wondered about Summer. She was even younger than Yolanda, but there was her Change power.

When the line folded around, Kerry was paired with Yolanda, leaving Becky without a partner.

Jennie called up, "Summer, we're starting warm-ups."

"I don't need to warm up," Summer replied. "I'll come down for the sparring."

"No warm-up, no sparring," Jennie said.

"This is just like school," Yolanda muttered. "I wish Ross hadn't invited her."

"I don't need to warm up," Summer repeated, louder. "When I'm attacked in the desert, I can't ask the bandits to wait around while I warm up, can I?"

Meredith rolled her eyes. "Get down or go home. What are you afraid of?"

"I'm not afraid of anything!" With a rustle of foliage, Summer landed in their midst, her black hair swinging.

Nobody made a move toward her until Ross left his partner, Mia, and stepped up to his sister.

"Go back to your *girlfriend*," Summer sneered.

"I can warm up by myself," Mia squeaked, backing away. "It's fine!"

Summer gave her such a scornful look that Mia took another step backward. Ross looked wildly from Summer to Mia. Summer clenched her fists and glared at Ross as if she wanted to fight him for real. Kerry felt bad for Mia and Ross, but she couldn't help also finding it funny that Mia, who could blow up buildings, and Ross, who had single-handedly won an entire battle, were so easily intimidated by a fourteen-year-old.

Jennie stepped between them. "Ross, go back to Mia. Summer,

please partner with Becky."

Kerry figured that Jennie thought that if she put Summer with the most timid person in the group, Summer would be ashamed to bully her.

That's not going to work with her, Kerry thought as Summer stomped up to Becky.

Poor Becky shrank back a step, then straightened up, her lips thinning as if she were bracing up to die well before a firing squad. She was wearing a pair of battered leather gloves, maybe to make her feel more like a fighter.

Mia relaxed, mirroring Ross's movements. The way he smiled down at her, both standing a little closer than the other pairs, intrigued Kerry. He was like that with Jennie, too. But once sparring began, he fought very differently. With Mia he was gentle, patiently slowing his movements so she could keep up. But Ross and Jennie were a real pleasure to watch, their clothes snapping with their lightning-fast punches, feints, and counter moves.

Kerry immersed herself in the rhythm of the familiar drills. But as soon as they broke apart to begin formal set sparring—one step and punch, one block—a commotion broke out.

Summer and Becky were rolling around on the ground together. Becky had obviously forgotten all her techniques in surprise and alarm, but was fighting on pure instinct, making Summer work hard to try to pin her. Kerry was impressed. Becky would never be a great fighter, but she'd come a long way from the terrified girl who ducked rather than blocked when someone threw a punch at her face.

"Break it up!" Jennie took two strides, and yanked each girl to her feet.

Ross stood right behind her, ready to intervene. Kerry smothered a flutter of laughter at the appalled expression on Mia's face as she flicked a glance from Ross to Jennie to Summer. Mia mumbled something to Ross, then backed away, edging out of the glen and into the orchard.

"Great spirit, Becky!" Meredith whooped.

Becky rubbed her wrist, her lips quivering as if she was about to burst into tears. Summer stood scowling, arms crossed tightly.

"This is set sparring," Jennie said. "Not grappling."

"Come on, Beck, be my partner," Brisa said, pulling Becky away.

Kerry saw Jennie's reluctance to send Becky back to Summer. And Mia had vanished, leaving Ross without a partner.

Kerry waited with interest. What would Jennie do now? Then Kerry became aware of Summer's gaze on her. Was that behind the girl's ploys — the desire to get the attention of a princess? That was something Kerry had dealt with all her life, but she decided not to intervene. No one in Las Anclas would appreciate the reminder that she was the daughter of a king.

"How about we all change up and start over?" Jennie suggested. "Brisa, stay with Becky. Yolanda, go with Ross. Summer, you can spar with Jose."

Summer rolled her eyes, but said nothing. Jennie signaled the start. Kerry worked with Yolanda, who was fierce and controlled.

They finished the set sparring, then Jennie said, "Open sparring."

With a challenging yell, Summer leaped at Jose. He bent down, put his hands on the ground, and made the earth surge under Summer's foot just as she landed. She yelped on a different note, and the two began grappling.

A smack on the arm brought Kerry's attention back to Yolanda. Kerry resisted the urge to create her weapons, and circled, looking for openings. The pose, the focus, always brought Santiago back to mind. She let the hurt pulse through her, then sidestepped as Yolanda dove at her in a whirl of wind.

Kerry didn't need all her strength to fight off Yolanda's attack, but Yolanda was determined. Then Jose let out a yell of surprise and anger, the ground under Kerry and Yolanda rippled, and Summer flew past them with a yelp. Summer twisted like a cat in the air and managed to land gracefully. Kerry staggered but recovered her balance.

Summer angrily stalked toward Jose, looking as if she intended to fight for real.

Jose raised his fists defensively. "That was against the rules."

Jennie stepped between them. "Break it up! What happened?"

"She cheated, using her power — " Summer said.

"He," Jennie corrected. "And powers are allowed in open sparring."

"He?" Summer repeated. "No, I grabbed her—"

Jose spoke up. "I was born with a girl's body. But I'm a guy. I've known ever since I was a little kid."

"Oh." Summer blinked, then shrugged. "Okay, so I grabbed his—"

"*Anyway*," Jose went on, "Grabbing private parts is against the rules."

Summer looked annoyed. "In a real fight, anything goes. What's the point of practice if you don't practice everything?"

"Sometimes we do," Jennie said. "But we talk about it first, so we all know what to expect. Right now, the rules are no eye-gouging, no biting, no clawing, and no below-the-belt attacks."

Summer rolled her eyes—and again glanced at Kerry.

Jennie seemed on the verge of a smile. "Let's change partners. Summer, spar with Kerry."

Summer snorted and stomped, reminding Kerry of Nugget in a bad mood. Well, Kerry could handle Nugget, and she could definitely handle a sulky fourteen-year-old.

They squared off. Kerry said, "If you want to spar anything goes, feel free."

Summer smirked, and Kerry waited for the attack she was telegraphing. Three, four steps, and Summer's hand darted in, grabbing Kerry's wrist, while her foot shot out in a sweep.

Kerry was ready for her. She jerked her own foot up, created a long looped cloth, caught Summer's foot in it, and yanked her off her feet. The girl slammed to the ground.

"Want to try that again?" Kerry asked, offering her a hand.

The anger on Summer's face dissolved into curiosity. "How'd you do that?"

"It's my power." Kerry created a short hooked cane and thrust it into Summer's open palm. "Hold on."

Summer's hand closed over the invisible cane, and she let Kerry pull her up. "Pretty cool power. Almost as cool as mine."

◆ ◆ ◆

At the end of sparring practice, Kerry said to Summer, "You're a good fighter."

"Of course." Summer smiled. For the first time, Kerry could see the family resemblance between her and Ross. It wasn't just the smile itself, which both brother and sister wore so rarely, but something about their eyes.

"You've got a beautiful style," Kerry said. "Like a dancer."

Summer's shoulders came up defensively, but then her mouth thinned and she sent a challenging look at Becky and Meredith, as if to say *See?*

"Want to ride one of the royal horses?" Kerry asked, laughing inwardly at everyone's surprise. Of course the entire group was listening in on their conversation.

Summer promptly turned her back on the others. "Let's go!"

Soon Nugget and Sally galloped side by side past the fields, then turned up a narrow path beside an arroyo. A stream tumbled nearby, running into the gully and toward the mill.

Whatever Summer knew about dancing, Kerry was glad to discover that she had not been making empty boasts about her riding. She sat a horse with trained ease. She was almost unrecognizable—as herself. Her smile, her half-shut eyes and long lashes, and her ribbons of glossy black hair again reminded Kerry of Ross, this time as he'd raced uphill to blow up the Gold Point dam.

A flash of color caught her eye. The stream contained a swarm of underwater bubbles, each as large as a plum. Kerry reined up to get a better look. The bubbles surrounded flat green leaves. Perched atop each leaf was a furry creature like a bright blue mouse, completely dry in its sphere of air. The mouse things seemed to be steering their underwater craft with twitches of their bare pink tails.

"Summer, look at these!"

Summer paused farther up the trail. "I've seen those. But they were green and pink, not blue. They only come out after the rains. When the streams dry up, they disappear. Once we—once I tried to catch one."

We? Kerry thought.

"I was pretty hungry," Summer went on. "Don't try it. They sting. Or maybe it's an electric shock. Anyway, it hurts."

An electric shock went through Kerry's heart at the thought that Sean would know where the mice went when the streams dried up. Summer was right: it did hurt. The one time he'd visited her in Las Anclas, he'd said he'd come back soon. But she hadn't seen him since.

"What's wrong?" Summer asked. "Did one sting Nugget?"

Kerry glanced down at his hind leg at the edge of the rilling stream. Nugget was fine, but this was a perfect opportunity to lure Summer into talking about Ross. "No. He just sensed that I was sad."

Immediately, Summer said, "What are you sad about? Do you miss being a princess?"

"No. I had—*have* an older brother. He disappeared when I was sixteen. I don't even know if he's still alive. I kept hoping someday he'd come back, but..." Kerry let her voice trail off.

Summer said flatly, "Well, at least he's not dead."

Kerry knew better than to respond to that. Summer's averted gaze and too-tight clutch on the reins were sure signs of someone sitting on a secret they'd almost blurted out. *We?* she thought again. She wondered who Summer had been traveling with who'd died. It couldn't be a brother—that was Ross. Or maybe someone the right age to be an older brother?

And why was it such a secret? Dead. Had Summer killed him?

When Summer spoke, her voice was testing again. "So what was it like, being a princess?"

"I had everything I wanted. Except friends. Everyone was scared of me, because I could have them executed. Everything I did—*everything*—was a test. And when I broke Ross out of prison, I knew that if I was caught, my own father would have me executed. As painfully as possible, with everyone in Gold Point forced to watch."

At Summer's look of horror, Kerry clucked to Nugget, who obediently began to canter. They dodged between clumps of hardy firs and copper-colored Manzanita bushes, then halted at a cliff overlooking the plains, and beyond them the sea. To the south lay the town, and to the north the crystal trees, shimmering like a sparkly haze in the sunlight and obscuring the ruins beyond.

Summer said abruptly, "That scar on Ross's throat. He won't

tell me how he got it. Nobody seems to know. Or maybe they just won't tell me. Do you know?"

A flock of hummingbirds swooped overhead. The leader signaled to the flock with three quick flashes of its reflective wings, and then the entire flock veered right and vanished behind the trees. Kerry watched the glints of light between the leaves as she considered her response.

She'd bandaged that burn on Ross's throat, and seen how he'd gritted his teeth in a way that spoke of more pain than that of the wound itself. He'd told her how he'd gotten it, and had never spoken of it again. Even now, he flinched if anyone's gaze settled too long on his scar. She was sure that he hated having people wondering what had happened to him, let alone actually knowing.

But she could also see how frustrated and unhappy he was with his long-lost sister acting as if she didn't even like him. Maybe if Kerry could get Summer to see Ross in a better light, he'd think whatever Kerry told her was worth it.

"What do you know about what Ross did in Gold Point?" Kerry asked.

"Just the stupid lies people were telling in other towns. About how he's this big hero." Summer snorted. "Even his girlfriend Jennie said none of it was true."

Kerry ran her fingers through Nugget's mane, letting the glittering strands catch Summer's attention. "Oh, some of it's true. Let's see. Did anyone mention that when he was first captured, he was temporarily blinded, and he escaped anyway and made it almost all the way back to Las Anclas, blind and on foot, before he was recaptured?"

To Kerry's secret pleasure, Summer looked impressed. "Nobody told me that. They don't tell me anything. And Ross keeps saying he doesn't want to talk about it."

"I don't mind talking about it," Kerry said. "But I wasn't there for that part. All I can tell you is what I saw myself. When I rode back into Gold Point, Ross was imprisoned for having tried to assassinate my father—the king—all by himself, when my father was surrounded by armed guards."

Summer whistled. "How many guards?"

"Ten," Kerry said. "Highly trained. The best of the best. And

Ross *still* nearly succeeded. But the guards beat him half to death, and threw him into the hell cells. They're cold stone, and so small that you can't stand up or lie down. Imagine being in one of those with a broken arm and ribs."

Summer winced. "Ow."

"Then my father sent Luis in. He was a torturer with the Change power to burn people with his hands." Kerry held up her hand, fingers slightly splayed, and placed it over her own throat. "And that's how Ross got his scar."

Summer leaned forward as eagerly as if she was listening to a traveling storyteller. "And then what happened?"

Kerry dropped her hand. "I broke him out of the cell. He was so badly hurt that he couldn't even walk. I had to carry him. But once I'd treated his wounds, he got up and told me that we were going to bring down my father's entire empire. I thought he was out of his mind. But he had a plan. We snuck up the mountain to the dam, and Ross blew it up."

"With his mind?" Summer said skeptically.

"No. With explosives. I wouldn't have had any idea how to do that, but Ross did. He was bleeding through his bandages and he couldn't use one hand at all, but he sat there calm as could be, doing calculations on a slide rule." Kerry kept her expression cool. Letting Summer see that the story was intended to impress her would ruin everything. But from her wide-open eyes and even wider open mouth, *bleeding through bandages* had been the perfect touch.

Kerry went on, "I helped him set up the explosives. When the dam collapsed, it took out the power for the entire city, and the flood ruined the army's stock of gunpowder. My father had no way to control the rest of his cities, and they all rebelled. Before he made the mistake of messing with Ross, my father ruled an empire. Now he only has Gold Point."

Summer said slowly, "My brother did that? But he looks so... well, he doesn't act like the sort of person who could *bring down an empire.*"

Kerry nodded seriously, hiding her satisfaction. "One thing I've learned, the most dangerous people are the ones who brag the least."

·17·
ROSS

WHEN SUMMER LEFT THE stable, Ross was waiting.

Once the barn fire had been doused, Sheriff Crow had come to the surgery to talk to her privately. When they were done, Summer had slammed out and not returned until Ross had gone to sleep. She'd avoided him entirely until martial arts training, when she'd jumped into the tree without a word. Ross couldn't bring himself to question her in front of everyone, and after the training she'd gone off with Kerry.

She had to be hungry and she liked Dr. Lee's cooking, so he figured he could walk with her to the surgery. But as soon as she came out, her lips curled into a familiar annoyed sneer. Like he was the last person in the world she wanted to see. How did Jennie manage in a house full of siblings? He couldn't even deal with one sister.

"Hungry?" he asked.

Her expression became slightly less hostile. "Starving."

That was reasonably polite, so he decided to get to the point. "That fire the other day —"

The sneer returned, angrier than ever. "I didn't start it."

"I know. I just wondered where you were when it happened."

"You and half the town," she retorted darkly.

"Half the town?" Ross echoed, appalled. He remembered distinctly how nasty and even threatening some people had been when they thought he was a claim jumper. "Mr. Horst? Mr. Preston?"

Summer shot him an odd look. "The sheriff. Dr. Lee. *You.* I was running. I was mad. When I'm mad, I run. When I saw the smoke—everybody in town saw it—I went to help. I thought I could put it out from the roof."

"I believe you." Ross did. She might make up stories about killing more bandits than had ever existed, but this sounded true. And setting a fire didn't seem like her. If she'd been mad around the barn, she'd have kicked the door down, and yelled a lot. But she was his responsibility, so he'd felt he had to at least ask. "Dr. Lee has dinner waiting. Let's go."

To his relief, either she forgave him or the idea of Dr. Lee's cooking distracted her. She gave a little bounce, floating forward a few feet. When Ross caught up with her, she said, "Did you know a foal can gallop within a day of being born? And that its legs are almost as long as they're going to be when it grows up? I didn't get to see Penny's colt born, but maybe I can see Acushla's. Mrs. Riley says the mare will drop any day now. Two foals! Will they play together?"

She chattered on until they reached the Lees' kitchen, where Dr. Lee and Mia waited at the table. Mia instantly fell silent. Frustration welled up in Ross. He loved talking to Mia over dinner, and Summer made her too nervous to speak. All he could do was look at her.

Mia wore her best white shirt and freshly ironed pants, and she'd brushed her hair until it shone with blue-black highlights. There wasn't a speck of dust or smear of engine grease anywhere on her. He remembered then that it was their date night. *He* hadn't dressed up, but Mia wouldn't care.

Once dinner was over, they'd go to her cottage just to be together. That gave him a strange feeling, intense but unidentifiable. It wasn't fear, and it was more than simple affection or even the rush of heat at the prospect of touching her. It felt...deeper. Whatever it was, it made him smile at her as he sat down at the table.

The corners of her mouth lifted in answer, making the feeling intensify. Then Mia gave a nervous jerk of her head toward Summer and avoided his gaze. Then any other feelings were washed away by the helpless worry that had become all too familiar ever since his sister had walked into his life.

Summer didn't seem to notice that Mia didn't talk when she was there. If she was in a good mood, like now, she did all the talking. If she was sullen, Dr. Lee would speak quietly about easy topics, as he had when Ross first arrived. Ross recognized now, and hoped his sister wouldn't, how similar Dr. Lee's tone was to Mrs. Riley's when she was calming a wild, plunging horse.

Summer rattled on about the royal horses as she shoveled in her dinner, pausing only once, her mouth full of daikon kimchi, to say, "This is really, really good!" At least, Ross assumed the last word was 'good;' it was lost in a very loud crunch.

The moment her plate was clean, she got up. "I'm going back to see Acushla," she announced as she ran to the door, and then she was gone.

"Sorry," Ross felt obliged to say. "I don't want to say anything about manners, or she might..."

"That's all right, Ross," Dr. Lee said. "She's a smart girl. When she settles down, she'll learn. Or remember what she was taught. I think her manners are a way of maintaining her distance until she feels she can trust us."

"Is that it? I thought she was doing it to get back at me for not being that gunslinger she imagined." With Summer gone, the room felt very quiet. Ross took a deep breath. He was alone with Mia and Dr. Lee, and *he* trusted them both. He still couldn't look either of them in the eye as he muttered, "I think she hates me."

"She may be angry and disappointed, but I'm sure she doesn't hate you," Dr. Lee said. "But also, being a rebel can be a normal part of being a teenager. Did you know that no one is allowed to move into Singles Row until they graduate from school?"

Ross considered that. "Oh, so it doesn't fill up with kids who got mad at their families."

Until Summer came along, he'd never thought he could get mad at a family member—or that one could get mad at him. When he'd been a lone prospector sleeping beneath the stars, sometimes he'd imagined a family for himself, and they had always been something like the Rileys.

"If there's a serious problem at home, we have fosterage," Dr. Lee replied. "But yes, we don't want kids bouncing in and out of

Singles Row because they are squabbling with their families." Then, as if speaking to himself, he murmured, "And sometimes it's not the obvious ones who need help."

Mia piped up, "Like Becky?"

Ross hadn't expected that. From Dr. Lee's expression, neither had he. Immediately, he turned to his daughter. "Is there something you know about her?"

"Not exactly," Mia said. "But before Grandma Wolfe left, every now and then she'd ask Becky how she was feeling, though she didn't look sick. Becky always said she was fine. And once she asked Becky to stay after school. I came back because I'd forgotten my lunch pail, and I heard Grandma Wolfe asking her if everything was all right at home."

"What did Becky say?" Dr. Lee asked.

"She said everything was fine." Mia shrugged.

Dr. Lee tapped his chopsticks against his plate. "Mia, Ross, please don't repeat this conversation. But if either of you hears or observes anything…"

Ross doubted that he would. Despite all the time he spent in the surgery, and how often he encountered Becky at the stable, the longest conversation he'd ever had with her had been on his very first day in Las Anclas, when she'd put aside her shyness to be kind. If something bad was happening to her, he hoped Dr. Lee would find out and fix it.

"I don't know her that well." Echoing Ross's thought, Mia said, "Which is funny, since she's your apprentice! But she was always part of Felicité's crowd, coming to school in party dresses. I never had much to do with her, though I like her. Especially now. She's the only other person at our practices as terrible as I am, but you should see how hard she tries."

"That's true," Ross said, thinking of Becky's red, determined face as she took fall after fall. But she always got up again.

Mia leaned forward, her eyes bright and curious. "Dad, is this why you took her as your apprentice?"

Dr. Lee held up a hand. "Whoa, whoa. Don't gallop down the wrong road! I have no proof that anything is wrong with Becky, and she apprenticed with me because she wanted to heal living things."

"I remember that," Mia said. To Ross, she explained, "When we were kids, if anyone found a wild animal that was hurt, they'd bring it to Becky. She'd do her best to fix them, but she mostly tried to tame them and make pets of them. The one who was good at the fixing part was Alfonso Medina. Especially broken bones. Even dead bones. Once I saw him putting together an old bleached snake skeleton like it was a jigsaw puzzle. Weird."

"Bones are the cogs and struts of the body," Dr. Lee pointed out. "Not so different from a machine. And you love putting those together."

"And blood is like oil!" Mia said excitedly. "Or, no, probably food and water is like oil used as fuel, and blood is oil used as grease. Okay, I guess the snake bones aren't that weird."

Ross laughed.

"Alfonso," Dr. Lee said, rubbing his chin. "The only word that boy has ever said to me was after I set his collarbone when he discovered that he'd grown too heavy to stick to ceilings. It was, 'Thanks.' Now there's a boy who never had a rebel phase. Hmm."

"Don't call Summer a rebel to her face, Dr. Lee," Ross said. "She'd love it. Too much."

Dr. Lee laughed. "She might regard it as a challenge to live up to. Don't worry. I'll treat her as the adult she seems to want to be." His smile disappeared. "But Ross, if you don't mind some advice, listen to her. I think there's a reason she's so distrustful. I think something very bad happened to her, and not so long ago. She talks and brags a lot, but it's always about people or events when she was younger. I've never heard her mention anything in the last year or so, except that she found out about you."

"I didn't notice that," Ross admitted, feeling as ignorant as he had when he'd first come to Las Anclas.

"There's no reason why you should have," Dr. Lee replied. "This is your first time dealing with a sibling. Whereas I've had lots of experience with that."

Dr. Lee has lots of experience with a lot of things, Ross thought. *Especially people.*

If anyone could tell Ross what was wrong with him, Dr. Lee could.

Before he could lose his nerve, Ross made himself say, "Dr.

Lee. You know—you must have noticed—there's a lot I don't talk about either, but it's because I don't remember it. And the memories I do have are in bits and pieces."

Even saying it aloud made him feel like he was about to have a building collapse on top of him. Like it had already collapsed. A band of pressure around his chest made it hard to get the words out.

Mia reached out across the table, slowly so she wouldn't startle him, then closed her warm hand over his. He held it tight, then managed to pull in a deep breath.

"Yes, Ross, I've noticed." Dr. Lee spoke gently, but not in his horse-taming voice. "Do you know when your memories that are in one piece begin? Approximately?"

Ross hadn't thought of it that way before. It wasn't something he liked to think about at all. "I'm not sure."

"Try going backwards," Dr. Lee suggested. "You remember everything that's happened since you came to Las Anclas, don't you? And you seem to recall your own solo prospecting days."

"Yeah, I do. I had some apprenticeships before that. I remember them." Ross tried to picture how his first one had started. He'd used his grandmother's map to find the nearest town. And before that—

Walking across the sand, leading Rusty. His clothes were soaked with sweat, and his arms and back ached. He didn't look back. He didn't want to see the grave he'd dug with a shovel taller than he was.

"My grandmother died," Ross said. Mia squeezed his hand. He looked at her, not her father, as he went on, "I think after that is when things stop breaking up. Nothing killed her. She was old, and one morning she didn't wake up. But I don't have a memory of that. I just know that's what happened. Somehow. I don't know if that makes sense."

"I understand," said Dr. Lee.

"If someone asks me something, sometimes I know the answer. But I don't know how I know. Or I'll get a piece of a memory I didn't have before."

"Like a disassembled engine," Mia said softly. "Only not laid out nice and neat. Like bits you'd find prospecting, all jumbled together and half of them buried. Right?"

"Yeah. It's exactly like that." Ross turned back to Dr. Lee. "Do you know why?"

"I have an idea," Dr. Lee replied. "Several people have told me that their memories of the battle of Las Anclas are like yours, out of order, with pieces missing. Most of them had something particularly bad happen to them. They lost a loved one, or they killed for the first time."

Ross caught Mia and her father exchanging glances. Dr. Lee didn't even ride out on patrol because he wouldn't take a life except in mercy. But Mia had killed in that battle. He'd seen her shoot an enemy who'd been about to attack him.

"I remember it," Mia volunteered. "Well, not every single moment. But all the important parts."

"And what was the most important part of the battle to you, Mia?" Dr. Lee asked.

A radiant smile lit her up like a bright-moth. Instantly, she said, "Saving Ross's life."

Dr. Lee gave her a proud pat on the shoulder. "And an excellent job you did of it." Then he turned back to Ross. "And that's probably why she didn't forget anything. The battle wasn't the worst thing that had ever happened to her. It had terrible moments, but the most important part was good."

Ross couldn't believe he was saying this, after he'd experienced the deaths of Voske's soldiers and nearly died himself, but he replied, "It wasn't the worst thing that ever happened to me, either."

"No," said Dr. Lee. "I didn't think it was. Sometimes people's memories break up when they have such painful experiences that they feel unbearable to recall. It's as if part of their mind is trying to protect them, but doesn't quite know how. They might lose some memories that wouldn't have bothered them, but keep some of the ones that do."

"Yeah." The vise around his chest made it impossible for Ross to say more. But Dr. Lee had to be right. Why else would Ross have forgotten most of the ordinary moments of his childhood, but remember finding his father's body? He pictured a person wildly swinging a club at a roach in a kitchen, and smashing half the dishes while the bug scurried free.

Dr. Lee went on, "Also, think of your age. Everyone's earliest childhood memories are fragmented anyway. Remembering our lives is something we learn how to do, like we learn how to speak. Ross, my guess is that your worst thing was losing your family. And because it happened when you were so young, and still learning to remember anyway, your memories just kept on breaking up and getting lost. When your grandmother died, that was probably the next worst thing. But by then you were much older and better at remembering, so that was the last thing you forgot."

Ross nodded slowly. When he tried to take a deep breath, he found that he could again. "Thanks, Dr. Lee. That makes sense."

He still didn't know if he'd ever remember his parents' faces. But that was all the talking he could stand do on that subject for one day. At least now he knew that there was a reason for the way he was.

More importantly, he wasn't the only person with holes in his memory. Dr. Lee hadn't mentioned who in Las Anclas had forgotten parts of the battle; he'd never repeat anything told to him privately. It could be anyone. The next time people stared at him for not knowing something about himself, he'd remind himself that maybe he wasn't the only one there with missing memories.

Mia gave his hand another squeeze, then picked up her plate. Grateful for the excuse to end the conversation, Ross put away his dishes and Summer's too.

"Let's go," she said in a low voice, glancing around in that sneaky way that always started a flutter of laughter behind Ross's ribs. "I want to show you something I made."

As they headed out, hands clasped, Ross felt better with every step he took. Soon they'd be alone together. He'd have something to focus on other than Summer and what he'd learned about himself. But more than that, he couldn't wait to be with Mia, whether they'd finally spend the night together or whether their date would consist of trying out a weapon she'd made. Ever since the ruined city, they'd barely been alone together. He'd missed her.

She opened the cottage door with a flourish. Ross stepped in, then stopped in surprise. For the first time ever, nothing was scattered across the floor. All her tools and metal scraps were hanging from her new tool rack or stacked on the table or crammed into bins.

Mia pointed behind him with a grin, indicating a set of iron bars she'd bolted on either side of the door.

"What are those?" Ross asked.

She lifted a board leaning against the wall and dropped it into the bars. "A lock. Now nobody can push their way in."

Mia drew him further inside. "I have something else, too. I don't know why I didn't think of it before. I usually work until I get tired, and I just curl up wherever I am. But some of the Lees sleep in a yo on the floor during summer, because it's cooler than a bed. It's a Korean mattress. But when we, um, tried the bed I put together, I thought, hey, this is comfy. And so, well, I rigged this."

She reached for a rope attached to a pulley, which was also new. A soft cylinder came down like a boat letting down a sail, and thumped gently to the floor. Mia unhooked and unrolled it, transforming it into a thin mattress already made up with sheets and blankets. "Ta-da!"

"Wow." Ross was impressed. Mia could make *anything*.

She pulled a pair of pillows from a box tucked behind her bin of hoses. "Instant comfort! And if anyone starts banging on the door, it only takes ten seconds to make it all go away. Want me to show you?"

Ross laughed, remembering how Tommy had barged in and Mia had flung her bedding in the soldering water. But even as he did, he felt a hollowness behind his ribs and at his knees that made him want to hug Mia to him.

She smiled at him expectantly, and he held out his arms. Mia came to him at once, and they kissed. Heat built up in Ross's body as his hands drifted over her back and down—

—and someone rattled the door.

Ross and Mia froze.

"Ross?" Summer's voice was muffled. "Ross, I know you're in there!" The door rattled louder.

This time it was Ross's turn to panic. He looked around wildly, but Mia had already sprung into action. A quick movement of her small hands, and the yo rolled up. A yank on the pulley, and the bedding vanished up to the ceiling.

"Mia!" Summer shouted. "Why are you barring the door?"

Ross snatched up the pillows and threw them into their box.

"Tommy Horst says you're making bombs," Summer yelled. "I want to learn how to make bombs!"

Mia opened the door. Summer looked accusingly at her, then him, then past them. "Where's the bombs?"

"There are no bombs. We were just..." Mia shot Ross a desperate glance, obviously begging for him to rescue her. But he was so horrified at the thought of his little sister guessing what they'd been about to do, his mind went completely blank. He stared at the floor, willing her to not look up and see the hanging bed.

But Summer clearly lost interest as soon as Mia denied the bombs. "That new compressor you made blew out at Luc's. Took the lights with it. Luc said he'd give me a plate of tacos if I fetched you."

That gave Ross an idea. "I think Mia has to do something else tonight. But I can give you scrip for tacos, Summer."

But Mia's look of wide-eyed panic only intensified. It was like she hadn't even heard him. She blurted out, "Tell Luc I'll be right there!"

It looked like this wasn't going to be the night for trying out the yo. Ross handed Mia her tool kit.

·18·
BECKY

BECKY SLOWLY PULLED ON the sterile kelp gloves as Dr. Lee laid out the instruments for the surgery. A memory flashed briefly — a man's hands setting the gloves on a surgical tray — and then she was back to the present moment. As far as she could tell, Dr. Lee hadn't noticed a thing. She was getting more control over her power, but it was no consolation when it returned her to a place she didn't want to be.

On the table, Mrs. Hattendorf mumbled something about keeping the tea cozy warm, then trailed off into a snore. Dr. Lee picked up her limp wrist, checking her pulse. "She's out. Ready?"

Becky swallowed, her throat dry as sand. She told herself sternly that she had assisted at hundreds of surgeries, including far more complicated ones than removing an appendix. She'd even threaded a needle and stitched up wounds. But picking up a scalpel and cutting into a living, breathing person made her stomach go cold.

"It's normal to be nervous about your first surgery," Dr. Lee said. "But being timid doesn't do the patient any favors. Your first cut needs to be bold. All the way through the layers of muscle."

Mrs. Hattendorf's stomach was painted with greenish antiseptic, but nothing could disguise the rise and fall of her breathing.

Becky picked up the scalpel. Her hand shook. She stiffened her fingers.

"One bold stroke," Dr. Lee said firmly.

The surgery would save Mrs. Hattendorf's life. But it felt so... violent.

"We don't want to keep her out for too long," Dr. Lee warned her. "It's not healthy."

Becky swallowed down an unreasonable flare of anger. Dr. Lee couldn't use his power to heal an inflamed appendix. If he sped up time for Mrs. Hattendorf, her appendix would burst and kill her. He had to wait until the infected organ was removed, and then make the incision heal quickly.

It was up to her.

She remembered what it felt like to slice through the slabs of meat Dr. Lee had made her practice on. Trying not to think about what she was doing, she let muscle memory take over and sliced into Mrs. Hattendorf's belly.

One bold stroke.

Blood welled up shockingly fast, but Dr. Lee quickly clamped down on the bleeding vessels. "Excellent, Becky. Now find the appendix."

She had seen the insides of people's bodies lots of times, but the mess of blood and pink tissue her scalpel had exposed looked alien and incomprehensible. Then she whispered the sequence of steps to herself, and her fingers moved obediently. Locate, isolate, clamp, cut, lift. Check, then stitch.

She took her first deep breath when she finished her neat line of seaweed stitches. Blood welled up between them. Dr. Lee laid his hand over the incision, and the wound closed and became a pink line: one week healed.

"Congratulations," Dr. Lee said, dabbing a few beads of sweat from his forehead. "Your very first surgery. Let's finish up, and I'll take you to Jack's for a celebratory dinner. The special tonight is liver and onions. You like that, don't you?"

A memory leaped into Becky's mind, almost as vivid as if it had come from something she'd touched: her mother slicing up a bloody, quivering slab of liver, then whipping around to smack Becky for standing around uselessly instead of helping.

A hot surge in her stomach sent her bolting to the bathroom. She barely made it to the toilet before everything came up. Then she huddled in the corner, cold, shaky and ashamed. What sort of surgeon's apprentice was she?

A lifetime of bold strokes stretched out before her, and her stomach surged again. She sank trembling to the floor, her entire body damp with cold sweat.

When Dr. Lee had invited her to become his apprentice, she'd imagined that being a doctor would be like doing the things that had made him notice her in the first place: splinting a cat's broken leg, and watching it run around easily a month later, or stuffing a pill down a sick dog's throat and seeing it get back its interest in life.

She stared down at her bloody gloves, remembering the shredded horror of Mr. Gonzalez's stomach as he lay on a table in the town hall while the Gold Point and Las Anclas soldiers killed each other at the gates. She could almost see Dr. Lee gently taking his hand and telling him that he could not recover, and using his power would only speed the infection. Dr. Lee had offered him a choice: painkillers for his remaining days, or a quick death. Becky saw the whitening around Mrs. Gonzalez' knuckles as she'd gripped her husband's other hand, and heard the ringing in her own ears when he'd said, "Make it quick."

"Becky, fetch me the poppy elixir," Dr. Lee had said.

Becky had fetched it, as she had when it would only be used as a sleeping drug. But when she handed it to Dr. Lee, she felt in her own knotted stomach that she was helping to kill a man. She'd thought she was safe from that in the field hospital, separated from the fighters outside, but she was doing the opposite of healing. The opposite of saving lives.

Becky hunched over the toilet and pressed her bloody gloves together, knowing that she never wanted to be the one to make it quick.

She did not want to be the one making one bold stroke.

A quiet tap at the bathroom door startled her. Becky jumped, then forced herself to her feet. She flung the gloves into the mulch bucket, then stood with her bare hands in the air, afraid to touch anything.

"Becky?" Dr. Lee called. "Should I come back later?"

"No." Using the tips of her fingers, she reluctantly opened the door.

Dr. Lee held out a glass of water. Grimacing against the lingering bitterness, Becky rinsed out her mouth, then gratefully drank down the rest.

"Mrs. Hattendorf is in the infirmary," Dr. Lee said. "She'll be fine. You did an excellent job. She would have died without the surgery, you know. That appendix was about to burst. Shall I show you?"

She grabbed his wrist. "No!"

He looked startled, but as she snatched her hand back and began to dither an apology, he said, "Come into the kitchen. Let's talk."

Becky knew he would be kind, but she still dreaded telling him. She felt like she was confessing some kind of crime. He'd be so disappointed in her.

She had to get it over with. Before they even reached the kitchen, Becky blurted out, "I can't be a doctor. I'm sorry. I wasted your time. Years of it! My mother is right. I'm a useless coward. But I can't do it."

"Sure you can," he said mildly. "You just did. And well, I might add. At least as well as I did on my first surgery. In fact, I think you did better. Becky, we all have moments like this."

He paused as they sat down, then leaned forward. "When my wife died, though I had done everything possible to save her, for a time I thought I was finished as a doctor. I no longer trusted myself. If I hadn't been the only doctor in town, I might have quit." He looked out the window into the garden, and let out his breath. "But my own mother had been there, too, as her midwife. She said she'd done everything she could, and so had I. Sometimes people die, no matter what you do."

Becky shook her head. "That's not it. I know I *can* do it, but I don't want to anymore. It's not what I thought it would be. Mr. Gonzalez…"

"I see. It's one thing to know what you might have to do, and another thing to actually do it. But I'd like you to take a few days and think this over. A first surgery can be a fairly traumatic experience." Dr. Lee smiled slightly. "Not only for Mrs. Hattendorf."

"It's not just that." She poured out the entire story of her Change. "I can never touch the surgery table again. I'd have to wear gloves all the time." Hot tears spilled down her cheeks. "I have to anyway. I can't stand touching anything in my house. I know I'm a disappointment—"

Dr. Lee held up his hand. "Stop right there. You are not a coward. It took courage to talk to me. It took courage to perform that surgery, and it took courage back in the field hospital. You don't have to force yourself to do anything you don't want to do."

"But what will you do? You wasted all that time with me!" Becky said, wiping her eyes.

"I learned to be a better teacher. And you still have your skills. They might come in handy." Wryly, he added, "Also, I'm not exactly doddering. I feel confident that I have many good years left. There's time aplenty to find an apprentice who will enjoy being a doctor. Still, please think it over. If you still feel the same in a few days, we'll decide what to do next."

Becky sniffled and nodded.

He cleared his throat. "I hate to bring this up, but I know how your mother feels about Changed people. Whatever you want to do, I'll support you. If worst comes to worst, you're welcome to stay here."

Relief made her giddy. She left, her feet carrying her home without her being aware of her journey. But when she got there, she realized that she still had no idea what to do.

I don't have to decide this minute.

Becky elbowed the door open, then stopped with one foot inside and one on the porch. She could hear Grandma Ida all the way from the kitchen.

"...and if you'd listened to me, your husband would still be here," Grandma Ida snapped. "You are such a fool, Martha! And the proof is that boy of yours, who can't stick to anything. He was dating Preston's daughter and he still didn't get into the Rangers! And that mouse of a daughter of yours—"

"My daughter," Mom retorted, "is the future Dr. Callahan. Dante Lee could have picked any brat in the schoolhouse, but he chose her."

"That makes me wonder what's wrong with those other

children," Grandma Ida said. "Future doctor, huh. You'd never think 'doctor' to look at her!"

"Stop it, Mother!"

"'Stop it, Mother,'" Grandma Ida mimicked. "That's all I've heard out of you my entire life. Everything is always someone else's fault. Who are you going to blame for the failure of your business?"

"My business is not failing," Mom shouted.

"So it's an accident that everyone's going to that fool Frank Kim for tailoring?"

Becky started to back out, but the warped floorboard under her foot creaked.

"Who's there?" Mom called.

"It's me." Becky reluctantly entered the kitchen, where two red, angry faces turned to her. She couldn't tell them—she just couldn't. "I finished my first surgery. Dr. Lee sent me home."

"Your first surgery! Congratulations." Mom's voice was thin and triumphant. "Let's get you something to eat. Was it Vera Hattendorf's appendix? How is she?"

"She's fine."

Grandma Ida got up. "Remember what I said, Martha. You have to be stricter with that boy of yours, or he'll never amount to anything. But you won't. You never do."

The door banged behind her.

"I don't need..." Becky trailed off at the sight of her mother leaning against the sink, wiping her eyes.

Sorrow nearly suffocated Becky. Mom was crying! She couldn't remember seeing Mom cry, even after it was obvious that Dad would never come back from his "trading trip."

"I'm sorry, Mom," Becky said, coming up to join her mother.

"It's all right. You didn't do anything. I just wish your brother..."

Becky spoke hastily, before Mom could get angry. "Shall I help you fix dinner? Or I could do it. You don't have to."

"No, it's too early. This bread won't be ready for another hour. But you can clear the table. I'll pop these muffins in with the bread. Then you can eat one warm with butter."

"Okay." Becky hesitated over Grandma Ida's half-empty coffee cup. She didn't want any of her grandmother's memories in her head. She took Jennie's gloves from her pocket and put them on.

Mom glanced up from the pan of corn muffins. "Are those Henry's fighting gloves?"

"They're Jennie's," Becky said.

Mom put the muffins in the oven, then straightened up. "Why do you have them? And why are you wearing them? The dishes aren't hot."

"I know." Becky tried to think of some explanation, but nothing came to mind. A headache she hadn't noticed before stabbed red-hot pain behind her eye. "I just...I can't..."

"Can't what?" Mom laid a hand on Becky's forehead. "Are you sick? You're all clammy! You need to go straight to bed. What was Dante thinking, making you work when you're feverish?"

It was the first time in months that Mom had felt like, well, like a mom. Maybe Becky had been frightened of nothing. Maybe Mom was just as scared as Becky. She'd been crying over the sink because her own mother had yelled at her.

"I'm not sick, Mom." And then the words came out. "I'm Changed. I have to—"

"What?" Mom yanked her hand away as if she'd been burned. "Changed!" She spat the word out as if it was poison.

Lights exploded across Becky's vision. She found herself lying on the kitchen floor, her cheek throbbing. Her mother stood over her, scrubbing her hand on a dish towel as if to rub the skin off.

"How *dare* you! How *dare* you!" Mom's breath whistled in her throat.

"Mom—"

"Get out!" Mom's face distorted into something unrecognizable. A purple vein ticked in her forehead. "Pack your stuff and get out of my house, you mutant!"

Becky scrambled up and ran to her room. But once she was there, she froze in the middle of the floor, looking from her bed to her trunk to the clothes pegs on the wall as if she'd never seen them before.

The floor creaked behind her. Becky spun around, flinging up her forearm to protect her face.

But it wasn't Mom. It was Henry. For once, he wasn't grinning.

Quietly, he asked, "Were you serious? What can you do?"

Her face throbbed in time to her thudding heart. Daring him to be nasty, she said, "I touch things. And I see a flash of whoever held them last."

She waited for him to call her a mutant or a monster, but he just stood there staring at her. She'd never thought about it before, but he looked so much like Dad.

"Say something," Becky choked out.

But he didn't. He was so loud everywhere else, but at home he shut down. No matter how much Mom scolded her about her monster girlfriend, Henry neither joined in nor defended her. He just sat there silently, then escaped to Felicité Wolfe, his perfect Norm girlfriend.

Mom shrieked from the kitchen, "Henry? Is that you? Get away from her! I don't want you catching it!"

Henry glanced back, then said even more softly, "Want me to help you pack?"

Becky shut her eyes. "You better go. Don't make it worse." The words *for yourself* died in her throat. A sob shook her.

Henry's steps retreated. Becky opened her eyes and sprang to close the door. But that wouldn't keep Mom out. She turned in a circle, unable to think of what to do next, until she heard angry footsteps in the hall. Mom!

Becky leaned against the door, sick with apprehension. Mom rattled the knob, then screamed, "This is your own fault, Rebecca Callahan. You chose this. You wanted to be like that monster girlfriend of yours. Well, go live with her!"

The footsteps stomped to the back bedroom.

Becky yanked her door open and ran into the street, startled to find it was still the middle of the day. It felt like years had passed. Everything was different. Brisa would welcome her, hold her, kiss her tears away. But she couldn't stay with Brisa. The Preciados already had four people in each bedroom. Becky felt like a burden when she ate over. She wouldn't be able to live with herself if she moved in with them.

Grandma Thakrar passed by, tugging a cart full of hops. Becky watched her go, her head like hot metal clanging with her heart-beat. She longed for Brisa's comforting touch, but Brisa would insist that she stay.

Oh. Whenever she and Brisa wanted private time, they used Aunt Rosa's spare bedroom. In fact, her aunt had said Becky could spend the night any time, with or without Brisa. Becky ran for the tree-lined lane where Aunt Rosa lived. She found her aunt in the quilt room, stuffing down into squares of leaf-green cloth.

"Becky!" Aunt Rosa exclaimed, her smile of welcome vanishing. "What happened to your face?"

Becky's hand flew up to her cheek. It hurt too much to touch. Her lips shaped the word *Mom* but no sound came out.

"Let's get a cold cloth on that." Aunt Rosa's expression was odd, unreadable. But her words made sense, and her voice was soothing.

Becky soon found herself lying in the spare room, the window shade pulled down, and a cool cloth laid over the side of her face. Aunt Rosa said she would bring some willow bark tea. Becky was glad to just lie there, thinking of nothing. She felt so strange, as if she were floating in water.

"Becky?"

She woke from a doze, wincing against the hammer in her head. "Oh, I'm sorry, I didn't mean to fall asleep." Her voice suspended when she saw that two people had joined Aunt Rosa in the shadowy room. A yellow snake eye gleamed in the darkness. "Sheriff Crow?" She sat up. "Dr. Lee!"

Aunt Rosa pressed a cup into Becky's gloved hands. "Here. It's cooled off, but I didn't want to wake you."

Becky obediently choked down the bitter liquid, her mind full of questions.

Dr. Lee motioned toward the shades, which Aunt Rosa raised. He bent over Becky, examining her as if she was a patient rather than his apprentice.

Then she remembered: she wasn't his apprentice any more. She was nothing.

"I'm all right," Becky mumbled, but her jaw and ear and eye throbbed like the worst toothache she'd ever had.

"What happened?" Dr. Lee asked.

"It's nothing." Becky's gaze slid to the sheriff. What was she doing there?

"I hate to contradict you," Dr. Lee said, "But someone struck you. There are fingerprint bruises on your cheek. Was it your mother?"

Becky's eyes filled with tears. "I shouldn't have told her. About my Change."

"Change?" Aunt Rosa said, but she sounded surprised, not angry. "When did that happen?"

"Last week. I didn't tell anybody. Except Brisa. And Jennie," Becky said quickly. "When I got home today, it just came out. I should have waited."

Sheriff Crow spoke for the first time. "Becky, it sounds like you're blaming yourself. You didn't choose to Change, and I'm guessing *you* didn't hit anyone." She smiled a little. "Did you?"

The absurdity of that question almost made Becky smile, but somehow all that came out was a sob. "I've never hit anybody."

Sheriff Crow indicated her cheek. "Has this happened before?"

"No." Becky shook her head, and winced. "Yes. Not like this," she said quickly, remembering her mother's fingers digging into her arm. Mom had shaken her, and once pulled her hair when Becky had come home from a schoolyard game with her new dress covered in mud. Her mother had slapped her many times, but never that hard. "She never knocked me down."

"And Henry?" Sheriff Crow asked. "Does she ever hit him?"

This time Becky managed to stop herself from shaking her head. "*She* never did."

Sheriff Crow and Dr. Lee exchanged glances, and Aunt Rosa said softly, "I was told never to interfere, or the children would be forbidden to visit me at all. And I haven't, though I've often..." Aunt Rosa turned away, blinking hard.

"It was only one time!" Becky spoke loudly enough to surprise herself. She quickly shut her mouth. Her jaw hurt. Everything hurt. Her ears were still ringing.

The sheriff stood up. "Once is enough. Your mother is about to spend the night in jail."

"No! You can't! I'm sorry I said anything—it's all my fault, I shouldn't have—"

The sheriff turned at the door. "Becky, when Ed Willet knocked Jack down, I put him in jail for a night. A blow is a blow.

Doesn't matter who did it to who." And she went out.

Becky covered her face. "Mom will blame me."

Aunt Rosa said crisply, "Let her try it. I'll knock her down myself. It would be worth a night in jail and a month feeding rotten meat to the eater roses."

Dr. Lee looked more upset than Becky had ever seen him. "Rosa? Can Becky stay here?"

"I was about to offer." Aunt Rosa still sounded angry, making Becky flinch. But her tone softened as she said, "Becky, as far as I am concerned, this bedroom is yours. I'll fetch my wheelbarrow and go get your things." With satisfaction, she added, "Your mother won't be there to stop me."

Dr. Lee gave her a spoonful of elixir. Becky flinched at the scent of poppy, but drank it down. She just wanted everything to go away. Then she lay back, sure that she was too upset to sleep. But the next thing she knew, she was opening her eyes to morning light streaming through an open window. She was still fully dressed, all the way down to Jennie's Ranger gloves.

Aunt Rosa came in with a tray. Delicious smells wafted from the steaming dishes. For what felt like the first time in months, Becky's stomach tightened with hunger rather than tension or nausea.

"Here you go, dear. Breakfast in bed. I always find that so relaxing. In fact, I sometimes make it for myself and climb right back into bed." Aunt Rosa poured out the tea, and the scent of mint filled the room. "Peppermint, your favorite. And when you're done, a hot bath will be waiting for you."

Aunt Rosa left, quietly closing the door behind her. Becky looked down at the tray on her knees. There were buckwheat pancakes drowned in mesquite syrup and butter, a dish of stewed apples, and eggs scrambled with bell peppers, cheese, and onions. *Everything* was her favorite.

An unexpected happiness filled Becky as she ate. It wasn't only that the food was good and warmed her inside. It was that Aunt Rosa had remembered what she liked. And more than remembered, she'd cared enough to cook it for her.

Becky took a long bath afterward, sinking into the hot water. Aunt Rosa had left clean clothing for her, a simple dress of her own that she'd taken in to fit Becky, and a pair of cotton gloves. Becky nervously pulled on the gloves, bracing herself as they touched her palms. But all she saw was her aunt's familiar hands measuring them.

Just right for Becky, Aunt Rosa thought. *She's such a little thing.* And, with a hot surge of anger, *How dare Martha strike that child!*

The vision ended, leaving Becky unsettled. She felt as if she'd been spying, though she hadn't done it deliberately. And it was strange to not just see someone's anger on her behalf, but actually feel it.

When she returned to her room, the closet door was open. Aunt Rosa had brought over her clothes, just as she'd promised. All those beautiful dresses her mother had made. All those ribbons and ruffles. A sudden rage flamed inside her, hot and bright. Ever since she was little, Mom had said, *Don't get dirty! Don't get mussed! You're my walking advertisement!* Becky had never had play clothes. She'd never dared to play after she came home in a muddy dress, the first and last time Becky had tried to be like the other kids.

With quick, furious jerks, Becky ripped every ribbon off every dress. It was only when the fragile lace ripped under her fingers that she stopped. The rich gleaming ribbons were spilled all over the floor in coils, like Mrs. Hattendorf's intestines.

A familiar mixture of nausea and guilt rose up in her. But rather than let it swallow her up, she fought it. The dresses were hers. It didn't matter what she did with them. She could even trade them for practical clothes. Pants, for the first time in her life! Plain tops, like the single one she wore to the surgery. And if she wanted to stomp a mud puddle or climb a tree, who would stop her?

But first, she'd repair the dresses. Ruining them was stupid. They were only clothes. And lots of girls—like Brisa—would dearly love one of Mom's fancy dresses, but could never afford them.

Becky spooled the ribbons so they wouldn't get crushed. But once she'd finished sewing them back on, what would she do next? She had no apprenticeship. She could never return home. It was as if her entire life had evaporated like a drop of water in a hot pan.

She stood before the closet, her mind a blank. Finally, she shook herself and went to ask her aunt for sewing supplies. But once she left the guest room—no, her new room—she heard voices in the parlor.

"Let's ask Becky," said Sheriff Crow.

Becky made herself go in, her feet dragging like stones. She found the sheriff sitting with her aunt.

"Hello, dear," said Aunt Rosa, her lips compressed. "Dr. Lee told us that you have been reconsidering your apprenticeship. You certainly don't have to make any decisions now. He said you need time to think it over. But for now, your afternoons are free, are they not?"

And Sheriff Crow said, "Becky, I'd like to ask a favor of you."

Becky couldn't imagine what she could do for the strongest person in town. "Me?"

"Dr. Lee also told us what your power is," the sheriff said. "I'm still investigating the fire in the old barn. If you don't mind, I'd like to borrow you. Maybe you can see how it was set. Not until you're ready, of course."

Becky looked doubtfully at the sheriff. "I can't pick the memories. I might just see cows."

Sheriff Crow shrugged. "If you do, you do."

Becky didn't mind helping the sheriff, but the chances of her being useful were slim to none. Probably they thought giving her make-work would help her feel better. "It's very kind of you. But I don't think I'd be very good at what you do."

Sheriff Crow smiled. "I'm not proposing to deputize you. This is just an experiment, to help me with my investigation of that fire. Think you can do it?"

"Sure," Becky said, relieved. That was small enough. "I'd be glad to try."

"And who knows? It might turn out to be interesting to see what a sheriff does," Aunt Rosa said.

Becky couldn't help blurting out, "Arresting people?"

Sheriff Crow's beautiful brown eye and slitted snake eye studied Becky with equal thoughtfulness. "There's much more to the job than that. You'll see. In the old days, sheriffs used to be called peacekeepers."

·19·
FELICITÉ

FELICITÉ HURRIED INTO THE dining room, relieved to find it empty. She still had time to prevent a scene. Felicité took the taper and lit the candles. Now Grandmère would have no excuse to use her power, so Daddy would have no excuse to get angry. They'd all have a pleasant dinner, and afterward she'd invite Henry up to her room instead of dismissing him. She'd worn his favorite dress, the crimson linen. It had lots of buttons that he liked to undo.

As she sat down to wait for him, she recalled yesterday's delightful surprise: Sheriff Crow marching the insufferable Mrs. Callahan through the town square to the jail.

But of course, it couldn't have been delightful for Henry. All day, she'd waited in vain for him to seek her out for consolation. When Mother and Grandmère took her to dinner at Jack's, on their way out they'd heard the tuneless yowling of "My Darling Clementine," which Rick Willet always sang when he got drunk and disorderly.

The racket faded abruptly when Sheriff Crow hauled him off to jail. Felicité had hoped that Mrs. Callahan had been treated to all ten verses at least a dozen times, but had hidden her smile in case Henry came looking for her. But he hadn't.

She hadn't seen Becky, either. Felicité could imagine what it must have been like for Becky to be publicly revealed as a mutant and have her own mother hit and disown her. She must feel so alone and ashamed. Maybe Felicité should visit her. But what comfort could Felicité give her when everyone knew how she felt about Changed people?

She imagined herself saying, "You couldn't help it," or "I like you anyway." And then she imagined hearing those words herself. Ugh! Anything she could say would only make Becky feel worse.

She doesn't need me, anyway. She has Brisa, Felicité thought, relieved. *Another mutant. What could be more natural? Let them be together, on the other side of town.*

Daddy stepped onto the porch and took off his shoes. It was the first time she'd seen him that day. He'd already eaten breakfast and gone off to the Rangers before the rest of the family rose. Felicité frowned. That wasn't like him. She'd looked forward to Grandmère coming back, but not if it meant Daddy had to avoid his own house.

"Hello, darling." He kissed Felicité on the cheek, then sat at the head of the table.

"Hello, Daddy," she said in her best social voice. Now if only Henry would show up, everyone could be together and have dinner like a proper family.

Will appeared next, banging his cast on the banister as he jumped down the stairs.

"William," Mother said reprovingly, and Will slowed down.

"Hi, Dad," Will said. "Where did you go today?"

"We rode out to Sepulveda Arroyo," Daddy said.

"When are you going to let me ride with the Rangers?" Will said. "Cousin Julio says that he rode with you when he was *ten!*"

"Cousin Julio has a poor memory," Daddy said, smiling. "When he was ten, he wasn't riding anything but his pet burro."

Will laughed and kicked the table legs as Mother sat down opposite Daddy.

It was a nice, normal conversation. Good. That made for a nice, normal dinner.

Grandmère came downstairs, her steps noiseless, as Henry's familiar knock sounded at the door. Felicité conducted him to his place. Here they were, all together, the candles safely lit, with Clara setting out the tray of covered dishes. She uncovered stir-fried green beans with garlic, a dish of assorted pickles, and a tangle of wheat noodles. Then Clara lifted the largest lid to reveal the main course: a huge, whole braised fish.

"Yum!" Will said.

"That looks wonderful," Henry said.

Felicité's stomach tightened at the sight of the bulging eyes and open gills.

Daddy picked up the big chopsticks and plucked out the cheeks. With a smile he deposited them on Felicité's plate. "Your favorite, darling."

"Thank you, Daddy," she managed. At her side, she felt Henry stirring.

As Daddy served everyone else, Henry whispered, "Are you okay?"

"I'm fine," she returned, and with concern, "How are you?"

Henry's smile didn't change. "Now that I'm with you, I'm fine."

"I'm so sorry about Becky," she whispered.

"Hey, Henry," Will said. "What power did Becky get?"

The serving chopsticks clattered to the fish plate. "Will," Daddy said. "Not at the dinner table."

Grandmère interlaced her long fingers. "There is nothing inappropriate about the topic of Changes, William. My understanding is that Becky gained the ability to see into the past of an object. Isn't that fascinating? We could learn so much from that. I was thinking of suggesting that she accompany young Ross when he next visits the ruined city. Perhaps if she can touch an artifact that has not been handled since ancient times, she could catch a glimpse of our lost history."

"Oh, history," Will said, sounding bored. Then, perking up, he said, "What if she touched a Ranger sword? She could see whoever they killed!"

"William," Mother murmured.

"Killing isn't for entertainment," Daddy snapped. "And Will, I told you not to talk about this."

"You never said I couldn't talk about killing," Will protested.

"Your father meant the Change," Grandmère said. With delicate sarcasm, she added, "Talking about killing is perfectly acceptable."

"Please, Mother." Felicité winced as her own mother laid a

hand on Grandmère's wrist. "Let us eat in peace, shall we?"

"There can be no peace without acceptance," Grandmère said. "Becky Callahan gained a power that is useful and harmless. She did not deserve to be struck down and disowned."

Felicité looked at her hands, then saw Henry's white-knuckled grip on his chopsticks.

"I'm not saying it was justified to hit the girl," Daddy said. "I will never approve of that. But Mrs. Callahan had the right to turn a mutant out of her own house!"

Grandmère stood up. "And I have the right to turn a bigot out of *my* house."

Daddy also got up. Felicité half-rose, trying to think of some way of stopping them.

Looking more flustered than Felicité had ever seen, Mother said, "Please sit down, both of you. Let us agree to disagree, and set an example by enjoying a civilized meal."

Grandmère retorted, "What is civilized about bigotry?"

"It's my house, too," Daddy snapped.

Grandmère seated herself like a queen. "This house has been owned by the Wolfes for generations. You used to work for the enemy. You came here with nothing. You don't even know who your parents were. Valeria chose you, but *I* did not."

Daddy looked straight at Mother as he said, "You know where I'll be." He threw down his napkin. In two steps, he was outside and pulling on his boots.

"Mother, stop him," Felicité said desperately. And to Grandmère, "Daddy saved this town!"

Grandmère turned to her. "One good deed does not excuse one bad one. Isn't Becky a friend of yours? Felicité, imagine if it was you."

Felicité backed away from the table where that hideous fish lay gaping its gills at her. She *was* imagining if it was her. Daddy would never hit her, of course. But he'd turn the mutant out of his house.

She shoved her feet into her shoes and dashed into the garden, stopping to look fearfully up at the sky. It was clear. Every star shone brilliant white. She stood breathing hard, then jumped as a warm hand slid into hers.

"There you are, Princess," Henry said. "Let's get away from them all, okay?"

Felicité gratefully squeezed his hand. "Henry, I'm so sorry about Becky—and your mother. That was awful."

"Well, I'm sorry about your family. Let's leave them to be awful together and go be civilized. In our way." He grinned at her in the darkness, tightening his fingers on hers.

"I don't want to go back in there."

"We can't go to my place," Henry said, grimacing. "I guess we could go to Jack's."

"I'd rather be alone with you." She could feel Henry's agreement in his grip. Where could they be alone, other than her bedroom? "I know a place. Come on."

She hurried him down the Hill and to the looming black shape of the town hall.

"Here?" Henry said doubtfully. But when they got inside the cold, vast room, and Felicité showed him where the lantern was, he grinned with anticipation. "There isn't a secret passage, is there?"

Felicité suppressed a start. He was joking, but he'd come so close to guessing the biggest secret in Las Anclas: the emergency exit should the town ever be invaded, the concealed tunnel that ran from the basement to the mill outside the town wall.

"It's better than that. It's a place where we can be completely alone."

"Oooh," Henry said. "That sounds great."

In the basement, Felicité led him past Jack's beer barrels and the jumble of old decorations and a broken wagon that concealed the tunnel's trapdoor, and finally to the shelves of emergency supplies. She unfolded a blanket and shook it out. A glowing bug dropped to the dirt and scuttled away.

Henry looked around appreciatively. "You've been holding out on me. Privacy, blankets—and beer! Do you have a siphon?"

Felicité stretched out on the blanket. "We're not touching Jack's beer. He has measure marks inside the barrels. Just appreciate the blankets and the privacy." *And dryness.* There was no chance of getting caught in the rain or of Henry suggesting that they take a bath together.

Henry lay down beside her and twirled one of her curls around his finger. "I'm appreciating! So, what's next, Princess? Shall we play Secrets again?"

"Sure. You go first." Felicité relaxed against the warmth of his body. For the first time that day, she felt safe. In five months of dating, he had always followed her lead. He'd ask for more, but he'd never pressure her or make her feel uncomfortable once she said no.

Henry lay back, looking upward. She watched the reflection of the lantern flame dance in his huge pupils. "You know all my secrets. I'm an open book."

"Think harder."

He was silent, then grinned. "Sometimes I imagine you, me, and Sujata, swimming in the ocean together."

"What kind of a secret is that?" Felicité asked.

He blushed. "Naked."

Felicité laughed and pulled him over for his kiss. His kisses had gotten better and better. There was nothing she loved more than lying beside him, enjoying the heat of his lips. She sank into pleasure as they each teased and nibbled. As the kisses deepened, she ran her hands up his sides, beneath his shirt. He'd gotten more muscular since he'd started Ranger training. Felicité liked that. She hoped he'd keep training, even though it wouldn't be with the Rangers.

Henry's breath caught. "Your turn," he whispered into her ear.

Felicité loved this game. She would never reveal the two most important secrets in her life—the tunnel and the one she wasn't going to think about—but others were so delicious. "Sometimes I imagine you and me in the shed behind Luc's, the one that doesn't have a lock. Kissing with one eye on the door, knowing that someone might open it at any time."

"Oh, let's do that. And if whoever discovers us is a girl, we can invite them in!"

Felicité bit his ear.

"Ow!" he squeaked. "Do it again."

She slowly unbuttoned his shirt, then took her kiss on his chest. His skin was so smooth beneath her lips. To her relief, he wasn't sweating yet. That always had to be her cue to stop.

"Your turn," she said.

"I'll tell you about my first kiss," he began.

"Yuki Nakamura," Felicité said, grinning.

Henry poked her indignantly. "No!"

"Are you sure?" Felicité teased. "You used to follow him around like a puppy."

Henry sighed. "Yuki was kissing before I ever thought about it, and it sure wasn't me. No, my first was Faviola Valdez." He sighed again. "She got bored with me pretty quick."

"Did you put a flying cockroach in her desk?"

"How did you know?" Henry asked with a grin. Then he admitted, "Grandma Wolfe blamed Tommy Horst for it, and I let her."

"That's two secrets. So you get two kisses."

"I can think of two places I'd like to kiss," Henry murmured.

His fingers lightly brushed against her collarbones, then slid down to unbutton her blouse. Felicité relaxed and let him. She knew now that whenever she said stop, he'd stop. Besides, she liked it when he kissed her there. And he knew now to stay away from her neck.

Felicité reveled in the building sense of urgency. She wished Henry would take off all her clothes. She wished she could rip off his. She wanted to press their bodies together, skin to skin . . .

"Your secret," Henry whispered.

Felicité gritted her teeth. She could never go all the way. He'd sweat, she'd sweat, and she'd Change. She forced her mind away from that repulsive image. She should just enjoy what she had.

She searched for a secret, opened her mouth to tell him another fantasy, and heard herself blurt out, "I wish Grandmère had never come back from exile."

Henry laughed, but it was forced. She knew he was thinking about Becky, and his mother. He rolled away from her and lay staring at the ceiling.

There would be no more Secrets tonight. No more kissing and touching that made her forget everything but the pleasure of the moment. She'd ruined that for both of them. And she had no one to blame but herself.

·20·
JENNIE

JENNIE RAISED HER HAND, and the patrol slowed behind her. "Water halt!"

Some of the teenagers cheered. It was a hot day. She swung off Sidewinder, and left him ground-tethered as she strode to the cliff. Jennie gazed across the peaceful town to the sea beyond, glimmering in the morning sunlight. She loved this promontory, one of the highest of the palisades above Las Anclas. A brisk breeze blew out from the ocean, carrying the scent of salt and seaweed.

Mia joined her. "I'm so disappointed that we missed the queen lobster. Of course what we were doing was much more exciting. If I'd had to choose, I'd have picked the ruined city. But it'll probably be another fifteen years before another queen lobster comes to Las Anclas."

"Do you see one?" Henry shouted, pointing out at sea. "Is that a claw?"

Everybody lined up along the edge of the cliff, gazing out under hands or hat brims, ignoring Mia's squeak of, "No! We were just talking!"

"I think I see one!" Yolanda yelled.

"It's a boat," an adult said in a squelching tone.

"I remember the last queen lobster," Ms. Salazar said. "That thing could have trampled the front gate, if they ever came on dry land. I hope I never see another."

"Mmm, someone is barbecuing," Tommy Horst said. "I'm so hungry."

Mia sniffed. "That's not cooking smoke."

Jennie spun around. A plume of white smoke rose from the rocky ridge behind them. From the size of the billows, the fire was nearby, and big.

"To your horses!" Jennie bolted for Sidewinder.

Everyone ran to their mounts and scrambled into the saddles. The horses' ears were flicking back and forth—nervous, but not panicking. Jennie's relief that they wouldn't have a stampede on their hands evaporated when she turned Sidewinder. In the few seconds it had taken her to reach her horse, the fire had crested the ridge above her.

The patrol was trapped between a wall of flame and a sheer cliff.

They couldn't douse the fire with water. There was none but whatever they had left in their canteens. But they didn't ride out on patrol unprepared.

Jennie shouted above the crackle of flames. "You six, hold the horses! The rest of you, get the entrenching tools!"

As she grabbed hers from her saddlebag, she saw that Henry was already passing them out. The diggers began scooping up weedy dirt and flinging it toward the edge of the fire. Even if they couldn't smother the fire, if they could remove everything that could burn, the fire would die before it could get to them.

Jennie had only managed two scoops before a puff of wind blew hot, smoky air so intense it burned her lungs. Bits of burning weeds and sparks floated through the withering heat. She slapped out a flaming leaf that stuck to her shirt.

Clods of dirt flew at the flames, halting their advance, but they couldn't get enough earth to put out the fire. Alfonso, who was busy scooping dirt with his gecko-padded fingers, could climb down the cliff, but it was far too sheer for anyone else, and too high to use ropes.

They needed another strategy. Then she remembered that you could fight fire with fire. They'd all been taught how to do it, but she'd never seen it done. It was risky enough to only use as a desperate last resort.

As Jennie opened her mouth to give the order, Henry shouted, "Jennie! Let's start another fire!"

He held up a box of matches.

"Do it, Henry." Jennie ordered, "Everyone, back up to the cliff! Take the horses!"

Henry faced into the wind, then knelt a scarce few yards from the flames, lighting matches and putting them down in a line below the roaring fire. His fire sprang up. As he bolted back to the crowd at the cliff, who stood ready with their entrenching tools in case a flame or even a spark headed their way. Jennie stood poised, biting her lip as his fire spread to meet the larger one.

If the wind changed, they'd all be dead.

The flames rose high, fed by the breeze from the sea, and raced toward the fire moving downward over the ridge. "Start burying it from this side," Jennie yelled, and everyone feverishly began dumping dirt along the line where Henry had set the fire. Jennie was aware of a small shadow working next to her. Without looking, she knew who it was. Jennie put her arm around Mia.

If the worst came to worst, maybe Alfonso could get Mia down the cliff. She was the lightest person there.

"It's getting bigger!" Yolanda raised her hands to send a whipping wind at the flames. It did nothing but make them roil and spit out sparks.

"No, it's working, it's working!" somebody yelled from the other end of the line. The smoke was so thick and the roaring of the flames was so loud that Jennie had no idea who was speaking.

The two fires joined in a blaze that seemed to blot out the sky. And then, almost as swiftly as the fire had come over the ridge, it began to die down, with nowhere to burn.

"Put it all out," Jennie croaked, her throat raw.

The diggers got back to work with redoubled energy. A few minutes later, the last of the bush fires was smothered.

Jennie leaned her hands on her knees, fighting to calm her breathing. It had all happened so fast and unexpectedly, and ended just as quickly, that it barely even seemed real. Everyone around her looked as stunned as she felt. But an acrid smell of smoke clung to her sweat-soaked clothes, reminding her that she still had a job to do.

Sidewinder sidled at her approach, but one of the patrol held him steady. Jennie gave him a soothing pat, then rode up the blackened slope to see if the fire still burned on the other side of the ridge.

The blackened area ended as abruptly as if it had been drawn with a ruler. The other side of the slope was nothing but rocks and gravel. The fire had begun at the only burnable area of the ridge.

That was strange. And it was strange for any wildfire to start without lightning. But the sky was a brilliant blue, free of clouds. Jennie swung out of the saddle and crouched to examine the edge where soot met rock.

Mia joined her, peering intently through soot-speckled glasses. "This is the second time in two months I've poked through ashes."

Henry wandered up, kicking idly at the ashes. "Find any drunken kids?"

Jennie tried to smile. "Not this time."

"Look, a match!" Mia pointed toward the toe of her shoe.

Jennie held out a hand. "Don't touch it. If this fire was set, Becky could see who held it last."

Henry followed Jennie's lead and held out his arm, too, blocking the crowd of curious patrollers.

"Mark off this area," Jennie said. "Use the rope in my saddlebag."

◆ ◆ ◆

The sun had reached its zenith when the patrol reached the gates. The stink of smoke rose from Jennie's clothes, and her arms and back ached from digging. She was exhausted and had a heat-headache, too. But none of that mattered. No one had died. No one was even hurt, other than scrapes and blisters.

She'd led her patrol through danger, and she'd brought them safely home.

As they passed through the gates, the memory of carrying Sera's body brought a familiar grief. Then Jennie realized that it was the first time she'd recalled that in days. Even when she'd been fighting the fire, in air filled with smoke and burning leaves, she'd thought of nothing but the people she was trying to save right then.

Now that she had remembered the battle, Jennie tensed,

waiting to be overwhelmed with guilt and memories so vivid that she could practically feel the blood on her hands. But she wasn't. She'd done nothing she regretted during the fire. And all she saw and felt was what was happening here and now.

From the sentry walk, Ms. Lowenstein called down, "We saw smoke. What happened?"

"We fought a brush fire." Making sure the entire patrol could hear her, Jennie added, "Everyone did well. Nobody panicked. Henry was especially helpful. He was the first one to suggest that we fight fire with fire."

Ms. Lowenstein repeated incredulously, "Henry?"

"Yeah," Tommy Horst called. "Henry was cool under fire!"

Felicité leaned over, her bobbing curls tempting the eater-roses into frantic, useless lunges. "Henry! You were a hero! I want to hear all about it."

To Jennie's surprise, Henry actually looked embarrassed. "Oh, I was just the first person to open my mouth. I'm sure Jennie was thinking of it."

Jennie smiled and said nothing. Let Henry have his moment of glory. Maybe he'd changed. People did.

·21·
BECKY

SHERIFF CROW MOTIONED TO Becky. "Go ahead. Take your time."

Becky crouched down, wrinkling her nose at the stink of burnt wood and weeds. The ash was still hot underfoot.

She'd used her power in front of Sheriff Crow before, at the burned-out barn. As Becky had predicted, she'd seen cows. And also Hans and Peter stealthily climbing the ladder, Kerry's secret party from when she'd been a hostage, Paco practicing the drums, Yuki and Paco kissing passionately (Becky had blushed and mumbled that it was nothing interesting; the sheriff had given her an extremely knowing look and dryly said, "Let's say it was more cows,"), and the barn being raised. But she hadn't seen any clues to the fire.

Becky braced herself to disappoint the sheriff again. But she was nervous for another reason, too. She knew it was just imagination, but every time she used her power, her cheek heated and throbbed where her mother had slapped her. It was throbbing already.

She extended a finger and touched the burned-out match.

Impatience flooded her as her slim brown hand, extending from the patched sleeve of a leather jacket, whisked over a smooth surface, knocking the blackened match away.

Becky blinked up at Sheriff Crow's intent gaze. "I saw someone touch it, but I'm not sure that's the person who lit the match. It was already burned."

"Can you touch it again and try to see who lit it?"

Becky took a deep breath, focused, and reached out again.

Concentration on a task. Hunger. *Twenty more matches and then I can have lunch.* A woman's hand dipped the match into the sulphur mixture, then stuck it upright in a ball of wax.

"I think I saw Mrs. Horst," Becky said apologetically. "When she made it."

Sheriff Crow gave an exasperated snort. "Someone's being very clever here. Who was it who touched the burned match?"

Becky hesitated. She doubted that Summer had set the fire, but once Becky spoke, Sheriff Crow wouldn't be able to keep what she said out of the town gossip. Becky had seen what people had been like to Ross when he'd been falsely accused of a crime.

Reluctantly, she said, "Summer Juarez. I recognized her jacket. But all she did was knock it off something smooth." Bringing the vision back in memory, she added, "Something wooden. A table, maybe."

Sheriff Crow put her hands on her hips and looked around. "Nothing smooth here. And you said the match was already burned. The whole town knows about your power. I think—" The sheriff broke off, looking curiously at Becky. "What do you think, Becky? What's your explanation of this?"

Becky's stomach fluttered nervously. "I only see things. I don't know what they mean."

"I didn't mean your power. What explanation can you imagine?"

Becky couldn't think why the sheriff cared what she imagined, but she said, "I don't think Summer set the fire. I think someone else lit that match, then put it where they knew she'd touch it. Maybe her chair or desk at school. And then they dropped it here."

Sheriff Crow's skull-side couldn't form expressions, but the beautiful side looked pleased. "I think so, too. And if we find out why, we might find out who."

"We?" Becky echoed. "Do you think you'll have more things for me to touch?"

"Could be. Why don't you tag along, just in case?"

Becky got to her feet and dusted herself off. To her surprise, she was glad of the invitation. It wasn't as if she had anything else to do. And she had been helpful. It wasn't just make-work. But more than that, she was curious. As they walked back down the burned slope, she turned over different possibilities in her mind.

Finally, she couldn't resist asking, "What do you think, Sheriff Crow? Why would someone set a fire here? Why do people ever set fires?"

"The most common reason is they're kids playing around. Fire is fascinating. Did you ever set tiny fires when you were little?"

Becky shook her head.

The sheriff smiled. "Well, lots of kids do. I did."

Becky tried to imagine Sheriff Crow as a child. She must been one of those little girls who hadn't been scared of anything, like Meredith or Jennie. Becky had always wished she was like that.

"But this couldn't have been a kid, right? They're not allowed this far out of town, and someone would have noticed if they'd gone out through the gates." As soon as Becky spoke, she thought, *What a stupid thing to say. Of course the sheriff already knows that.*

But Sheriff Crow didn't give her a scornful look. Instead, she nodded as if Becky had said something smart. "No, I don't think it could have. As for fires people set on purpose, the usual reasons are to destroy something that belongs to an enemy, or get rid of something they need to hide. But this area doesn't belong to anyone, and we didn't find the remains of anything. Can you think of any other reasons?"

The sheriff sounded as if she genuinely wanted to hear Becky's thoughts. Timidly, Becky suggested, "Everyone knows about my power now. And they know you had me touch things at the barn. Maybe someone wanted Summer to be blamed for the fire."

The sheriff nodded. "Someone seems to have gone to a great deal of trouble to arrange that. So if all the arsonist wanted was to harm Summer, then who hates her enough to endanger the entire patrol?"

"She broke Will Preston's arm. He couldn't have set the fire himself, but maybe someone—" Becky caught herself before she could say "someone in his family." She couldn't accuse the mayor or the Ranger chief or an elderly council member or even Felicité of arson.

"Go on."

Becky cleared her throat. "Everyone says the story Summer told, about how her town was destroyed when the Norms turned against the Changed, cost the election for—"

"Tom Preston," the sheriff said, smiling. "Interesting how all theories lead back to him."

Becky didn't dare to voice her thought, but she was dying to ask Sheriff Crow if she believed he might have done it.

Sheriff Crow took pity on her. "I don't think it's his style. But you're right to ask the questions. Speaking of questions, I agree that Summer is probably the victim here, but we still have to check. Let's find out where she was when the fire happened."

♦ ♦ ♦

Sheriff Crow had Jennie check the week's student roster for Saturday morning jobs. Summer had been assigned to assist Mrs. Riley.

But when Becky and Sheriff Crow arrived at the corral, Mrs. Riley was alone. And annoyed. "Yes, Summer was here. For about three minutes. I left her to rake out the back corral while I fed the horses. When I came out, she was gone with nothing done."

As they walked away, Sheriff Crow remarked, "And sometimes our neat little theories blow up in our faces. Let's see if anyone in town saw her."

"Should we start with Ross?" Becky asked.

"Just what I was thinking."

They found Ross hammering stakes into the ground in the Vardams' orchard. He'd half-finished the raccoon-proof electric fence Mia had designed.

In the few days since Becky had last practiced martial arts there, the raccoon city had gotten even larger. The biggest and best raccoon house had acquired a fourth story, and nearly every tree had at least one raccoon-crafted vine-bridge or swing. And the raccoons had once again diverted the stream into their city.

"But why won't you take me into the ruined city? You took your girlfriends!" Summer was saying loudly.

Ross's hammer came down extra hard on a stake.

Summer's voice rose above the banging. "I could protect you.

You wouldn't get all beat up, like you did the last time. I bet your *girlfriends* never killed an armored bear. Well, I have. Two!"

"I told you before, it's too dangerous. It's not the armored bears, it's the crystal trees. I can't." His voice trailed off as Ross returned to his work.

"What else is there to do?" Summer demanded. "This town is so boring."

"They'll have a dance for Lunar New Year," Ross said.

"And what, hop around in a circle while somebody plunks a banjo? They don't even have a theater!"

Ross pounded the hammer harder, then saw Becky and Sheriff Crow. His frustrated expression changed into one of relief. "Hi. Are you looking for Sujata?"

Summer picked up an apple and flung it at a raccoon who was trying to steal the coil of electric wire. It caught the fruit in its clever paws, hissed viciously, and hurled it back. She ducked, and the apple smashed against a tree.

"Summer!" Ross exclaimed. "I told you, stop bothering the raccoons."

"It was stealing your wire."

Sheriff Crow turned to Ross's sister. "Summer, where have you been all morning? You were supposed to be at the corral."

"The foals were with their mothers, and it was boring. I didn't want to rake poo." In a jeering tone no one else in town would have dared use on the sheriff, Summer asked, "Are you going to arrest me?"

Sheriff Crow didn't smile. "Ross, has she been with you all morning?"

Ross wiped his damp forehead on his sleeve. "I think so. Most of it, anyway. Why?"

"I want to know where she was when the fire started," said Sheriff Crow.

Becky could swear that Summer's eyes widened in genuine shock. She waved a stick at the nearest raccoon house and snapped, "I didn't set it! Why would I do that?" She poked the stick into the wall of hardened mud. "Why would anyone do something that stupid? Do you think *I'm* stupid?" Poke, poke, poke, right into the raccoon's front door.

"Where did you go when you left the corral?" The sheriff's tone was calm, not accusing, but the girl reacted as if she'd been threatened.

"I looked for Ross! I figured I could help him, if I had to do something. I notice *he* never has to rake horse poo."

"I raked it last week," Ross put in. "We all have to."

Summer jabbed the stick angrily into the raccoon house. "Well, I—"

A loud hiss emanated from within, and the stick shoved itself back. Summer stumbled backward as a raccoon leaped out and lunged at her, teeth bared. She jumped into the air, rising up and up until she landed atop the town wall.

She stuck out her tongue at the raccoon, then leaped into the corn fields and vanished. Leaves rustled as she ran off. The raccoon glared with its beady eyes, then retreated back into its home.

Ross broke the silence. "Sheriff, do you really think she set the fire?"

"I don't know. If she didn't, someone went to a great effort to make it seem that she did. Know anything about that?"

Ross muttered, "A lot of people went to a great effort to get me in trouble when I came here." He wiped his forehead again. "But not like that. I wish I'd noticed when she got here. But Mia might have. She was here when Summer arrived. But then she, um, left."

Becky could imagine why. She wouldn't want to face Summer's glares, either.

As they went to find Mia, Sheriff Crow said, "I'd like to keep you with me for the day."

"More things to touch?" Becky asked.

"Could be," the sheriff replied. "But also, I like the way you think. You might be able to add something to my report to the council, since you've been with me for the entire investigation so far. Are you ready for that?"

Becky's stomach churned with the old, familiar terror. "I have to speak in front of the council?"

"Not if you don't want to. But if you think of anything I missed, you can mention it to me."

"Okay." Becky's fear didn't wear off instantly. But a different feeling also shivered through her, more in her nerves than in her stomach. It was…excitement. And curiosity. Being a sheriff wasn't just about arresting people, or even keeping the peace. It was also about solving mysteries.

And there were some mysteries that Becky had wondered about for a long, long time.

◆ ◆ ◆

"…and according to Mia, Summer showed up about half an hour after the time Mrs. Riley thought she'd left the corral," Sheriff Crow concluded.

"That might have been enough time for her to set the fire and get away, as fast as she is," Mr. Horst said. "I hear she's always running off. Especially if she is asked to do chores."

"There is at least a partial explanation for her disappearances," Mr. Preston said.

When Sheriff Crow had brought her to the town hall, Becky had been surprised to see Mr. Preston sitting in his old place beside the mayor, even though he was no longer on the council. Maybe nobody had the nerve to throw him out. He was in his old chair, too. Mr. Horst sat in a new one.

"What's that?" the mayor asked. "Where does the girl go?"

"Luc told me he's been hearing footsteps on his roof whenever he has musicians playing or even rehearsing," Mr. Preston explained. "He thinks she's dancing. The footsteps keep rhythm with the players."

"Why would she dance on the roof instead of inside?" Mr. Appel asked.

"Why does she do anything, except to be annoying?" Mr. Horst looked straight at Mr. Preston as he said sarcastically, "Maybe she set the fire in between rooftop dance shows."

Sheriff Crow held up her hand to catch everyone's attention. "I haven't finished. Another possibility is that the purpose of the fire was to frame her. In which case we should ask, who in town has that much personal animosity against Summer Juarez?"

Becky's breath drew in a quiet gasp as everyone but the mayor looked at Mr. Preston.

He didn't look guilty. Nor did he seem worried or defensive. Instead, he addressed the council in the same calm, interested tone Sheriff Crow had used to discuss the reasons for setting fires. "If you're looking at motivation, I've got one for you. Maybe someone wanted to be a hero. I've seen that before. And one person was very noticeably heroic, *from what I hear,* because I was nowhere near either fire. That was Alfonso Medina. Not only that, but he was the only person capable of being heroic in that barn fire. Furthermore, he was the only one who could be sure to survive being trapped between a fire and a steep cliff."

"As usual, Thomas blames the Changed person," Grandma Wolfe said tartly. "I've taught Alfonso his entire life, and nothing in his character leads me to believe him capable of such a thing. Moreover, being a hero doesn't benefit him. He's not trying to get into *your* Rangers," she glared at Mr. Preston in a way that made Becky want to duck, "which is the only motivation I can see for being perceived as a hero."

Mayor Wolfe said smoothly, "One never knows what people may want, or what they're capable of. Let us stick to facts rather than speculation. Sheriff, please continue your investigation."

Mr. Horst raised his voice. "What about that Changed girl? I'm not happy having her wander loose around the town causing trouble. Especially when she can get into anything, grasshoppering from roof to roof. At the very least, she should be under restrictions."

"I agree," said Judge Lopez.

"I do as well," said the mayor.

"What sort of restrictions are we talking about?" Dr. Lee inquired. When no one spoke, he continued, "I would vote for having her brother or some other responsible adult watch her, at least until the question of the fire is cleared up."

"You're calling Ross a responsible adult?" Mr. Horst demanded. "For all we know, he held the match so she could strike it."

Grandma Wolfe gave Mr. Horst a cold look, then turned away. "A splendid idea, Dante. I call for a vote."

Mayor Wolfe said, "All in favor raise your hands."

All the adults but Mr. Horst raised their hands. Mr. Preston began to raise his, then quickly changed the movement to adjusting his glasses.

"The ayes have it," Mayor Wolfe announced. "From now on, Summer Juarez is to be watched 24/7 by either her brother or some other adult he hands her off to."

Becky was relieved that Summer hadn't gotten in worse trouble. But when she imagined being with that girl 24/7, she felt sorry for Ross.

·22·
ROSS

ROSS AND PACO SAT on the beach, doing the breathing exercises Yuki had taught them. He didn't enjoy them—Ross was never going to like feeling suffocated—but the more he practiced, the more precious seconds he gained.

"I can hold my breath longer than you," Summer called. "When are you going to teach me to swim?"

"Now, if you want," Ross said, glad that she was asking for something he could actually give her, for once. "I'll walk you back so you can get something to swim in."

Summer glanced over her shoulder at the distant town walls shimmering in the heat haze. "Ugh. What a slog! By the time we get back, you'll tell me you have something else to do."

Ross looked at his hands, unsure what to say. She was right. He'd promised Mia that he'd do the oil-collecting, taking people's used oil and replacing it with fresh jugs, once he was done with the sea cave. And Summer would have to come with him.

Much as he loved Las Anclas, sometimes the rules and expectations still made him feel like the walls were closing in.

"I'll go first." Paco's voice broke into his thoughts. He jerked his sharp chin at Summer.

"Right." Ross would much rather dive with Paco. He didn't feel entirely secure diving to the cave alone. But now he wasn't allowed to leave Summer unattended.

Kerry came riding up on Nugget, leading Penny. Gold and copper coats gleamed in the brilliant sunlight. "There you are!"

Summer's pout vanished. "Kerry!"

"Hi, Summer," Kerry said. "Ross. Paco."

A splash behind Ross made him turn. Paco was gone.

Ross tried to find a way to word his question without starting another argument. "Summer, are you going to ride with Kerry?"

Kerry shrugged, smiling at them both. "She can ride with me or watch you dive. Up to her."

"I'll ride," Summer said instantly. "This is boring."

She leaped into the saddle in one graceful move, and the girls galloped off.

Ross watched his sister leaving him just like Paco had fled from Kerry. Six months ago, neither he nor Paco had known they had sisters. And though Kerry seemed to want to get to know Paco and Ross was trying hard to be a brother to Summer, neither of their siblings seemed interested.

Not that he blamed Paco. Maybe he'd feel the same after finding out that his father was none other than King Voske—and that Kerry had been raised to attack the town and take it for her own.

"But I'm not Voske," Ross muttered. Though probably Summer would think he was cooler if he was.

He grimaced, torn between being glad his sister had never known Voske and worry that if she stayed, she might. Desperate for a distraction, he dove under a wave. The icy shock was a relief after the heat of the sun and the unsettled way he always felt around Summer, as if she were unstable dynamite about to ignite.

Paco's dark head surfaced, and he took a deep breath. Ross didn't miss his look of relief when he saw that Kerry was gone.

Treading water, Ross asked, "Find anything?"

Paco shook his head. "I didn't go inside. Something's stirred up the water."

A whiskered head popped up between them. Ross started, thrashing in water that he'd forgotten how to swim in. When he caught his balance, he heard Paco laughing. That was a sound Ross hadn't heard in a long time.

"It's the harbor seals," Paco said. "I'd forgotten that they come back to Las Anclas for the winter. I guess the water's warmer here than wherever they live for the rest of the year."

The whiskery head blinked huge black eyes at Ross. He looked down through the water at a cylindrical body with spotted fur and four flippers. One of the flippers gave him a light whack on the thigh.

"They're harmless?" Ross asked doubtfully, remembering the soulful blue eyes of Princess Pit Mouth.

"Completely. Follow me." Paco dove beneath the surface.

Ross gulped in a breath and followed. He slitted his eyes for a quick peek. The seal had friends; at least twenty sinuous shapes moved gracefully through the water. They clustered around Ross and Paco, bumping them with their muzzles and prodding them with their flippers. Ross put out his hand, palm out. A seal slapped it with a flipper. Ross had to stop himself from laughing underwater.

Paco and Ross surfaced to catch their breath. Several sleek heads popped up around them.

"Ark, ark!" A seal barked.

Others added their voices, from babies no longer than Ross's arm to one almost the size of a fishing skiff.

"Watch this." Paco flung his arms around the neck of the nearest seal. The creature gave a powerful flick of its back flippers. To Ross's amazement, seal and Paco went skimming over the water together, diving in and out of the breakers.

Several seals nudged Ross, gazing at him in a way that he couldn't help reading as hopeful. Imitating Paco, he caught the nearest seal in his arms. It was wet and furry and warm, contrasting with the chilly water. Slippery, too. He almost lost his grasp as the powerful muscles bunched under his arms. He tensed as the seal took off.

Then he was flying across the water, fast as a horse could gallop, cold spray in his face. But the movement was far smoother than a horse's gait, and unlike any horse he'd ever encountered, he had the feeling that the seal found it fun to have Ross ride him. Ross hung on tight as the seal leaped into the air, then came down with a huge splash. Salt water flooded Ross's mouth as he laughed with sheer delight. It was the first time he'd enjoyed riding anything but his burro Rusty.

The rest of the seals followed as Ross's seal caught up to Paco's.

"This is amazing!" Ross shouted. "How did you know about

this?"

"Yuki taught me. He used to ride dolphins. The way he described them, they're sort of like seals and sort of like big fish. They live in the deep ocean." Paco glanced over his shoulder at the open sea beyond, as if he was imagining Yuki out there.

Ross looked back for Summer. He bet she wouldn't be bored by this. Maybe she'd take off her jacket and swim in her clothes to ride a seal. But Kerry and Summer were nowhere to be seen, and were still gone by the time he returned to the beach.

He went back to town, collected the oil cart, and headed for the schoolhouse, hoping to find Jennie making lesson plans. Ross found her alone in the schoolyard instead, doing pull-ups on the monkey bars. She'd taken off her jacket, leaving her arms bare. Ross admired her shoulder muscles as they worked under her smooth dark skin. His breath caught as he remembered that he could touch that skin any time he wanted. All he needed to do was ask. Or say yes...

Then Jennie saw him. Her intent expression melted into to a welcoming smile as she dropped down.

"Come with me?" Ross asked.

"Sure." Jennie fell in step beside him, and they headed along the street.

During the long walk from the beach, Ross had been thinking about how to word his request. "Jennie, you have a lot of siblings."

She grinned. "You noticed!"

He grinned back, then pushed on, still unsure. "I know your family fosters kids whose own families kicked them out when they Changed. Or for other reasons."

Her smile faded. "Do you want Ma and Pa to foster Summer?"

Ross loved that idea—for about two seconds. "No. She's my responsibility. And I don't think she'd do it. But I've seen how everybody gets along so well at your house. How do you do that?"

"It's Ma and Pa, mostly. They never get angry. Even when the kid is. Especially when the kid is. Pa told me after Yolanda came that anger comes from the grief of betrayal. And anger only begets anger. The deeper it goes, the more dangerous it is."

Ross grimaced. "Summer is angry, all right, but I don't know if she's been betrayed. Though she acts like I betrayed her. Dr. Lee thinks something bad happened, something she's hiding. Have you ever had anybody like her?"

"Once," Jennie said thoughtfully. "It was when Yuki came."

"Yuki was like Summer?" Ross couldn't think of two people with less in common. Except, he supposed, for their long black hair.

"It wasn't that Yuki was like Summer, but that he was the one kid my parents couldn't get through to. Even with angry kids like Yolanda used to be, at least we all knew each other already. None of us could even speak Yuki's language. Everyone he knew was dead or gone, and we had no idea what had happened to him."

Ross could *almost* imagine that. For half his life, everyone he'd known had been dead or gone. But at least most places he'd gone, he could understand what people were saying. His sister, too, must have believed she'd lost everyone she'd ever known.

"Summer never said how she ended up here," Ross said, stepping on to Grandpa Guzik's back porch. "Sometimes she talks like Mom had her the whole time, but sometimes it sounds like she was alone in the desert, like me. When I ask her, she gets mad. I guess with Yuki, he told you everything as soon as you could understand each other."

"Not really." Jennie hefted the stinky jug of old oil Grandpa Guzik had left on the porch. Ross replaced it with a clean one. "Yuki picked up English and Spanish pretty quick. But he never fit into our family. The harder Ma and Pa tried to make him feel welcome, surrounding him with people, giving him lots of affection, the more he retreated. He'd do what he was told, but as soon as he was done, he'd shut himself in his room or go to the beach and stare out at the sea."

Ross hauled the cart between the longhouses along Jackalope Lane. He could imagine how tough it had been for Yuki to be in the Rileys' crowded kitchen, no matter how friendly everyone was. "How did he end up with the Lowensteins?"

"I got the measles," Jennie said. "Dr. Lee said if Yuki had never been exposed to it before, it could be really dangerous for him to catch it. Meredith had already had it, so he moved in with the Lowensteins. It turned out he did a lot better when people weren't constantly trying to talk to him and pat him on the shoulder. Ms.

Lowenstein's way of making him feel welcome was to give him a crossbow. Meredith's was to set up a target in the backyard and start shooting, so he could join in if he wanted to and not if he didn't. For Yuki, the way to get him to come to you is to back off."

"Do you think I should back off with Summer?" Ross asked.

Jennie smiled. "I think you've already tried that. I was thinking more of how different Yuki was at our house and at the Lowensteins'. He wasn't a different person, he just needed a new environment. Actually, there's another thing he and Summer have in common. Sort of. They're not good with crowds. Yuki just didn't like them. But they seem to inspire Summer to put on her worst behavior."

"That's true," Ross said slowly. "She can be a lot calmer when it's one on one. She seems...normal...when she's with Kerry."

Jennie snapped her fingers. "What about taking her to prospect in the desert? Even one afternoon alone together outside of Las Anclas might make a big difference."

"That's a good idea. I'll ask her."

He was still thinking about it when he lugged the laden cart into Mia's yard. Getting away had always been his first defense. Maybe that was one way that Summer was like him.

Mia's head popped out through the cottage window. "Ross!" She leaned out further, looking around shiftily. "You're alone," she added with relief that she couldn't quite hide. "Come on in!"

Ross glanced up at the yo on its pulley. Mia turned red.

Before things could get awkward, Ross said, "I know you and Summer don't get along. Summer and I don't get along. But Jennie thought that might change if I took her out of Las Anclas."

"Oh, right, I heard Summer talking about that in the schoolyard, when I was fixing the water pump."

Alarmed, Ross said, "You couldn't have. I haven't asked her yet. What did she say?"

"She didn't say she was going with *you*. She said she was going to go on a snake hunt. You know, for giant rattlesnakes. Half the kids volunteered to go with her."

Ross thought grimly, *Angry kids might be dangerous, but bored ones are even worse.* He had to take his sister out of town before she got in even more trouble. He'd ask her as soon as Kerry brought her back. But even an overnight prospecting trip would just postpone her terrible snake hunt to the next day.

Then he got a better idea. "Hey, Mia, wasn't your dad telling us the Catalina Players would be in the Saigon Alliance around now?"

Mia nodded, looking puzzled. "Yeah, they go up and down all those coast towns for Lunar New Year. We used to be one of their stops. Not any more, of course."

"That's perfect. How would you like to see them again?"

Her lips parted in astonishment, as if taking a trip out of Las Anclas had never occurred to her. Maybe it hadn't. Ross still wasn't used to the idea that people here didn't just pick up and leave whenever they wanted to. *Or had to.*

"I'd love to!" Mia said belatedly.

"I want to take Summer," Ross warned her. "She keeps talking about how boring it is here with no theater. But I'd ask Jennie, too. And maybe Kerry, if she wants to come along. Summer likes her."

And she doesn't like anyone else, Ross thought.

"Isn't that a crowd?" Mia's smile was completely unconvincing.

"A small one. With two of your friends. Look," he said, lowering his voice. "You and I might have better luck being alone than in town. No one seems to have anything better to do here than bang down your door."

Though they'd only been interrupted twice, Mia had gotten so nervous about it happening again that they'd spent all their subsequent dates at Luc's or working at the cottage with the door open so she could see if anyone was coming.

Mia brightened. "Yeah. And hey, I could take my cloud viper gun!"

"Cloud viper gun?" Ross echoed, baffled.

"Yes!" Mia whipped a cloth from her work table and snatched up a gun. It was the smallest pistol he'd ever seen, almost toy-like. But it fit Mia's hands perfectly. "It paralyzes people with darts filled with cloud viper venom. That is, I hope it does. I still have to test it. But I could do that now that you're here!"

"You want to test it on me?" There was a lot Ross would do for Mia, but the thought of being paralyzed — trapped inside his own body—made his palms sweat.

"No, no, of course not." Mia grabbed his shoulders and moved him into the center of the room. "Just stand here."

Ross moved obediently, looking for the target as she raised the pistol.

"It doesn't use anywhere near as much gunpowder as it would if it fired bullets, because the darts are fragile," Mia explained. "They're filled with liquid, you see. Okay, watch this."

Before Ross could react, she shot herself in the arm.

Her eyes rolled back into her head, and she started to topple. He lunged forward and caught her. Her body was stiff as a board. His heart pounding, he laid her down on the floor and put his ear to her chest. She was breathing as deeply and evenly as if she were asleep.

He gently tugged the pistol from her rigid fingers and laid it on the bed beside the engine parts. Then he took her hand, rubbing it and wondering if he ought to run and fetch Dr. Lee. But he was afraid to leave her. What if she stopped breathing? And he wouldn't be able to get her out the door, stiff as she was.

Her fingers twitched. Ross laid her hand down, and watched as her toes wriggled, then her head turned. The paralysis was wearing off, though not fast enough for Ross. He didn't relax until Mia smiled up at him and said, "I hope I didn't drool."

"No, but you should have warned me! You keeled over like a tree falling. I hope you tested that on an animal first."

Mia didn't seem to hear him as she scrabbled for her pocket watch.

"Ah! Three minutes for a one hundred pound person. But most people are bigger than me. And it needs to knock out the largest people for at least one minute to be useful, so I'd better double the dose." She glanced at Ross as if she'd suddenly remembered that he had spoken. "Oh, it wouldn't have been practical to test it on an animal. My cats only weigh a few pounds. Too risky. Even a tiny overdose might kill them."

"You should have tested it on a cow, or something."

Mia shook her head. "How would you know if a cow was paralyzed? They never move anyway!"

·23·
KERRY

THE HORSES AND ROSS'S little burro plodded southward alongside the broken slabs of the ancient road.

Kerry wiped a trickle of sweat from her forehead. Each of their three days of travel had been hotter than the last. Ross had given Summer her knives back as soon as they'd left, and they'd all ridden out watching for danger. So far, they'd scared off two coyote packs that had wanted horse for lunch, and avoided half a dozen pit mouths. But those moments of excitement had been brief and separated by long stretches of boredom.

When Kerry had said as much, Ross had commented, "That's desert life for you."

"*Yours* might have been boring," Summer had retorted. "*Mine* was non-stop adventure! Have I told you about the monster I fought in an alkali lake? Well, it's not there anymore, not after it met me! We—I was riding along…"

There was that *we* again. But in the entire long and clearly imaginary tale of tentacles and underwater battles that followed, Summer never again let a clue slip about her mysterious companion.

Kerry mostly rode beside Mia, enjoying her chatter about explosives and weapons and dancing dresses. But by the end of the third day, in which nothing happened but a whole lot of riding, even Mia and Summer had fallen silent.

Kerry stifled a yawn and tried to think of something amusing.

For instance, how desperate the town council must have been

to get rid of Summer and buy a week or so of peace in Las Anclas. Apparently they'd agreed to the trip almost as fast as it had been proposed. Kerry hadn't been at the meeting, but Sheriff Crow had told her friend Ms. Lowenstein all about it. Meredith had overheard, then reported the story to the martial arts group.

Grandma Wolfe had reminded the council of Mr. Horst's election promise to invite the Catalina Players back to Las Anclas, and suggested that this would be a perfect opportunity. Meredith passed on Sheriff Crow's vivid description of Mr. Horst's sour look as everyone else (except the mayor, who abstained, and Mr. Preston, who no longer had a vote) instantly endorsed that idea.

The martial arts group had whooped and clapped. But Kerry hadn't forgotten that except for Dr. Lee and Sheriff Crow, that same town council had once voted to execute her. Kerry hoped they'd all go for a swim the next time a queen lobster decided to pay a visit.

She scanned the barren sands for something interesting. Nothing moved but heat waves. Summer looked ready to pass out from boredom. Mia's eyes were glazed. Kerry bet that for the first time in her life, Mia had run out of new weapons to imagine. Ross and Jennie were clearly keeping a lookout for danger, but even they seemed to be struggling to stay focused.

Which reminded Kerry of something that did amuse her, watching Ross trying to juggle two girlfriends and a little sister who made loud retching noises if she so much as caught him holding hands.

If anyone had been mean or jealous, it wouldn't have been funny. Kerry had grown up watching her father's many wives subtly jostling for power for themselves and their children. Ross and Mia and Jennie were nothing like that. It was just a hilariously awkward situation, and in ways Kerry was sure Ross hadn't envisioned when he'd planned the trip.

For instance, the nightly game of musical bedrolls. When they camped the first night, Kerry set her bedroll near the fire. Ross waited for Summer to lay hers down, then put his next to hers, no doubt meaning to be close enough to protect her should something attack in the night. Summer instantly picked up her bedroll and dumped it beside Kerry's, as far from Ross as possible. Jennie, with cool poise, set hers down next to Ross's before going to check for desert creatures.

Mia laid down her bedroll on Ross's other side. They glanced at each other, then reached out. Their fingertips brushed, and then—

"BAAAARF," Summer announced.

Mia and Ross yanked their hands back like they'd been burned. And that was the last touching either of them attempted that night. Jennie never even tried.

The next morning, Ross said he'd go get firewood. Jennie went with him. They were gone for an hour and returned with wood they could have gathered in ten minutes. Ross was flushed under his brown skin, with a silly little grin. Jennie, of course, was completely deadpan.

That night, Summer pawed through their food. "Why is everything so gross? Ugh! This jerky makes me want to puke!"

Mia stared at intensely at Ross, then informed him in a squeak that she'd get the firewood. He got up and followed her. Fifteen minutes later, they were back, both looking uncomfortable.

"Finally!" Summer declared, fists propped on her scrawny hips. "Did you *walk* back to Las Anclas? How'd you miss all those dry branches right over there?"

Mia blushed scarlet. To distract them both, Kerry said, "I wonder what's at the end of the road. The desert can't go on forever."

"I was expecting something more like the ruined city," Mia said wistfully, laying her bedroll next to Ross's. "Not exactly like it, of course. Just interesting and different. But we haven't seen anything yet that we don't have right outside of Las Anclas. Pit mouths, coyotes, jumping cactus, vampire trees. It's like a three-day patrol."

"It'll change soon," Jennie promised as she pitched her bedroll in an expert snap of her wrist on Ross's other side. "There's a reason nobody lives here: no water. Things should change once we hit our first stream."

"When do I get to ride Sally?" Summer demanded. "I ride better than any of you. Except Kerry, of course."

Calmly, Jennie said, "You get your turn with Sally tomorrow if you do your part with camp chores tonight."

"Like?" Summer crossed her arms belligerently.

"How about feeding the horses?"

"That's no chore!" Summer sprang to Rusty's side. She clucked to the little burro as she rifled through the luggage, then triumphantly produced the feedbags. "That's *fun*! I thought you'd make me get firewood."

"Ross and I will do that," Jennie said.

As Ross and Jennie took off, Mia began shredding jerky for soup. Kerry watched Summer long enough to see that she was doing an excellent job with the horses, then excused herself to check for tarantulas. Once she was out of earshot, she let herself laugh. Jennie obviously had plenty of experience dodging siblings at the "romance is gross" stage, but it looked like Mia would have to wait for her turn with Ross till they were back in Las Anclas.

◆ ◆ ◆

The next morning, they awoke to a low gray sky that promised rain. Summer roused them by banging pots and pans, yelling, "Wake up!" *Bang, clatter!* "Let's eat as we ride. The jerky doesn't taste any better fried, now that we're out of potatoes."

Nobody objected, so they set off. Kerry didn't mind eating on the road, especially when all they had was hard jerky and harder trail biscuits. Hills loomed in the distance, but otherwise the terrain was the same as it had been all along, a black road with weeds sprouting from every crack, and bleak desert stretching infinitely to either side.

She worried off a strand of jerky. If she'd been home, cooks would have accompanied them and made pancakes and coffee.

If she'd been home, Santiago would have ridden beside her, his dark eyes turned up to the sky in the hopes of rain.

If she'd been home, she and Santiago wouldn't have had to "look for firewood." They'd have had a royal tent that no one would have dared approach at night.

Enough "ifs."

Gold Point was no longer her home. She'd never ride with Santiago again. Thinking about it did nothing but cause pointless hurt. Her brother Sean had assured her than Santiago was all right.

That was all that mattered. She should be grateful that she even knew that much.

"Look at that!" Ross pointed.

A brilliant pink bird dropped out of the clouds. It circled overhead, then veered off and soared back the way it had come.

Jennie shaded her eyes and watched it go. "The Saigon Alliance uses those birds to send messages. That must have been a scout. So we're near the border." She indicated the cracked remnants of a cement bridge. "I think three of us should wait under this overhang, and two should ride ahead."

"Why don't we all go?" Summer asked.

"Las Anclas doesn't have a good reputation," Jennie explained. She bit off the end of the sentence, presumably for Summer's benefit; Kerry supposed it would have been something like, *thanks to Tom Preston.* "The last thing we want to do is look threatening, so the fewer, the better. Ross is used to coming into strange towns, so he should go with me."

Summer scowled. "I'm used to coming to strange towns, too."

And what happened after you got there? Kerry thought. *Something involving the mysterious "we?"*

But she wasn't about to go there. Summer's sulkiness was probably easier to deal with than whatever emotion lay underneath it. Instead, Kerry said, "If *they're* threatening, we need to split up the people who can fight. So you should stay here."

At the word "fight," Summer's scowl vanished, and she gave a short nod.

She needs purpose, Kerry thought. *Or trust. I bet someone betrayed her, and she doesn't want to trust again. But she wants to be trusted.*

Kerry knew betrayal well. She could almost see Father's merciless smile. Whenever it widened enough to show his teeth, someone always died.

She forced the image from her mind and watched Jennie and Ross ride ahead. Rain began to splat down, making shiny dots on the dusty road. Kerry led the royal horses under the bridge. They didn't mind getting wet, but she didn't want to groom mud out of their coats.

"This is boring," Summer said, as she'd remarked every few hours for the entire trip. No one ever responded. Kerry wondered if Summer said it as a test—and what she was testing for.

Mia walked into the rain and crouched to peer at the road. Curious, Kerry followed her. "See something shiny?"

"Yes, actually." Mia cupped her hand around a crack in the road, then blew gently into it.

Summer joined them as Mia lifted her hand to display a delicate insect like a copper-colored butterfly. Its metallic wings spread wide and fluttered gently. Rain fell on them, but was absorbed rather than rolling off. With every drop, its wings grew bigger and brighter.

"It's a rain-catcher," Mia said. "We have them in Las Anclas, but not as colorful. They blend into the sand."

The rain-catcher flapped its wings, which were now bigger than Mia's palm, and soared away. As the three of them watched it spiral up into the sky, cool rain spattering their upturned faces, Kerry felt a companionship that she'd had with Mia and Summer separately but never with both together, delicate as a soap bubble.

The beat of hooves caught their attention. Mia whirled around. Summer tensed, poised to leap. From the sound of it, there were far more horses than would make sense for a welcoming committee.

"Weapons ready," Kerry said. "It sounds like trouble."

"Yesss," Summer hissed with satisfaction. "Finally."

Kerry, Mia, and Summer stepped apart so they wouldn't foul each other's aim with their crossbows. Jennie and Ross rode up with an escort of ten hostile-looking armed people, most visibly Changed. They looked resigned rather than frightened, so Kerry relaxed a little. This was clearly going to be *Get out and don't come back,* not *This way to the execution platform.*

The leader, who wasn't much older than Kerry, had tightly curled black hair and wore a shirt cut to expose four small, gauzy wings. They fluttered as he spoke, reminding her of the rain-catcher. He announced, "Your Mr. Preston made it quite clear that Changed people are not welcome in Las Anclas. Well, citizens of Las Anclas are not welcome in Palos Verdes. Get on your horses and ride away from our border."

Tom Preston had been voted out of office, but he was still ruining things for everyone. At least they were just getting kicked out, not attacked. But the detour would add days to their trip.

"Las Anclas held an election recently," Jennie said. "Mr. Preston is no longer the defense chief. Changed people *are* welcome in our town."

Winged Guy seemed unmoved. "Sure they are. Is he still there?"

"Yes," Jennie admitted.

"Then take off." His gauzy wings flapped in emphasis.

Summer stiffened. Kerry caught her eye and gave her a quick head-shake. The last thing they needed was to get into a completely unnecessary, two-to-one battle. Summer scowled, but didn't attack.

"We understand," Jennie said in a tone calculated to be calming but not condescending. Kerry suspected that she intended it for both the Palos Verdes escort and Summer. "We'll ride east and go around."

"Go right ahead," the winged leader said with a sneer.

Kerry went to the underhang and rode Nugget out to join the others. Summer followed her on Sally, and Mia on Buttermilk. A chorus of gasps and exclamations rose up from the Palos Verdes patrollers at the sight of the royal horses. Kerry materialized a sword, ready to defend them. A detour was one thing, but nobody was going to steal her Nugget.

"They're like Yuki's horse!" a woman exclaimed.

That was the last thing Kerry had expected. The sword wavered in her hand.

"You know Yuki? Yuki Nakamura?" Jennie asked.

The winged guy sounded a whole lot less hostile as he said, "Why didn't you mention him?"

"Any friend of Yuki's is a friend of ours!" exclaimed a girl. The tendrils she had instead of hair waved enthusiastically.

A woman whose auburn hair crackled and sparked with static electricity said, slightly suspiciously, "You *are* friends of his, right?"

"Of course we are. I'm Kerry, the one who gave him Tigereye." Kerry put on her most practiced smile, hoping that if they knew Yuki, he'd at least told them the name of his horse. With any luck, he'd also mentioned hers.

To her relief, her guess was correct. The winged guy turned to his people and said, "Lower your weapons. Only the real Kerry Cho would know the name of his horse."

And I bet the entire royal horse stud that Yuki didn't tell you where I came from or what my name used to be, Kerry thought as she ladled even more sincerity into her smile. "Yes, that's me."

Mia unslung her crossbow and peered up at Winged Guy. "How do you know Yuki?"

"He saved my little brother's life," the girl said. Kerry admired her tendrils, which were silvery on top and a deep blue underneath. They rippled like the sea as she spoke. "He came through town a couple months ago. He just said he was a prospector. We didn't know where he was from."

"*We're* always happy to see prospectors," Winged Guy said, with a significant glance at Jennie. He'd obviously pegged her as the representative of Las Anclas.

"And so is Las Anclas. Now," Jennie said. "We have Changed people." She emphasized her words by extending her hand toward the ground. A rock flew up to smack into her palm.

"Well, come along!"

They introduced themselves as they rode south. Kerry was surprised when Ross went first, then realized why when he didn't give his surname: he didn't want the attention he'd get if anyone realized he was the legendary Ross Juarez, who could blow up dams with his mind. Picking up his cue, Jennie smoothly introduced herself, Mia, and Summer by first name only. Summer didn't protest; Kerry supposed she didn't care if Ross got any glory or not.

Shireen, formerly Tendril Girl, continued her story. "Yuki didn't have anything to trade, so he offered to give the town half the value of any finds he made if we let him explore our sea caves. He was on my family's fishing boat, on the way to the island with the caves, when a kelp tentacle lunged up from the water, grabbed my brother by the ankle, and yanked him overboard. Yuki dove after him before I even realized what happened. Then we all dived in, but the water was so murky, we couldn't see them. And we had to fight the kelp."

"Cool," Summer breathed.

Shireen went on, "They were under so long, we thought they were both dead. Then Yuki surfaced with a knife in one hand and his other arm around my brother. We hauled them both back into the boat. A piece of the biggest kelp tentacle I'd ever seen was still wrapped around my brother's ankle!"

Another patroller chimed in, "Of course, after that, the town elders told him to just keep anything he found. But he was so honorable that he refused to go back on his bargain."

"Yuki stayed with *my* family," the winged leader, whose name was Adebayo, added. "He had amazing stories. He said Tigereye was a gift from a girl named Kerry Cho, who rode like the wind. But he never told us Kerry was from Las Anclas."

Kerry smothered a laugh as Jennie said as diplomatically as ten Mayor Wolfes, "Things really are different in Las Anclas now."

"About time," exclaimed Shireen. "What are you doing here, anyway?"

Summer spoke up. "We want to see the Catalina Players!"

"Oh, too bad," the woman with electric hair remarked. "You missed them! They were here last week. Keep heading south, and maybe you'll catch them."

Adebayo added, "But first, you're invited to a feast. And you have to tell us about your travels."

Shireen put in, "And the battle with Evil King Voske, and how you got rid of Evil Preston!"

Kerry smothered a laugh at Ross's look of horror at the prospect of public speaking; he obviously hadn't figured out yet that with Summer around, he'd never have to open his mouth if he didn't want to. But Jennie's flinch wasn't funny at all.

Quietly, Jennie asked, "Mia, if I tell them about the election, could you do the battle?"

Mia leaned over the saddle to pat Jennie's hand. "Of course."

As if daring Jennie to argue, Summer said, "I can tell stories. Lots of them!"

"That's a great idea," Kerry said. Summer grinned.

Palos Verdes was a small oceanside town, divided between houseboats and adobe buildings. But they didn't see much of it, as they were taken straight to the nearest patrol outpost. There a group of patrollers took their horses to the stables, then invited them to a lavish meal of asparagus and crab soup, steamed fish with ginger and lemon grass, egg rolls stuffed with shrimp and herbs, fried flatbread, sauteed mustard greens, and a sponge cake topped with candied apricots. Kerry enjoyed the fresh seafood, which was still a novelty to her. At Gold Point, the only sea fish came from traders, and was dried or smoked.

Once everyone was finished, Adebayo said, "Now let's hear your news."

Summer stood up eagerly. "Before we talk about the battle, let me tell you how I crossed the great desert." With relish, she began recounting a series of implausible but hair-raising chases, duels, and animal attacks. Ross looked alarmed, and Kerry figured he expected accusations of lying. But the younger patrollers clearly preferred a good story to the truth, cheering and laughing in all the right places.

When Summer paused to drink from her lemonade, Shireen remarked, "Some say that famous gunslinger Ross Juarez rode through Las Anclas after he blew up King Voske's palace and ran off with his beautiful daughter. Any of you ever meet him?"

"*No,*" Jennie said firmly.

Ross scrambled to his feet, muttering something about checking on the horses. No one gave him a second glance, not even to joke about him and the gunslinger sharing a first name. He'd been so silent, they'd all probably forgotten it.

Kerry stood as well. If they expected everyone to talk, she'd be better off gone. All that friendliness would evaporate in an instant if they learned the truth behind the legend. "I'll help Ross. Nugget is temperamental."

The last thing Kerry heard was Summer's voice, "So there I was, in the middle of the desert, wearing nothing but the hide of a sand tiger I'd killed with my bare hands, when a horde of fifty cannibal bandits, armed to their filed teeth..."

Outside, Kerry said, "I thought I'd take a closer look at the houseboats. Want to come with me?"

Ross shook his head. "I want to see the stars."

The outpost was near a promontory like a rocky finger stretched out into the ocean. Kerry walked out along it. The full moon shone down brightly, so she didn't miss a step. At its end, she sat on a large flat rock and gazed out at the fleet of long boats, bobbing gently on the dark water. Some had strings of lights festooned along the rails, while others' windows glowed white or gold. She wondered what made the rail lights shine. Electricity? Globes of bright-moths? Something she'd never even heard of?

Behind her, someone cleared his throat. She spun around, a sword and shield materializing in her hands. Then delight flooded her when she recognized her brother Sean, picking his way over the rocks to join her.

"Sean," she whispered, letting her weapons vanish. "How did you know I was here?"

"I always seem to be walking in your footsteps," he replied in a voice pitched so low that it rumbled in his broad chest. "I went to Las Anclas to find you, but you'd already left. Took me this long to catch up."

They ran the last few steps toward each other and hugged, Sean lifting her off the ground and spinning her around before setting her down again. Then they sat on the flat rock. Sean had pulled his cornrows back into a short ponytail. His white shirt was stained, like Kerry's clothes, from the dust and dirt of the road.

Sean's sharp profile reminded her abruptly of Paco as he glanced at the houseboats, but the resemblance vanished when he turned back. Paco's expression was always closed off or hostile, but Sean's was warm and open. Kerry was so glad to have a brother who was actually happy to see her.

"So what are *you* doing here?" Sean asked.

Kerry explained quickly, then said, "Have you been back to Gold Point?"

Sean nodded, but his eyes flickered away: there was something he didn't want to tell her.

Her heart banged painfully against her chest. She could barely get the obvious question out. "Is Santiago...?"

"He's fine, he's fine," Sean said quickly. "It's just that he was hurt when Father retook Lake Perris. When I arrived in Gold Point, he was in the infirmary. I couldn't get close enough to get the details, but apparently he'd jumped in front of Father."

"Again," Kerry said grimly. If Santiago hadn't protected Father when Ross had tried to kill him, he wouldn't have been injured now, and she and Santiago would never have been separated. But there was no use wishing the past away. "How bad?"

"Can't be too serious." Sean laid a reassuring hand on her shoulder. "I saw his name on the list to go back to duty the next week."

Kerry was relieved, but not as much as she'd have liked to be. She knew Sean too well to miss the tension in his posture, and she knew Gold Point too well to not guess the reason for it. "What else?"

"My mother is the new governor of Lake Perris. Father has a really short chain of command now. He doesn't trust many of his old commanders. The only people left with real power are his wives."

"And my mom?" Kerry asked.

"Head of the guardians."

"Guardians?" Kerry repeated. "What's that?"

"From what I heard people whispering, it's the replacement for Pru. Your mother is running a spy network inside Gold Point. There won't be a revolution there any time soon."

Sean looked more unhappy than that news should warrant. Kerry had never imagined that there would be a revolution in Gold Point, and she doubted that Sean had either.

"What else?" Kerry asked again.

Her brother's throat bobbed as he swallowed. Now he was coming to something that scared *him*. He glanced around, then lowered his voice before he replied. "Father's been paying traders to hire anyone who owns a boat. Sailors. Captains. Shipwrights."

"But Gold Point is landlocked." Then years of Father's lessons came back to her, and Kerry knew why he wanted boats. The night wasn't cold, but fear chilled her. "He's going to invade Las Anclas from the sea."

"I think so, too. And not just Las Anclas. Catalina doesn't have an army, but they do have a lot of ships. It'd be easier for Father to conquer it and take their ships than buy that many. That is, if he took them by surprise."

She looked at her brother's boots, dusty and worn from all that walking back and forth through the desert. "Not while you're around."

Sean managed a faint smile. "No, I already warned Catalina. We have an agreement with the Saigon Alliance, so I'm sure they're making arrangements to send soldiers right now. And we'll have plenty of time to set up defenses. It'll take Father months and months collect enough ships to launch an attack."

Kerry looked out at the brightly lit houseboats floating on the dark sea, aware of her own lack of surprise. She'd always known, from the moment she'd decided to stay in Las Anclas, that Father would come back. And now that idiot Mr. Horst was in charge of town defense, when all he knew how to do was forge metal and complain. She could pass on Sean's warning, but Mr. Horst wouldn't believe her. And even if he did, he wouldn't know what to do about it. But she knew someone who did.

She had to tell Tom Preston.

·24·
MIA

MIA ONCE AGAIN TOOK out her imaginary scale as the horses plodded up yet another steep hill, no doubt with yet another lagoon beyond it. That was a word she'd learned in Palos Verdes. It meant a bay that opened into the sea and was surrounded by palisades. The good thing to be weighed on her scale was that lagoons were beautiful, and undoubtedly would just be one of the many amazing new things she'd see on the trip.

Bad: It was hard to appreciate scenery or anything else after Kerry had told them about the trader from Catalina that she'd run into at Palos Verdes, and how he'd mentioned that Voske was buying ships. Mia hadn't immediately understood the implications, but Jennie's eyes had gone as glassy and unseeing as they had right after Sera had been killed. Which was *really* bad. The battle might not have been the worst thing that had ever happened to Mia, but it sure had been for other people, and everyone said a second attack by Voske would be much worse than the first.

Good: Kerry and Jennie had agreed to tell Mr. Preston, and that he'd have plenty of time to prepare a defense.

Bad: That hadn't cheered up either of them. Or Ross, for that matter. Only Summer had looked excited, and that was because she *wanted* to fight.

Good: Nothing came to mind.

Okay, that wasn't working. So she'd try something personal, not about battles and politics.

Good: No one had interrupted Ross and her when they went

to "collect firewood."

Bad: Nothing had happened *to* interrupt, and it was all Mia's fault. A first time was supposed to be special. Perfect. And once she started thinking about that, her mind filled with a bee-swarm of what-ifs about everything that could possibly go wrong, making her too nervous to even enjoy kissing Ross. And she used to love kissing him. She'd ruined that for herself. What was wrong with her?

Mia swiped at a fly that kept settling on Tucker's ears, then stayed bent to hide her face, which she could feel turning fiery red. As it did every time she thought about sex. Anything about sex. Even the absence of sex.

And who was to blame for that absence? Mia. Jennie and Ross had no trouble finding nice places to be together (Mia refused to think beyond that), judging by how long their firewood expeditions ran. But Mia's were always wrecked by bugs or sand or the worry that they were too close to camp and someone would pounce and laugh at her. The fact that Ross kept on accompanying her and even still seemed to like being with her made her feel worse.

Ross took Rusty to a stream tumbling from a palisade; like all burros, he could detect poisoned water. Rusty sniffed, brayed, then bent to drink.

"What's that noise?" Summer called from farther up the hill.

Kerry's fingers curled around an invisible hilt and Jennie's around a visible one. Ross snatched a knife from his belt.

Mia belatedly grabbed for her cloud viper darts. "Is it Voske attacking?"

Kerry turned, the chiseled lines of her profile cut out against the sky. "He wouldn't attack this far south. No secure supply line. And he doesn't have enough soldiers to hold any of these towns against the rest of the Alliance."

Mia hoped she was right. But Kerry didn't let go of her invisible sword.

"Wait for us, Summer," Ross shouted, then tried to urge his horse to catch up with her. Buttermilk didn't cooperate, clopping upward at a leisurely pace no matter how much Ross dug in his heels.

As they crested the hill, the distant boom, wash, and hiss of the ocean below the towering palisade grew louder. But then came another sound, long, low and sustained, reverberating like the world's biggest horn. It seemed to come from the sea, which glimmered blue-green in the brilliant light.

"Look!" Summer stood in the stirrups, pointing at the sparkling water.

Mia shaded her eyes against the sun on its downward arc, and made out a grayish shape far out to sea. A spray of white shot up from it, then fell in a lacework of glittering water.

"It's a whale," Jennie exclaimed in wonder. "It must be enormous!"

Green waves, measureless from wing to wing, rippled shoreward until they broke in crystalline whiteness, then spread in sheets of lacy foam to slide back to the water again.

"There's at least twenty of them," Summer exclaimed, her awed voice unrecognizable.

A brassy note that might have been blown from an immense tuba echoed from cliff to cliff. It was followed by one on a higher scale, as if winded from a trumpet. A smaller shape lifted from the water, arced, and dove, followed by two larger whales.

"No," Jennie murmured, shading her eyes. "There's hundreds."

The whales leaped and splashed down, tumbled and rolled and floated, maybe playing, maybe dancing. And all the while, they sang in eerie, melancholy, lovely long notes. When many sounded at once, they resonated in chords.

"We have to stay," Summer said, turning pleading eyes to Ross, then Jennie. "It's so beautiful."

Mia turned hopefully to Jennie. The higher whale notes reminded her of her meditation flute, magnified a thousand times.

There was no discussion needed. Everyone quietly set about making camp, pausing frequently to watch the whales leaping and diving in slow majesty, blowing geysers and singing their chorus. At sunset they shared out jerky, fresh persimmons from Adebayo, and a rare delicacy, sweet-sticky rice balls wrapped in cabbage leaves from Shireen. Everyone was quiet, listening to the ocean music.

Before the sun vanished, Summer leaped to a cliff below them that only she could reach. She sat there alone, her knees under her chin, her arms tightly wrapped around her legs. Jennie, closest to the cliff, opened her mouth, probably to warn Summer about tarantulas or slips in the dark, then closed it again. The bright stars would be out, and Summer could leap away from any danger and float safely down. Even when the whales were lost against the inky sea, they could still hear the singing.

"I'll take first watch," Jennie said, and sat by the cliff above Summer.

Kerry headed off toward the horses. Mia went in the opposite direction, walking dreamily by starlight, searching for the best place to listen. She wasn't there for long before she heard Ross's footsteps crunching the parched earth. His arm slid around her, warming her everywhere with that one little touch.

As the whales sang far out to sea, Mia's feelings for Ross flooded back, stronger than ever. And like the way her favorite wrench fit her hand, everything about them felt so *right*.

The sand and the interruptions and all the rest had been excuses. Every time she thought about sex, it made her feel like the little girl who got laughed at on the schoolyard, and the older girl who still believed every mean thing anyone had ever said to her: that she'd never have a date with anything that wasn't made out of metal, that she'd grow older but she'd never grow up, that she was terrible at anything involving other human beings.

But Ross's fingers tracing up and down her spine said otherwise.

Everything had felt scary and weird when she'd thought of sex and how she was supposed to feel about sex and how she was definitely going to do sex wrong. She'd gotten so obsessed with sex, she'd forgotten about *Ross*.

No what-ifs. No forcing myself to do anything because I think I'm supposed to. This is just me and Ross.

And there was nothing scary or weird about that.

She tucked her shoulder under his arm, and his hand tightened around her. And when he bent his head, his breath soft on her cheek, she turned her lips up to meet his.

And so, when he whispered, "I know where we can go to be

alone. Only if you want to," she whispered back, "I want to."

"My sleeping bag is over there." Ross laid his hand on her cheek, then slid it down in a caress that made her breath catch.

His hands were so warm and strong, and she knew every inch of them, from the tiny raised scars on his knuckles to the soft pads of his fingers. He'd trusted her enough to let her measure his disabled hand for the gauntlet. He could throw a knife faster than her eyes could follow. He'd held her hands and spun her in the air, he'd touched her chest through a rip in her shirt, and the way he was running his fingers through her hair right now made her feel like she was about to burst into flames. But in a good way.

"How about we share it?" Ross went on quietly. "There won't be sand, or bugs, or anything to interrupt us."

And there wasn't.

·25·
JENNIE

I'M A TEACHER, JENNIE thought. *I should know what to say to a fourteen-year-old girl.*

But she didn't. She didn't even know if she *should* say anything.

When she sat on the cliff above Summer, Jennie heard her sobbing her heart out as the whales sang their mournful songs of the sea. No doubt Summer thought her weeping would be lost against the whale-song and the crash of the surf, but a trick of acoustics carried it to Jennie as loud and clear as if the girl were crying on her shoulder.

When the whales finally swam away, their singing fading into the rhythm of the waves, Summer leaped back up, then went to sleep without a word. Jennie debated telling Ross, but that would do nothing but transfer the burden of decision-making to him.

Jennie watched Summer covertly as they proceeded southward the next morning. All that day, Summer barely said a word. The next day, she was equally subdued, and did her chores without being asked. The day after that, just as Jennie was beginning to get seriously worried, Kerry said it was Summer's turn on Sally.

Summer's rare, brilliant smile transformed her face. She floated into the air and settled atop the silver mare, light as a feather. As they set out, she chattered to Kerry about horse training, sounding completely normal.

Jennie was glad she'd kept Summer's secret. If the girl ever decided to confide in anyone, it would be Kerry. Or maybe Ross.

She certainly wouldn't appreciate her teacher butting in.

◆ ◆ ◆

They encountered two more Saigon Alliance towns in the next few days. Like Palos Verdes, they were on small lagoons sheltered between high cliffs, with some buildings on the land but most houseboats connected with little bridges. This time they knew to display the royal horses and mention Yuki immediately. Along with the inevitable news that they'd just missed the Catalina Players, the royal horses and Yuki's name netted them a warm welcome, a good meal, and more stories about Yuki's courage, cleverness, and way with animals.

Jennie was happy for Yuki, but also sorry for all the years he'd spent feeling trapped within the walls of Las Anclas. These towns appreciated him more than Las Anclas had, where he'd been respected but not hailed as the greatest guy ever. Then again, prospectors didn't need to fit in, since they were always only visiting; the differences that had made some people in Las Anclas regard Yuki as not quite one of them only made him seem cool to the Saigon Alliance towns.

She was glad that he was clearly having a good time prospecting. But she knew he'd eventually tire of the towns and strike out for less populated territory. He'd never much cared what others thought of him. It was the idea of new lands and new discoveries that had drawn him away from Las Anclas. And from his family. And from Paco.

Jennie also enjoyed seeing new places, but the longer they traveled, the more she wanted to get home and report Kerry's news about Voske buying ships. If they didn't catch up with the Catalina Players soon, they'd have to give up and turn back. Mr. Preston needed to know, so he could have the Rangers investigate. Without her. After all this time, she still felt a hole in her days that had once been filled with training and patrolling, and a hole in her heart that had once been filled with camaraderie. Would she ever stop missing those empty spaces?

Then they reached the top of the hill they were climbing, and the sight below drove all regrets from Jennie's mind. Inland, a blue lake spread out, surrounded by more greenery than Jennie had seen in her entire life. On the sea side, a huge lagoon joined the sapphire ocean.

A city rose up from the stretch of land between the two bodies of water, much bigger than Las Anclas. Every building was on stilts at least ten feet tall, and many were much higher. The platforms extended over the edges of the lagoon and the lake, so part of the city seemed to hover above the blue water.

Most of the homes were round, with roofs of woven reeds, built of wood rather than heavy adobe. Some platforms had gardens instead of buildings, lush with greenery or bright with flowers. Others were bare wood, and seemed to be gathering places like the town square of Las Anclas. A maze of interconnected bridges and staircases joined the buildings and gardens and platforms, and roads ran below the ones on dry land. A rainbow cloud of messenger birds circled high above, diving and chirping.

It was awe-inspiring. After she'd seen the other Saigon Alliance towns and heard the whales sing, not to mention the ruined city, Jennie had thought she'd had her eyes opened to the wonders that lay outside of Las Anclas. But now she truly comprehended that there was a whole world out there that she had barely even begun to glimpse. For the first time, she understood why Yuki had been willing to leave everything to travel.

Summer leaped up and stood on Sally's saddle, poised like a dancer. "Prettiest town yet!"

"It looks like a raccoon village," Mia said doubtfully.

"You don't think those are cute?" Kerry asked.

Mia shoved her glasses defiantly up her nose. "Not if you've spent the entire year trying to move it out of the Vardams' orchard."

Kerry laughed. Nugget tossed his silky mane as she turned to Ross. "Have you ever seen anything like this?"

Ross shook his head. "Closest I came was that ruined city by Gold Point. You couldn't see it from the outside, but inside it was green and wet."

Summer settled gracefully back into the saddle, then lifted her chin, the signal that she was about to brag. Jennie waited for her to announce that she'd seen fifteen lakeside bridge-cities and had killed a hundred bandits in every one. But all she said was, "I've seen a lot, but nothing like this. I hope we can explore those bridges. They look cool."

Summer had gotten much less prickly since the whales had sung. And that wasn't the only change that had happened that night. From the little touches and looks between Mia and Ross, Jennie suspected that they had finally found their mathematical formula. All their lives, Jennie had been the leader and Mia the follower, even when it came to dating the same guy. It made her feel off-balance to realize that Mia had caught up with her in so many ways.

Well, good for Mia, Jennie thought firmly. *Ross, too.*

He smiled a lot more now, and seemed more relaxed than he'd been since his return from Gold Point. It was one of the most complicated relationships Jennie had ever had, but it was also one of the best. They'd gone through so much together, it was worth some awkwardness to make it work.

They rode down a switchback trail leading to the city, past hillside terraces with a crop that looked like giant stalks of grass. That had to be rice. Jennie stared at it, fascinated. Yuki had drawn her a picture of rice cultivation, but it had shown the stalks sprouting from boxes full of water. Both previous towns had served rice at every meal, as if it were as common as corn was in Las Anclas.

And here is where they grow it, thought Jennie.

The chatter of messenger birds filled their ears, along with the distant sounds of human voices. A splash of pink caught Jennie's eye. A flock of flamingos hopped along the rice terraces, their long beaks diving into the water. They were as bright as in the one picture Las Anclas had of them, in an ancient children's book about birds, but larger, and though the book had said they were pink or white, a few were brilliant blue or emerald green.

"Look at the colors!" Mia exclaimed. "They're like the bugs in the car in the ruined city. Except they're too big to run up my leg."

"Lucky for you," Jennie said with a grin.

"Is that a hippo?" Kerry peered at a fat gray creature in the lake. "I thought they were bigger."

"Big enough to eat you," Mia remarked as it opened its gaping jaws, displaying a few sharp teeth and a vast pink mouth.

"They're herbivores," Jennie said. "At least, they were in ancient times."

Smaller hippos, the size of medium dogs, seemed to be pets or working animals, trotting at people's heels like a dog or a rat would in Las Anclas.

Jennie waited for someone to accost them. Shouldn't there be guards? Or patrols? The town was completely open. It couldn't possibly be as defenseless as it looked. The houseboat towns could pull in their bridge-ramps and pole seaward if threatened, but this stilt city wasn't going anywhere.

The first building they reached was an enormous stable. A girl their age popped out and ran up to them. Her rumpled black hair and overalls reminded Jennie of Mia, though the girl was taller and didn't wear glasses. "Hi, I'm Lin. And there's the horses! You must be Yuki's friends. Welcome to Dai La!"

Not for the first time, Jennie mentally thanked Ross for inviting Kerry. Without her and her royal horses, the entire trip might have been a complete disaster.

Lin chirped to Nugget and Sally. Their ears twitched toward her, then they trotted up to snuff at her palm. Rusty and the other horses followed, and she patted noses all around. Jennie wondered if Lin was like Ma, either Changed to communicate with horses or so good with them that she might as well be. A wave of homesickness washed over her. Travel was exciting, but if it had been up to her, she'd have turned around then and there. Never mind the Catalina Players, she just wanted to see Ma and Pa.

"I gave Yuki Tigereye," Kerry said.

"Oh, you're Kerry Cho," Lin said with deep respect. "Yuki told us how you gave him your only alpha mare so he could fulfill his dream. It's an honor to meet you. And the rest of you, of course," she added quickly.

It was strange how they'd traveled in Yuki's footsteps. Everywhere they went they heard more about him, until he felt like an invisible companion.

I wish he hadn't left, Jennie thought, remembering Kerry's grim news about Voske. Yuki was one of the best fighters she'd ever known. And he'd been the only person in Las Anclas with training in sea battles. He'd mentioned that to Jennie, but she'd never thought to have him teach it to her. And now it was too late. He might be gone for years.

While they introduced themselves, Lin rubbed Nugget between the eyes. "I hope Yuki comes back soon. He taught me to ride dolphins. You have to be a good rider and a good swimmer. We all swim, but not everybody rides. Only traders own horses here."

The horses eagerly followed Lin as she led them to the stable. "Leucadia sent parakeets to let us know you were coming. But we thought you'd be here yesterday. Did something hold you up?"

"We stopped to listen to the whales sing," Kerry said. "Do you hear that often?"

"No, you were lucky." Lin glanced out to sea. "They only go north once a year, and usually they don't come close enough to hear them from the land. I'd have stopped, too. But it's a good thing you didn't wait any longer. The Catalina Players are having their last performance tonight. Their ship sails out tomorrow."

Jennie winced at the close call. If they'd missed the Players one more time, she'd have had to decide whether to make everyone turn back. She probably would have, given Kerry's news. And then Summer would have had a tantrum, and Ross would have been upset, and Mia and Kerry would have been disappointed.

But instead, everyone was happy and excited. Rusty let out a bray that sounded almost like a cheer. Summer snickered.

"What can we trade to take care of our animals?" Ross asked.

Lin shrugged, clearly willing to take anything that Yuki's friends had to offer. "What have you got?"

As he displayed their trade goods, Jennie again checked for guards. She couldn't believe this prosperous town had no defense.

"Are you hungry?" Lin asked. "If you go up that catwalk to the town square, you'll see booths with—"

An unearthly shriek split the air. Jennie's sword was in her hand before she was even conscious of drawing it. Mia fumbled her crossbow off its shoulder sling, Ross snatched the dagger at his belt, Kerry brandished what had to be an invisible sword, and Summer tensed to leap.

Lin gave them a puzzled look. "It's just the captain's peacock screaming to call a militia drill. Want to watch?"

People burst out of the round houses, ran along the catwalks, and swarmed into two fleets of canoes, one floating on the lagoon and one on the lake. Others leaped into defensive formations along the streets and catwalks. Most were armed with swords and crossbows, but a few bore rifles. There were more people in the militia than the entire population of Las Anclas.

With advance warnings by the bird messengers, Jennie reflected, Dai La would never be taken by surprise. No wonder it was so open. She bet the drill had been timed for their arrival, so they could bring the news back to Las Anclas that the town was prepared. It was disconcerting to realize that Las Anclas's reputation was bad enough for Dai La to think it might attack them. Did they really see no difference between Mr. Preston and King Voske?

At some inaudible order, the canoes all skimmed out into the lagoon and in along the lake. The canoers pulled in perfect synchrony, with archers balancing at the prow and the stern.

"They're fast," Ross said.

Lin laughed. "They have to be, or they'll be doing it again tomorrow, and Auntie Hoa says we're due for a thunderstorm."

There was no way they'd have to do it again tomorrow. The drill ran far better than any Jennie had seen in Las Anclas. Given Kerry's news, that was also disquieting. Dai La was probably safe from Voske, but Las Anclas wasn't. And it wasn't likely to get any help from the Saigon Alliance, either.

Kerry interrupted her gloomy thoughts. "Did Yuki say where he was going?"

Lin's round face took on an ominous look, as if she was about to tell a ghost story. "The Burning Lands. We warned him, but he was set on it."

"The Burning Lands?" Mia echoed. "What are they?"

Lin lowered her voice to a menacing whisper, reminding Jennie even more of scary campfire tales. "A deadly place where fire shoots from cracks in the ground and they have earthquakes every day. All the houses are made out of paper, or they'd collapse and kill everyone in them."

Dubiously, Jennie said, "If fire shoots from the ground, wouldn't that burn the paper houses?"

Lin waved her hand as if that was a silly question. "I guess they rebuild them every day. Anyway, it's way too dangerous to go there. Everyone knows that. But Yuki was determined. He went around asking if anyone had ever been there."

Jennie knew the answer already. Paper houses and burning earth had all the marks of a legend, not a firsthand report. Sure enough, Lin went on, "Of course we haven't. No one could survive out there!"

Except the people with the paper houses, Jennie thought. *Yep. Legend.*

"But where is it, exactly?" Ross asked. "I've never heard of it."

"Southeast. Somewhere," Lin said vaguely. "But don't worry, I'm sure Yuki won't actually go there. He's much too smart for that. Once he gets to the border, he'll take one look at the fountains of flame and falling boulders, and go around."

Jennie summoned all her willpower to keep a straight face. "I'm sure."

Lin gave the horses a final pat as they contentedly munched their hay. "I have to get back to work. You'd better get your seats now if you want good ones. The play is on Sunset Terrace. Just ask along the walks. Anyone can direct you."

They thanked her, and Summer eagerly led the way up to the highest level of the city. They bought snacks from the line of booths selling food, and carried them along the catwalks over the lagoon. Ross and Summer got heaping platefuls of tacos, Kerry got cold rice noodles with shredded pork and cucumber, Mia got an oozing grilled cheese sandwich, and Jennie got skewers of broiled meat and vegetables.

Parakeets fluttered in and out of the wide windows, and landed on the wrists of people outside. It seemed most long-distance communication was done by messenger birds. Jennie spotted people extracting tightly rolled scrolls from containers on the birds' legs, or summoning a bird with a shrill whistle to dispatch their own message. Dai La didn't seem to have rats, but hippos patrolled individual houses like guard dogs; their trotters made the bridges quiver as they clopped along.

Catwalks stretched out in a bewildering webwork around and below them, some wide, some narrow, some made of wood and some of rope and some of reeds. Kids swung through the air on vines and ropes, laughing and sometimes letting go to dive into the rippling waters.

It was all so different from anything Jennie had ever seen. And this was just one city out of the hundreds — maybe thousands — that must exist. No wonder Yuki, who had sailed the seas, had found Las Anclas so small and confining.

Troops of flamingos wove fearlessly between the humans at every level of the city. Jennie couldn't figure out if they were pets or working animals or wild animals that knew they wouldn't be harmed. Summer tried to pet a brilliant blue one, but it ducked its sleek head in an unexpectedly cat-like way.

A tug at her belt startled Jennie. Something invisible pulled at it the same way she used her Change power. She slapped the pouch flat to her hip, but it pushed up against her fingers. A ruby-red flamingo was staring at it with intent and beady eyes. As it flapped its wings sharply, she felt the tug again.

Jennie clapped her hands. "Shoo!"

The flamingo squawked at her and bounded lightly away. Now that was something familiar: an animal trying to steal her stuff. Laughing, Jennie ran to catch up with the others.

Sunset Terrace was a huge platform covered with timber worked into geometric patterns. Much like the town square of Las Anclas, the open space was surrounded by buildings and small gardens, though here plants were grown in boxes of earth.

The stage was set up in a building with only three walls. Benches faced the open side in a semi-circle. The front rows were already filled, mostly with kids, but Jennie and the others found seats with a good view of the stage. She could see a little bit of the backstage, with a rack of costumes and a box of masks. Jennie remembered sitting with her family in the town square, eagerly waiting for the show to begin. It had been so wonderful and magical — when she was seven. She wondered if any of the magic would remain, or if it would be like finding a doll she'd loved when she'd been four and seeing only a corncob wrapped in rags.

The benches filled rapidly as the sun touched the ocean

beyond the floating world of houseboats. A forest of masts heaved slowly on the waves that rolled in to crash below, sending up a scent of brine.

Summer sat swinging her feet and nibbling on her last taco. Ever since the whales, she'd seemed less angry and more like Ross when he'd first arrived, wary and skittish. And just as Jennie had that thought, she spotted Ross shifting uncomfortably as more and more people pressed in around and behind him. His right hand clasped tight around Mia's and his gauntleted left curled into a fist in his lap.

Jennie laid her palm on his back. He stiffened, then relaxed and cast a brief smile her way. Last summer he wouldn't have been able to tolerate either the crowd or being touched. Now he leaned into her hand so she could rub between his bony shoulder blades.

Mia nudged Kerry. "I loved the Catalina Players when I was a little girl. Did they ever come to Gol—ah, to you?"

Jennie thought, *Of course they didn't. Nobody goes to Gold Point if they can help it.*

Smoothly, Kerry replied, "No. We had our own theater troupes."

"What were they like?" Mia asked.

"Oh, lots of fun."

Mia persisted. "But what sorts of stories did they tell?"

Jennie thought, *Everyone's head ended up on a pike.*

"All sorts of stories. Dramas, adventures, romances, comedies..." Kerry glanced skyward at an arrow of bright little birds heading south. "But they all ended the same way. Just when everything seemed hopeless, the king would come in and fix everything. If it was an adventure, he'd scare off the bad guys or defeat them single-handedly. If it was a romance, he'd order whoever stood in the couple's way to let them get married. He rewarded the good and punished the evil."

Ross touched the scars on his throat with his gauntleted fingers, then dropped his hand like it was red-hot. Jennie was sure he was thinking of the heads, too.

Stiffly, Kerry finished, "Well, we all enjoyed them."

A horn blew a flourish, and a middle-aged woman strode onstage.

"This play is adapted from an ancient book," she intoned, her voice carrying across the square. "Ten thousand years ago, the evil government controlled everything."

A slim man dressed in black took his place on a stool at the far end of the stage.

The woman went on, "Color is banned!"

The man gestured, and the white backdrop upstage turned to a dull gray. The vague shapes of a gray city appeared. Like a rabbit illusion, it was hazy and more convincing when you didn't focus on it.

"But most oppressive of all, the government controls love."

Now the backdrop showed vague human shapes, everyone walking about with their heads down. They all wore clinging one-piece gray garments.

Dramatically the woman announced, "All but the ruling aristocracy must wear...*the unitard!*"

The actors stepped onstage. A bright light shone on a teenage girl whose Change had given her beautiful pearly scales and a ruff around her head like a lacy crown. The players mimed the action as the narrator recounted the story of Madison, a girl of the oppressed Norm class, who had unexpectedly Changed.

"And so Madison will now ascend to the Changed aristocracy. Her family was so thrilled that they cast away their unitards and dressed in forbidden colors to celebrate Madison's good fortune."

Thunder and lightning! Bright colors shimmered over the players as they danced in a ring around Madison, who spun in perfect pirouettes in the center.

"But the government was watching," the narrator announced ominously.

As Madison ran to and fro, miming horror and clasping her hands pleadingly, masked unitard-clad minions marched onstage and grabbed her family, holding their hands behind their backs.

The audience gasped as a new actor stomped onstage with footsteps of doom—someone pounding a drum in time to each step. Jennie stuffed her knuckles into her mouth to stop herself from laughing. The 'terrifying' actor had his face painted bright red and wore red feelers attached to a headband. Best of all, he held giant wooden lobster claws on poles.

He clacked and snapped the claws over the heads of each of the family members. At every snip, the actor slumped down and lowered their head, while players in the background waved scarlet streamers, presumably indicating spraying blood. As the final touch, stage hands hurled fake heads across the stage. They bounced.

Jennie forced herself not to look at Kerry. But she had to see if anyone else thought this was hilarious rather than tragic. Apparently not. Mia was actually mopping her eyes with her shirt. Summer was totally engrossed, her fists clenched as if she wanted to leap on stage and do battle with the lobster man. Even Ross was staring glumly at the heads.

"Alas, poor Madison," the narrator intoned, "Witnessing the tragic deaths of her entire family made her lose her voice forever. She is now The Princess Who Cannot Speak."

Jennie heard each capital letter, and bit her lip. At that point the other actors began to talk, rather than just mime to narration. But Madison only communicated with interpretive dance. Jennie wished there was more dancing, which was quite beautiful, and less dialogue. Especially when the government assigned Madison two potential boyfriends, one the sweet aristocratic boy she'd known from childhood and the other a prince who appeared to be evil but was secretly a tormented rebel.

As Madison danced between the two boys, miming her anguish at having to choose between them, Jennie couldn't resist glancing at Kerry behind Mia and Ross's backs—at the same moment that Kerry leaned back to look at Jennie. Kerry rolled her eyes, and Jennie bit her lip against a laugh. If they'd been sitting together, they'd have nudged each other in the ribs.

Then Madison met Kayleigh, a blonde Norm girl who introduced her to the secret underground rebellion. They had much better chemistry than Madison had with either of her assigned boyfriends. Jennie was pulled into the story as the girls danced together, secretly wearing forbidden colors, and fought side by side to overthrow the evil government. She even caught herself leaning forward in excitement during the final battle, as the colorful rebels tumbled and whirled, some dying under fluttering crimson streamers, and Madison and Kayleigh fought their way to their society's shadowy rulers.

Cheers rang out from the audience when the villains crashed to the stage amid a sea of red streamers. Madison and Kayleigh got engaged and established a new and more just government, Madison's assigned boyfriends declared their love for each other, and there was a grand dance finale with every player wearing a different color.

As the actors took their bows before a hazy rainbow background, Summer turned to Jennie, her eyes wide and shining. "That was wonderful! I'm so glad we came. I wanted to kill that lobster guy! He was so evil!"

Mia mopped her eyes again, smiling happily. "Those lobster claws were really clever." She added under her breath. "But I could give them better rotation."

I'm never saying a word, Jennie decided. *Except maybe to Kerry. In private.*

But while the bouncing heads and designated boyfriends had made Jennie want to snicker in a way that she was sure the Players hadn't intended, the dancing and mock-fighting had been every bit as magical as she'd recalled. Jennie would never be seven again, but she appreciated the Catalina Players' skill and effort in a way she couldn't have before she, too, had spent years and years training her body.

"Come on. Let's talk to them before they pack up." Jennie led the way to the stage and stopped the first actor she saw, the boy who had played the tormented rebel. "Excuse me. We're from Las Anclas—"

The teenager flung back his beautiful hair, his expression haughty. "I've heard all about Las Anclas." His eyes went from warm brown to ice blue. "I'm surprised you'd condescend to mingle with us Changed folk."

Jennie held out her hand and pulled a wooden stage sword into it. "Some of us are Changed ourselves. Anyway, things are different in Las Anclas now. Can I talk to whoever is in charge?"

The boy's eyes shifted to spring green, and he gave her a tentative smile. "Okay. Grandma Jing is over there."

Grandma Jing, who was surrounded by a crowd of townspeople complimenting her on the show, reminded Jennie of

Grandma Wolfe. She was tiny, but carried herself as if she were much taller, and moved with the same commanding elegance. She even wore her hair in a similar style, upswept and held with mother-of-pearl combs.

Jennie waited for her turn to speak, while Mia wandered off to inspect the lobster claws, and Kerry struck up a conversation with the girls who had played Madison and Kayleigh. Ross watched his sister cautiously, but she was silent, apparently fascinated by Madison's actor. Jennie supposed Summer was impressed by her beautiful Change.

"May I help you?"

Jennie started. The crowd had thinned, and Grandma Jing approached.

Avoiding the dreaded *I'm from Las Anclas*, Jennie said, "We all loved your play. I'm the representative of a town up north, and we'd like to ask you to come visit us and put on a show."

"Is that the town that doesn't help its own neighbors if they're Changed?" Grandma Jing's voice, precise and melodious, carried across the stage.

A heavy silence fell. Jennie had been eight when Mr. Preston had made the Rangers throw out the delegation from Catalina that had come to Las Anclas to ask for help during a drought, but a burning rush of shame washed through her at Grandma Jing's words.

She chose her words carefully, both for Grandma Jing and for the listeners she could feel behind her. "We recently had an election. Mr. Preston is no longer the defense chief. In fact, he doesn't hold any elected position anymore. The new defense chief is Mr. Horst..."

Jennie tried not to pause too long while she tried to figure out if Grandma Jing had heard of him. She hoped not. Grandma Jing didn't react, so Jennie went on, "Part of his campaign was a promise to invite the Catalina Players back to Las Anclas. That's probably why he won."

Grandma Jing's severe expression eased into a slight smile. "I see."

A tall man stepped up next to her. "I for one would like to see my old friend Sam Riley again."

"That's my Pa," Jennie exclaimed, delighted. "I'm Jennie Riley."

Grandma Jing's smile softened, becoming real. "Welcome, Jennie. I must say, this is pleasant news. We shall have to arrange a special performance for our first visit in ten years. So, Mr. Preston no longer holds power in Las Anclas?"

"His wife is the mayor, and he heads the Rangers," Jennie said, glad her voice stayed steady. "But he has no vote on the town council."

"I remember Mayor Wolfe," Grandma Jing said. "And their little children. A toddler boy, and a little girl who would be about your age. What are they like now?"

Jennie tried not to obviously look around, but she knew everyone was listening.

Be diplomatic, Jennie told herself, crushing the vision of Felicité tied up, gagged, and furious in the fruit shed.

"Will Preston is a good-natured, energetic boy. Felicité is as elegant as her mother. She's the town scribe..." Jennie fished for something positive or at least not insulting to say. Nothing came to mind. Finally, she said, "She wears very stylish hats."

"*Huge* hats. Like this," Summer broke in, throwing her arms out to either side. "And she hates Changed people. She called my brother a mutant!"

Jennie suppressed a groan, wondering who had passed on that story. Probably Mia had told Kerry, and Kerry had told Summer.

Summer went on, "And her stupid grinning boyfriend Henry hates us all, too!"

Jennie longed to agree, but since she was the official representative of Las Anclas, she forced herself to say, "She hasn't used that word in a long time. And she did apologize."

Mia piped up, "I still don't trust her. She claimed that word 'just slipped out,' but I think she meant it."

Summer said fiercely, "Oh, I can believe *that.*"

Jennie was losing control of the conversation. Forcing her gaze from Summer, she addressed Grandma Jing. "As I said, Defense Chief Horst invites you all to Las Anclas. You don't have to have anything to do with the Prestons and Wolfes if you don't want to."

"Oh, I don't think we'll avoid them," Grandma Jing replied.

"They sound like a charming family. We accept your invitation. We'll see you in Las Anclas in two weeks. That should give us plenty of time to rehearse."

·26·
BECKY

BECKY LUGGED A SEWING basket overflowing with her repaired dresses into her aunt's workroom. With a gigantic sense of relief, she set it on the shelf. She'd see them again on some other girl, but at least Becky wouldn't have to wear them.

"Done already?" Aunt Rosa asked from her seat at the quilting frame. "Good job. They'll sell in no time—I already have some buyers. And then you can have Frank Kim make you some nice new dresses, exactly how *you* like them."

Becky didn't want to contradict her aunt, but the last thing she wanted was another dress. Every ruffle and flounce reminded her of her mother. Maybe Mr. Kim could make her a plain skirt and blouse. She could buy one now with scrip from her apprenticeship. Which she no longer had.

That thought left Becky stuck in the doorway, uncertain what to do with herself. Brisa was on patrol. Aunt Rosa was working. After school, everyone in town had something to do, from the littlest kids to the oldest great-grandparents. Except Becky.

Aunt Rosa glanced up. "Would you mind running an errand for me?"

"Sure," Becky said, grateful for the make-work.

"Take that quilt to Sheriff Crow, would you?"

The waiting quilt was one of Aunt Rosa's best, her difficult winding paths pattern worked in shades of blue and green. Her aunt had devoted most of her time to it ever since Becky had come to stay with her, leaving other projects undone. Aunt Rosa's satisfied smile as she sewed, and her firm statement to the sheriff that there would be no charge, made Becky suspect that it was a "thank you for throwing my sister-in-law in jail" quilt.

Becky headed out with the quilt folded in a basket. Though she knew her nagging sense of a lack of purpose would return once she'd finished her delivery, it still felt good to know that at the end of the day, she wouldn't have to go back to her house—her old house—and face her mother and grandmother.

It was bad enough seeing Mom delivering clothes, which she had to do herself now that she couldn't make Becky do it. Becky always ducked and hid until her mother was out of sight. Las Anclas was so small that you were always running into the people you least wanted to encounter.

She glanced around quickly. A few people worked in their vegetable gardens. A patrol rode down Main Street toward the gates. She was safe.

Becky wondered how Henry was doing, alone with Mom and Grandma Ida. Aunt Rosa had told her that Sheriff Crow had asked him if he'd like to move in with Aunt Rosa or some other family, but he'd refused. Becky hadn't seen him since they'd faced each other in her bedroom, with her head pounding and that strange look in his eyes. Now that she'd Changed and been disowned, she supposed he was avoiding her.

Maybe that should make her angry, but it only brought on a dull, weary sadness. She didn't want anything bad to happen to him, no matter what he thought about her. But nothing would. He'd always been stronger than she could ever hope to be. Henry would do what he always did to cope: turn it into a joke and laugh at it.

At the jail, Becky found Sheriff Crow cleaning her rifles with the same practiced skill as Aunt Rosa plied her needle.

"I brought your quilt." Becky hoped the sheriff wouldn't say anything about why she got it.

"Thanks. Would you mind setting it on the table?" Sheriff Crow held up an oil-smeared hand.

Becky laid it down, then stood awkwardly by the table, waiting out of what she belatedly recognized as the hope that the sheriff would ask her to come along and help investigate something. Appalled at herself, she darted for the door. The sheriff didn't need her any more.

"Becky, wait." Sheriff Crow set the last rifle in the rack and wiped her hands clean. "Is there something you're supposed to be doing right now?"

"No."

"Good. I was hoping you could come with me to—"

"Sheriff!" The door banged open, and in dashed stout Ms. Vasquez from the dairy. She leaned against the wall, panting, and spluttered, "Someone—or some*thing*—has invaded my house!"

Becky's heart sped up. Her lips moved soundlessly to shape, "Voske?"

"Oh?" Sheriff Crow inquired, not even bothering to get up.

Her complete lack of alarm made Becky relax, then hate her own stupidity. Of course Voske wouldn't invade one house in the middle of the day, then sit there waiting for its owner to return.

"I've been...out. For a few days. And nights. Completely out." Ms. Vasquez shot an embarrassed glance at Becky.

Becky dropped her gaze. She knew exactly where Ms. Vasquez had been. Everyone knew that she and Miss Chen the butcher had fallen madly in love.

"Anyway, I came back just now, and my door was ajar," Ms. Vasquez went on. "There were strange sounds coming from inside. I peeked in, and I saw movement. Stealthy movement! I thought to myself, this is a matter for the sheriff."

"Let's take a look." Sheriff Crow turned to Becky, "Want to come along? We can go from there to the thing I want you to touch."

"Sure." Becky smiled to herself. So the sheriff had wanted her after all. Her self-loathing dissolved as she considered Ms. Vasquez's description. It sounded like a stray cat. Maybe Becky could make friends with it.

Ms. Vasquez talked all the way to her house, adding more and more details in a way that reminded Becky of Summer's stories. By the time they arrived, she'd convinced herself that a posse of armed bandits had moved in and made themselves at home. She gestured dramatically to the front door, which did indeed stand ajar. *"There!"*

Sheriff Crow flung the door wide open. Ms. Vasquez screamed.

Becky jumped, but in surprise, not fear. She was sure nothing dangerous could be inside. Sheriff Crow would have warned her. When the sheriff beckoned, Becky walked right up—and stifled a giggle.

In the middle of the main room, all of Ms. Vazquez's furniture and bedding had been used to construct a tiny city. It looked as if a bunch of very strong five-year-olds were having a sleepover. Beady red eyes glowed from the depths of the furniture city.

"Well," Sheriff Crow said. "Now we know where the Vardams' raccoons went."

Ms. Vasquez screamed again. "What am I going to *dooooo?*"

"Lay a trail of tempting food from the front door to well outside your garden," the sheriff said. "Wait for night. The raccoons will follow it. When the last one's out, shut the door and clean up."

Ms. Vasquez snorted. "Or maybe I'll just move in with Amy." She stamped off in the direction of the butcher shop.

Once she was safely out of earshot, Becky couldn't help laughing. "I had no idea sheriffs had to deal with raccoons."

"Oh, we do all sorts of things," Sheriff Crow replied. "It's not like a lot of jobs where one day is pretty much like the next. I don't think I've ever done exactly the same thing two days running."

"I've done the same thing two *years* running."

"Not with me, you won't." The sheriff smiled at her. "Come on. I've got more work for those fingers of yours."

Before they'd passed two gardens, the sheriff peered up at the town hall roof. "Wait a minute. That's Ed Willet. Isn't he supposed to be on the walls?" She cupped her hand around her mouth. "Hey! Ed! What are you doing up there?"

Becky caught the glint of glass before a head popped up.

"Oh, um...I was checking the floodlights."

"With a beer jug?"

"I just happened to have it with me," Ed Willet said. "The floodlights are fine. I think I'm late to the wall. Don't want to keep Julio waiting."

As Ed Willet scrambled down the ladder, Becky asked, "Do

you have the roster for the entire town memorized?"

"It's not hard," Sheriff Crow said.

Becky realized that she, too, always remembered the sentry and patrol schedules for the teenagers. The difficult part would be daring to call up and confront people, knowing that they could yell. Or lie. Or get angry. What if Ed Willet had thrown that beer jug? Her stomach tensed at the thought.

But Sheriff Crow didn't have to worry about that sort of thing. She was the strongest and fastest person in Las Anclas. If Ed Willet had tried to fight her, she could have picked him up in one hand and thrown him into the jail from right where she was.

"Something bothering you?" Sheriff Crow asked.

Becky was going to shake her head and apologize, but she stopped herself. She'd lived her whole life telling people she was sorry. She didn't have to apologize when she hadn't done anything wrong.

"I forgot how strong you are. Nobody bothers you. They all know you could beat them."

"*Now* they know," Sheriff Crow replied. "But I haven't always been this strong. And none of my deputies are. Oh, sure, strength is useful. But it's not here." She touched her strong right arm. "It's here." She ran her fingers from her temple to her eyes to her mouth.

"I wish I was strong anywhere," Becky said miserably.

Sheriff Crow stopped walking and studied Becky with her mismatched eyes. Her two black braids fell on either side of her face, hiding nothing. "You could be."

"But..." Becky broke off. She couldn't stand saying one more word to the sheriff in her weak little voice.

"Let's try something. I'm going to walk across the square. You stay where you are, and you get my attention." She winked at Becky with her yellow snake eye. "Pretend you're Ms. Vasquez and you've just discovered a raccoon city in your bedroom."

Before Becky could protest, she walked away, her shiny braids swinging.

Becky gulped in air. "Sheriff Crow."

The sheriff's step didn't falter.

Becky clenched her hands into fists. She glanced around, afraid that someone would hear—that someone would stare—just afraid.

But the patrol was long gone, their dust slowly settling. The gardeners weren't watching her. They were working.

"Sheriff Crow?"

No one reacted. Sheriff Crow stood with her back turned, pretending to look at the carpenters' shop.

Becky tried to imitate Ms. Vasquez. "Sheriff Crow!"

The closest gardener glanced up, then went back to weeding. Becky wondered if Sheriff Crow had even heard her.

Why is she doing this to me? Becky thought miserably. *It's humiliating.*

Her mother's voice spoke in her head. *"What are you whining about?"*

Mom was right about her. The sheriff of Las Anclas was taking the time away from her busy day to be kind to Becky, and Becky couldn't even do one little thing for her. Sheriff Crow would be disgusted, and rightly so. She'd despise Becky for the weakling and coward that she was, and she'd never ask Becky to do anything for her again.

Knowing she'd fail miserably, Becky made one last try. *"Sheriff Crow!"*

The sheriff glanced over her shoulder. To Becky's surprise, she didn't look horrified at Becky's ugly screech. She actually looked proud.

"That's it!" Sheriff Crow's voice easily echoed across the square. "Now try it again. But louder!" She turned her back again.

Becky drew in a deep breath. "Sheriff Crow! Sheriff Crow! LOOK AT ME!"

All the gardeners raised their heads. Becky froze, her throat raw and her heart pounding. But once they'd looked, two went right back to weeding, and old Grandma Garcia smiled at her, then wheeled her barrow away.

Sheriff Crow strode back to rejoin Becky. Her half-smile was as wide as it could get, and the skin around her brown eye crinkled with approval. "Did you see what you did, Becky? You gave an order, and you got the entire town square to obey."

Becky opened her mouth to deny it or say it was a fluke or that it didn't matter. Then she fell in step with Sheriff Crow, hoping she'd get a chance to do it again.

·27·
ROSS

ROSS HAD THE FIRST watch of the night. Leaving the fire burning down and everyone asleep, he went to check the horses and Rusty. The burro huffed with contentment as Ross scratched behind his rabbit-like ears.

He walked up the little hill above the campsite and sat down, tipping his head back to gaze at the blazing stars and full moon. At Gold Point, the electric lights had blotted out the stars. And in the play set in ancient times, they'd said it was like that everywhere. He'd have hated to live back then.

Footsteps crunched up the hill. Mia started to settle down by him, but her cloud viper gun banged into his ribs.

"Oops." She snatched it up and re-holstered it on her other side, but didn't blush or apologize or flee.

He smiled and put his arm around her waist, pulling her in close. Her hand snaked around his shoulders. Neither Mia nor Jennie did anything more than exchange a quick kiss with him while they were on watch, but it was good to just sit companionably. It was especially good to sit with Mia without the jittery awkwardness that had ruined all their dates before the night the whales had sung. And he could feel in the soft lines of her body that she felt the same way.

"Look, Ross, it's the Seven Puppies!" She pointed at the constellation, which, as winter moved toward spring, appeared a little earlier each night. "Tipping out of their basket."

He laughed.

"How did you hear that story?" Mia asked. "They don't tell it in Las Anclas."

An unpleasantly familiar anxiety heated his face. "I don't know. I don't remember who told me."

Mia squeezed his hand. "Maybe your grandmother."

"Maybe," Ross said, though it was unlikely. Grandma mostly talked about useful things and how the day had gone. Her few stories were about people who'd done stupid things she wanted to warn him about, or clever things she wanted to teach him. She hadn't spun tales about dogs who changed into men or babies that became stars.

"You should get some sleep, since you have the dawn watch." Ross added in a low voice, "We'll have time when we get back."

"When we get home," Mia said, looking earnestly into his eyes. The distant campfire reflected in her glasses.

"Home," he repeated. That word hadn't been in his vocabulary before this year. It still didn't come without thought.

"Okay. Back to my sleeping bag."

Ross smiled, watching the moonlight shine on her hair and glint at her paralyzer gun as she picked her way down the hill.

"Mom told you."

Ross leaped to his feet, snatching his knife from his belt and spinning around. Summer was perched on a boulder a few feet away.

Ross let out his breath in a whoosh. "*Don't.* Do that." Then he remembered her words. Cautiously, he said, "What was that about Mom?"

Summer leaped from the boulder, floated through the air, and landed beside him with a soft thud. No matter how many times he saw his sister do that, it always amazed him. "Mom told you about the Seven Puppies. She had stories about all the constellations."

He wanted to ask about them, but kept silent. Asking her about his past, or hers, never went well.

"You really don't remember?" She sounded accusing, but he caught a slight tremble beneath the anger.

Ross slid his knife back into its sheath. "No. I wish I did."

She settled down beside him and hugged her knees tight. "It's so weird that you don't remember. Mom had so many stories about *you*."

"I remember some things," Ross said slowly. He was surprised that she hadn't stomped off as she usually did, angry with him for being something other than what he was. Or some*one*. "They're like the fragments you find in ruins. Pieces of all sorts of things, all scattered. You can try putting them together but nothing fits."

Summer rocked back and forth. "That's funny. I remember things I wish I could forget." Her voice was fierce again. "But not Mom. Can you remember her face?"

He drew a breath, trying to get his heart to stop pounding. "No. Sometimes I hate myself because I can't. And now I never will."

She stopped rocking. "Do you want to?"

That's weird, Ross thought. But it was better than arguing.

"Of course I do," he said, keeping his voice even. "I'd give the best find I ever prospected to get a single memory of her back."

Summer went so still that he thought he'd infuriated her. Then she spoke in an odd tone: low, flat, quick. "She said I should tell you."

Ross wanted to ask who "she" was, but managed to keep his mouth shut. Whatever was going on, speaking would ruin it for sure.

Summer slowly unslung her backpack and dug inside it. With infinite care, she pulled out a cloth-wrapped package. She glanced up at him, her face solemn in the bright moonlight, then removed the coverings, her hands trembling.

It was a book.

His sister kept a book in her backpack, a book whose very existence she'd hidden, a book that was clearly her most precious possession.

So had he. An ancient book that he couldn't read, which had almost gotten him killed, set Voske after him, led him to Las Anclas, and changed his life forever.

Like me, Ross thought in amazement. *My sister has a book, just like I did.*

He wanted to tell her, but the words caught in his throat. Of all the things he'd imagined they might have in common, this was the last one he'd expected.

He glanced up at her, sure that she'd noticed how dumb-founded he must look. But Summer's attention was on the book, not on him. Ross tried to force his gaze away from her and on to it, but all he could see were her fingers, slim and brown against the white page. It was a sketchbook. Then he looked down in the blue-white light, and saw the drawing.

His breath stuttered in his chest as if someone had punched him. The woman in the sketch was Mom.

How could he have ever forgotten that face? All the scattered memories of his mother brushing his hair, leading him by the hand, giving him a bowl of steaming acorn mush—all those memories now had her face.

"She looked a little like you." Ross glanced from Summer's round cheeks to Mom's thinner ones, from Summer's streaming hair to Mom's braids.

"She looked a *lot* like you," Summer said. "You got the same smile. *Exactly* the same."

"Who made that picture?"

"I did." Her voice was flat. "She taught me how to draw. She said she taught you, too."

Once she said it, Ross could almost feel a hand over his own, guiding his fingers holding the pencil. "She did. But I can't do anything like that. Do you have any more?"

Summer let out her breath, then looked upward. "I promised." She jerked her chin down again. "Okay. Here goes."

That was the girl he was used to, angry and resentful. But her hands were careful as they turned to a new page; she obviously had every one memorized.

Summer's face looked out of the paper with a lopsided grin that Ross had never seen on the real girl. She only seemed a little younger in the drawing, but her hair was as short as Mia's. There was no way it could have grown that long in a year, or even two.

Ross glanced up at his sister. She stared back, unblinking. "How old were you then?"

"That's not me." Her voice had flattened even more. Summer sounded as if she was daring him to react when she said, "That's my twin sister. Spring."

Her tone sent a chill through him. Spring was dead. He knew it without asking. "What happened?"

Summer slammed the book shut and pulled it against her chest, rocking back and forth in silence. Her face screwed up and her teeth clenched as if she was holding her breath underwater.

Then an angry sob exploded out. She dashed her eyes against her shoulder. "I *promised*. I promised Spring. When the whales sang."

Ross was stunned. He'd noticed that her eyes had been red the next morning, but she'd blamed it on salt spray. He didn't pretend to know Summer, but there was one thing he was sure of: just like him, she would hate being pitied.

"She was there?" Ross tried to make it sound like an ordinary question.

"Yes. In a way. I could *see* her, sitting right beside me." Her accusing tone didn't quite mask the tremble in her voice. "She would have *loved* hearing the whales sing."

Ross wouldn't give Summer pity, but he could give her the truth. "Until you came I thought I was alone, and I couldn't reach any memories. And now you're here, and there was another sister?" He heard his voice rise, but didn't try to hide how unsettled he felt.

She started rocking again, still clutching the sketchbook, then glanced down the hill. Ross could see that she was within a heartbeat of bounding away—maybe for good.

He didn't know what to say to make her stay, so he asked for what he wanted. "Can I see her again?"

She let out an angry sob, then jerked her head in a nod. "I promised her. She said…she said me not telling you was making her never be real."

Ross kept quiet, letting his sister speak.

"She *is* real," Summer insisted, as if daring him to deny it. "Sometimes just before I wake up, I can feel her sleeping beside me. That school, I know she would have loved it. When Dr. Lee cooks her favorite food. She's everywhere. Always. With me—but when I turn to see her, or talk to her, she's *gone*."

Whatever Summer expected, Ross had no impulse to tell her she was wrong. With his own shattered memories, he was hardly in a position to say what was or wasn't possible. And whether

Spring was a ghost or a memory, she was obviously real to Summer.

"And she wants...she wanted...you should know about her." Without looking at him, she opened the book. "Here's our tenth birthday. That's her with her pet iguana. Here she is, levitating him."

Spring looked like a happy Summer, skinny and knock-kneed. Her hands were raised high, and a resigned-looking iguana floated above them.

"What's the iguana's name?" Ross asked.

"Fluffy."

Ross laughed in surprise. Then he choked it off, afraid Summer would take it wrong, but she, too, gave a shaky chuckle.

"It's a perfect name for an iguana," Ross said.

"That's exactly what Spring said," Summer replied. "She said if we ever got a cat, she'd name it Prickly."

She turned more pages, showing Ross different scenes. Mom washing clothes on a river bank. Spring catching fireflies. Spring gathering acorns. Ross shut his eyes, struck by another vivid memory: stuffing acorns into his shirt. He couldn't have been more than four.

"I remember Mom making acorn mush," he said. "Sheriff Crow asked me what my tribe was. I didn't even know if I had one. Do you know?"

"Mom's people came from all over. If she had a tribe, she didn't know about it. Dad's mother taught her to make acorn mush, years and years before you were born," Summer replied. "But Dad was Miwok. His clan—"

Automatically Ross said, "Coyote. We're Coyote clan."

"That's right. Spring and I went looking for them, because we knew they'd take us in, but we never got that far. Mom said they were way up the northwest coast."

She turned the page. A village of flat-roofed adobe buildings and a fence of interwoven cacti. A donkey. Spring riding and laughing and gradually getting older, until Summer stopped with her hand flat on a page.

"Mom worked to get us horses," Summer said, her voice low. "This is Mom with Pepper and Salt."

Mom stood with her hands on the polls of a black horse and a white one. Her smile was just like the one Ross occasionally saw in mirrors.

"We were riding in the desert, and a rattler spooked Salt. Mom got thrown. Broke her neck." Summer pressed the book against her chest, avoiding his eyes. "That was a bad winter. Spring and I were alone. We barely got to high ground ahead of a flash flood. When we finally found a town, they wouldn't let us in because they had some sickness. By the time we found a camp, we were starving."

Her voice came quicker, with the angry edge Ross was used to. "They welcomed us. Fed us. Pretended to be friendly. It was a big family—twenty of them, uncles and cousins and so forth. The youngest was sixteen. They said if we were Changed we didn't have to hide it."

Summer opened the book to show him sketches of people. "Alice, the mother, could teleport little things. She showed us and laughed. Said she was like a squirrel. So we showed her what we could do. The next morning, we woke up with Don holding a pistol to Spring's head. Turned out they were bandits. They said we had to help them rob people, and if we tried to fight or run away, they'd kill Spring."

Ross's fists clenched until his gauntlet scraped and his nails bit into his other palm. "I wish I'd been there."

"Well, you weren't." She gulped.

"I'm sorry, Summer. If I had known any of you were alive, I'd have searched for you everywhere. I never would've stopped."

"I know," she said, low-voiced, surprising him. "I mean, I know now. We would have kept looking, too. But Mom was sure you and Grandma were dead."

"What happened?"

Spring appeared again in the sketches, no longer smiling. "We were with the bandits for two years. It felt like forever. Sometimes they robbed travelers in the desert. Sometimes they went to towns. They'd make one of us go with their son Joe to rob churches and rich people's homes while the other stayed with an adult. I could jump through windows and Spring could pull things out of them. They never let us be alone together."

Ross had been a captive for a few months, and he'd nearly lost his mind. He couldn't even imagine being held hostage for two years. He wanted to say something to his sister, but before he could, she started talking again.

"One day they decided to rob some jewel traders." She shut the sketchbook and pressed her knees to her chest. "We were going to distract the guards while Spring snuck up on the caravan and floated the jewels out of the trunks. But there were way more guards than we expected, and they fought hard. Alice sent me to steal the horses. Joe should have been guarding Spring, but he was off fighting someone to get their horse. Somebody in the caravan shot her. I ran to her, and Joe screamed at me to get back to my job. I jumped on him and broke his neck. But Spring was already dead."

Ross's breath hissed in his throat.

Summer fiercely wiped her eyes on her sleeve. "There was nothing keeping me there anymore. I grabbed Joe's gun and shot as many of the bandits as I could until I ran out of bullets. Then I jumped on the horse Joe had been fighting over and rode out of there. Everyone was still fighting for their lives, so they couldn't follow me."

In the long silence that followed, Ross swallowed in an aching, dry throat, then forced himself to speak. "I know it doesn't help. But I'm sorry."

"Yeah, well," Summer muttered, but she didn't sound angry. "When I finally had to stop, I found a pouch of diamonds in the horse's saddlebag. The jewels hadn't been in the trunks at all. That was what Joe had been trying to get."

"They let Spring get killed for a bunch of diamonds?" Ross's entire body flashed hot with fury. He wanted to reach back in time to finish off the bandits.

Summer wiped her eyes again. "I didn't care about the stupid diamonds. And I didn't even get to keep them. The horse, either. A couple weeks later, I took a bath in a pond. When I came back, the horse was gone and everything with it. The only thing I had left was my backpack, because I always kept that with me. So I started walking. And the very first town I came to, everybody was talking about you."

"I'm glad you found me," Ross said. "Even if I can't kill a hundred bandits with one bullet."

Summer gave a snort of laughter. "That's okay. I can do it for you!"

Ross turned to the last drawing before the blank pages. A mean face glared at him. It belonged to a hugely muscled young man bristling with weapons, aiming a rifle straight out of the page. His weather-beaten, hard-featured features reminded Ross of the bounty hunter, though the man in the drawing was much younger. "Who's this guy?"

"You," Summer said. "That's how I imagined you after I heard all those stories."

Ross could see why she had been disappointed. Then, after a second look at the scowling guy with the muscles nearly ripping through his shirt, he was tempted to laugh. But he was also impressed by her skill. "You imagined someone and you drew him? But he looks like a real person!"

Summer snorted. "Yeah, Ross. I can do that. If you described someone for me, I could draw them so you could recognize them."

"But you didn't draw him looking like you."

"I could do that. Easy."

She took a pencil from her backpack and turned the book to a blank page. With quick, sure strokes, she drew a man. Long black hair, sharp black eyes, high cheekbones, a blunt nose, broad shoulders, and narrow hips. Ross couldn't stop looking at the sketch. The young man seemed so familiar, and not just because he resembled Summer.

"Could you make him older?" Ross asked, not knowing why he was asking. "Like...with lines around his eyes. And here." He drew his finger down either side of his mouth.

The pencil moved, shaded. Ross bent closer. He did know that face. "That's my father—*our* father."

Summer's head jerked up, and her black eyes met his. "You said you didn't remember him. You told me you didn't even know what he looked like."

"I didn't. Until now."

Summer looked down at the drawing. In the distance a coyote ululated. "I guess now we both know."

·28·
KERRY

HER SISTER, SPRING, KERRY thought as they rode northward. She'd been right that Summer had lost someone before she reached Las Anclas.

That was another unexpected thing that she and Summer shared: a dead sister. But out of all her siblings, Kerry had liked Deirdre the least, even before she got her power. Afterward, Deirdre had become impossible to live with. From the anguish underlying the jumbled rush of the story Summer had told that morning, she and Spring had been as close as Kerry and Sean. But once Summer had revealed her twin's existence, she seemed glad to be able to talk about her. The "Spring and me" stories had been going non-stop since they'd started riding.

"...and then Spring and me looked into the canyon, and saw an entire ruined town at the bottom!" Summer concluded.

"Did you climb down?" Mia asked.

"No. It was completely surrounded by singing trees." Summer turned to Ross. "How about taking me into the ruins by Las Anclas? I've never been inside a real ruin that hasn't been picked down to dust."

Ross's shoulders hunched up. To spare him having to answer, Kerry said, "I know you strangled a sand tiger with your bare hands, but I don't know if you want to fight a thousand giant bees."

"Not a thousand," Summer said. "And I didn't kill a hundred bandits, either. I wish I had. I only shot three or four of them, and I don't know how many survived the attack." More cheerfully, she added, "But I did strangle that sand tiger."

Ross exclaimed, "I wish I could've seen it."

Summer flashed a smile. "I got pretty scratched up. You see, Spring and me were walking at dusk beside this huge rock formation, when this shape leaps out and knocks her down..."

Kerry listened intently, amazed. Fourteen years old, and she really had shot bandits. She'd fought for her life and survived. Even Mia had had to fight—both Jennie and Ross had told Kerry separately that Mia had saved Ross's life during the attack on Las Anclas. Kerry was the only one there who'd never been in a battle, though her father had killed many people and ordered even more deaths.

Summer and Ross were survivors of people like Father.

The closest Kerry had come to battle was when Jennie and her group had captured her. But she had always known they were trying to take her prisoner, not kill her.

Father had offered her leadership of an army, and she had run away rather than lead that army to kill harmless citizens. Kerry still believed she had made the right choice. Sean had also made it. The weird thing was, she knew she would have to fight for her life sooner or later, but it would be against that army of Father's. It was so easy to picture them swarming out of their ships and on to the beach.

"There must have been an earthquake," Jennie said.

As Nugget topped the rise, Kerry saw the rubble in the dip below. The concrete bridge had collapsed, blocking the road that ran between two hills. Huge chunks of fallen cement lay scattered as if some giant had torn up the bridge and flung it down in pieces.

"I can jump over it," Summer said.

"But the horses can't. We'll have to lead them into the arroyo." Jennie pointed to a deep ravine a little way off the road.

They rode into the arroyo and proceeded two by two along a shallow stream of rainwater. Gravel crunched beneath hooves.

Ross glanced up at one of the wide cracks that split the granite walls. "Looks like that crevice I hid in after I got kidnapped."

By Santiago's patrol, Kerry thought. *And they're all dead but him.*

If Ross's first escape attempt had succeeded, Santiago would be dead now, too. He and his patrol would have died trying to get Ross back rather than be executed for losing their captive. Father would be teaching Kerry about sea battles so she could lead or at least participate in the attack on Las Anclas.

She almost wished she hadn't run into Sean. Knowing about Father's plan wouldn't stop him. All it did was bring home to her exactly how brief her life in Las Anclas was likely to be. And not just hers, but Mia's, Ross's —

Nugget's ears flicked.

"Above!" Jennie yelled.

Rifle muzzles appeared over the edges of both sides of the arroyo. Kerry flung her arms over her head to shield herself, then remembered her friends. She gritted her teeth, extended the shield to its maximum reach, covering Jennie and Mia in front of her, and Ross and Summer behind.

A shower of bullets and arrows bounced off the shield. The acrid smell of gun smoke stung Kerry's nose.

"Fire!" someone yelled from above.

A second round, this time all arrows, clattered against the shield. Kerry trembled with effort. She'd never created anything this big before, or held it this long. Her body and mind strained.

Summer yelled, "I'll go after them!"

As Ross grabbed her arm, a woman's head appeared over the edge. "*There* she is!"

"Finally!" a man bellowed in triumph.

"Thought you'd lost us, running south then doubling back, eh, you stinking little thief? But we've got you now!" the woman snarled.

"Don? Alice?" Summer shrieked.

The man demanded, "Where are our diamonds?"

"Let me go!" Summer screamed at Ross. "I'm gonna kill them!"

As Ross struggled to hold her, Jennie spoke so softly that Kerry barely heard her. "How long can you hold this?"

Kerry tried to pitch her voice low, but it was hard when it took all her concentration to maintain the shield. "I don't know. Not long."

"Fire!" Don shouted.

Kerry braced, every muscle vibrating. Her heart pounded. But her shield held. Bullets bounced off and rolled to the side, joining the heap of arrows and bullets suspended in midair.

Black spots bobbed nauseatingly at the edge of her vision. But Kerry forced herself to yell, "It's fine, Jennie! I can keep this up all day!"

"Flank 'em!" Don yelled.

The bandits' heads vanished, replaced by the sound of footsteps and hooves as the bandits split up to attack from either end of the arroyo. With immense relief, Kerry released the shield. The suspended bullets and arrows showered into the mud all around them.

Kerry's head was splitting, but she tightened her belly, drawing on whatever strength remained to create another shield that would protect everyone. But it was like reaching into an empty barrel. Giving up on the shield, she tried for something smaller: her sword. Her hand closed on empty space. She had nothing left.

As the howling mob of bandits charged into the arroyo from either end, Kerry's mouth dried. She had no other sword. Why should she, when she could create her own?

"Kerry!" Jennie shouted. "Take mine!"

Jennie tossed Kerry her sword in its scabbard. Kerry caught it in both hands. It was heavier than she expected. Clumsily, her fingers shaking, she slid it out of the sheath.

Jennie raised her crossbow and shot the lead bandit. In a single movement, she slapped in another bolt and cranked it.

Mia took aim with her paralyzer gun, holding it steady with both hands, and fired. A bandit toppled out of the saddle. Behind her, Ross took out two bandits with a pair of blindingly fast knife throws.

An arrow zipped an inch away from Kerry's ear. She recoiled, almost falling off Nugget. It was hard to fight with a sword made of metal whose hilt had been designed for bigger hands. She was used to wielding her own weightless swords, whose hilts molded perfectly to her grip.

Everything was a blur of confusion. She had no idea what anyone else was doing or who was winning. The only thing she was sure of was that they were outnumbered. She could do nothing but swing that heavy sword at the nearest enemies.

Then she remembered Father's advice. *It's easy to get tunnel vision when you're in the middle of a battle. Always look for the big picture. Then you'll know your next move.*

Kerry took a deep breath, forcing herself to calm, and tried to widen her field of vision. Summer had jumped from Sally's back to hurtle overhead, leaping from one tiny foothold on the wall to the next as she slashed with long knives held in either hand. Jennie shot steadily, but only had a few bolts left in her quiver. Ross had dismounted and was fighting on foot against the bandits attacking from behind. He threw his last boot knife, then snatched his crossbow gun from the saddle holster as he faced off with four mounted bandits.

"Bolts!" Jennie called breathlessly to Mia, who started rummaging through her backpack.

"Jennie!" Ross shouted. As Kerry swiveled her head, metal flashed by her other ear as Ross tossed his naked sword through the air. The hilt smacked into Jennie's outstretched hand.

A blur of movement swung toward Kerry's head. She ducked instinctively, then forced her sword upward. Metal screeched against metal as a sword slid against hers. The bandit jerked her sword back, and swung it around at Kerry from the side — using both hands, just as Kerry did.

Kerry might not be familiar with the sword in her hands, but she was extremely familiar with that move. With the ease of long training, Kerry brought her sword under the girl's — she had a second to see that the bandit was a teenager like herself — before she arced her sword down to bury it in the girl's ribs.

Kerry jerked her sword free, and watched as the girl fell from her horse, landing face down in the stream.

I killed her, Kerry thought, unable to quite believe it. *She's dead.*

She forced herself to look away. Jennie faced three bandits, all men, one of whom was trying to get at Mia as she frantically dug into her pack. Kerry clapped her knees to Nugget's sides, pushing him up on Mia's other side. She used both hands to bring Jennie's sword down toward the attacker as Mia reloaded her cloud viper gun.

Summer whirled over Alice, her knife slicing across the

screeching woman's throat. Alice pitched lifelessly into the mud. Mia shot her venom gun, recoiling in her saddle as a huge man stiffened and fell on top of Alice.

Jennie took out the last two bandits with a powerful figure eight swing that embedded a sword in one and buried a knife up to the hilt in the second.

There were no more enemies that Kerry could see. The rest must be behind her. She spun around.

Ross leaned against the side of the ravine, breathing hard. Blood ran down his left arm and dripped from the steel fingers of his gauntlet. Four bandits sprawled dead on the ground before him, each with a bolt in their heart or throat.

As suddenly as the battle had begun, it was over.

Groans rose from some of the fallen. Two bandits lay stiff on their backs but seemingly unhurt, glassy eyes wide open. Both had tiny darts sticking in their flesh.

Summer landed in a crouch and stooped over one of the paralyzed bandits, bloody knife ready.

Jennie caught her wrist. "Leave them."

"Why?" Summer said, her voice high and shrill. "They got Spring killed! I'm sending them to Hell after Joe!"

Father's voice again spoke in Kerry's mind. *Spare the wounded when you're conquering a city, unless it's someone you would have to kill anyway. Then mercy has a purpose. But anyone who attacks you, don't leave them alive.*

"That is not your judgment to make," Jennie said. "They can't harm us now. And they won't come back."

"I'm not afraid of them." Summer raised her dagger, but Jennie again pulled her back.

Kerry didn't care about the bandits, but the last thing she wanted to see was more killing. "They'll suffer more if you leave them alive. Just imagine, Summer. Once they unfreeze, they'll have to get up and bury their family. They can't do that if they're dead."

Summer sobbed and scrubbed her eyes on her shoulder. "I bet they didn't even bury Spring." But she turned away.

Jennie glanced at Mia. "Can they hear us?"

Mia nodded violently. "Oh yes. They're completely aware. I

was when I shot myself."

Jennie's eyebrows rose, and Mia hastily added, "As a test! Not by accident. I wouldn't be careless like that."

Jennie smiled faintly. Then her expression hardened as she leaned over the nearest paralyzed bandit, her red-smeared sword brandished over him. "We showed you mercy this once. But if we ever see your faces again, you'll get what you tried to do to us. Leave this land. And don't come back."

Summer stood at her shoulder. "Those diamonds are gone. I got robbed right after I got them. Somebody is probably robbing somebody else for them right now!" She gave the bandit a vicious kick in the ribs and stomped away.

Ross, ignoring his wound, bent to collect fallen weapons.

Mia turned to Kerry. "Want me to clean that for you?"

"Clean what?" Kerry followed Mia's gaze, and was startled to see a long slice on her forearm, and another on her thigh. As soon as she registered them, they began to sting fiercely.

"Let's get out of the ravine first," Jennie said. "We've still got to ride around all that concrete."

Tired and aching as they all were, they caught the bandits' horses and collected their weapons and arrows. Jennie led the way out of the arroyo, sword in hand. Ross took the rear, crossbow gun at the ready.

When they emerged, the concrete bridge loomed before them, perfectly intact. All the fallen rubble was gone. Kerry stared, baffled.

"I should have seen that," Summer exclaimed. "Cousin Elias could create illusions. Good ones. Not rabbit illusions."

Jennie laid her palm on the girl's shoulder. "There was no way you could have known that was him. This wasn't your fault."

"I know that," Summer declared. But she didn't shake off Jennie's hand.

◆ ◆ ◆

They reached Las Anclas as the sun began its slide toward the sea. Teenagers clustered on the sentry walks as they rode up, leading their string of new horses.

Brisa shouted down, "Was it fun?"

"Are the Catalina Players coming?" Alfonso called.

As they rode through the gates, Kerry wished she could go straight to her room. Her entire body itched. She longed for a bath, clean clothes, a bed, and hot fresh food. But mostly a bath.

"Hey, why's Summer got knives?" Tommy Horst bellowed from the other side of the sentry walk.

"Tommy, back to your place," Ms. Lowenstein ordered sharply.

"I don't have to," Tommy called back. "My dad is defense chief, and that girl wearing those knives is defense business!"

Tommy's bullhorn voice attracted the attention of the field planters who were streaming in through the gates. They clustered around, blocking the road.

"Step aside," came Sheriff Crow's crisp voice. "Coming through."

She was accompanied by a blonde girl. For a surreal second, Kerry didn't recognize her. Then she saw that it was Becky, but a Becky who had transformed herself. Not only was wearing cotton pants and a shirt instead of a dress, she had pulled her hair into a ponytail, instead of letting it hang forward to hide her face. This new Becky walked with her back straight and her chin high, her gaze steady as the sheriff's rather than cast downward.

What did Sheriff Crow do with her? Kerry wondered. *Teach her to fight?*

That couldn't be it. Months of martial arts training in the Vardams' yard had done nothing for Becky but make her a timid girl who could punch harder than she could before.

Mr. Horst thrust his way through the crowd. "Now, what is all this?" He glared at Ross. "You were in charge of this girl. Why is she armed?"

Ross visibly forced himself to look Mr. Horst in the eyes—Kerry could almost feel the effort he made. She decided to rescue him. After all, he'd done the same for her when she'd returned to Las Anclas after blowing up the dam at Gold Point.

She pitched her voice to reach every listener, even those peeping out from windows. "Summer fought heroically when we were attacked by bandits. She used those knives to protect us. But of course, if she must turn them over, she must." Kerry eyed Sheriff Crow, willing the woman to go along with her ploy. "Oh! We confiscated these horses from the bandits. I'll take them to the stables."

"That's at least a dozen horses," Meredith called from the wall. "How many did you fight?"

"About twenty. Maybe more," Summer said airily.

"Thirteen," Jennie said. But she spoke under her breath.

Sheriff Crow gave her a slight smile, then motioned to Summer, who dismounted and approached with some of her old wariness. "What do you intend to do with your knives? They're not permitted in the schoolhouse."

"I'll leave them in my room when I'm at school," Summer replied. "And they're just in case something attacks me."

"Jennie, Ross, I'd like your opinion," Sheriff Crow said. "Should she should be allowed to bear weapons?"

"Yes," Jennie and Ross said at the same time.

Mr. Horst snapped, "That's a council decision."

Sheriff Crow inspected the crowd. "We have a quorum right here. Dr. Lee? Guildmaster Appel? Shall we let Summer Juarez keep her knives—and lift the restriction on her while we're at it?"

"I'm here as well," Grandma Wolfe spoke up cheerfully, from beside Felicité and Henry. "Summer, it's good to see you taking responsibility. Sheriff, you have my vote. "

"Mine, too," Dr. Lee said.

Guildmaster Appel hooked his thumbs into the pockets of his considerable waistcoat, rocked back on his heels, and rumbled, "If the sheriff thinks it a good idea, I'm for it."

"I do," Sheriff Crow said.

As Mr. Horst scowled, Jennie spoke up. "Mr. Horst, I have good news for you. The Catalina Players are coming to Las Anclas!"

The crowd burst into cheers. Kerry didn't miss the sour look that puckered Mr. Horst's face before he forced a smile and addressed the crowd. "See? I kept my promise to you voters!"

Felicité stepped forward. She was dressed for a party, as was Henry. She tipped her huge straw hat back and said in her tinkliest voice, "Why don't we combine my graduation dance with their performance? I will provide the refreshments, of course."

The teenagers shouted with enthusiasm, and Felicité smiled benignly around, as if the Players had been entirely her idea.

Kerry nudged Nugget to step near Felicité. Smiling in her sweetest Min Soo manner, she said, "Would you like a reminder about recording the quorum decision in the council records? I'd be happy to help."

Felicité's smile turned poisonous. "Oh, I never forget anything."

Kerry laughed silently all the way to the stable, where she handed off the tired horses. She rubbed Nugget's nose, then stretched one arm around his neck as she reached into her pouch for the last stale, broken horse cookie. Nugget accepted it regally.

From Penny's stall, mother and colt nickered in welcome. Kerry was glad to see their coats shining and clean, the stall spick and span, but she had expected no less. She wound her fingers in Penny's mane and kissed her soft muzzle.

"I can come back."

Kerry turned around. Paco stood behind her with buckets of feed. He was about to carry them to the next stall when she said, "Wait. Did you come back with the Ranger patrol? Is Mr. Preston here?"

Paco paused, glancing over his shoulder. Kerry could never get used to his resemblance to Father. Except that Paco never smiled. "He's on his way home."

"We heard some news about Yuki," Kerry offered.

Paco didn't speak, but he didn't go away.

"He's famous up and down the coast. He rode dolphins. He saved the life of a kid who was drowning. Everyone loved him. Just thought you might like to know."

Paco still didn't smile, but he looked like he was thinking of it. "Rode dolphins, huh? Did he make any good finds?"

He was actually talking to her. Marveling, Kerry said, "No big ones. Last anyone had heard, he was headed for a place with a weird reputation. The Burning Lands. No one had actually been there, but they'd all heard stories about it."

"Yeah, that sounds like somewhere Yuki would want to go." Paco paused, seeming to undergo some inner struggle. As if the words were forced out of him, he said, "What *were* the stories?"

"I have to make a report now, but can I tell you later?"

Paco shrugged and walked away. At least he didn't say no.

Jennie appeared at the stable door. "You can go find Mr. Preston now. Ma will see to Rusty and the horses."

"Do you want to come with me?"

Jennie shook her head, her expression somber. "There was a time when he would have believed me. But that's over now."

Jennie had lost Mr. Preston's trust on Kerry's behalf. If Jennie, Yuki, and Mia hadn't let her go, Kerry would have been executed by a firing squad, ordered by the man she was about to report to.

Life could take some strange turns.

Kerry spotted her target halfway up the Hill. "Mr. Preston!"

She still didn't like him any more than she liked his daughter, but he was the only person with power in Las Anclas who she was sure would believe her. He waited silently as she dashed up. In her mind, Father's cool, amused voice instructed her: *Only tell enough of the truth to serve your purpose.*

And then it was her mother's sweet voice that echoed in Kerry's ears: *There are more subtle forms of flattery than simple praise. Make a person think you're confiding in them and them alone, and they'll believe anything you say.*

Kerry glanced around, making sure no one was in earshot. Mr. Preston's pale eyes flicked upward, no doubt looking for hawks, and then back to her.

"I learned something on the trip that you need to know," Kerry said. "I told everyone I was with that I spoke to a trader. Everything I said was true, but I heard it from someone else. I want to tell you who. But I have to know that you'll keep that one part a secret. If anyone finds out who it really was, it could put them in danger."

"Hmm." Mr. Preston rubbed his chin with one finger. "I can't make promises without knowing what they are. But I have my own informants, and I never endanger them. I'll consider yours as one of mine. How's that?"

Kerry looked down, as if she were thinking it over, then nodded. "That's fine. While we were in the Saigon Alliance, my brother Sean showed up."

Mr. Preston stiffened. His gaze darted around again, but this time to the surrounding area. She knew that scan: *Is Sean here?*

"He's a fisher now," Kerry went on, pretending not to have noticed his reaction. What she would never tell him was that Sean had been to Las Anclas. "He lives in Catalina and trades with the Alliance. He saw the royal horses in a stable and went looking for me."

She gave him the full report. His eyes narrowed as he listened.

"I've told the council that Voske will return," Mr. Preston said when she finished. "I've told the entire town. Few seem to believe me."

"I do," Kerry said fervently. "I *know* he'll be back. Even before Sean told me."

"Thank you, Kerry. I'll take care of it." Mr. Preston gave her an approving nod, then strode toward his home.

Mom had been right again: *Tell people what they are already sure is true, especially if they've tried in vain to convince others. When they feel beleaguered, they look for allies.*

Now that Kerry had made her report and had been believed, her sense of urgency faded away. In fact, she felt more relaxed than she had in a long time. Father was still coming. But Las Anclas would be prepared.

With an odd mixture of relief and dismay, Kerry realized that she actually trusted Mr. Preston. At least, she trusted him to defend Las Anclas. He might not officially be defense chief any more, but she was sure that wouldn't stop him from doing his best.

As she headed back down the path, she wondered about the election. She'd been so convinced it was a sham that she hadn't bothered to vote.

Had the election been real after all?

If they are, I wonder if I could win one?

She was the daughter of the town's worst enemy. But she'd also helped bring down his empire. And by the time she'd be old enough to be a viable candidate—assuming Father hadn't conquered Las Anclas by then—her opponents would also be people her own age. Like Jennie. Or Felicité.

Kerry was still thinking over whether holding office was

something she'd enjoy, or if it only intrigued her as a test of the system, a challenge to herself, and a way to humiliate and crush Felicité, when a woman's voice called her name.

Trainer Crow stood smiling at her, with two of her ever-present rats at her heels.

"Hi, Trainer Crow," Kerry said, then bent to offer her hand to the rats. "Hi, Al. Hi, Ren."

"Peach's pups opened their eyes the day you left," Trainer Crow said. "They're old enough to bond now. Would you like to come meet them?"

Kerry froze with her arm extended. Joy swept away the tiredness. "Of course!"

In the excitement of Katana's birth and then the trip, Kerry had forgotten her months-old request to the rat trainers for a pup. She'd had no idea that any of the rats had been pregnant. But rats had a short gestation period, and people in Las Anclas were super-stitious about discussing pregnancies, preferring to wait for a healthy birth.

As they headed for the trainers' home, Kerry asked, "Are any already reserved, or do I get my pick?"

Trainer Crow's ironic smile reminded Kerry of her daughter's. "None are reserved. And you don't pick. The pup does. If you're compatible, they'll sense it. If none of them choose you, you'll have to wait for the next litter and try again."

Kerry hadn't heard anything about that before. "Aren't all of yours bonded to you and Trainer Koslova?"

The trainer made a tilting, yes-and-no gesture with her hand. "Some are. The rest obey us because we trained them, the way any working animal would, but we don't have a connection like the one between Yuki and Kogatana or Felicité and Wu Zetian. They bond as a pack instead, like wild rats. But if a person is only going to have one rat, it isn't fair for either of them to live together without that bond."

Kerry had known the rats of Las Anclas were special, like the royal horses of Gold Point, but she'd had no idea how special. She hadn't even known that wild rats had a pack bond.

I bet Sean knows, she couldn't help thinking. *He'd love a rat pup.*

If he were here instead of her, all the pups would probably

want him. They'd have to fight for the honor. Or he'd get his very own pack, and spend the next five years paying the trainers. A rat cost almost as much as a horse. Luckily Kerry's gold crown, which she had offered to Mr. Preston in exchange for the two horses she'd taken from Las Anclas and left in Gold Point, had been worth three horses and scrip to spare. Between that and the scrip she'd been earning as a patroller and in the stables, she could afford one rat.

They reached the trainers' home. Trainer Crow led Kerry to the room where her wife, Trainer Koslova, waited. Peach, a hooded rat with a black head, a white body, and a black stripe down her back, was curled up in a nest of soft cloth. The pups were on the floor, tussling or exploring.

Trainer Koslova's crown of white-blonde braids was bright in a shaft of sunlight from an open window. "Welcome, Kerry."

"What do I do?" It was all Kerry could do to stop her voice from shaking. Animals loved her, and she was never afraid to approach one. But this felt different. More important. Less straightforward. Exactly what had Trainer Crow meant by "compatible?"

"Just sit down with them, as you would with a litter of kittens," Trainer Koslova replied.

"How will I know if one picks me?" Kerry asked.

Trainer Crow smiled. "You'll know."

Kerry settled down on the floor, taking a deep breath and forcing her mind to calm. If there was one thing she knew about animals, it was that they could sense anxiety and they didn't like it. And besides, if Felicité could get a rat, anyone could.

One pup was gray as smoke, moving with unusual grace as it explored the corners of the room. Another, drinking daintily from a water bowl, was the same brilliant gold as Wu Zetian. Kerry couldn't decide if she'd rather have the smoky rat or the golden one; both were beautiful, and while she admired the fluid movements of the gray one, the idea of Felicité no longer owning the only golden rat in town—and Kerry having the other—tickled her enormously.

Two pups were hooded like their mother, but one was a rare reverse-hood, with a white head and stripe against a black body, and the other's hood and stripe were a rich chestnut. They were play-fighting, rolling and nipping in an impressive show of courage and strength for pups that young. Surely one of those was compatible with her, but which one?

Kerry held out her hand, not to any particular pup but to the litter as a whole, and made a soft clicking noise with her tongue. The rats all looked up, Peach included.

The golden rat tilted its head, blinked its long-lashed eyes, and went back to drinking. It was a clear rejection. Kerry wasn't sure whether to be disappointed or amused: a tiny Felicité! Anyway, she had a golden stallion. That was much more impressive than a golden rat.

The smoky rat slipped up to her, its paws moving soundlessly across the floor, and sniffed her hand. Kerry held her breath. Was this the one?

The rat gave her a brief lick, then wandered off to visit its mother.

Kerry had been right. If she was to get any rat, it would be one of the hooded fighters. Both had stopped their sparring to approach her, their bright eyes curious. She noted more details as they came closer: the white-striped pup was male, with a thicker coat, and the chestnut one was female, with a few stray spots near her rump.

Just before they reached her outstretched hand, the chestnut pup turned on her brother and nipped him, making him squeak and jump away. She stood in front of Kerry's hand as if guarding it and watched, her pink tail lashing, until her brother edged all the way back to the water bowl, where he began to lap with an admirable display of unconcern. Only then did the chestnut pup turn back to Kerry, her competition vanquished.

Kerry smiled. Now she understood what Trainer Crow had meant by "compatible."

"You're a fighter," she murmured. "Of course."

The pup sniffed her fingers, then licked them with a quick swipe of her rough pink tongue. Kerry petted her furry head.

The pup shook herself, then went bounding away to the water bowl. As Kerry watched in disbelief, she proceeded to do the exact same thing with it that she'd done with Kerry's hand: bite her brother and sister till they squeaked, guard the bowl until they retreated, and only then drink from it herself.

"What?" Kerry's words burst unbidden from her throat. "She's nothing but a bully! And *none* of them want me?"

Something soft nudged her hand. Not the one she still held outstretched, though her arm ached by now, but the one dangling at her side.

She looked down. A rat pup was nuzzling her.

He was undersized compared to the rest of the litter, his fur a plain light brown, like a wild rat. She'd seen herself how wild rats could be almost invisible against the desert sand. But the floor was polished black wood, so she had no idea how the pup had managed to get so close without her even noticing that he existed.

"Hey, little guy," Kerry said. "Where were you hiding?"

The pup blinked his shining black eyes at her in an expression that she couldn't help interpreting as a fake-innocent *Who, me?*

He jumped into her lap. She scooped him up and cradled him to her chest. He was small enough to cup in her hands. His claws prickled her palms, and when she lifted him higher, he stretched out his neck to brush her chin with his whiskers. The pup made a series of whiffling noises so quiet that she could barely hear them, as if he was telling her a secret.

"I'll take it to my grave," Kerry replied solemnly.

The pup gave a soft snort, as if he understood her joke. The way the light shone in his eyes even made him look like he thought it was funny.

Could he have understood? Just how smart are these rats, anyway?

"Whisper," Kerry said. "What do you think of that for a name?"

Whisper licked her palm. If he did understand, he certainly didn't seem to object. Then he curled up into a velvety ball, closed his eyes, and fell asleep.

Kerry didn't know how long she sat holding him silently, marveling. She'd gotten very fond of Kogatana, and she'd been impressed with Wu Zetian's beauty and intelligence. They were why she'd wanted a rat of her own. But Whisper was so much more than she'd ever imagined. She was so lucky that he'd chosen her!

"I thought he might be the one," Trainer Koslova said.

Only Kerry's years of training prevented her from jumping out of her skin. She'd completely forgotten that there were other people in the room. She did twitch enough to rouse Whisper, who glanced around, then yawned widely, displaying a rose-pink mouth and sharp white teeth, and went back to sleep.

"He's a throwback," Trainer Crow said. "Looks just a wild rat, doesn't he? And he's stealthy like one, too. Very unusual. We haven't had anything like him for three generations now."

"Why wouldn't you breed to get more rats like him?" Kerry asked. "He's perfect!"

The trainers exchanged amused glances before Trainer Koslova replied, "Our rats are working animals. We don't need them to be stealthy, we need them to be obedient. Besides, we don't want our rats to be mistaken for wild ones. Those are dangerous, and lots of people think they're vermin. Someone might shoot first and think later."

"We'll give Whisper a collar, so people will know he's trained," Trainer Crow assured Kerry. "And just to make sure, we'll spread the word that we have a throwback pup that looks like a wild rat. He'll be fine."

But Kerry wasn't worried. Bending her head to nuzzle Whisper, she murmured, "I'll protect you. And no one will see you if you don't want to be seen. I know someone like that. You'll meet him some day. I think you'll like each other."

·29·
BECKY

"YOU'RE STUPID!" BELLOWED ED Willet. "Isn't he? Jack is stupid!" He swayed. "He can't cut me off. I've got scrip!"

"Yeah," his brother Rick echoed. "He's got scrip." He turned to face Ed. His feet tangled with each other, and he sprawled on the ground. "Hey, who pushed me?"

Becky glanced at Sheriff Crow, who murmured, "Let's give Jack a chance. He's good at this."

"Go home, boys," Jack said from the saloon doorway. "Sleep it off."

"You pushed me!" Rick yelled, stumbling to his feet.

"You heard Jack," Sheriff Crow said. "Knock it off."

Ed squared up, chest puffed out. "Nobody touches my brother. Only me!" Both brothers raised their fists.

Sheriff Crow stepped forward. "Ed. Rick. You've got a choice. Sleep it off at home, or sleep it off in jail."

"Nobody tells my brother what to do," Rick yelled. Now his fists were aimed at the sheriff.

Becky's stomach lurched. Sheriff Crow could easily fight off a pair of drunks, but Becky still tensed at the prospect of a fight.

Sheriff Crow didn't move an inch. She stared hard at Rick. "Jail it is. This way." She lifted her hand slowly and pointed at the jail like she was aiming a gun.

Rick swayed, his fists starting to move up, but the sheriff never broke eye contact. He dropped his fists and staggered toward the jail.

Sheriff Crow turned to Becky. "You take Ed. Do it just like I did."

Becky stepped back, her breath tight in her throat. Ed was twice her size. He could knock her flat. She wasn't strong like the sheriff.

Sheriff Crow spoke softly. "Remember, Becky. Strength is here." She touched her eyes, then her mouth.

The gesture made Becky recall her voice tearing through her throat as she shouted, "LOOK AT ME!" Her whole body had seemed to vibrate. And everyone had obeyed.

Becky stepped forward, bringing her shoulders down and her chin up. She stared into Ed's bleary eyes and commanded, "Come with me. We're going to the jail."

Her voice rang out like it had never occurred to her that he could say no. Apparently it didn't occur to Ed, either. Becky forced herself to keep her amazement off her face as he dropped his fists. She strode toward the jail, and Ed obediently stumbled along beside her.

Once they were inside, the brothers each shuffled into a cell and flopped down on the waiting cots.

"They know the drill. Just like whistling for a dog." Sheriff Crow locked them in, then smiled at Becky. "Good job. Your first arrest."

Becky warmed inside, as if the sheriff's smile was a bright fire on the hearth. Then she understood the words. "First?"

"Could be." Sheriff Crow led Becky to her room, where she sat on the bed and gestured to Becky to take a chair. "Have you thought about your apprenticeship with Dr. Lee?"

"Yes. I haven't changed my mind. I was going to talk to him, but..." Normally Becky wouldn't have continued, but Sheriff Crow was so understanding. "I feel guilty."

"You do need to talk to him. I think he already has another candidate."

Becky had been dreading the conversation she owed Dr. Lee, who had been so kind, patient, and encouraging. Now she brightened. "He does?"

Sheriff Crow nodded. "As for the work here, you've got a

knack for it. And it's not just those fingers of yours. Most of this job is about understanding people, and you've learned a lot of that from Doc Lee. You're observant, and you've got common sense." Dryly, she added, "Well, we call it 'common,' but as I'm sure you've noticed, it can be sorely lacking in this town."

"But what if Ed and Rick had fought? And what if they hadn't been drunk?"

"That's a good question. If this is what you want, you'll need to learn to fight. I hear you've been training at the Vardams' orchard. How's it been going?"

"I'm the worst one," Becky admitted, her heart sinking. For a moment, she'd imagined a whole new life for herself. But obviously, it was impossible. She could never beat anyone in a fight. "The only one as terrible as me is Mia, and she's even smaller than me. It was kind of you to think of me, Sheriff, but this is just like being a doctor. When it comes down to the one crucial thing, I can't do it."

"It's true that you couldn't wrestle Ed Willet. Yet. But you won't be stopping fights for a while. As one of my deputies —"

"Me, a deputy?" Becky exclaimed.

Sheriff Crow smiled, her snake eye crinkling. "If you want."

Much as Becky liked Dr. Lee, she'd enjoyed her brief time with the sheriff more than she had her entire two years in the infirmary. Like Sheriff Crow had said, each day was different. Becky had never once been bored. And everything she knew about the people in town, just from a lifetime of being quiet and paying attention, had suddenly become useful and valued.

"Yes," she murmured. Then louder, with intent, "Yes! I *do* want that. But do you really think I could fight?"

"You've got the spirit." Once again, Sheriff Crow drew a finger from her eyes to her mouth. "Ed Willet felt it, and that's why he obeyed. You spent years believing that you were powerless. It takes time to think of yourself differently. Next time you train, watch Meredith. She's almost as small as Mia, but I'd back her against the Willet brothers any day."

"That's true," Becky said. "She can throw Paco if she catches him right. Jennie, too, and they're the strongest people I know. Except for you."

Sheriff Crow smiled. "So, you'll work on that. In the meantime, you need some kind of equalizer. *We'll* work on that. Maybe fighting sticks. Tomorrow I'll set time aside for us to practice."

Us, Becky thought, marveling. *Sheriff Crow and me.*

Sheriff Crow peered at the window. "Day's over. You've put in a good first day of work, Deputy."

Becky felt lighter than a cloud as she left the jail. Even Rick Willet bawling, "Ohhhh my darrrrling, ohhh my darrrling," made her grin.

She couldn't believe it. She had a job. And not just any job — she was a sheriff's deputy! She was going home to have dinner with Aunt Rosa. Maybe Brisa would be there. Aunt Rosa had said she was always welcome.

Dinner and no dread of what she'd find when she walked in the door. Becky was so lucky!

Her happiness dimmed as she peered anxiously toward Mom's dress shop, but the windows were dark. Her mother was surely at home. Did Henry have to cook every day now?

She wasn't going to ruin one of the best days of her life by thinking about home. *Not home.* Her old house. Aunt Rosa's was home.

As she approached the house, she saw several silhouetted heads against the gold-lit windows. Aunt Rosa had company? Brisa! And maybe her favorite cousin? She opened the door, a smile ready —

It was like she'd stepped on thin ice and plummeted into freezing water. There was no Aunt Rosa in the parlor, no Brisa. Mom stood on the rag rug, arms folded across her chest, with Grandma Ida ramrod-straight and forbidding beside her. Both wore their best dresses like battle armor.

"About time," her mother said. "Where have you been gadding about? Never mind. Go put on some proper clothes. That pink silk I made for Christmas will do nicely. We are going to Jack's for dinner, and to hear some music afterward."

Becky's stomach lurched. Probably they'd been standing there, waiting for her, the whole time she'd been talking to the sheriff. How could she have been so stupid, to imagine that she could change her life? Mom would never let her.

"Don't stand there like a lump," Mom said, anger spots appearing on her cheeks. She took a step forward, hand upraised. Becky flinched, her face tingling. Mom stopped short and dropped her hand, but the crimson splotches spread to cover her entire face. "Go get dressed. We're meeting Henry at the corner. This town is going to see a civilized family dinner."

Grandma Ida said, "You've already done enough harm to this family. The least you can do is make an effort to put it right."

Becky walked to her room like a doll on strings. She couldn't feel her feet hitting the floor. Jack's food was delicious, but the thought of eating anything now was sickening. She wouldn't be able to eat a bite, and then they would glare at her for wasting food. They'd lean across the table and hiss, because they couldn't yell at Jack's. And every hateful look, every threat and warning and comment about how disappointing and worthless she was would cut pieces out of her. By the end of the dinner, there would be nothing left of her but threads and tatters.

She opened her closet in automatic obedience, though she knew that the pink dress was gone. All her old dresses were gone. Her room contained nothing but the clothes Aunt Rosa had given her and the ones Becky had bought for herself.

Becky had begun to feel tall and strong at the jail, or at least like maybe one day she'd be tall and strong. If she gave in to her mother and grandmother, they'd make her small and weak again.

She remembered Grandma Wolfe quoting from a book in the schoolhouse, "No man can serve two masters."

Becky could serve the sheriff, or she could serve her mother. She couldn't serve both.

She returned to the parlor in her pants and shirt, walking like she did with Sheriff Crow. Her feet hit the floor hard with every stride, sending a vibration all the way through her body.

Becky faced her mother and grandmother. "I'm not going."

"What?" Her mother sounded like she couldn't believe it.

In the voice Sheriff Crow had taught her, the voice that made people obey just because she expected them to, Becky said, "I'm. Not. Going."

She forced herself to meet her mother's blue eyes. Mom and Grandma Ida were much scarier than Ed Willet. The worst Ed could do was hit her. Mom could rip her to shreds inside. And when Becky had faced Ed, she'd had Sheriff Crow backing her up.

Becky was alone now. But she pictured the sheriff touching her eyes, then her mouth.

Power comes from within.

Becky raised her chin and straightened her back. "You go to Jack's. I'm staying here. I have a new life. Don't come back to this house unless Aunt Rosa invites you."

For an ice-cold moment, Becky was afraid her mother would hit her again. Mom's hand twitched. But this time Becky didn't flinch. If Mom knocked her down again, Sheriff Crow would arrest her again. Either way, Becky wouldn't have to face her across a dinner table.

Grandma Ida caught Mom's arm. "We'll leave the ungrateful brat here. Don't let her ruin our evening."

Becky didn't let her breath out until her mother slammed the door behind her. Then she collapsed into a chair, trembling. She'd done it! She'd stood up to her mother! They'd go to Jack's and say how ungrateful and worthless she was to anyone who would listen, but she didn't care.

"I don't care," she said aloud. Her voice came out strong and clear. And at the sound of it, she knew that she'd meant every word.

Becky sat and savored that feeling for a while. Then she remembered who she'd expected to meet. Where *was* Aunt Rosa? She went to the kitchen, and found a message on the chalkboard.

Having dinner with friends. Help yourself to the meat pie in the larder. Hope you had a good time with the sheriff. Love you! Aunt Rosa.

Becky's eyes prickled with tears. The note was so sweet, and so different from what Becky was used to. Brisa's family was always asking if they'd had a good day and telling each other they loved them. She'd seen them argue and get angry, but they never got *mean*. The Rileys were like that, too. And so was Felicité's family, and Sujata's.

What was wrong with her family?

With Becky's Change power, she could actually find out. They'd lived at the same house for generations. And it would be empty for hours.

The thought of being there alone made her sick. But if she wanted to be powerful, she had to face it. Becky took a hesitant step toward the door, then stopped. Being strong didn't mean facing everything alone. Even Sheriff Crow had deputies. And Becky had Brisa.

She ran all the way to Brisa's house.

"Of course I'll go with you," Brisa said, as Becky had known she would. "Race you!"

They arrived at her old house flushed and breathless. Brisa looked it up and down as if she'd never seen it before. "Do you know this is the first time I've ever been here?"

"We never invited anyone," Becky said. "Felicité's never been here either."

"Felicité? Really? I always thought you could only be friends with people on the Hill. Until that day you smiled back at me." Brisa hugged Becky. "My favorite day! One of my many favorite days."

"You're in my favorite days, too. Until we started dating I didn't have favorite days. It seemed normal, never to have company. Grandma Ida had feuds going on with so many people, starting with Grandma Alice. Mother, too." Becky's eyes moved over the tall blind windows that should have let in air and light. She'd always remembered the rooms as dark and cheerless, and yet the same sun shone on this house as on Aunt Rosa's. But here, the sun was shut out. "I didn't know that Mother forbade Aunt Rosa to set foot in this house more than fifteen years ago."

Brisa's eyes widened. "I always wondered why we could visit her at her house, but never here."

"Mother always said nasty things about interfering spinsters. How they know nothing about raising children, and how nosy they are, always poking into others' business." Becky crossed her arms, feeling a chill that had nothing to do with the temperature of the room. "It never occurred to me that she meant Aunt Rosa. But when you're small, you don't put things together. Especially if asking questions can get you punished just for asking."

Brisa wordlessly hugged her again. Becky hugged her back, then straightened her spine. She was a sheriff's deputy now. She could do this.

She opened the door, then flinched back from the smell: starch, dried roses, cleaning lye, in a stuffy, stale atmosphere. It was the same aroma the house always had, but she'd been away long enough to have forgotten about it. Becky had smelled much more unpleasant odors in the infirmary, but none carried that weight of emotion. It was the smell of fear and misery.

What's wrong with my family?

"I'll get a light." Brisa felt her way toward the kitchen table.

"Let's not. I want to do it this way." Becky held up her hands.

Brisa's profile was half-lit against the window, her cheeks glowing gold in the light of the neighbor's house. "Sure, Beck. My eyes are getting used to the dark anyway."

Becky didn't need to see at all to get around the house. She was used to sneaking in late at night, hoping to avoid her mother's wrath. She knew the shadowy furniture by heart, every silhouette menacing with years of remembered fear. Maybe if she could get a sense of how it looked to Brisa—just chairs and tables, nothing more—it would lose its power over her.

"No. I changed my mind." Becky lit the lamp. "Tell me what you see."

Brisa's bright eyes took in the old kitchen table that Becky had scrubbed a million times, the gray tile floor she'd swept and cleaned. The four straight-backed chairs, hard a cheerless. The stove, splattered the way Henry always left it. Brown ceramic dishes stacked in the sideboard. The pantry door closed, and the tightly shut curtains over windows with the tiniest crack in case the stove got smoky.

Brisa put her hands on her hips. "Huh. It's not that different from my place. I always pictured your house like Felicité's, full of beautiful things. Like your dresses! When I was a little girl, they made me jealous of you. They were so pretty, and you had so many of them."

"I hated every single one. I wish I could've given them to you." Becky pulled off her gloves, stuffed them in her pocket, and ran her fingers through Brisa's hair. It was cool and silky, smoother than satin. The sense of peace she gained helped her to breathe deeply, and lay her palms on the kitchen table.

The most vivid images were the most recent. Mom sat in her

green dress, sawing through a piece of tough meat. Becky saw her through Grandma Ida's eyes, nearly overwhelmed by corrosive bitterness and disappointment.

That stupid girl should have done better. But Martha was always her father's brat — and he was the most worthless loser in town.

Becky squared herself, and pressed deeper into the past. She found Dad, first seen through Mom's eyes…then his mother's, Grandma Alice's…and then Becky's. Dad leaning back in his chair, smiling with a glass of red wine in one hand. Dad frowning, elbows on the table, ignoring the plate of food before him. Dad pushing his chair away from the table, about to stomp out of the room. In each successive image, he looked younger.

A distant part of Becky's mind, the part that was solely her own, thought, *I'm getting so much better at this. I can sort through them now, without getting stuck in one when I don't want to.*

She stopped at one where Dad was as young as Julio Wolfe was now. He was smiling as he held up a plump baby with a fuzz of yellow hair.

Mom's thoughts were warm with unexpected happiness. *He's already got such a strong personality. Tommy Horst isn't even crawling yet. Henry Callahan, future mayor of Las Anclas.*

That's so Mom, Becky thought. Always looking to an impressive future that never happened, and furious at what she actually got.

She reached deeper.

A teenage girl flinched, cowering away. But not fast enough. A strong hand blurred and struck her, and pain flashed through Becky as in memory she fell away from the table to land on the floor. A middle-aged woman — could that be her grandmother? — sobbed in the corner. A man's bitter rage, acid with contempt, scoured through Becky with toxic power. It was her grandfather's rage, her grandfather's anger at his useless daughter, his coddling wife, his family that did nothing but defy and disappoint him —

Becky jerked her hands away from the table. The room swung around her, the emotions and images dissipating in a wash of dizziness and nausea.

A pair of warm arms encircled her shoulders, and she smelled the scent of crushed flower petals. "How are you doing, Becky? What did you see?"

Becky leaned into Brisa's comforting softness. "This didn't start with Mom. Or even my grandparents. I think something's been wrong with my family for much longer than that. But I still don't know why."

"Want to keep looking?"

Becky nodded. "I have to know. If I don't know what went wrong..."

I won't know how to stop it from happening to me.

"I have to know," Becky repeated.

To her relief, Brisa didn't ask her to explain. She followed as Becky moved further into the house, touching walls and furniture and household items. Becky skimmed past memories, not dipping too deep into any, but even the most ordinary moments had a pall over them, a faint dusting of unhappiness or frustration or boredom or disappointment. Sometimes fear. And anger.

But not always.

When Becky touched the coat rack, she saw her mother as a bride, hanging up her veil. It was a good memory, bright with happiness and hope.

It left her unprepared for the gut-punch of bitterness she felt when she touched the latch to her grandmother's room. *I deserved better than this little dump.*

Becky snatched her hand away. Her heart thumped hard against her ribs as she eased Mom's bedroom door open. She didn't need to have a Change power to know that bad things had happened here.

Even Brisa seemed to sense it. Uneasily, she said, "Beck, are you sure you want to be here?"

Becky nodded. She already knew this wasn't a good place. But maybe she'd finally find out why.

She touched the dresser. Pain flashed across her shoulder as a woman fell against it; she saw thin hands clutch at the wood. A woman stared back at her from the mirror, blood trickling down her face. A man loomed behind her, his fist raised to strike again.

Becky staggered backward, her heart pounding, her breath crowing in her throat. She'd never seen either of those people in her life. Who were they? Her great-grandparents? They had to be relatives—the man had blond hair and blue eyes the exact shade of

Becky's own.

She leaned against the wall, as she had so often in the past, pressing her aching head against the cool adobe. This had been a terrible idea. All her ideas were terrible. She'd upset herself, she could see that she'd also upset Brisa, and she'd learned nothing but the totally unsurprising information that her ancestors had been just as horrible as her parents. Yet she still didn't know why.

But she'd come this far. She'd make one more try.

"Henry's room?" Brisa asked as they went inside.

"Yeah. Don't worry, Brisa. Whatever I see, this'll be my last try. We're almost done."

Becky reached out at random. Her palm touched the wall.

She was half-sitting, half lying. Her back and head hurt—she'd been thrown against the wall.

Her vision was blurred with tears. But she saw a tall man, looming over her—Dad, but a much younger Dad. She was in Henry's mind and body, scared and angry and desperately trying to figure out what Dad wanted from him. What could he do to make the pain stop?

"Smile, Henry," Dad said. He raised his fist. "If you pout, I'll give it to you again. Smile!"

Henry forced his lips to stretch into a grin.

Becky jerked away from the wall, pulling her arms tight into her body. She didn't want to touch anything in this house, ever again.

"This is awful. I wish I hadn't come." A tear slid down her cheek, burning like acid. "Dad hit Henry. A lot. More than the couple times I saw when I was little. Henry never told me—I never asked—"

Brisa reached out, her arms wide open, ready to pull Becky into her warmth. Her love. There was nothing Becky wanted more, but she forced herself to step away.

"Don't!" Becky saw Brisa's confusion and hurt as Becky backed away from her, but that made her even more sure that they shouldn't touch. Brisa was sweet and loving and kind, and Becky had repaid her by dragging her into this house of cruelty.

"There's something wrong with us." Becky's voice shook as she forced the words out. "Not you and me. My family. It goes way back. My mother and father loved each other once. And they loved me and Henry. That love was real. I felt it. But they stopped loving each other, and I don't know why. And Dad hit Henry and Mom hit me, and I don't know how that happened, either. All I know is that I don't want to do that to you. But I don't know why any of this started or why no one stopped it, so I don't know how to stop it from happening to us."

"It's not going to—" Brisa began.

"No!" Becky's voice rose, not with anger but with desperation. "Don't tell me it won't happen, because you can't know that! Just wanting something doesn't make it happen, or my family wouldn't be like this! None of us sat down and decided to be horrible, but we are. I'm broken and awful and I don't want to hurt you, but I will because I don't know how to stop it!"

Tears ran down Becky's face, and her chest heaved with sobs. Brisa opened her mouth, then closed it. Creases appeared between her black eyebrows as she seemed to think hard about something. Finally, she said quietly, "Come outside, Beck. I want to show you something."

Becky struggled to stifle her sobs as she followed Brisa out. Becky had ruined everything, without even meaning to, just as everyone else in her family had. She'd never touch her girlfriend again, and it was all her fault. Her entire world was falling apart.

But instead of leaving her, Brisa caught her by the shoulders and gazed steadily into her eyes. "Listen to me. You're not broken. You're not awful. And you're not going to hurt me. I don't care about your family. I care about you. Let me show you how I see you."

Brisa untied one of her ribbons. "I was wearing this on a day I'll never forget, and I remember you touching it. I remember every single thing you've done the entire time we've been together. Here."

She pressed the scarlet ribbon into Becky's palm.

Love suffused Becky, warm, sensual, joyous. It took a moment for Becky to recognize her own face, it was so different from what she saw in the mirror. In Brisa's eyes, her ugly freckles were charming, and her washed-out blue eyes sparkled like a sky after rain. Her hair didn't look like old straw, but shone like sunlight on summer hay. Becky had never even known that she had a smell, but to Brisa, Becky carried the scent of fresh laundry, both comforting and enticing.

I'm the luckiest girl in the world. Becky likes me!

Becky saw her own face come closer. She let the ribbon drift from her palm as she sank into her own memory of their first kiss.

When she opened her eyes, Brisa's arms were around her shoulders. "I wish I could show you what you look like to me," Becky said.

"Oh, I think I can guess," Brisa said blithely, and somehow, Becky found a bubble of laughter deep inside, watery as it was.

Relief came next, and gratitude so overwhelming she was almost dizzy. But Brisa held her tight. Finally Becky sighed. It was stupid to throw everything away because of what might happen.

Then she remembered the sheriff, and what she had said about strength.

I'm going to be strong, she thought. And it started today. Now.

"First thing in the morning, I'll talk to Dr. Lee," Becky said. "I *don't* want to be a doctor. And Sheriff Crow hinted that someone wants to take my place, so I guess I won't be leaving him without an apprentice."

"You won't," Brisa said.

"How do you know?"

"Who's my brother Rodrigo's best friend?"

"Alfonso Medina," Becky said automatically. Then she considered it. "Really? Alfonso?"

"Rodri says Alfonso always wanted to be a doctor, he was just too shy to ask. But when you said you might quit, it got Dr. Lee thinking about who else he could take on. So he asked Alfonso if he was interested. Said he could start even if you decided to stay. Alfonso's thrilled." Becky giggled. "Quietly."

Becky was immensely relieved. "If I'd known that quitting would make someone that happy, I'd have talked to Dr. Lee before."

Unexpectedly, Brisa laughed.

"What?" Becky asked.

"Listen to yourself, Becky," Brisa said. "You care about people, and you always have. I remember when I Changed, and I showed off my power in the schoolyard. Everyone else looked at the explosion. But you looked at me. And you didn't smile till you saw that I was excited and happy. If you were like the rest of your family, you wouldn't love me, and I wouldn't love you. I don't think any of them sat down and decided to be horrible, but one thing I do know: they have always tried to make you think that everything is your fault."

"But it..."

"Isn't," Brisa said, her gaze steady. "Do you see it, Becky? You have *always* had what my dad calls a sense of responsibility. You tried to fix every fur and feathered thing in town, then you tried to learn to fix people. Do the rest of your family do that?"

"I—I don't want to claim I'm something special. Not when I have so much to learn. And I make so many mistakes!"

"And you own up to them," Brisa said, still serious, her face so close as she watched Becky's eyes that Becky could see her own reflection in Brisa's pupils. "Beck, my great-granny told me on my quinceañera that being a real grownup isn't about age, or being stronger or smarter or richer than everyone else. She said it means owning up when you mess up. Then you go and fix it. The ones who go around blaming everybody else for everything that goes wrong are still angry little kids inside. Even if they've got gray hair and wrinkles."

Becky drew in a slow breath. *It's all your fault...it's his fault...well it's her own fault...YOUR FAULT.* She had heard those words all her life.

Becky wasn't sure which one of them reached out for the other first. But their lips met, soft and sweet and warm as ever. Not a long kiss, not a deep kiss, just a kiss that said that there would always be a kiss waiting for them, whenever either of them wanted one.

Then they walked away, clasped hands swinging, leaving the empty house behind.

·30·
FELICITÉ

FELICITÉ DRIBBLED HER BASIN of wash water around the edges of her tub, wetted the part of her hair that didn't touch the skin, then rubbed herself vigorously with a barely dampened towel before patting herself dry. Satisfied that she was clean, she hung up the towels. Anyone who came in or saw her would think she'd just bathed.

She was dressed and dabbing perfume on her wrists when she heard a call from downstairs. "Felicité, Henry is here!"

"Send him up!"

She opened the door for him, then stepped back to admire his new shirt and pants. The shirt beautifully matched her sapphire dress and set off his blue eyes. He looked like a young man, not a boy.

Felicité stood on her tip-toes to kiss him. His breath was sweet from the mint leaves she'd told him to chew when she'd explained her plans for the evening. The appalling dinner where Daddy had walked out would be redeemed by this one, in which Henry would demonstrate his maturity and convince Daddy to let him into the Rangers.

"Remember," she said. "Even though I'm the hostess, serve Grandmère first."

"I know," Henry said. "Use the outside forks and work your way in. The two-pronged fork is for the clams."

She bent to chirp to Wu Zetian, who leaped up into Felicité's arms, her gorgeous sapphire bow neat as a pin. No other rat in town would allow a bow to be tied around its neck, or look so pretty in it if it did. Certainly not Kerry's peculiar rat pup, the worst of Peach's litter, that she'd been showing off all over town as if it was the greatest creature to ever be born. Come to think of it, that was the perfect metaphor for Kerry herself.

With her lovely Wu Zetian riding in the crook of her arm, Felicité took Henry's arm with her other hand, and they walked downstairs together.

She was delighted to see that Daddy had acceded to her request to wear his best shirt and his greatcoat. He'd even shined the pearl buttons. She knew what a sacrifice it was for him to take even a single evening away from patrolling the beaches with the Rangers, watching for Voske's ships. Mother was perfection itself in her hundred-button dress, and Grandmère was exquisite in a silk coat embroidered with chrysanthemums.

Better yet, Grandmère was smiling as Daddy poured more wine into Mother's glass. Felicité had spoken to them both, and just as she'd asked, they had called a truce in honor of her graduation.

"Shall we go into the dining room?" Felicité asked, with an elegant wave of her hand. She knew it was elegant. She'd practiced it in the mirror.

They went to their places at the table, where the candelabra was already burning. She'd lit it herself before Henry's arrival.

"Thank you all for joining me at my first dinner party as an adult," Felicité said. "I think you will enjoy tonight's menu." She rang the crystal bell, and Clara came out in her best apron. She set the roast beef down before Henry, who carved it expertly and offered the first slice to Grandmère.

"I must say, darling, I will miss your lovely face when I stop by the schoolhouse," Grandmère said.

"But your loss is my gain," Mother said. "I've needed extra help since her father stepped down from the council."

"Always tactful, Valeria," Daddy murmured.

Grandmère chuckled. "I was about to say, I was delighted to second your nomination as mayor's aide."

As the conversation moved on to guesses at what play the

Catalina Players would present that evening, Felicité sat back and admired Henry. He looked grown up and very handsome, his golden hair burnished by the candlelight. She let herself indulge in a little daydream: Henry sitting at the head of the table opposite her, in their own house.

By the time dessert was finished, everybody was in a genuinely good mood, not just pretending for her sake. Daddy had even offered Wu Zetian tidbits, which he almost never did, saying that you shouldn't treat a working animal like a pet.

"Tonight's special," he'd said, leaning down to offer her a bit of cheese. "You won't get spoiled, will you, Wu Zetian?"

It was easy to suggest that Mother walk ahead with Grand-mère to get good seats. Felicité and Henry fell in with Daddy as they walked into the balmy twilight air. Even the weather was cooperating. The dry winds that had blown all morning had died down, but Felicité knew how quickly they could start up again. Although the rainy season was probably over, she wore her broadest hat with a ribbon knotted under her chin. A blue silk scarf protected her throat, and two hidden clips held it tight.

Felicité coughed to cue Henry.

"Mr. Preston," Henry said. Felicité was glad to hear the humility she'd suggested. Henry didn't sound at all like the arrogant boy who Daddy had said didn't live up to his talk. "About the Rangers. I won't ask what's going on, but I've seen you all patrolling the beaches day and night. I've changed a lot since Ranger training. It seems to me you might be able to use another hand. I'd like to try again."

The hours they'd spent practicing had paid off. His speech was word-perfect.

Daddy looked at Felicité. He knew. Embarrassed, she glanced away. Maybe the words weren't Henry's, but Daddy should be able to see that they were true anyway.

Daddy turned back to Henry. "I can see that your attitude has improved. You don't need to convince me of that. But it seems to me that a real sign of maturity would be working with your strengths. You're well-spoken and you've learned to get along with all sorts of people. What about helping Jack at the saloon? He's got his hands full, and he's got scrip to spare. It would be an interesting job, never a dull moment."

As Daddy spoke, Henry visibly struggled to conceal his disappointment and frustration. It was true that Jack was wealthy and respected, but Henry wanted to ride with the Rangers, not fetch drinks and clear tables. How could Daddy keep holding him back just because he'd been a little immature when he'd been younger? Indra Vardam had sucked his thumb till he was seven!

Will came racing up with the two friends he'd had supper with. "There you are! Come on, everybody's ready!"

Daddy walked off to join Mother.

"I'm sorry," Felicité said. "We can always try again."

He flashed his familiar grin at her. "Don't worry, Princess. I haven't given up."

"You're so determined." It was something they had in common. Between her and him, there was no way they wouldn't succeed. Eventually.

"Don't let this ruin your graduation party."

"I won't," she said. He was considerate, too, always thinking of how *she* felt. She couldn't have chosen a better boyfriend. Felicité squeezed his hand as they entered the town square.

The Catalina Players had set up a raised wooden platform in front of the town hall and rearranged its floodlights to shine on the stage. The town hall itself would be their backstage area. She didn't see any of the players, so presumably they were inside.

Felicité turned her attention to the two picnic tables of refreshments she had provided for her party. Teenagers were already crowded around, eating and drinking and laughing, dressed in their best clothes. The balmy air, the golden light before sunset, and the music from the band reminded her suddenly of the dance last summer.

She glanced up at the sky. Not even a cloud marred it. And Voske wouldn't catch the town by surprise again. The Catalina Players were doing three shows, so people on guard tonight could see the play tomorrow or the next night. Daddy had divided the Rangers so each night one-third could see the play while the other two-thirds patrolled.

Grandma Thakrar was selling beer from a stall, calling, "Ice cold and refreshing!" Felicité spotted Peter and Hans attempting to sneak into line, but Grandma Thakrar did, too. "Haven't you two learned your lesson? Lemonade's over there!"

The boys sulkily wandered off.

Near the beer stall, the Rileys and Lees were swarming around a horseshoe of picnic tables laden with food and drink. Felicité had invited everyone her age to her party, regardless of whether she actually liked them, but she was relieved to see that Ross, Jennie, and Mia were planted at those tables.

Ross and Jennie were dressed normally for a party, but Mia wore a bizarre fluffy dress embroidered with purple orchids. The sleeves were gigantic puff balls, and ribbons hung everywhere, fluttering even in the still air.

"What is that *thing* Mia's wearing?" Felicité muttered.

Mother, who had come up beside her, replied quietly, "I believe that's her aunt Olivia Lee's old party dress. It was in fashion twenty years ago. I have a dress with puffed sleeves and red ribbons in our attic." As Felicité shook her head in disbelief, Mother patted her arm. "But *you* look very stylish. Come greet your guests."

Felicité put on her best smile to receive the compliments of the gathered adults. To her dismay, Mrs. Callahan and her mother pounced on Henry and struck up a conversation. Felicité had no desire to speak to either of them, so she hurried toward the teenagers in her party.

Kerry was among them, no doubt just to annoy Felicité. She stood tall in high-heeled black boots, wearing one of the weird suits she'd designed herself and had Mr. Kim make for her. They all consisted of a tight blouse and pants with a short jacket, but this one was fancier than usual, of black linen embroidered in silver.

Felicité was even more irritated to see that Meredith had imitated Kerry, in a green and white version of the same outfit. Then Nasreen stepped out from behind a cluster of people. Felicité stared. Nasreen was wearing it, too! Kerry had actually managed to start a fashion trend. And of course it was a hideous one. *She* certainly wasn't going to wear any such thing.

Indra followed Nasreen, whom he was escorting. From the admiration on his face, he didn't think that awful outfit was ugly. And her indigo suit matched his pants and tunic. They'd plotted it out in advance!

Felicité wasn't going to stand there watching them. She looked out at the square. Once again, she was reminded her of the terrible evening of Voske's attack, even though so much had changed since then. Voske's daughter and Ross's sister were present, and a number of people who had been at the visitor's dance were absent. Sujata and Paco were patrolling, along with two thirds of the Rangers. Yuki was gone. Sera Diaz and Mr. Vardam and Grandma Alice Callahan were dead, along with so many others. Ken Wells and Estela Lopez, who would have been sixteen this year. Laura Hernandez, who had helped Jennie in the schoolhouse. Laura, with her black claws...

Unsettled, Felicité turned back to her party. She nearly bumped into Becky—in yet another Kerry suit! And a scarlet one, at that. Felicité could not believe it: Becky Callahan in tight pants instead of ribbons and lace. She was nearly unrecognizable as the girl Felicité had grown up with.

The disorienting sense that Becky had become a stranger only grew when she spoke in a clear voice that easily carried over the party chatter. "Hi, Felicité. Congratulations on graduating."

"Thank you." Felicité searched for a polite topic of conversation. "Did Brisa get to come with you, or is she stuck on the wall?"

"The wall. Ms. Lowenstein didn't want to repeat the mistake we made at the last town party." Becky said nothing more, but her cool regard reminded Felicité strangely of Sheriff Crow's, who often kept quiet to encourage people to fill the silence with whatever it was that she wanted to know.

Felicité could guess what Becky might want to know. Or rather, to hear. She knew perfectly well that she shouldn't have avoided Becky all this time, but she still couldn't think about Becky's Change and every awful consequence without imagining herself in Becky's place. Of course Daddy would never strike her. But it was easy to imagine him walking past her in the streets as if he didn't even know her, the way Mrs. Callahan walked past Becky.

Felicité had always known Becky was unhappy, and had even assumed it was because of her family. But she'd imagined nothing worse than having to live with unpleasant, complaining people.

I should have asked, Felicité thought.

Finally, she found something to say that was both tactful and honest. "I was glad to hear that you're working with Sheriff Crow. You like it, right?"

No matter what else had changed, Becky's answering smile was the same one Felicité had known all her life. "I love it. I learn something new — do something new — every day."

"I never would have guessed you'd want to do that." Felicité glanced at Becky's skinny body in those form-fitting clothes. "You must be training hard."

She hoped she hadn't made Becky self-conscious. The two of them had always avoided training. In fact, they'd gotten to be close that way, standing on the sidelines and whispering while everyone else sweated in the sun.

But Becky only nodded. "I'm working on it. Sheriff Crow and I are practicing with different weapons. She says I still haven't found the right one. But there's time." She caught a clip that was sliding out of her fine hair and clicked it firmly back into place. "Congratulations on being the mayor's aide."

"Thank you. Being town scribe was the perfect training for it. I'll have a lot more to do, of course."

"You've always been good at organizing things. Running a town is a bit like planning a party, isn't it?"

"I've always thought so," Felicité admitted. At last, they were talking like they used to, back when they'd been friends. "Who knows? Maybe someday I'll be mayor and you'll be sheriff, and we'll be on the council together."

"Me, the sheriff? I'm just one of her deputies. I'm not her apprentice!" The words sounded more like the old Becky. But she didn't talk to her shoes. Instead, she laughed.

Felicité hated to end Becky's cheer, but if she didn't say something now, she never would. Before she could have second thoughts, she blurted out, "Becky, I wanted to say — I'm sorry about what happened. With your mom. And I'm sorry I didn't say anything until now. I'm sorry I didn't *know* anything."

Then Becky did look down at her shoes. "Nobody did. I didn't want anyone to." She straightened up. "But it's over."

Felicité wished Henry wasn't still living with Mrs. Callahan.

She knew his mother didn't hit him, and that Sheriff Crow had asked him if he'd rather move in with a foster family and he'd refused, saying he'd be in Singles Row soon enough. But he'd be so much happier away from his awful mother and grandmother.

Felicité checked to see if they still had him trapped. Mrs. Callahan was talking to her mother near the table where Jack was selling refreshments. Henry had vanished. He probably hadn't come to Felicité because he wasn't sure what to say to his sister, and of course he wouldn't want to talk to his mother any longer than he had to. Who would?

But Felicité couldn't say any of that. Belatedly, she said, "I'm glad it's over." That was awkward. She tried for something more graceful. "Have you had anything to eat yet? I ordered extra crumble because I knew some people would be on the wall. You could take a napkinful to Brisa after the play."

Felicité was rewarded with the return of Becky's smile. They went to the table to collect the crumble. Becky's happiness gave Felicité an uncomfortable pang of jealousy. What had happened to Becky was terrible, but at least she had no more secrets. Felicité still had to hide for the rest of her life, even from her own boyfriend.

She gave Becky the dessert, then took refuge in greeting her party guests and making light conversation in Mother's style.

Mr. Horst's booming voice rose above the chatter. "Look how happy everyone is, Tom! Shame you didn't do this years ago. Who knows where you'd be? No, I know. We'd all be sweating on the walls in one of your endless drills, instead of having fun!"

Some people chuckled, but Grandma Lee's eyebrows arched in disapproval. "Aren't you supposed to be the defense chief, Noah? Doesn't it concern you at all that Voske is preparing to attack us from the sea?"

Mr. Horst let out a loud laugh. "What's he going to sail in, conches? A few months ago Gold Point was underwater. And that was a first, because it's landlocked! His entire empire has fallen apart. And now he suddenly has a war fleet? I'll worry about that five years from now. If he's still alive."

Daddy took out a handkerchief and polished his glasses, then deliberately glanced southward, in the direction of the black singing trees that had once been the soldiers sent to murder the town council. But Mr. Horst didn't seem to notice, let alone understand the implications. Subtlety was lost on him.

Felicité was sure he thought Daddy was stepping on his toes, with Kerry making her report to Daddy rather than to him, and with Daddy using *his* Rangers to execute *his* coastal defense plan. Like Mother said, Mr. Horst swung in the wind like a weather vane.

Mr. Horst went on, "I feel sorry for your poor Rangers, parading up and down the beach. But don't worry, Tom, they might have some excitement yet. I saw a dead jellyfish this morning. They better investigate! It might be a spy from Voske!"

A roar of laughter met this sally. Felicité shook her head in disgust. But Daddy was too dignified to get into a fight. He merely said, "I'm sure you'll enjoy watching your new Changed friends put on a play, Noah. In fact, it looks like it's time to take our seats."

Mr. Horst pushed through the crowd toward the center of the front row. But when Ms. Salazar seated herself there, her halo of golden light sparkling, he retreated to the end of the row rather than sit next to a Changed woman.

Swinging in the wind, Felicité thought.

Daddy and Mother took their seats with quiet dignity. As Felicité sat next to Daddy, Henry appeared at last, holding a napkin.

"Sorry I'm late. There was a huge line for the churros. One for me, one for you, and one for Wu Zetian." He sat down beside her.

She inhaled the delicious aroma of the fresh-baked pastry sticks coated in cinnamon and sugar, then gave him a kiss. "That's so sweet of you."

The crowd quieted down in expectation as a horn tooted. A middle-aged woman stepped out onto the stage.

"Nowadays," she intoned in a portentous voice, "Changed people are persecuted and discriminated against—even driven away from towns where they sought help."

Felicité's pleasant anticipation died into a chill that formed into a heavy lump in her stomach.

"But long ago, it was different," the player proclaimed. "Then, it was the Norms who were oppressed and the Changed who ruled with an iron fist! The Changed Capulets rule, headed by the tyrant King Capulet, and the Norm Montagues are their ill-treated servants."

The stage filled with actors. Foremost was a tall man wearing fake horns and a long fake tail attached to his butt. Rage burned through Felicité as the lights glinted off a pair of wire-rimmed glasses exactly like Daddy's.

How dare they write an entire play just to mock him! And no one could say so, because they'd reply, "Of course King Capulet isn't supposed to be Mr. Preston. Mr. Preston isn't Changed...is he?"

If Daddy got up and walked out, she'd follow. Felicité hoped he would. But he sat like a statue, his arms folded.

"But true love defies prejudice," continued the narrator. "The Changed Prince Capulet and a lowly Montague Norm saw each other at a ball, and made arrangements to meet in secret."

A young couple tiptoed onstage, looking back over their shoulders, then clasped hands and swore their eternal love. At the sound of footsteps, Prince Capulet exited and a girl swept onstage. A chorus of rustles and snickers rose from the audience at the sight of her gigantic hat, which had holes cut into it to accommodate a pair of fake rat ears, and a scarf so long that it dragged on the ground behind her like King Capulet's tail.

The rat-eared princess ordered the poor Norm girl to scrub and clean. "Get busy, while I get ready for the ball!"

Felicité didn't want to believe her eyes, but the hat and scarf were unmistakable. That ridiculous-looking villain was supposed to be *her*.

The Norm heroine's friends came to meet her, giggling and chattering. The Changed girl snapped her fingers. "Your job's not done. Get moving, *Normie!*"

The heroine's friends gasped dramatically. "I can't believe you used that word!"

Felicité's stomach lurched. That had to be a direct slam against her for calling Ross a mutant at Luc's. Jennie must have told the Catalina Players when she'd conveyed Mr. Horst's invitation. And they'd spent all the time since plotting to publicly humiliate

Felicité at her own graduation, for one word that she'd said six months ago. And apologized for!

With patent insincerity, the Changed princess said, "Oh, my goodness. How did that slip out?"

A hand touched her arm. Daddy whispered, so low no one else could hear, "This is the price of power. Don't let them win."

Felicité hadn't realized until then that she'd been poised to get up and run away. She forced her muscles to unclench and smoothed out her face. Everyone who looked at her—and she knew people were looking—would see the future mayor smile. Just like the one Mother wore right now as she held hands with Daddy.

Felicité took Henry's hand. He squeezed hers, then whispered against her ear, "Shall I punch them in the nose for you after they take their bows?"

"No," she whispered. "Let's pretend we thought it was wonderful."

Henry grinned. "I get it. They'll hate that."

Felicité made her smile even broader. She wouldn't let anyone see how upset she was. A breeze tugged at her hat—the hat that that was being mocked onstage right now. Nervously, she wondered if she shouldn't call attention to it by adjusting it. Then she decided that it was a perfect opportunity to demonstrate how much she didn't care. She straightened the brim, then fluffed her scarf. Daddy was right. The Catalina Players thought she was important enough to write an entire play about, just to hurt her feelings. If you thought of it that way, it was almost flattering.

But that didn't mean she had to listen to their hateful play. Felicité broke off a tiny piece of churro and fed it to Wu Zetian. She'd play a game of how long she could make a single churro last. By the time she was done, with any luck, the play would be over.

Felicité was engrossed in watching how Wu Zetian's whiskers twitched as she waited for her next bite when another puff of wind rustled her hat, bringing a smell of smoke harsh enough to sting her nose. Those stupid players must have set something on fire. But she certainly wasn't going to look.

A distant voice shouted, "FIRE!"

Felicité glanced up. Nothing was burning onstage, and both

actors and audience were looking around in confusion.

"I smell smoke!" someone yelled from the back of the audience.

Daddy jumped to his feet an instant before the town bell began to clang the pattern for fire. Felicité's mind blanked. Then she remembered that her fire post was to relay messages, so she was exactly where she was supposed to be — with Daddy.

Everyone else seemed caught by surprise, either freezing in place or milling around before they finally started hurrying toward their fire posts. It wasn't just being at a play for the first time in ten years that confused everyone. They hadn't had a fire drill since Voske's attack — they'd only had attack drills. Before that, they'd had fire drills every three months. It had been at least six months since the last one. No wonder everyone was rusty.

Mia belatedly leaped up, flailed her absurd puffed sleeves, then ran madly away, purple ribbons trailing after her.

Everyone turned to Daddy, who used to lead the fire drills. Before he could speak, Mr. Horst raised his big voice. "Where is the fire?"

"It smells like it's somewhere in the south or east," someone yelled.

Mr. Horst turned to Daddy. "With the wind coming up, it could spread fast. Why don't you take charge at the south end of town? The north end has always been my post."

"Good thinking," Daddy said. He turned to the waiting crowd. "I'll set up my command post at the sentry tower at the main gate. Everyone to your posts!"

Ross and Summer and Kerry, who had never been present for a fire drill, stayed where they were. Jennie didn't move either. She had nowhere to go, now that she'd been thrown out of the Rangers. Felicité hoped Daddy wouldn't put her back with them, even for this one emergency. She didn't deserve another chance.

Felicité held her breath in anticipation as Daddy eyed Jennie. She stared right back, squaring her shoulders like she wanted to challenge him to a duel.

Mr. Riley stepped up. "Jennie, why don't you join my fire team?"

Jennie broke her staring match with Daddy and left with her

father.

Mia bolted up right then, puffing and clanking. She'd buckled an elaborate leather harness with hundreds of tools attached to it over her ridiculous dress, and rattled at every step. She skidded to a stop, patted at the tools, then looked down in surprise at a strange-looking gun. "Oh. I forgot that that was on there."

Mia turned in a circle, purple ribbons fluttering in the smoky wind. "Ross? Oh, but you won't be fighting." Then she saw Becky. "Yes!" Mia unclipped the weird gun and offered it to her. "Becky? I won't need my cloud viper gun, but you might."

"What's its range?" Becky asked.

"Best is twenty yards. Here's the darts." Mia pulled a pouch from the harness. Becky calmly clipped the holster to her belt, then pocketed the pouch.

Felicité felt as if the entire world had turned unreal. Becky asking about weapons range—Becky with a gun!

Daddy said to Mia, "You're with me. I'll need you to coordinate fire teams with water, once we know where the fire is." Then he pointed to Ross, Summer, and Kerry. "You come along, too. I'll assign you as soon as we know more."

"What about Whisper?" Kerry asked. "I haven't had time to train him to do anything but come when I call and go to my room. Will he be safe if I send him to Singles Row?"

"Your rat?" Daddy asked, looking around. "Where is he?"

"Whisper!" Kerry called. Felicité would have sworn the plain creature was nowhere around, but the rat pup appeared at Kerry's heels seconds later.

"Animals are taken to safe places, unless they're well-trained and we might need them." Daddy indicated Mr. Tsai, who was headed toward the veterinary building with seven leashed dogs in tow, and the veterinarian Ms. Segura and her apprentice, who were coming from the same direction with armfuls of empty cat cages and bags of cat treats to lure them in. "Singles Row is fine for your rat if you're sure he'll stay. Otherwise, give him to Ms. Segura."

"He'll stay." Kerry bent to her rat. "Whisper. Go home. Stay there."

The brown rat took off. Felicité lost sight of him as he passed behind someone, and no matter how hard she looked after that, she couldn't find him again. She shrugged. Her own rat, unlike Kerry's, was both well-trained and needed.

Grandma Jing stepped offstage. "What can we do to help?"

Felicité was surprised that Grandma Jing's hair didn't burst into flames at the look Daddy gave her. Then he unclenched his jaw and assigned the Catalina Players to join the closest fire teams.

Henry spoke up eagerly, "I'll lead a fire team. I fought that fire at the cliffs, and I know what to do."

Felicité's heart sank at the annoyed crease that appeared between Daddy's eyes. "How about you assist Felicité? She might need a runner besides Wu Zetian." And he walked away.

Henry started after him, but Felicité grabbed his arm. "Don't make it worse."

"But I do know how to fight fires," Henry protested. "We put that one out at the cliffs, and it was more dangerous than this one."

"Maybe you'll get your chance," Felicité said, deciding not to point out that nobody knew yet how bad this fire was. "Remember, Daddy doesn't like it when people don't follow orders."

"Right," Henry said. "Okay."

They hurried to catch up with Daddy. He stopped when Trainer Crow ran up, followed by two rats. "The abandoned cornfield north of the black trees caught fire," she said. "It's heading toward the wall."

Daddy dispatched fire teams all along the wall. Last, he turned to Felicité. "I want you at the mill as a lookout. Send Wu Zetian if there's anything I need to know."

Henry looked like he was going to argue, but Felicité dragged him away. As they ran past the stage, she was glad that at least they didn't have to sit through any more of that hateful play.

·31·
BECKY

BECKY WATCHED HENRY AND Felicité run off hand in hand, Henry grinning as if he'd pulled the best prank ever. Nobody else was smiling. Maybe he was happy because he was with his girlfriend.

Sheriff Crow beckoned to her. "Let's make sure everyone actually gets to their posts, without stopping off to help themselves to Grandma Thakrar's beer."

Becky stationed herself by the barrels as Sheriff Crow moved through the dispersing crowd. The wind kicked up dust, bringing the stronger scent of burning leaves, which mixed with the yeasty smell of beer.

Ed Willet began to fake-casually stroll past the barrels. He stepped up close, deliberately looming over Becky. "Aren't you supposed to be on a fire team?"

Becky's heart thumped, but she looked him right in the eyes and deliberately fingered Mia's dart gun. "I'm supposed to be right here."

Ed looked away first.

Rick shouted, "C'mon, Ed. They'll give it out free after the fire's done for."

Ed brightened, and loped off to join his brother.

Becky covered her nose as another gust of wind eddied through the nearly deserted town square. She wondered what had started the fire. It couldn't have been lightning. She hadn't seen a cloud all day. Maybe someone hadn't put out a cook fire, and a spark drifted in the breeze.

Or maybe someone had set it. Again.

Sheriff Crow reappeared at a run. "Town square is secure. Let's do a wider perimeter through the streets."

They set out past the infirmary toward the schoolhouse. Sheriff Crow said, "It's too early in the season for spontaneous fires. We're barely out of winter."

Nothing could be read in her skull face, but Becky knew her tone. "Do you think it was set, too?"

"Let's consider the facts."

It was a favorite phrase of Sheriff Crow's. Becky had heard it often enough now that it instantly set her mind going. Facts — like Henry's grin. It hadn't been his happy grin, it had been his distinctive "just kidding!" grin. It had caught her attention because it was so strange to see it during an emergency. What trick could he have possibly pulled?

Her mind leaped to the fire on the cliff — which Henry had been at.

He'd been at the barn fire, too.

No. That was pure coincidence. Plenty of people had been at both. Like Alfonso. Becky remembered what Mr. Preston had said about heroes. He'd hinted that Alfonso might be that type, but Becky didn't believe that. Mr. Preston didn't really know Alfonso, other than the fact he was Changed, but Becky knew him. Alfonso was quiet. He never seemed to want others' attention, not like Henry...who'd bragged about his heroism at the battle.

The old sickness roiled inside her.

Facts, she told herself. Henry used to put cockroaches in desks and honey in people's shoes to amuse his friends and get attention from girls. But those were all harmless pranks, and he seemed to have stopped doing them recently. Anyway, he'd been in the town square when this fire had started. The entire town had been there, except for the sentries and some of the Rangers.

Then she remembered her conversation with Félicité. Becky had been watching her mother and grandmother out of the corner of her eye, so she could avoid them. She'd seen them talking to Henry, then Henry had run off. The next time Becky saw him, he returned with a napkin full of churros, sweating like he'd run a long way. But Luc had been selling those churros right behind Grandma Thakrar, fifty feet to Becky's right.

So maybe he'd run off to play a prank. Henry would never do anything that could get people killed.

Or would he? Becky had never quite believed in all those enemies he'd bragged that he'd killed during the battle. And even if he had, it had been in defense of the town. But she hadn't liked the way he'd looked when he'd talked about it. Like he'd wished it was true. He'd had the same grin when he talked about snuffing enemies that he had when he stuck a roach in a girl's desk.

Her stomach lurched. It was too easy to imagine Henry setting a fire, then saying, "Just kidding!"

"Becky?" the sheriff asked. "What are you thinking?"

"I'm not sure..." But it was more that she didn't want to be sure. Maybe if she said it out loud, the sheriff would see where she'd gone wrong. And Sheriff Crow would know who the real fire starter was. Becky was being stupid, worrying about accusing her own brother just because she so badly didn't want it to be true. The lightest punishment for arson was exile. If anybody died in the fire, the arsonist would be executed.

"Have you ever had to arrest someone you like?" Becky's voice came out the way it used to, shaky and small. She hoped Sheriff Crow wouldn't ask the obvious question, which was "Why?"

She didn't, but Becky was sure she was thinking it. "I have. And not very long ago, either. It was Jennie, Yuki, and Mia. Of course, they turned themselves in. But I would have had to be the one to escort them out the gates if they'd been exiled."

"Could you do it if..." *If it was someone in your own family?* Becky couldn't say the words. She had no proof—only her own fears.

"Let's turn down Jackalope Row." As soon as no one else was in sight, Sheriff Crow said quietly, "What were you going to ask?"

Becky shook her head, unable to speak.

The sheriff looked down at her thoughtfully. "This is the tough part of the job. In a way, arresting Jennie and Yuki and Mia was less complicated than it could have been. They broke a law, but they did it to prevent the town from murdering an innocent girl, and they owned up to it right away. All I had to do was lock the cell doors on them. But around that same time, I found out that someone else I cared about had done something that I did think was wrong."

Becky blinked up at her. "What? Who was that?"

"Furio Vilas. You probably thought of him as the bounty hunter." Sheriff Crow was silent for a few steps, then said, "We were...close. Until I found out that he'd taken Mr. Preston's order to murder Ross. He would have done it, too, if Jennie hadn't stopped him. And I would have arrested him."

Becky nearly said, "But even if Henry set the fires, at least he didn't murder anyone." But she didn't know that yet. People could still die in the fire burning now.

"Let's consider the facts," the sheriff said again. "Together, this time. We'll begin with the physical evidence."

"There isn't much. Just the match on the hillside."

"Which seems to have been planted. So let's look at our suspects. Peter and Hans were at the first fire, but they were at archery practice during the second fire."

Becky nodded. Swallowed. Said firmly, "Alfonso, Henry, and Mia were at both fires, but the only one who could have escaped from the second was Alfonso."

"Go on," Sheriff Crow said.

"But today I saw Alfonso helping Mr. Medina carry baskets of food while I was having a conversation with Felicité, and after that he and I talked about the surgery until the play started. And then he sat with his family. I'm pretty sure Mia was there the entire time, too." Becky hated to go on. But a sheriff's deputy had to think of the entire town. "But Henry disappeared for a while. I didn't see him again until right before the play started."

"So he had an opportunity," the sheriff said. "What about motive? Alfonso and Mia don't seem to have any reason to start fires. Do you think Henry has?"

"I know he has," Becky admitted. "He wants Mr. Preston to think he's a hero, so he'll get into the Rangers. That praise he got after the second fire—it was important to him. And to our mother. Mom's been telling him he's a failure every day since he didn't make the Rangers. I know what that's like."

"Yes, but you didn't set fires."

"We don't know that he did," Becky said quickly.

"Why don't we find out? Once we establish where the fire started, you can use your power to look for who set it. But Becky," Sheriff Crow added. "If it does turn out to be Henry, don't confront him. We need to do this right, by the rules."

·32·
MIA

MIA TUGGED AT AUNT Olivia's dress, which tried to crawl up her harness at every step, as she panted in Mr. Preston's wake.

Every time there was an emergency, she always seemed to get stuck running after someone with much longer legs. In a dress. In the worst possible dress! Why had she had given in to Grandma Lee, who had insisted she wear Aunt Olivia's lucky dress? There was no such thing as a lucky dress. These stupid ribbons were tangling with every single tool, and how did this always *happen* to her? She wore a dress maybe once a year!

Twice a year. Two disasters.

At least this time, she wasn't lugging her flamethrower.

Ross ran easily beside her, not out of breath at all. "Can I carry something?"

Mia nearly tripped over her feet as she tried to look down at her tools. The problem wasn't that any particular one was heavy. It was that there were so many of them. She handed him the two that were closest to her hands, which turned out to be a podger spanner and a drift pin—two of her lightest ones.

Ross flashed a quick grin as he stuck them in his belt. "I could take more."

"Later...maybe," Mia gasped. If she tried to extract one more thing while she ran, she'd fall flat on her face.

Kerry had no trouble running. As for Summer, she floated along. Literally. Her feet only touched the ground every ten to fifteen feet. She had the best power. *Ever.*

Kerry tapped Mia's shoulder. "What are we doing?"

Mia gulped in air. "Command post's at the gate. Mr. Preston can see better there. Send the fire teams. He'll put you and Ross on one."

"And you?"

"I know the pumps. We send the fire teams to them. The big hoses have to go..." Mia determinedly sucked in a breath. "...where the water pressure's best."

Kerry looked impressed. "In Gold Point we had a whole team in charge of that. But here it's just you?"

For about two seconds, Mia was thrilled to imagine the job to come. Then misgivings fell on her head like a twenty pound sledge hammer. "I guess. I've never done it before. I haven't even run a fire drill. But Mr. Rodriguez, who used to do it, is sick..."

By the time she staggered up the steps to the command post, she wanted to collapse to the floor. But with Mr. Preston there, she didn't even dare to lean against the wall.

"The fire is thickest that way," Ms. Lowenstein reported, pointing toward the abandoned corn fields. "But the wind is carrying it northwest."

"Toward the Vardams' orchard. Sparks can jump the wall." Mr. Preston turned to loom over Mia, his blue eyes cold behind wire rimmed glasses. Mia vividly remembered him on the other side of the jail bars, telling her she'd never grown up and never would, and he'd been a fool to ever trust her. She barely stopped herself from cringing back.

"Mia," Mr. Preston said. "We need to fight this fire in two ways. One is to prevent it from spreading. We need teams all along the wall inside the Vardams' orchard to watch for sparks and put out any flames. We should also attack the fire from the south, where it's burning strongest. But we don't know how far it's spread, and there's no way to investigate without being slaughtered by the crystal trees. Any ideas?"

Mia's hand popped up as if she was still in school. Mr. Preston stared at her incredulously, and she yanked her hand down, her face burning.

"There is a way to investigate." She stopped herself before she could blurt out how, and tried to shoot Ross a meaningful look without Mr. Preston noticing.

Mr. Preston clearly noticed. Ross gave Mia a resigned nod. To Mr. Preston, he quietly said, "I can look right now."

"Too risky. I know you're..." Mr. Preston visibly forced out the words. "...safe from the crystal trees. But you could easily get surrounded by the fire."

Ross shook his head. "I can look from here."

Mia saw the exact moment that Mr. Preston figured out what Ross meant. He looked as if he'd bitten into an apple and found half a worm.

Ross glanced around, and Mia knew he wanted privacy. But there were so many people on the platform, there was barely room to move. He lowered his head and shielded his eyes with his gauntlet, leaving nothing visible but the fall of his black hair.

Mia edged up close to him, trying to find a way to touch him without attracting even more attention. All those stares were making *her* nervous. Imagine how poor Ross must feel. This was the first time he ever contacted the trees in front of anyone but her or Jennie. Since there was no hope of stealth, Mia grabbed his free hand and glared defiantly at Mr. Preston.

Mia was glad she had when Ross swayed, then steadied himself against her. He dropped his other hand and looked up. "There's scattered fires all around the trees, but they're small. But there's sparks floating on the wind, and I saw new fires starting."

Repulsion briefly tightened Mr. Preston's face. Then he turned to address the others without even thanking Ross. Mia wished she had the nerve to do *something* to him. Stomp on his toes, maybe. With all it cost Ross to use his power, and in front of everyone, too, he deserved more than that 'ugh, a Change' face!

"We need to put out those scattered fires," Mr. Preston announced. "If we don't, they'll blaze through the abandoned corn fields. It'll create a monster fire to threaten the entire east wall." He pointed at the brown smoke billowing up beyond the dairy barns. "The fastest way to attack the fire from the south is impossible — through the singing trees. We'll have to —"

Ross interrupted him. "I can do that."

Mr. Preston stared at him. Then he said, "I know you can get through the trees. But it takes an entire team to hold a hose. Can you take a team through?"

"I can only take two people." Ross was staring at the floor again, his words barely audible. "How heavy are the hoses?"

Too heavy, Mia thought. They were made of the thickest canvas possible, in three layers, with wire mesh to protect the seams against the water pressure. Even then it was impossible to keep water from leaking through completely, which made them wet and hard to hold onto. Fire teams always included several very strong people to carry them. The rest of the team stamped out the fire beyond the reach of the hoses.

"Too heavy," Mr. Preston said, startling Mia with his exact echo of her thought. "But you and two strong people might be able to handle one of the smaller hoses." Then he addressed Mia. "So we use the Vardams' well for the north end of the fire? And Horseshoe Pump for the south?"

Mia had been scared that she would fail, but once she heard the questions, she felt confident. Nobody knew those pumps and how their water flowed better than she did, after all the times she'd fixed them. "Not Horseshoe. It's on the same pipe as Vardams'. There won't be more than a trickle. We'll have to use Santa Lucia Well instead. With the biggest hoses, because it will take two of them to reach the wall."

"And in the very south, Ross and his team will use the dairy pump?" Mr. Preston was asking, not telling.

"Yes. And if we have to, extra hoses from the south forge pump."

Mr. Preston addressed the waiting fire team runners, "You've got your orders. Go!" As they took off, he said, "Now we need volunteers to go with Ross."

Immediately, Mia said, "I'll go."

Mr. Preston gave her an irritated look that was getting all too familiar. "Two *strong* people. Two strong people who aren't needed right here."

His cool blue gaze slowly traveled across the strongest people in the crowd. Every single one of them looked downward, or away, or at each other. Nobody wanted to go near those singing trees.

Summer stepped forward with her head held high and her

black hair whipping in the wind. "I'll go. And I'm *plenty* strong."

"I will, too," Kerry volunteered. She too stood straight and proud, but Mia knew her well enough to recognize her 'arrogant princess' expression as a mask over fear.

Mr. Preston looked doubtfully from Summer's skinny arms to Kerry's slim figure, then eyed the crowd with disapproval. His gaze lingered especially on Mr. McVey, muscular from a lifetime of kneading dough, and on Miss Chen, who was equally strong from butchering. "Really? Nobody else?"

Nobody else met his eyes.

Shaking his head, Mr. Preston turned to Ross. "Over to you."

Mia sidled up to Kerry. "You'll be fine. Ross won't let you get killed by those singing trees. He'd only do that if he wanted to—I mean if he was trying—like if you were an enemy—well, anyway, don't be scared." It was only when she'd finished speaking that she realized that she'd forgotten to whisper. Everyone was staring at her.

"Huh." Summer curled her lip at the crowd. "Hope you all aren't as scared of the fire as you are of my brother."

Ross caught Summer's hand. "Let's go."

·33·
FELICITÉ

FELICITÉ PULLED A FOLD of her scarf over her nose. It didn't help much. Smoke billowed up in choking gray clouds. Here and there smoldering sparks whirled wildly, like angry eyes. She could barely see the orchard beyond the trees they stood beneath.

"I can't see anything," Henry said. "Let's climb up."

She didn't want to climb—it had to be even hotter up high. Heat rose, and she was already sweating. At least the smoke gave her an excuse to hold her scarf over her face. But no matter how fast she wiped away the sweat, more formed as soon as the cloth left her face. She hadn't yet felt the prickle of scales, but it was only a matter of time.

She tried to think of an excuse, but Henry was already halfway up a tree. He bent down and held his hand. "I'll pull you up. It's perfectly safe. This is a sturdy branch."

She was going to exclaim that she wasn't scared—but that was just it. *But.*

Felicité raised her hand to his. He clasped her wrist and pulled. Distracted, she admired his easy strength. Then her feet scrabbled and found purchase on the branch beside him, while her thoughts kept speeding like a runaway horse.

She couldn't let Henry see what she was. She had to find some way to hide herself, or get away, or get him away. But he seemed determined to do a good job. He leaned out dangerously, holding on with one hand and wiping his eyes with the other.

Her own eyes stung with smoke and sweat, making it even

harder to see. But that was good. She'd just remind Henry that his vision was bad, so anything he saw, he'd dismiss as distorted. "I can barely see. Everything's a blur from the smoke."

"I know," Henry replied. "That tree over there will get us to the wall. We can see from there."

Felicité ground her teeth. That hadn't been what she'd intended at all!

Somewhere behind her she heard a fire team shouting orders, and the thud and scrape of trowels digging in the dirt.

When she turned back, Henry was swinging down onto the wall. "Come on, Princess. I'll catch you."

She hesitated, searching for an excuse.

"Don't worry," Henry said. "You know I'm strong enough. I won't let you fall."

Felicité wiped her face again, trying desperately to find something, anything, to make him leave her behind. But what could she say when Henry was strong enough to catch her and determined to protect her? And also to do a good job. And help her do her job.

Henry was the perfect boyfriend. Except for his dreadful family, he was exactly what she wanted. But if he ever saw her hideous scaled face, his admiration would turn to disgust and horror. She wouldn't be the princess he adored, she'd be the monster he loathed.

She forced herself to swing from a low branch to the wall, and stood beside him as he peered out into the beating red glow.

"There's the fire," Henry said. "It's going north."

Felicité wondered how he could tell the direction of the fire. Everything was gray around them. Except for the silhouettes of the trees behind them and the vague shape of the mill a few hundred yards away, it was as if the entire town had vanished.

Henry turned to Felicité. "I don't hear any fire teams out there. I think ours is the farthest north."

"I'll send Wu Zetian." Her rat had curled tightly around her neck, making her even hotter. She was relieved to send Wu Zetian to safety—and get the fur muff away from her face. Felicité scribbled a message, tucked it into the collar case, and said, "Go to Daddy."

Her clever rat scampered away along the wall. Felicité turned her back on Henry and loosened her scarf in the hope of getting a little air to dry her neck. A hot gust of smoky air blew over her, singing her nose. She broke into a coughing fit.

Henry knelt beside her, patting her back. "You stay and keep watch. I'll go fight the fire."

"With what?" Much as she wanted Henry gone, it would be suicide for him to try to fight a wildfire alone. "It's too big for you to smother with dirt. You'd need a whole team. Anyway, Daddy said to stay here and keep watch. Maybe we should get down and try where the smoke isn't so thick." She pointed back toward the orchard.

"We won't see anything from there. The wall will be in the way. Felicité, you can stay here, but I'm going to jump down. If I can get ahead of the smoke, I might be able to see more. Only for a bit. I'll be right back."

Felicité was positive that he was planning to heroically fight the fire by himself. There was no way she'd let him get himself killed. She grabbed his sleeve. "Let's go together. But let's get to the mill and climb up. We might be able to see from there."

"Great idea." Henry took her hand. As they ran along the wall, she heard someone shout from the orchard, "More wet blankets!" The voice broke into a harsh cough.

"We need trowels," someone else yelled from farther away. "There's sparks everywhere!"

The blurred shape of the mill resolved into detail. There were no sentries on duty—they'd all have reported to their fire teams. Felicité and Henry hurried inside. She'd hoped it would be cooler inside the thick adobe walls, but it was like stepping into an oven.

Soot covered the railing and the floor. As Henry peered out over the rail, Felicité scooped up a handful and smeared it over her face and throat. If the worst happened, maybe the soot would conceal her scales.

Henry leaped up the stairs to the lookout tower, taking them three at a time. Felicité followed him, mopping uselessly at her face. Her scarf was drenched in sweat. It was only useful now for hiding her face, not drying it. Her heart lurched in terror as she felt a familiar prickle beneath her skin. All along her spine and chest and face, scales were forming. She yanked up her skirt and scrubbed frantically at her face, but she knew it was useless. The skin split along both sides of her throat. Gills.

Terrified, Felicité wrapped her soaking scarf along her throat, then threw the end over her head, draping it over her face like a veil. She'd claim it was to keep out the smoke. But once the skin closed over her nose, her voice would change. And then there would be no hiding it.

She had to get out of there.

Henry was gone. He'd climbed onto the roof. She could hear his shoes scrabbling on the tiles. She could demand that he come down and leave with her. If he wouldn't, she could go alone. She'd rather he think she was a coward than a monster.

But if she left him, what would he do?

She didn't trust him to keep himself safe. He'd do anything to impress Daddy. Maybe she could convince him that she was so terrified that he had to escort her back?

"The fire's jumped the stream!" Henry yelled.

A series of thuds overhead resolved into Henry swinging inward and dropping down beside her. As she tightened her veil over her face, he exclaimed, "The fire's jumped the stream! I'm going to fight it!"

Felicité caught his arm. His muscles were clenched like steel. She could feel how much he wanted to go. He was so brave. And his courage would kill him.

She snatched desperately at an idea to save them both. "No! Remember Daddy's orders." Her voice was already thickening. She coughed loudly. "The smoke. It's getting in my throat." Felicité pointed at a whirl of sparks flying upward over the wall they'd been standing on a minute ago. "We have to go and warn Daddy. Now."

Henry didn't pull away, but neither did he agree. She could feel him reaching for reasons to go try to be heroic. To get himself killed proving himself. And if she didn't get out of the mill's blistering heat, her life might as well be over.

Then she remembered the tunnel. The one place in Las Anclas that was sure to be cool was the passage from the mill to the town hall, running deep underground. Cool, dry, and dark. She'd never told anyone about it—unlike Mia, who had told her boyfriend, and not even for a good reason! Well, Felicité had a good reason. It would save Henry's life, it would save Felicité's secret, and it really was the fastest way to warn Daddy.

She tugged at Henry's hand. "Want to be a hero?"

That caught his attention. She couldn't see his face through her scarf, but she could feel his gaze. "What do you mean?"

"There's a secret tunnel under the mill. It's the fastest way to get the news back to Daddy. You can't tell anyone about it. Ever. I'll explain why later."

"A secret tunnel?" Henry said. "Cool!"

He followed her to the boards that concealed the trapdoor. She lifted them and slid aside the catch, and together they pried it open.

"Wow," Henry whispered. "I've done a million boring stints on wall duty here and never knew about it."

"Nobody knows," Felicité said as they felt their way down the ladder. "Except the council. We'll have to tell Daddy we used the tunnel, but we have to do it in private, after the fire is put out. You'll have to swear to keep the secret."

"I can do that," Henry said, laughing. "And you never even hinted when we played Secrets. Think of the kisses we could have had."

Felicité was thinking of her scales, which were already receding. Her gills tickled as they began to close up. She loosened the wet scarf to help the dry air do its work as they felt their way along the walls of earth.

"What's it for?" Henry asked. "Where does it come out?"

"It's the last resort, if we ever get invaded," Felicité said. "Remember my job in the attack?"

"Sure. You took the little kids to the town hall basement."

"And that's the other end of the tunnel. If the town falls, at least I can try to save the children," she said grimly. "It's my one job that I hope I never, ever have to do."

"I had no idea." Henry sounded excited, not horrified. But during the battle, he'd been out fighting, not waiting to find out if he'd have to leave people he loved to die while he fled with a bunch of crying brats.

Her fingers finally bumped into the ladder. She touched the skin of her face and throat. Smooth. Normal. She was safe.

"Here we go." She led the way up. They felt their way along the stacked barrels, then up the ramp. Felicité held up a hand to stop Henry before he could throw it open, then put her ear to the door. She heard nothing, but she still eased the door open a crack and peered through.

The town hall was deserted except for the clutter of the Catalina Players' tawdry props and costumes. As she led Henry out, she couldn't resist stepping on and crushing a fake crown that had fallen to the floor. "Oops!"

The town square was also deserted, a sight made even eerier by the huge red sun hanging in a smoke-gray sky. They ran hand in hand to the gate, where Daddy stood at the command post.

"You tell him," Felicité suggested.

Henry leaned over to kiss her. When he turned away, he had soot smeared over his lips. Only then did she remember that she'd deliberately made herself filthy. But it didn't matter. She'd kept her secret.

Henry vaulted up the steps while Felicité waited below.

"What are you two doing here?" Daddy asked.

"The fire has jumped the stream," Henry said. "I climbed to the mill roof and saw it myself."

"It has? Why didn't you report to Horst?" Then Daddy shook his head. "That's right, he's up in the hills fighting the fire from the east side." Felicité rejoiced at the approval in his tone as he said, "Good work, Henry. You followed orders. Horst's people are with him, and I dispatched my last backup team. Run to the dairy. They have three teams there. Recall Ling Vargas's team and send them to the stream."

Henry turned to the steps, then glanced over his shoulder. "Can I go with them?"

Daddy smiled grimly. "Go ahead. You earned it. And I'm sure they can use your help."

Henry rushed down, his blue eyes shining. Felicité watched him proudly as he ran away. All her plans had paid off. Not only had she saved his life and preserved their relationship, but he'd finally managed to impress Daddy.

Her pride faded slightly at the recollection of how she'd done it. It was the first town secret she'd ever broken. But it would be all right. They'd explain when the emergency was over, in private. It might even turn out to be a good thing, after Henry's help with the fire. If Daddy didn't appoint Henry into the Rangers on the spot, surely he'd at least let him try out again.

She mounted the steps to the command post. Daddy gave her a proud smile and a pat on the shoulder, then offered her his handkerchief. "Water's over there. I can see you've been working as hard as Henry."

Felicité took the handkerchief and turned her face away, scrubbing quickly at it without touching any water. The handkerchief darkened with smoke grit. Felicité's face burned from the dry rubbing.

She stuffed the handkerchief in her pocket so that her father would not wonder why it was not wet. She backed away, then stilled when she spotted a girl watching her. Humiliation and anger burned through her when she recognized the actor who had made a mockery of her onstage, but she forced herself to give the player Mother's best cool, unconcerned glance. Felicité had a town to be concerned about. Who cared what some stranger thought about her, anyway?

Sheriff Crow and Becky appeared at the base of the stairs. The sheriff called up, "Everything's quiet at the west end. Becky and I are going to investigate the cause of the fire. I'd like to get a look at the evidence before the entire town stomps all over it."

Evidence? Felicité had assumed it was a natural fire. Despite the heat, a chill made her shiver. Who would deliberately try to burn down the entire town? Would the Catalina Players do it for revenge? Felicité spun around to glare at that actor, but the girl was gone.

·34·
KERRY

IF THERE WAS ONE place in Las Anclas that Kerry had never wanted to be, it was the grove of black crystal trees.

Everybody else avoided them for fear of an agonizing death. Kerry did, too, but also because she knew who those trees had been. She'd known every one of Father's elite team by name. She hesitated atop the wall, probably right around where they had been supposed to breach. Father had ordered them to kill the town council. Instead, Ross had killed them through his crystal tree.

She glanced at Ross as he peered into the smoke, his prominent shoulder blades ridging his shirt. Though she knew what he'd done—even though she'd seen him fight—it was still hard to believe. It was his little sister who stood with the arrogant pride that Kerry would expect in someone who had killed thirty soldiers at one blow.

Summer put her hands on her skinny hips and glowered contemptuously at the rope ladder Mr. Riley's fire team had thrown over. "I don't need that." She leaped off the wall and floated down through the smoky air, light as a feather.

Ross yelled, "Stay there, Summer!"

Her voice rose indignantly from the smoke. "I'm not stupid!"

Kerry grinned, expecting Ross to share her amusement, but he seemed unaware of her. His expression, etched against the drifts of smoke, was the one she'd never thought to see after he left Gold Point: closed in and grim. Kerry wondered if she ought to say something, but before she could, Jennie appeared with the hose.

Jennie dropped it over the wall, then put a hand on Ross's shoulder. "I know it might not seem like it, but Summer really is listening to you. She's not going to run off and do something dangerous by herself. Besides, Kerry will look after her."

"Of course," Kerry said. But she wondered why Jennie had said that. Ross would protect his sister himself, wouldn't he?

Ross dipped his head in a nod and stepped onto the ladder. His gauntleted hand couldn't quite close around the rope, forcing him to descend slowly. Kerry followed. The heat and smoke were much more intense once they hit the ground. Within seconds, her nose and throat burned, her lungs labored, and her eyes felt dried out.

Mr. Riley and his team were lined up atop the wall, wavering like ghosts in the smoke and fading light. Ross peered up at Jennie, then bent to examine the brass-nozzled hose.

"I'll take that," Summer said.

Ross shook his head. "Kerry, will you lead? Summer, you've got to hold the hose still. I don't think I'll be able to help any."

That also surprised Kerry. Of the three of them, Ross was probably the strongest. She wanted to ask, but his expression unnerved her. Instead, she lifted the hose. It was even heavier than she had expected, and there wasn't any water in it yet.

Everything about this mission was unsettling, from the dragging weight of the hose to Ross and Jennie's odd remarks to the crystal trees themselves. She didn't like how limited their visibility was, either. All she could see was dirt, and that for only a few yards, except for the wall behind them. In the other direction, where they were headed, was another wall, towering skyward, made of brownish gray smoke.

Kerry remembered how the Gold Point fire teams had drilled, and put one arm around the hose to grip it and the other under it to hold it against her hip, and to guide it. Summer stepped behind her and copied her.

Ross took a stance between them. "Kerry, I'll guide you." He took off his gauntlet and locked its fingers around his belt, then laid his right hand on her shoulder and reached back with his left to do the same with his sister. "Summer, whatever you do, don't shake off my hand. I don't know if I can keep you safe from the trees when I'm not touching you."

Summer's eyes widened in the dim light, and she gave a firm nod. "Got it."

"And I can't talk to you while I'm talking to them," he added.

Talking to them? Despite the hot breezes, a chill tightened Kerry's gut.

On Opportunity Day, Ross had described to her how the last thing a woman had seen was Father's face before she died in agony and became a crystal tree. At the time, Kerry hadn't asked for more detail because she hadn't wanted to believe him. Later, she didn't inquire about his power because he obviously hated discussing it. Now she wished she'd asked anyway.

Ross closed his eyes. His expression shuttered, still and distant, as if he was listening to something very far away. He couldn't possibly mean to walk blind through fire and crystal...could he?

"Ready?" Mr. Riley shouted from the wall.

Kerry had no idea. But Summer yelled, "Yes!"

Mr. Riley called, "Release the water!"

"Oh!" Summer gasped.

A second later the hose stiffened in Kerry's arms and almost got loose, as if a dead thing had become alive, writhing like a snake. She planted her feet wide, clamped her arms firmly on the hose, letting her hip take most of its weight as water gushed out in a stream. Now she knew why the fire teams gripped the hoses as they did.

Ross's hand tightened on her shoulder. Kerry plodded, one foot at a time, in the direction he pushed her—straight toward the singing trees. The smell and the smoke thickened on the left. Ross nudged her that way until she made out a cherry glow within the boiling smoke. She shifted her hips and set her feet hard, pulling at the unwieldy hose to direct the water straight into the crackling flames. With a whooshing hiss, the smoke thickened briefly, then wavered and thinned. The scarlet glow vanished; the fire had gone out.

Ross's hand pulled her to the right. The hose jerked as Summer stumbled, then regained her balance, once again matching Kerry's steps. Between the two of them they were just barely able to control the heavy hose. But they managed to douse another small fire.

Ross guided them to another fire. By then they'd found their rhythm. Step, grip, douse. Kerry could see nothing but roiling gray smoke and the red glow of flame. Kerry's arms and lungs and legs burned, her eyes watered, and the skin of her palms rubbed raw. She could feel a huge bruise forming on her hip, where the hose ground against the bone.

Her foot came down on empty air, and she almost pitched forward. Ross yanked her back. Her heart pounding, she felt out with her foot. They were at the edge of a slope.

"Watch your feet," Kerry called. "We're going down the ridge."

"Oooh!" Summer's voice shrilled between fear and excitement. "Where my brother's tree is! I'll finally get to see it! Everyone says it's *blood red!*"

Ross stiffened, and crystal tinkled sweetly ahead. Kerry almost jumped out of her skin. The hose promptly tried to fight loose. She wrestled it back under control.

"Quiet, Summer," Kerry hissed. "I think you're distracting Ross."

A tiny voice came from behind. "Oh."

Summer fell silent as Kerry edged her way down, step by step, spraying water in front of her in a wide arc. Even if there was no fire on the slope, she'd make sure that sparks couldn't catch.

When they reached the bottom, Ross directed her to the left. Kerry tried to breathe shallowly, but her lungs still filled with the acrid smoke that was all that she could see. She had to be close to Ross's red tree, and the black trees that were all that was left of Father's team.

Kerry wondered if the singing trees knew they were there. Then she wondered if they knew *her*. Ross had told her they remembered the moment of their deaths, but did they remember more? Which one was Santiago's cousin Bernardo? He'd been like an older brother to Santiago, and Kerry had known him well. After she'd begun dating Santiago, Bernardo had often joined them for lunch when he had the palace watch.

As Kerry edged forward, steadying the heavy hose in aching arms, she remembered asking Santiago if he'd told Ross about Bernardo. She'd meant to warn Santiago not to mention him, but it hadn't been necessary.

Santiago had shaken his head fiercely. "Tell Ross he killed my cousin, who I loved like a brother? No. Not a chance. The king ordered me to make friends with Ross. Besides." Kerry hadn't understood his expression at the time, but now she thought that Santiago had felt sorry for Ross and guilty about his own role. "He's got enough to think about."

Bernardo was here—or all that was left of Bernardo. Ross kept turning his head as if he was listening. What could he hear?

Silvery chimes rang out all around Kerry. She froze, clutching the hose so tightly that stabbing pain shot from her forearms to her shoulders. She felt Summer stop behind her. Ross gave her an insistent prod. Gritting her teeth, Kerry took a step forward.

A sudden gust of wind hit her in the back, snapping her clothes in front of her. The smoke before her blew away, and she could see everything.

They were surrounded by singing trees. A black branch, thick with razor thorns, loomed inches in front of Kerry's face. She jerked aside. Ross's fingers tightened painfully on her shoulder. The obsidian branches swayed, knife-edged leaves clashing together. Chimes rang out in sweet and deadly chords.

Kerry dared a glance over her other shoulder. She had to make sure that Summer wasn't about to panic and run. Summer's soot-spotted face was fixed in terror, her black eyes stark.

"I'm scared," Summer whispered.

Putting more confidence in her voice than she actually felt, Kerry whispered, "Ross has done this hundreds of times. He'll keep us safe."

She didn't know whether to be relieved or even more scared when the wind died down, once again cloaking the trees in smoke. All she could see was the thorny black branch in front of her. Ross nudged her forward, and Kerry ducked low and stepped under it. The branch bent on its own, and a loose lock of her hair brushed against a razor-edged thorn. The lock fluttered to the ground, sliced away by an edge so sharp that Kerry didn't even feel a tug.

Kerry shuddered, terror making her hands tingle and her breath catch. She wondered if she felt like Santiago had when Father made him go with Ross past the singing trees at Gold

Point's ruined city. As she sprayed the red glow of a fire to the left, she decided that it must have been far worse for Santiago. At least she knew that Ross was trying his best to keep her safe. As far as Santiago had known, he and Ross were enemies. Ross had stood to gain nothing and lose everything by keeping Santiago alive.

The smoke stayed heavy, concealing the trees, as Kerry and Summer doused smoldering, fitful fires. Kerry couldn't decide if it was more frightening to be able to see the trees, or to know they were present but not see them. Every now and then, eerie chimes rang out, always from unexpected places and always making her jump. Kerry lost all track of time in a haze of terror and exhaustion.

Then: "We're clear." It was Ross's voice, weary and hoarse.

His hand slipped from Kerry's shoulder. As she turned back, another gust of wind scoured past them, driving the smoke before it. Ross stood swaying, his eyes still closed, and then his knees buckled. Summer let go of the hose and caught him around the chest. He clutched at her shoulders, trying to steady himself. The wind whipped their hair together in black streamers.

Kerry also dropped the hose. Before it could go berserk, she stepped on it with both feet, so only the nozzle twitched back and forth. They were surrounded by black stubble, all that was left of the abandoned cornfield. Two glowing walls of fire leaped skyward, one close to the wall a couple hundred yards to the north, and a much bigger one burning its way up the palisades a quarter mile away. She heard orders shouted from the palisades, so someone was already fighting that fire.

Ross opened his eyes and managed to get his feet under him. Like Summer—like Kerry, she supposed—his face was covered in soot, cut through with runnels of sweat. He looked utterly exhausted, but his voice, though roughened by smoke, was calm and steady. "We're done. Can you tell Mr. Riley to send his fire team?"

Summer peered down at him worriedly from behind, her arms still tight around his chest. "Are you sure you're all right? Kerry could go."

Ross detached her hands like a pair of clinging barnacles. "I'm fine. And you're faster."

Summer ran toward the wall, leaping like a deer.

·35·
JENNIE

JENNIE COUGHED, HER EYES and lungs burning.

A gust of wind eddied through the smoke, and from it Summer emerged. It looked as if the girl was flying. She landed lightly, shot up again, and lit down on the wall.

"The fires are out around the crystal trees," she reported.

"How's Ross?" Jennie asked urgently.

Summer seemed puzzled. "He said he was fine. He got a little dizzy from the heat, but he wasn't burned or anything."

Of course Ross hadn't told her how difficult it was for him to deal with those trees. "I don't think it was the heat. Talking to the trees wears him out. But if he said he's fine, then he is."

"Oh," Summer said, her eyes huge. "I am *so* glad I don't have that power."

As Pa's fire team gathered, Summer straightened up, throwing her hair back. "My brother was amazing. He took us straight through that impassable forest of killer trees! They tried to stop him, but he fought his way through."

Jennie had a feeling that any fighting had happened inside of Ross's head, but she didn't argue.

Summer went on, "And while Ross was battling those deadly trees, Kerry and I fought through a wall of flame three stories high!"

"I'm glad you're all okay," Pa replied. His tone was serious, but Jennie saw the hidden smile in the quirk of his eyelids. "Good job, Summer. You can go back to Ross now. Tell him that my team will pull in the hose. We'll bring shovels for you and him and Kerry."

Summer leaped down from the wall and vanished into the billowing smoke.

Pa turned to his team. "We'll start from where Ross left off, and fight the fires all along the wall, moving north. Jennie..." He hesitated. She'd always been with the Rangers, and had done all her fire drills with them. Pa's team was used to working with each other, and didn't have a place for her.

The rumble of footsteps walking south along the wall preceded the appearance of a group of Rangers. Jennie's heart twisted when she spotted Indra in the lead. Paco and Sujata ran behind him, carrying shovels. All of them were covered in sweat-streaked soot from the firefighting they'd already done.

"We're supposed to start where Ross left off and fight north," Indra said to Pa.

"Here's your hoses." Pa indicated the hoses wrapped around wheels. "You can deploy parallel to us."

Indra stepped up to Jennie, so close that she could feel the radiant heat of his body. Still hot, even in this firestorm. She didn't know how to react, so she didn't move at all, not even to blink. No other Ranger would have come quite that close to her.

"Mr. Riley, may I borrow Jennie?" Indra asked.

He smiled at her as if he was sure that she'd be thrilled to join them. She *was* thrilled. She was also certain that Mr. Preston had authorized no such thing. She glanced at Pa, who had to know that.

Looking at Jennie rather than at Indra, Pa said, "Jennie, if you'd like to join the Rangers for this, my team can manage without you."

So it was her decision. Jennie shrugged off thoughts of consequences, especially when she saw the smile brightening Sujata's tired face and the relief in Paco's somber expression. She was needed with the Ranger team, whereas she was a fifth wheel on Pa's team. "I'd love to join the Rangers."

Indra grinned and beckoned at her, then turned to the rope ladders. His long braid dangled down his back. Jennie started to reach out to give it a playful tug, then dropped her hand. They didn't have that kind of relationship any more, either romantic or as Rangers. A flush of heat burned her face, and she was glad her skin was too dark to show it. This was just a one-time job.

The Rangers and Jennie swiftly descended on the rope ladders. The last on the wall handed over the hoses, and these were passed along from hand to hand. Next came the shovels. Jennie was given one of these. The Rangers and Pa's team ran the hoses out into the muddy ground north of the crystal trees. The smoke there was thinner, sometimes blowing away in gusts of wind coming off the desert, then drifting back again to partially obscure people.

At Indra's direction, they turned north, Pa's team spraying to the left, and the Rangers to the right. They fought into the thick of the smoke, where the fire had burned down from solid flame to a flickering carpet. They made sure it was completely put out as they worked northward, with no stray pockets waiting to flare up again behind them.

Jennie fell into the familiar pattern of drill and training, moving in step with Indra, who guided the hose. She and Indra worked as if they were two parts of a perfect machine. They didn't need to talk. They didn't even need to look at each other. She knew what Indra was doing because they'd done it so often before in drill. He was never in her way, but she could feel his presence whether she could see him or not.

It was great to be with the Rangers again; it was great to be where she belonged. Her arms and legs ached with fatigue, but her heart filled with light. It had been so long since she'd pushed her body to the limit that she'd forgotten how good it felt. And she wasn't fighting enemies. No one would die on her watch. Yet she was working to save the town.

She jabbed the shovel into another patch of muddy ground, tossed the load onto the red-glowing remains of cactus, then smashed it down. When she searched for the next hot spot, a hand came down on her shoulder, startling her. She glanced up into Indra's warm brown eyes.

"This is as far as the hoses reach," he said. "We've met the mid-wall fire teams. We're done."

Jennie leaned on her shovel and wiped the sweat from her face. That last bit of fire she'd stomped out really had been the last one, as far as she could see. Sujata and Paco and the other Rangers stood with hoses and shovels, tired but exhilarated. The fire team from Santa Lucia's well was also there, and also resting.

Sujata clapped Jennie on the back. "That was fun. Let's do it again!"

Jennie laughed.

Indra laughed, too, but ruefully. "I don't think it's over yet. There's still smoke that way." He pointed northward. "We'll have to carry the hoses back and get new orders."

Jennie took a deep breath. It burned a lot less. The wall of smoke in the distance was still thick, but around her the steam rising from the drenched ground looked ghostly in the lurid light of the setting sun.

She fell into step beside Indra. "I'm good. I've got a second wind."

Indra smiled. "I'm working on my third."

"Water!" Mrs. Callahan's hard voice caused a sudden silence. She marched up, carrying a bucket. All smiles vanished as people took turns dipping the ladle and getting a drink. As Mrs. Callahan's hands lifted the bucket, Jennie pictured those same hands slapping Becky's face.

When Paco reached for the ladle, Mrs. Callahan jerked the bucket so the water slopped over his feet. "Sorry," she said insincerely.

Jennie wondered how long she was going to carry a grudge over Henry not getting into the Rangers. Forever, probably. To draw Mrs. Callahan's attention away from Paco, Jennie said in her politest voice, "That water looks really good right now. Thank you."

The woman thrust out the bucket, but gave Jennie a look even more sour than the one she'd directed at Paco. "What are *you* doing with the Rangers? Aren't you supposed to be banned for life?"

Indra stepped up to Mrs. Callahan, deliberately looming over her. "She's here on my orders. There's thirsty people over there." He pointed behind him.

As Mrs. Callahan stalked away, she muttered in a tone calculated to be overheard, "Don't blame *me* if His Majesty complains. It wasn't *my* idea. But no one ever listens…"

Jennie watched her retreating back, feeling suddenly weary.

Indra stretched a hand toward Jennie, then dropped it to his side. "Thanks for helping out. You were great."

Jennie smiled at him, but the lightness inside her had vanished. When she scrubbed the soot and sweat from her eyes, she spotted Ross, Kerry, and Summer stiffening as Mrs. Callahan approached. They gulped their water and then quickly backed away. Summer had her arms folded as defiantly as when Jennie had reproved her for breaking Will Preston's arm.

The moment Mrs. Callahan turned her back, Ross leaned on his shovel, obviously exhausted. Jennie glanced from him to Indra, wondering if she should go to Ross or stay where she was. It felt so right to be standing with Indra again, with their old wordless understanding connecting them, but she wanted to be there for Ross, too.

Indra was no longer smiling. He lifted his voice. "Come on, team. Let's report back."

·36·
BECKY

BECKY BENT OVER THE blackened ruins of the abandoned cornfield, then straightened up, her back aching. To the south, the singing trees glittered against the muddy, still-steaming earth. To the north, a line of smoke beyond the mill marked where the last of the fire was being put out. The town was no longer in danger—

Except from whoever had started the fire. Becky's stomach clenched. She didn't want to think of anybody as an arsonist, but she couldn't help hoping she'd find evidence that it was anyone but her brother. Maybe it was one of the Willets. She could believe they'd do something careless and stupid, especially while drunk.

Sheriff Crow had identified the direction the fire had burned in. Much of the evidence had been trampled by the fire teams, but that didn't stop Becky from using her power to search through time. She hadn't seen anyone setting a fire, but at least they'd found out where the fire *hadn't* started.

"What do you think?" Sheriff Crow asked. "Where should we look next?"

Becky knew the sheriff had her own idea, but rather than try to figure out what it was, Becky did as she'd learned, and considered the evidence.

She turned in a slow circle, surveying the area. Though it seemed to be where the fire had started, no one had dropped a match that she'd seen. But there were other ways to set fires. Last week she and Sheriff Crow had stuffed rags in bottles of oil, like the ones Jennie had used to blow up King Voske's ammunition.

They lit the rags and threw the bottles, observing what those small, controlled fires looked like and how they spread. And how far an ordinary person like Becky could throw.

Becky pointed to a grove of jacaranda trees that stood inside the town walls and rose at least ten feet above them. "If I climbed one of those, I could throw a bottle to where I'm standing now."

"My thought exactly," the sheriff said. "Let's go look."

When they reached the wall, Brisa's voice rose above the hubbub of everyone talking about how they'd fought the fire. "Becky!" She was leaning precariously out, hanging onto a shield with one hand. "I thought it would be boring being a sentry and missing the play, but I got to be on one of the very first fire teams sent out! And it looks like you've been doing something exciting, too!"

"Investigating the cause," Sheriff Crow said.

Brisa actually squealed. Becky couldn't help laughing, the tightness around her heart easing for the first time since the fire had started. "I don't think it's as exciting as you think it is."

Brisa hung even farther out. "Oh, I bet it is! Can I join you?" Glancing at the sheriff, she added, "I could help. I might be able to, um, explode some rocks for you."

Sheriff Crow smiled from Brisa to Becky, the skin around her brown eye and her yellow one crinkling. "Would you like Brisa to come along?"

"Yes," Becky said fervently. If the worst came to worst, Brisa was exactly the person she wanted by her side.

Sheriff Crow called up to the fire team commander, "May we borrow Brisa?"

"Sure."

Brisa squealed again. Becky followed Sheriff Crow up the rope ladder, then down the other side of the wall. People backed off to give them space—not just from the sheriff, but from Becky. It was strange to not only be noticed, but to have people make way for her as if she were someone important.

Felicité approached, grubby with soot, her hair in a tangle. Becky tried not to stare as Felicité cupped her hands around her mouth, and called up to commander, "The defense chief—" She broke off. "My father says the fire teams are dismissed. Sentries back to duty. We're on the night shift now." Her eyes flicked to

Becky. "Did you figure out who set the fire?"

Becky swallowed past a lump in her throat. Henry wasn't just her brother, he was Felicité's boyfriend. And as far as she could tell, the two of them had gotten really close. Maybe even as close as she and Brisa. How would Becky feel if she found out that Brisa had done something terrible — something that would get her exiled from Las Anclas?

Sheriff Crow cleared her throat warningly. Becky couldn't meet Felicité's eyes as she muttered, "Not yet."

"Your father will be the first to know once we find out," the sheriff said.

"I'll go tell him." Felicité took off.

The sheriff led the way into the jacaranda grove. The thick trunks and corrugated bark stood like dark pillars around Becky. The frond-like leaves and purple blossoms of spring and autumn had fallen, leaving the trees bare. Thin twigs crooked out like a witch's fingers. Becky turned to Brisa, hoping to be cheered by her girlfriend's excitement, but found Brisa with an unusually solemn expression.

"What's going on, Becky?" Brisa glanced at Sheriff Crow. "Ooops. Wait. This is secret, right?"

"Until we're sure." Sheriff Crow nodded at Becky. "Go ahead."

Brisa clasped Becky's gloved hands in a warm, firm grip. "Whatever's going on, I'll be right here."

Becky took a deep breath to settle her churning stomach. She wouldn't feel any better waiting. She examined the cluster of trees. If she wanted to throw something as far as she could over the wall, she'd pick the jacaranda to the right. It wasn't the tallest, but it had thick branches high up, so she wouldn't risk a branch breaking beneath her.

She walked to the tree and started climbing. She got to the highest branch that could support her weight, though it swayed beneath her. She started to pull off her glove with her teeth, then reconsidered. Anyone heavier than her wouldn't have climbed this high. She lowered herself to the highest branch that would support someone. *Henry's weight,* she couldn't help thinking. If there was nothing there, she'd try higher.

Becky glanced down at the upturned faces far below. It was a view she'd never seen before. She'd never been allowed to climb trees, which might tear her dresses. And she'd never done the advanced training that involved climbing, as Brisa had in Ranger training.

If I fall out of this tree, I'll break my neck.

But she'd climbed without even considering the danger. And even now that she had, she wasn't afraid of falling. She was afraid of what she was about to find out.

Becky braced herself between two higher branches and pulled off her glove. Her hand trembled in the air before she forced her palm down on the branch she sat on.

Excitement, satisfaction, and a delight in his own cleverness surged through him. And beneath that a simmering anger—a familiar anger.

I don't belong in this family. I'm meant for something better. Everyone will see it now.

A strong, pale, freckled hand reached out. The anger flared through his belly, surging out in a flash of heat. A white-hot fireball exploded from his palm, shooting out over the wall and falling into the bone-dry cornfield.

Now I'll be a hero.

Becky opened her eyes and clung to the branches as she fought against the sob threatening to tear from her ribs. Poor Henry. She buried her eyes against her sleeve. Ever since it had occurred to her that he could be the arsonist, she'd known in her heart that it was true—that she'd seen little signs all along. She'd wanted so much to be wrong.

But she'd never guessed that he was Changed. How long had he been hiding *that* secret? In their family, nobody really talked to each other, because nobody trusted anybody, not with blame constantly hurled around. Henry must have felt terrible when the Change came, every bit as terrible as she had. And then he'd seen what had happened to her when she'd told.

All he'd wanted was to be respected. She'd wanted that, too. He was angry. So was she. She'd just been too scared to show it. If she'd gotten his power and he'd gotten hers, would she have been the one to throw fire over the wall?

"Becky?" Sheriff Crow called. "Have you found anything?"

Becky pretended not to hear. For the first time, it occurred to her that she could keep a secret, too. No one could see what she'd seen. All she'd have to do was claim that she'd seen nothing. She could talk to Henry privately and warn him to never set a fire again.

She could imagine that conversation. Henry would deny it, but if she pushed, he'd grin and say, "Don't be so serious, Beck! It was a joke that got out of hand, that's all. Of course I'll never do it again."

But this was his third fire. His first would have killed Hans Ruiz if Alfonso hadn't arrived on time. But instead of stopping or even being more careful, Henry had gotten more reckless. His fire on the cliffs could have killed the entire patrol. And his third fire was the biggest and most dangerous of them all. Would *anything* make him stop?

Becky remembered Henry talking about how many soldiers he'd killed in the battle. That didn't prove anything about him, of course. Half of Las Anclas had fought that night, and many of them had killed. Jennie had. Ross had, and Becky had heard him cry out in his sleep while he'd lain ill and delirious in the infirmary. Even Mia had.

Brisa had told Becky how strange it felt to know that she had killed people when she'd blown up Voske's ammunition dump. Her usually cheery face had been uncharacteristically solemn, her words stumbling as she'd tried to express feelings she didn't quite understand herself.

"I don't feel guilty," Brisa had said at last. "I know I did the right thing. I was protecting Las Anclas. It just feels...strange. Especially since I never saw the bodies close up. I don't even know how many there were. Maybe if I did, it would've given me nightmares. But...I kind of feel like maybe I *should* have seen their faces. Like I owed them that." Brisa shook her head, sending her ribbons flying, but in confusion rather than denial. "I guess if I become a Ranger, I'll find out what that's like. *They* fight up-close."

Becky herself had helped to take a life, handing Dr. Lee the poppy elixir. Mr. Gutierrez had glanced up as she'd arrived with the bottle, and he'd actually tried to smile at her. He'd been dying anyway; all she'd done was ease his passage. But it would haunt her till her own dying day.

It wasn't the act of killing that was important, Becky thought. It was the reason for it.

Henry had *bragged* about the number of enemies he'd snuffed. Even if he was making a show of unconcern to seem tough and brave, Becky had sensed that deep down, he'd meant it. It was as if those soldiers hadn't been people to him.

Becky glanced down at the sheriff's upturned face. "Just a moment!"

She gazed out at the blackened field. Sheriff Crow had sent away a man she loved because he'd tried to kill a citizen of Las Anclas. Henry had endangered every person in the town. For the first time, Becky understood that that meant her, too.

She slowly began to climb down. The bark felt as cold as the bottle of poppy elixir. She'd thought she never wanted to be involved in that kind of decision again. And yet here she was, holding another person's life in her hands.

Becky hoped that by the time she felt solid ground under her feet, she'd know what to do. Then she was stepping away from the tree, with no better idea of what she was going to say than when she'd first started climbing down.

Hot tears welled up in her eyes, blurring her view of the sheriff's face. "It was my brother. He's got a Change power."

"I see," Sheriff Crow sounded completely unsurprised. Becky wondered how long she'd suspected that. "Good work, Becky. And I'm sorry."

Silently Brisa slid an arm around Becky, who leaned gratefully into her warmth. She hadn't even noticed that she was shivering. That sob was trying to get out again, and her throat tightened.

"I know it feels like your responsibility, as if you're exiling him," Sheriff Crow said, echoing Brisa's words from her great-grandmother. "But this fire was not your choice. Henry was the one who chose to set fires and risk other people's lives. He must deal with the consequences of his action."

She handed Becky her canteen. Becky wiped her eyes on her grimy sleeves and took a drink. "I'm all right now." She wasn't, of course. But she still had a job to do.

"Then let's go report," the sheriff said.

·37·
FELICITÉ

FELICITÉ CLIMBED WEARILY UP to the command center and once again mopped her face, though the air had cooled considerably. But she felt grimy and filthy, and the memory of those scales changing her skin made her constantly want to scrub at it. Her father gave her a concerned glance, and she yanked her hand down.

"Sheriff Crow and Becky said they hadn't found anything yet," she reported.

Indra and his team of Rangers walked up below the platform. "Fire's out," Indra called.

A cheer rose. Daddy smiled. Then his smile faded. "Jennie Riley, what are you doing with the Rangers?"

It took Felicité a moment to spot Jennie, who wasn't standing tall and stuck-up the way she normally did. She lurked behind Indra as if she'd snuck into a place where she didn't belong, and knew she ought to be ashamed of herself. As indeed she should!

"I needed her on my fire team." Indra sounded neither apologetic nor defensive, but simply stating a fact.

"The fire is out," Daddy said, echoing Indra's tone. But his angry gaze was directed at Jennie as he said, "You're done here."

Jennie walked away without a word, her face expressionless. Only then did Daddy congratulate the Rangers.

Felicité knew then that Daddy would never forgive Jennie. She'd sometimes wondered if Jennie could worm her way back into Daddy's good graces with some especially heroic deed, which

Felicité had to admit Jennie was entirely capable of. But now Felicité knew that nothing she did would ever be good enough. Daddy knew Jennie was brave and capable, but he'd always known that. It didn't matter. There were some things that Daddy would never—could never—forgive.

Felicité didn't miss the tightening of Indra's face, or the other subtle ways that the Rangers showed their anger. It was obvious that they all thought Jennie deserved to be commended, too, and equally obvious that none of them would say so. They might not approve of Daddy's actions, but they would never speak against them. He'd disciplined them well. That discipline would be good for Henry, once he got back into Ranger training.

The crowd below parted. Sheriff Crow appeared, followed by Becky and Brisa. Becky was once again staring at her feet, and though Felicité couldn't see her face, every line of her body reflected the old Becky, timid and miserable. A sparkle fell to the ground. Was Becky crying?

"Do you have anything to report?" Daddy asked.

"Yes." But Sheriff Crow didn't look triumphant. In fact, she seemed grim, though that might only be her ghastly face. When she reached Daddy's side, she spoke so quietly that Felicité could barely hear her. "I don't want this spread across town before we can do something about it."

Daddy stepped to the rail. "Rangers, dismissed. The rest of you, go home. Good job."

Everyone left, except Mia, who stood looking nervously from Daddy to the sheriff to Felicité.

Brisa piped up, "I already know."

Daddy gave her an irritated glance, then turned to the sheriff. "Do we need her?"

"We might," Sheriff Crow replied.

The only reason anyone would need Brisa was for her power to explode stone. What in the world was going on that they might need a potentially lethal Change power?

"Henry Callahan is Changed," Sheriff Crow said. "He can shoot fireballs a distance of ten yards. He started this fire, and probably the others as well. Seems like he wanted to be a hero."

"He did not!" Felicité heard her own voice rise in an ugly

shriek. "You're crazy!"

"Becky saw it," the sheriff said.

Felicité turned on Becky, and there were the twin tracks of tears running down her cheeks. Felicité's fury froze into cold shock. Becky would never make that up.

Felicité turned desperately to Daddy, hoping he would explain why Becky was mistaken. But he didn't even look surprised. "We'd better go find him."

Mia had started to slink away, but Daddy said, "Mia. You'd better stay."

She jumped, the tools on her ridiculous harness clattering. "Oh! You might need...water? Engineering advice? Explosions?"

"I hope we won't need explosions," he said grimly. "Or water, either. But we might."

"Let's try to avoid backing him into a corner," Sheriff Crow said to Daddy. "I think he was specifically trying to impress you."

"Then I should be the one to talk to him," Daddy said. "I'll take him aside. I should be able to get him to surrender peacefully, once we're alone. The rest of you follow in case I need backup, but hang back out of sight."

"What if I talk to him?" Felicité offered.

From the surprise in Daddy's eyes, she realized that he'd actually forgotten that Henry was her boyfriend. He patted her shoulder. "No, darling. That boy is not what you thought he was. He's dangerous. Stay here."

He walked down with the others. Felicité lingered on the platform, watching them go. She wanted to believe that everyone was wrong, but like Daddy, once she'd gotten over the shock, she wasn't really surprised. Henry did want to be a hero. He wouldn't have meant to hurt anyone. He didn't intend to do this much damage. He was impulsive. She could all too easily imagine him grinning and saying, "Just kidding!"

Felicité's shock gave way to hurt, then anger. How could he have not told her? If he'd only trusted her enough to confide in her, she'd have warned him not to do anything crazy. He didn't need to start a fire to be a hero. Felicité could have made up some story about him saving her life and coached him on it.

Of course he had a Change power. His sister was Changed.

And Becky had been thrown out of her own home. He'd probably thought Felicité would hate him if he told her.

She ground her teeth, remembering every conversation they'd had about Changed people, and how they'd assured each other that they hated the people and their powers. They'd each lied so the other wouldn't reject them.

If he'd only told her, she could have revealed her own secret. What if Henry had been The One after all? He might not have cared about her gills and scales. Maybe he'd only said he thought physical Changes were ugly because he thought she believed it. She could have had one person who knew everything and loved her anyway.

Maybe she still could. His secret was out now, so she *could* tell him hers. She just needed to think up some excuse he could give Daddy so he wouldn't be exiled. People got away with all sorts of stuff in Las Anclas. Jennie, Mia, and Yuki had locked her into a fruit shed all day to cover up their treason, and they'd gotten off with a mere two weeks in jail.

Treason was worse than arson. If those three could weasel out of exile, then Henry certainly wouldn't have to go. Felicité could still salvage things. She just had to get to Henry before Daddy did.

She raced down the stairs. Daddy had gone toward Main Street. Felicité knew that Henry had been fighting the fire with the team sent to the stream beyond the mill. They would be coming back into town now that the fire was over.

Daddy would know that, too, but he and his group were trying not to attract any attention. They'd walk normally, and with any luck, they'd be slowed down by the usual busybodies trying to start conversations. But it didn't matter if anyone saw Felicité running. She was a messenger. If anyone asked, she'd invent a message.

She ran behind the buildings to make sure Daddy didn't see her, and reached the gate at the same time as the fire teams coming back to town. Felicité scanned their sooty faces until she spotted Henry, tired but triumphant. Her heart twisted at the sight of him, and again, even more painfully, when he saw her and gave her that familiar joyous grin.

"Felicité! You came to meet me!" Henry called.

"I did!" She plastered on a smile. Turning to the fire team captain, she said, "Mind if I take him?"

If the captain had refused, Felicité would have invented a message from Daddy on the spot. But the woman shrugged. "Go ahead. We're done here."

Felicité silently hustled him to the north wall harvest barn, which was the nearest place with any privacy.

"What's wrong?" Henry asked. "You look—"

"Shh." Felicité pulled him inside.

As soon as she closed the door, Henry laughed. "Oh! That's what you wanted. Any time." He put his arms around her and bent to kiss her.

She braced her palms against his chest. "Not now. This is important. Daddy is coming right now. To talk to you." Felicité swallowed, the words burning in her throat. While she tried to figure out what to say, she backed up to light the lantern that always waited by the door.

"About the Rangers?" he asked hopefully, following her. "You should have seen me out there. I put out more fires than any three people—"

"Henry, Daddy knows," Felicité said.

His smile vanished. He stared down, the light of the lantern flame flickering in his eyes. "Knows what?"

"About you. And your Change."

His eyes widened in an expression she had never seen before. Then it was gone, replaced by a *"You're* kidding, right?" grin. "What Change? Felicité, that's not funny."

Felicité wanted to shake him. "We know you set that fire—all the fires."

"Set it? I *fought* it!"

"Daddy knows about everything, Henry. Stop arguing. He's on his way. You've got to tell him you didn't know you were Changed. You only realized that you must have accidentally set those fires when you started this one."

Henry froze, his face gone blank. Like shutters had slammed down and closed him off.

She talked even faster. "Say you get dizzy. Feverish. Then it's like you wake up, and you don't remember the last few minutes.

But today, you realized what must have happened. You were afraid to say anything while there was a crisis, in case it distracted people from their work. But you were going to confess as soon as it was over. And you fought that fire harder than anyone. Maybe you felt so guilty, you didn't even care if you got killed fighting the fire that you *accidentally* started."

"Felicité," Henry said, reaching for her.

The door slammed open, shocking them both. Henry pulled her to him as they turned —

"Felicité!" Daddy stood in the doorway, the lantern light shining on his furious face. "Get away from my daughter, you monster!"

Henry backed away, his eyes wild. Felicité watched in horror, the word *monster* echoing in her ears.

"Stop!" Felicité shouted, not knowing if she was yelling at Henry or at Daddy.

A white light gathered in the palm of Henry's hand.

Daddy lunged at him, yelling, "Felicité! Drop!"

Henry raised his hand. And then toppled, crashing into a pile of empty crates.

Stunned, Felicité whirled around. Sheriff Crow and Daddy were skidding to a stop on either side of Henry. And in the doorway, silhouetted against the floodlights, Becky Callahan stood holding the cloud viper gun, tears dripping down her face.

·38·
BECKY

THE SHERIFF PICKED UP Henry from the splintered crates. He was stiff, his eyes closed. The only movement was a thin trail of blood trickling down his face.

He was Becky's brother. And she'd *shot* him. She leaned against the barn door, shadows swimming at the edge of her vision.

Mia's urgent voice spoke at her shoulder. "Are you okay?"

Brisa's arms slid around Becky, holding her up. "You saved Mr. Preston's life. Whatever Henry was going to throw was aimed right at him."

Becky gulped in a breath. Her fingers trembled as she tried to give the gun to Mia.

"Keep it, Becky," Mia said. "You were terrific."

"That's right," Sheriff Crow said as she passed by the girls with Henry in her arms. "She was. How are you doing, Becky? Do you want to go home?"

Becky couldn't run away now. She had to follow this all the way to the end. "No. I'll come."

The sheriff waded into the crowd that had gathered outside the barn, shouting, "Stand clear!" To Mia, she asked, "How long is he going to be paralyzed?"

Mia eyed Henry. "Um, looks like he weighs about one seventy-five, so I'd guess four minutes thirty seconds. Approximately. You've got one minute twenty seconds left." After a pause, she added, "Approximately."

Sheriff Crow bolted for the jail, using her full Changed speed. Becky followed with Brisa at her side, leaving Mr. Preston behind to deal with everyone's questions.

When they reached the jail, the sheriff had laid Henry on a cot in a cell. She'd already put the manacles Mia had made for Kerry on Henry and was wrapping cloth around his hands, binding his palms together. Uneasily, Becky remembered that they'd done that to Kerry, too.

Henry began to twitch and stir just as Sheriff Crow finished. She quickly backed out of the cell and locked the door behind her. Becky scrubbed her eyes on her sleeve. But no matter what she did, the tears kept welling up.

"Come on, Becky." Sheriff Crow led the way to her private room on the other side of the jail. To Brisa, she said, "Do you mind staying out here with the deputy? She'll be right out."

"Sure," Brisa said instantly. "I'll help guard."

"Thanks." Sheriff Crow led Becky into her room and closed the door. Aunt Rosa's quilt covered the bed, and two chairs sat at a small table under the window. Becky dropped into one, her knees wobbly.

The sheriff sat in the other. "I'll tell you one thing. There is nothing you'll ever do in this job that's harder than what you just did."

"I had to," Becky said. "I don't think Henry meant to attack anybody. But he was going to. Brisa said I saved Mr. Preston's life."

Sheriff Crow nodded. "You also saved your brother from becoming a murderer. He's done things he can't take back, but at least he didn't do that."

"He's going to be exiled, isn't he." It wasn't even a question.

"Afraid so. But at least he won't be executed for murder." Encouragingly, Sheriff Crow said, "This isn't the end of his life. It's more like a new beginning. We'll give him supplies. He's young and strong. He can make a good life somewhere else. Maybe he'll find a Changed town where he'll be welcome."

The anvil that had been pressing on Becky's heart lifted. The sheriff was right. Henry would get a second chance.

"And now we come to you," the sheriff said. "Your work with

Meredith and Jennie has really paid off."

"But they can both still beat me. Everyone in our practice group can."

"Not everyone can shoot straight," Sheriff Crow said. "Even after far more practice than you've had. Very few people, adults included, can hit a moving target on an instant's notice, with people rushing around in front of them, when they're under a huge amount of pressure. You did that, Becky."

Becky knew the sheriff well enough by now to be able to read the subtle changes in her expressions. Sheriff Crow was proud of her. She was impressed by her. Despite Becky's sadness, a tentative smile tugged at her mouth. Not many people impressed Sheriff Crow.

"You went above and beyond today," the sheriff continued. "But even before that, I've been thinking about you. Your integrity, your intelligence, your aim, your grace under pressure — those are all qualities I'd want in a sheriff. I've only had this job a year, and Tom Preston was sheriff for most of my life. There's not much precedent for how a sheriff chooses an apprentice. I always figured I'd tap one of my deputies, but none of them ever seemed quite right. But you do."

Becky was so amazed, she didn't know what to say. The sheriff had plenty of deputies. She'd even temporarily deputized Ross and Mia during the battle. But she'd never had an apprentice.

"Think about it, Becky," the sheriff said, and she smiled. "You don't need to decide right now. I know you're under a lot of stress —"

"Sheriff Crow, I would love to be your apprentice." Becky gulped, aware that she'd actually interrupted the sheriff.

Sheriff Crow laughed, leaned forward, and clapped Becky on the shoulder. "I'll see about getting you a badge —"

The door banged open.

Becky whipped around. Her stomach cramped as her mother charged in, Brisa's yell echoing behind her: "Wait!"

"Rebecca Callahan, how *dare* you!" Mom screamed. "Just because you're a mutant, you *dare* to accuse your brother? You probably started those fires yourself!"

Becky had frozen at her mother's sudden appearance. For a

heartbeat, all the old terror kept her in place. But she was not at home. She was the sheriff's apprentice. She had just saved a life. And her mother had barged into the sheriff's private space.

Becky stood up. "Get out."

It was her mother's turn to freeze in shock.

"Get. Out," Becky said louder, advancing on Mom. "This is Sheriff Crow's room. You don't belong in here."

Sheriff Crow stood at her shoulder, but said nothing. Becky knew with the instinct she was beginning to trust that the sheriff was letting her resolve this on her own.

She took another step. Mom backed through the door, her face mottled with rage. Then she turned to Henry. He was standing by the cell door, his face pale and his lips pressed tight together as if he'd never smile again. The image of him forcing a grin to placate Dad flashed before Becky's eyes, churning up her stomach.

"You *chose* to be a mutant," Mom shrieked. "That's the only way it can happen. You betrayed me and your entire family." She spun to shake a finger at Becky. "And you, with your monster girlfriend, you probably put him up to it!"

The cold nausea in Becky's stomach turned to hot rage. Her entire body burned with it, as if she'd been engulfed in one of Henry's fires.

"If anyone is to blame, it's *you*." Becky spoke so loudly that her last word echoed. "You're the one who always told him he wasn't good enough. He had to be a Ranger, he had to be a hero, he had to be defense chief someday. You made life so miserable that we could never tell the truth. We would've been safer outside the walls at night than in our own home."

Mom gasped. "I did *everything* for you and Henry! And all I've heard all my life is ingratitude. Everybody takes advantage of me..."

Becky remembered walking through the house at night, seeing all the anger and pain of years. Grandma Ida sneering at Mom. Dad hitting Henry. Becky felt sorry for Mom, but mainly she wanted to never see her again.

"I grew up hearing every mean thing Grandma Ida said to you, and what you and Dad said to each other. And I know what Dad did to Henry." Becky held up her gloved hand. "I saw it with my Change power. No one's ever been happy in that house. You could stop yelling at us right now. You could take responsibility for your own mistakes. But you're not going to, are you?"

Mom stood still, breathing hard, her face brick red. Becky looked into eyes as round and blue as her own, and saw the young Martha staring back.

Then Mom's eyes narrowed. Angrily, she muttered, "This is all your father's fault. If he hadn't run off and left me to raise two children..."

Becky turned away. There would always be someone else to blame. Always.

But she wasn't going to accept that blame. Not anymore.

·39·
FELICITÉ

Felicité slipped away from the crowd around the barn.

The entire town seemed to have gathered, and everybody wanted their opinion heard. Especially by Daddy. Mr. Horst had shoved his way to the front, but no one paid any more attention to him than they would to an ordinary citizen. She was certain that half the people there had literally forgotten that he was the defense chief now.

He should have held a fire drill the day after the barn fire, Felicité thought. But he'd been too busy patting himself on the back for the new, *better* weapons that would be made at his forge.

She walked to the jail, intending to see Henry. But she didn't know what to say to him, and when she arrived, she could hear Mrs. Callahan all the way through the closed door. There was no chance of a private conversation.

Felicité stood outside, at a loss. She felt terrible, inside and out. Her head throbbed, her entire body ached — even her hand hurt. A big red patch and small blisters covered her wrist and the back of her hand. She didn't even remember getting burned.

She headed for the infirmary, where a long line of people snaked over the porch and spilled into the street. She circled around the line. Surely she'd be tended before all those perfectly well people who just needed a little water. To her dismay, the lobby was equally packed. Ross was slumped in a chair, his eyes closed and his head tipped back, with Summer and Kerry hovering over him. Everyone was always so concerned when something happened to Ross. Where was the concern for her and her injuries?

Alfonso Medina stood over Ross, stitching a long cut on his arm. Felicité shuddered at his gecko fingers. She certainly didn't want them touching her.

"Please get in line, Felicité," Alfonso said. "It starts outside."

Felicité glared at all four of them. She couldn't decide who was the best representative of how unfair everything was in this town. Alfonso, the mutant doctor's new mutant apprentice, ordering *her* around? Kerry, the daughter of the town's worst enemy? Summer, who had broken Will's arm and gotten off free? Or Ross, who had broken practically every rule in town and also gotten off free? Mia had even shown him the tunnel under the town hall.

The tunnel!

Felicité had completely forgotten that she'd taken Henry through it. Fear chilled her. If Daddy found out now, he'd have Henry shot. There was no chance that he would let an exiled criminal leave town with that secret.

She had to warn Henry not to say anything about it. Felicité pushed past the crowd and ran into Main Street. She peered through the gloom toward the jail on the north side of the town square,. A huge crowd had collected around it. There was no chance that Felicité would be able to get past that mass to talk to Henry in private. She'd have to come back later. With any luck, Henry would have way too much on his mind to even remember the tunnel.

With no better options, she decided to go home. She could get a bandage there after she cleaned up. Now that she was aware of the burn, it hurt more than ever, and she felt gritty and grimy and filthy and sweaty. She wanted to burn her clothes and never see them again.

Felicité walked home the long way, avoiding the few people she met. She found Wu Zetian waiting for her. She kissed her rat, then locked herself in her bathroom.

It took three towels, barely dampened, before she was sufficiently clean, her skin smooth and normal. When she emerged in a fresh dress, she found Daddy and Mother in the dining room. They too had bathed and dressed, but the air inside still smelled of smoke. Or had it soaked into Felicité's pores? She resisted the urge to sniff at herself.

Clara had laid out a cold dinner of potato salad, fish salad, crisp bread, smoked fish, fresh cheese, pickled turnips, and fish dip. Fish again! There were only three table settings, so Grandmère and Will were elsewhere. Instantly, Felicité knew what she was in for. Daddy and Mother would never humiliate her by scolding her in front of Will. Felicité's neck tightened and her mind raced.

Mother waited until Felicité sat down. Then she said, "Darling, I am concerned that you deliberately put yourself in danger."

"Disobeying an order," Daddy said.

Mother touched him on the wrist. "I am sure you had your reasons. We felt we should discuss this quietly."

"I wanted to make sure Henry would surrender without a fight. I thought he'd listen to me. I was afraid Daddy would scare him, and that's exactly what happened." Felicité was proud of her even voice. "Henry wouldn't have done anything if we'd had more time to talk. He was scared when the door slammed open. *I* was scared."

Daddy's lips compressed. "Felicité, you don't seem to realize that that boy has been lying to us all along. Lying to *you*. You haven't considered what he might be capable of."

"But he had to lie —" She stopped. She'd meant to point out how horrible and prejudiced Mrs. Callahan had been. But anything she could accuse Mrs. Callahan of, short of actually hitting Becky, could also be seen as an accusation against Daddy.

"What do you mean, he had to lie?" Daddy asked.

"He knew how I felt about Changed people. How we all felt." Felicité glanced at her mother, who looked distressed. She was probably thinking of Grandmère. Feeling sick, Felicité turned her gaze to Daddy.

He gave her a nod of approval.

An unexpected angry heat flared up in her belly. Daddy liked knowing that she hated Changed people. He was completely fine with Henry feeling forced to lie about his Change to keep her love.

"He should never have dated you in the first place," Daddy said. "Then he never would have put himself or you in that position. Don't blame yourself, darling. Henry chose everything he did, and he's the one who will bear the consequences."

Consequences like exile, Felicité thought. *Consequences like Daddy killing him if he finds out about the tunnel.*

Well, Daddy's choosing what he's making me *do.*

♦ ♦ ♦

After checking the jail several times, only to be foiled by crowds outside or people inside, Felicité finally had the perfect excuse to be alone with Henry. She wished she didn't.

When the council had voted to exile him, Felicité had volunteered to take the news to him, saying, "I think it's better if he hears it from me."

She hated the thought of it. But anyone else doing it would be even worse. Besides, she still had to warn him never to mention the tunnel. The Rangers would escort him a day's journey out of town, and if he let his knowledge slip, they'd never let him go.

Felicité scanned her closet, frowning at her prettiest dresses. She'd worn them all on dates with Henry. She couldn't wear one to tell him that his life in Las Anclas was over. She reached for a plain blue dress, then stopped. Mrs. Callahan had made that. She knew Henry could recognize his mother's work. He might even have seen her making it. She didn't want to show up in anything that would seem like an ironic reminder of what he'd lost.

She rummaged through her closet, realizing how many of her dresses Mrs. Callahan had made, or Henry had seen her wear and admired. Practically everything. She finally located a dress Mr. Kim had made that she hadn't worn in years. Its green dye had faded to an unpleasant shade that reminded her of mold. Felicité sniffed at it. Despite the sachets in the closet, it smelled slightly musty. Well, it would have to do.

She squirmed into it, barely managing to roll it over her hips. It was much too tight, and not in a flattering way. But at least it didn't have anything that would make Henry think of things he'd never see again.

Except her body. Felicité glared at her reflection in the mirror, trying to crush all the lovely memories of kissing Henry that had popped up at that thought. Angrily, she grabbed a handful of scarves and draped them around her shoulders and her neck.

When she was done, she looked like she'd been huddling in the attic against a freezing winter. But she couldn't put it off any longer.

Felicité once again set out for the jail, trying not to meet anyone's eyes. When people looked at her now, surely they weren't thinking "Felicité, the most stylish girl in Las Anclas" or "Felicité, the future mayor." They were probably thinking, "Felicité, the naive girlfriend of the mutant fire starter."

She was stopped by two teenage girls from the Catalina Players, both in pretty, perfectly-fitting outfits. One was the blonde who'd mocked her onstage as the rat-eared princess. The other had scales like mother of pearl and a crest that rose from her head like a filigree crown. Lots of people would find the scales and crest beautiful, Felicité knew, and she hated the girl for it.

Felicité hid her rage and practiced her mayoral smile. "Yes?"

The scaled girl stepped close and spoke in a breathy whisper. "We saw you after the fire. We could see you'd been fighting hard."

"We wanted to let you know that we'll be asking the company to pick another play," the blonde girl said.

In her strange, soft voice, the Changed girl said, "Grandma Jing says that a ten year old grudge rightly belongs to ten-year-olds."

When Felicité didn't answer — she had no idea what to say — the filigree girl dropped her gaze, looking disconcerted. Felicité wondered what had got past her control.

"See you later," the blonde said, and the two walked away.

It was only then that Felicité saw that her fists were clenched at her sides. She shook them out, wiped her sweaty palms on the awful mildew dress, and continued on her way.

She kept her head down until she reached the jail. A handful of busybodies still lurked outside. But for the first time, Felicité ignored them and went inside. Sheriff Crow emerged from the side room. "Hold on, Felicité. Becky's talking to him."

The two blonde heads were close together, separated by iron bars.

"I wish you'd told me," Becky was saying.

"How would that have helped anything?" Henry replied, his

voice flat.

"Maybe if you'd had someone to talk to. I mean, someone who knew about you. You wouldn't have done that stuff." Becky sounded as miserable as Felicité felt.

"I didn't need one more person nagging me," Henry retorted. "You were always such a goodie-goodie. Perfect little Becky."

"I was always afraid." Becky's voice was so soft, Felicité almost couldn't hear the words.

"Of what? Dad never hit *you*."

"I know. But I was always scared he was going to. The way he yelled at Mom. And you. I should have told Grandma Wolfe. Or Dr. Lee. They both asked. Maybe they could have done something."

Henry shrugged. "And have the whole council blabbing about us? Make the whole family look bad? Then I never would've had a chance with the Rangers."

Becky was silent. Felicité was sure that she, too, was thinking that Henry's actions had exposed everything that was wrong with the family more effectively than any gossip.

Then Becky spoke louder. "Listen, Henry, we don't have to be like the rest of our family. I've promised myself I won't be. You can be different, too."

"Easy for you to say." Henry jerked his head at the cell bars. "Look where *you're* standing."

Silence fell again. Finally, Becky asked, "Henry, why did you set up Summer?"

"What is this, sheriff practice?" Henry replied in a strained attempt at a joking tone. "Let's have the apprentice try an interrogation!"

"No. I just wondered." But Becky's expression had gone thoughtful at her brother's words. She admitted, so softly that Felicité could barely hear, "I guess it is the sort of thing a sheriff would wonder."

"Fine, Sheriff Becky. I'll confess!" Then Henry dropped the forced humor. "Since the sheriff was investigating, I had to point her at someone who wasn't me. Who cares about Summer? She's not a citizen. She broke Will Preston's arm."

"She's Ross's sister," Becky protested, then seemed to hear her own words. "Oh. That too."

"Yeah. That too. Sheriff Becky."

Becky walked away. Tears glittered under her eyes, but she kept her head high. Then she and Sheriff Crow went into the sheriff's room and shut the door, leaving Felicité and Henry alone.

Up until then, Becky had blocked Felicité's view of Henry's body. His hands were bound together with cloth, and his wrists were manacled. How humiliating. He wouldn't even be able to feed himself. Maybe they took them off and held him at rifle point while he ate. That was even worse. The treatment for a dangerous *mutant*.

She hurried up to his cell. She had to speak quickly, before someone else came in. "Henry, come close. I have something important to tell you."

He stepped up to her, but his expression was wary. As if he no longer trusted her.

Felicité whispered, "Henry, remember that tunnel I took you through? Never say anything about it to anyone. It's a town secret. If Daddy finds out that you know about it, he won't let you leave. He'll have you killed."

Henry's blue eyes widened in shock. "Oh. Okay." Then he looked at her with the same...was it actually love? Now he looked like the Henry she'd loved when they'd been alone together, kissing and playing Secrets. "Thanks for telling me, Felicité."

"I tried to get in earlier. I couldn't. But that's what I was trying to tell you at the barn."

Henry gave a deep sigh. "Wish you'd gotten there one minute sooner." Then he frowned. "Why are you here? Besides that, I mean? The council—"

"Voted for exile," she said quickly. "I didn't want anyone else telling you. I'm so sorry."

"I figured they would. It was either that or..." Henry pointed to his throat. When Felicité flinched, his grin vanished, and he gestured with his bound hands to a backpack. "Mom threw that in yesterday. It has all my clothes."

"The Rangers will escort you, then give you supplies and a map. Henry—" Her voice suspended.

"Come with me." His face pressed to the bars. "Felicité, if you go with me, I'd be happy. We could go anywhere. We could get married at the first town we come to."

Felicité closed her eyes and leaned her forehead against the bars, their faces separated only by the iron. For one wild, blissful heartbeat she imagined that: she and Henry would be together. She could do anything she wanted. They could go to a Changed town, where no one would care about him.

And no one would care about her.

But what would that "anything" be? She knew what she wanted—what she'd wanted her entire life: to be mayor of Las Anclas. As a stranger in some other town, she'd be nobody. Like Ross. Or even like Yuki. He'd been a prince, but once he got to Las Anclas, the highest he ever rose was captain of a bow team. Nobody would respect a Wolfe for their family name anywhere but here.

She'd never see Mother again. She'd never see any of her friends or family. She'd never see Daddy.

And Henry. Did she love him enough to marry him?

Did she really want to marry someone who'd endanger the lives of an entire town—including her—to look like a hero?

What would Henry say if he saw her Change? She didn't have a cool power. It was a hideous, pointless Change. He might take one look and scream, "Mutant!" She certainly felt that way when she looked in the mirror. And if he even saw it once, could he ever forget it? Or would he see it again every time he looked at her?

She reached through the bars and took his hands. "I'm sorry, Henry. I can't."

He stood very still, his blue eyes widening. Then his breath huffed on a sound suspiciously like a sob, and he pulled his hands away and walked across the cell. He threw himself on the bunk.

"Have a nice life, Felicité," he said to the ceiling.

She hated herself for her clumsiness. Hated to part angry. "Henry," she said, holding onto the bars. "Becky was right. You get to start over. You can do anything. Think of it that way, okay?"

He didn't answer. When the pause became a silence, she turned away, sick at heart. And angry. Henry really did get to start over. No more secrets, unless he chose to keep them of his own free will.

That was a choice she'd given up forever.

·40·
ROSS

ROSS KNOCKED ON MIA'S door. She flung it open, then stood in the doorway to let him get a good look at her. She wore the blue and gold hanbok Kerry had given her for Christmas. Like her ripped shirts, it covered most of her skin, but in a way that made him long to touch the bits that were left bare. The long-sleeved blouse called attention to her deft hands, her pretty face, her warm brown eyes, and her soft black hair. All he could see of her lower body were her slim ankles and her little feet in green slippers, but that made him think about her legs under the skirt.

Ross wanted to tell her everything he was seeing, but all he managed was, "Wow."

Mia stepped out, making her bell-shaped skirt sway like a morning glory opening at dawn. "I hope me in a dress doesn't mean another disaster. I double hope it, because I didn't care so much about Aunt Olivia's dress, but I'd hate to ruin this one. Well, technically it's not a dress, so maybe nothing will happen."

Ross nodded vigorously. Every time he saw Mia after they'd been separated for a little while, he lit up inside, whether she was in pink silk or oil-smeared overalls. But she looked dainty and graceful in the hanbok, which suited her much better than ruffles, and he loved how excited she got whenever she dressed up.

"It was a tossup between this and the dress Jennie gave me, but Jennie thought I should wear the one Kerry gave me first. So I am." Mia grinned. "So we match! You look great in your new shirt. I'm so glad you didn't wear it the night of the fire."

"I would have, except I'd seen your dad making beet-flavored pumpkin kimchi, and I was afraid I'd slop beet juice on it."

"I don't know how you can like that stuff," Mia said.

"It's delicious."

"You think everything is delicious."

"Not lizard eggs. Or lizard." Ross might have forgotten a lot, but he definitely recalled the nastiest meals he'd ever forced down.

"Ugh." Mia's eyes crinkled in disgust. "I bet not even Dad could pickle that until you liked it."

They laced their fingers together and let their hands swing as they headed into the crowded town square. Everyone was dressed up, from the oldest citizens to the Nguyens' baby, who wore an embroidered cap with holes cut out for his antennae.

"Jennie!" Mia waved at her from across the square.

Jennie was at the Riley table, gorgeous in his favorite red dress that hugged all her curves. A welcome inward warmth flowed through Ross as she looked up, saw them, and smiled. How was it possible to feel so differently about Jennie and Mia, but care so much about them both? He still didn't completely trust that kind of...

He cautiously tested the word *love*. Like *home*, it still wasn't quite part of his vocabulary.

"Ross?" Mia asked. "Is something wrong?"

He started to shrug, then made himself speak. Pretending feelings weren't there didn't make them go away.

"I was thinking about some things," he said slowly, considering each word before he spoke it. No, he wasn't quite ready to trust *that* one out loud. "They feel dangerous, because they can be taken away so quick."

"They?" Mia looked worried. "Ross, is something wrong?"

"No. No." Why hadn't he kept his mouth shut? But once he started, he had to go on. He couldn't leave her hanging.

"Things like love." His entire body prickled with awkwardness. He muttered, "Summer and Spring. And, well, I don't like them, but Félicité and Henry."

"Yeah, I guess they *were* in love. Or in something."

"I think they were." He'd seen them together, and he was sure of it. "But she still didn't go into exile with him. And it's not just losing someone. Henry's parents must have been in love once, right? Nobody in this town is forced to marry anyone. But it didn't last."

"That's sad," Mia said.

Jennie strode up to them. "What's sad?"

Ross was ready to shut up about it, but Mia said, "We were talking about love. And how it..." She waved her hands. "Doesn't always fix things, I guess."

Jennie's dark gaze flickered to the side, then back. Ross didn't have to look. He could hear Indra's laughter from the far table. And he'd seen Jennie and Indra together during the fire, standing close enough to touch. But they hadn't.

"Gather round!" Mr. Horst's huge voice boomed, quieting the crowd. "Time for the wedding!"

Only then did Ross remember that Brisa's brother Cisco and Alfonso's sister Tania were getting married. Jennie had told him that Tania had adored the Catalina Players as a little girl, and had moved up the date of their wedding so the play could be a part of their celebration.

The Preciados swarmed on to the stage, almost swallowing up the smaller Medina family. The Preciados' finest clothes were nothing compared to the most casual outfit that the wealthier families of Las Anclas could afford. But they wore what jewelry they had, and those who had none wore flowers or ribbons. The Medinas' clothing was far more expensive, and they all wore precious jewelry. But though the families differed in size and wealth, they seemed united in happiness.

Ross stood at the back of the crowd, too far to hear Cisco and Tania's soft-spoken vows. But he could see their joyous expressions. He hoped their love would last.

A familiar cadence broke into his reflections. "Our Father, who art in heaven, hallowed be thy Name."

Ross recognized that prayer from church with the Rileys. Voices rose from the crowd, joining the wedding party in prayer. "Hail Mary, full of grace, the Lord is with thee..."

He spoke before he even realized that he knew the words. "Blessed art thou among women, and blessed is the fruit of thy womb, Jesus."

Though many of the crowd had fallen silent, Ross continued with the ones who hadn't. They all must be Catholics, like the Preciados and the Medinas. Like him. He knew the entire prayer.

"Holy Mary, Mother of God, pray for us sinners..."

Summer spoke with a reverence Ross had never heard from her before. Her eyes were squinched shut and the fingers of one hand were curled.

She's holding Spring's hand, he thought.

"...now and at the hour of our death."

Summer's eyes opened and looked straight into his. Together, they said, "Amen."

Ross felt as if he was praying with both his sisters, the one he'd found and the one he'd never known. And though Summer said nothing, he sensed that she felt so, too.

The crowd erupted into cheers, making Ross jump. Then people began throwing flower petals. A few purple and red petals stuck in Summer's black hair. The newlyweds walked off the stage, hands clasped tight, followed by their families.

Once the stage was empty, a fanfare pealed out and a man with a powerful voice called out, "The play is about to begin!"

Ross, Jennie, and Mia moved with the crowd toward the benches. Summer sat with Kerry and Meredith.

Mayor Wolfe stepped onstage, tall and imposing in The Button Dress. Ross was surprised that she'd have anything to do with the play after the mockery the Catalina Players had made of her family.

"Citizens of Las Anclas," Mayor Wolfe announced. "Ordinarily our town celebrations begin with a meal, with the entertainment following. But in thanks to our guests from Catalina, who all pitched in to aid us in fighting the fire, we've decided to have the entertainment first, so they may join us for the feast afterward. Which will include dancing."

A wave of applause went up as the mayor joined her family in the front row. Ross didn't particularly care for her, let alone the rest of the family. But he knew what it was like to be publicly humiliated, and he hoped the Catalina Players wouldn't do the same play as last time.

The actors who entered wore plumed hats, capes, and swords.

The girl with pearly scales, the blonde girl, and a guy with bright green eyes played 'musketeers,' swashbuckling their way through a story of disguises and spies. The fights were fun, he enjoyed the witty exchanges between the heroes and villains, and there were no rolling heads. Ross liked it better than the unitard play, and much better than the play mocking the Wolfe-Preston family.

When it ended, he said, "Now I know why everyone was so excited about the Catalina Players coming back. I'd travel a long way to see more plays like this one."

Mia nodded so enthusiastically that light from her glasses flashed in his eyes. "Great fights. And a happy ending! The heads in the last play were so sad."

Jennie's full lips twitched in a way that Ross recognized from when they'd watched the unitard play. He wondered what she was thinking. But all she said was, "I'm starving. Shall we help set out the food so we can get a plate faster?"

They raced to the table.

When Ross sat back, satisfied at last after his third helping, the musicians took the stage. The bandleader paused to talk to Paco, indicating a drum set. But Paco shook his head, then vanished into the crowd.

"He won't even drum with the Catalina band," Jennie said, her smile vanishing. "A year ago he'd have been thrilled to get the chance."

Ross remembered how Paco hadn't liked the folklorico shirt Ross had given him at the Christmas party. Now he realized why: it was a reminder of the last time Paco had seen his mother alive.

Kerry appeared with Whisper on her shoulder, his pink nose twitching curiously, and Summer and Meredith in tow. "I've never seen Paco play."

"Doesn't look like you're going to," Meredith said. "It's a shame. I used to love dancing to his drumming. Come on, let's grab the middle before the old folks do." She elbowed the other two toward the empty space in the square.

Jennie held out her hands to Ross and Mia. "Shall we join them?"

"Sure. I can't wait to dance in this." Mia twirled, making her hanbok flare out.

The band struck up as they went to where the teenagers were gathering. Becky and Brisa were already slow-dancing.

"Are you kidding?" Brisa was saying to Becky. "I *love* being the sheriff's apprentice's girlfriend. I can't wait to kiss you while you're wearing your badge!"

Becky's reply was too soft for Ross to catch, but he heard Brisa say hopefully, "You could wear it on a ribbon around your neck. I mean, just that and nothing else."

Ross's face heated up. Jennie stifled a snicker.

Mia must not have been listening, because she didn't blush. Her gaze was fixed on Becky's waist, where she'd wear her holster. "Becky's only got forty-eight darts left. I'm sure she won't waste them, but I'll need to get her more cloud viper venom eventually."

Summer, who stood nearby, said, "I can get some for you."

"You can?" Mia grinned at Summer for the first time that Ross had ever seen. "Wow, that would be terrific."

Summer looked gratified. Ross wondered how she'd manage it, then decided that if there was a way, his sister would find it.

Kerry was dancing solo in her unique martial arts-influenced style, her high-heeled boots stamping patterns into the dirt, her gaze fixed far in the distance. She too had been hurt by love. Ross wondered if she was thinking about Santiago.

Closer to the edge of the square, Sheriff Crow was dancing with Jack. They'd broken up before Ross had come to Las Anclas, but they moved in perfect synch, pressed as close together as Brisa and Becky. Maybe love was still alive for them.

And then Ross stopped watching other people, because Mia and Jennie grabbed his hands and began to dance. Jennie led, and Ross and Mia copied her steps. She was adapting a two-person dance for three, but she made it feel easy. He lost himself in movement until the music stopped.

The next tune was quick and lively. The younger Catalina Players started doing gymnastic dances. Meredith joined them with a rapid series of cartwheels.

Mia poked Jennie. "Show them how good you are."

"This is a dance, not a competition." But Jennie looked tempted.

"Come on," Brisa called. "Go, Jennie! *You* won't sprain your ankle!"

Jennie laughed, then stepped into the midst of the whirling and kicking and flipping. Shouts, whistles, and claps went up as she and the blonde player did back flips. They landed and grinned at each other, then slapped their hands together. If it had been a contest at all, it had been a friendly one, ending in a draw.

Beyond them, Ross glimpsed Felicité sitting with her parents, her posture elegant and a smile fixed on her face like a mask. When the band struck up a waltz, Mr. Preston pulled the mayor into the square, leaving Felicité alone.

Ross waltzed with Jennie, and then he and Mia spun in the fast dance that followed. The next tune prompted an excited squeal from Mia, and she and Jennie paired up for a dance they'd learned as little girls. Ross kept an eye out for Summer, but she stayed perched on the edge of the stage, head cocked and black hair sheeting down as she watched the musicians.

It was getting late when Jennie nudged him. "Look at that!"

A crowd had gathered at one side of the dance square. A solid wall of people hid whatever they were watching, but between them he glimpsed a flare of green.

Summer was wearing green.

Alarm tingled through Ross's nerves. Of course something had gone wrong. Of course the peace and fun of this evening had been too good to be true. He rushed into the gathering crowd, ignoring the press of bodies around him as he searched for his sister.

Mia followed him, catching his hand. "It's okay. Look."

Ross broke through the crowd. In the center of an open space, Summer twirled and leaped, almost too light and graceful to be real. Everyone was watching her with awe, even the Catalina Players. But Summer seemed unaware of the crowd. Her eyes were half shut, one hand open, sometimes reaching, sometimes clasping air, as if she danced with an invisible partner.

She is, he realized. He knew without asking that she was dancing with Spring, if only in her mind.

It wasn't only a beautiful dance, it was about love. He could feel it, and others could, too. He saw it in clasped hands, and bright eyes, and soft smiles. Spring was gone, but Summer's love for her endured.

Ross felt a warm presence on his other side. Jennie had followed him, too. Ross held the girls' hands, and watched his sister twirl and leap, then land as soft as snow.

RACHEL MANIJA BROWN IS the author of the memoir *All the Fishes Come Home to Roost: An American Misfit in India* and *A Cup of Smoke*, a collection of short stories and poems. She works as a therapist specializing in the treatment of PTSD (post-traumatic stress disorder). She lives in Southern California, and her website is www.rachelmanijabrown.com.

SHERWOOD SMITH HAS PUBLISHED more than forty novels for teenagers and adults, including *Crown Duel* and the Mythopoeic Award Finalist *The Spy Princess*. A retired teacher, she lives in Southern California, and her website is www.sherwoodsmith.net.

ABOUT BOOK VIEW CAFÉ

Book View Café Publishing Cooperative is an author-owned cooperative of over fifty professional writers, publishing in a variety of genres such as fantasy, romance, mystery, and science fiction.

BVC authors include *New York Times* and *USA Today* best-sellers; Nebula, Hugo, and Philip K. Dick Award winners; World Fantasy Award, Campbell Award, and RITA Award nominees; and winners and nominees of many other publishing awards.

Since its debut in 2008, BVC has gained a reputation for producing high-quality e-books, and is now bringing that same quality to its print editions.

CPSIA information can be obtained
at www.ICGtesting.com
Printed in the USA
LVHW041712051118
596009LV00002B/430